THE
MARRIAGE
RULES

BOOKS BY SAMANTHA HAYES

The Reunion

Tell Me A Secret

The Liar's Wife

Date Night

The Happy Couple

Single Mother

The Trapped Wife

The Ex-Husband

The Engagement

The Inheritance

Mother of the Bride

Her Housekeeper

THE
MARRIAGE
RULES

SAMANTHA HAYES

bookouture

Published by Bookouture in 2025

An imprint of Storyfire Ltd.
Carmelite House
50 Victoria Embankment
London EC4Y 0DZ

www.bookouture.com

The authorised representative in the EEA is Hachette Ireland
8 Castlecourt Centre
Dublin 15 D15 XTP3
Ireland
(email: info@hbgi.ie)

ISBN: 978-1-83618-543-7
eBook ISBN: 978-1-83618-542-0

PROLOGUE
FIONA

I was suspicious of his weird rules from the get-go – right from when he first mentioned them to me in the pub. The most unusual chat-up line I'd ever had. But there was just something about him – something so appealing, so magnetic, so charismatic. We seemed to vibrate on the same frequency. There's no denying that.

I suppose I should have listened to my gut, spotted the red flags sooner, realised that something wasn't quite right. I mean, who actually lives by a list of strict rules every single day?

It had never been my way, that's for sure, and until I met Jason, I'd lived a fairly normal, if not sometimes chaotic, life – ducking and diving, living from one pay day to the next, bailing myself out of one disaster after another, whether that be a relationship, a job or a living situation. OK, so maybe at age forty-three I should have been settled with a family of my own, a mortgage and a nursing career that I wasn't holding onto by the skin of my teeth. But I'd been doing what *I* wanted, whenever *I* wanted to do it, and that had suited me fine.

Except now it didn't.

Because I'd fallen in love.

And love makes you do stupid things. Things that go against every rule ever written.

So here I am, living under the umbrella of my husband's marriage rules – a system he swears will keep us safe, help us achieve our goals and make us happy. It's a fresh start, doing things Jason's way – or rather, his *father's* way, as he keeps reminding me. It's only because my husband cares for me so much. At least there's that.

Rule 1: No lying.

Rule 2: Never talk about *You Know Who*.

Rule 3: Family confessional every day at 6 p.m.

Rule 4: No leaving the house without good reason.

Rule 5: Bedtime confessional.

Rule 6: Never talk about the past.

Rule 7: No alcohol, apart from one drink at the weekend.

Rule 8: Grieving hour every Sunday at 5 p.m.

Rule 9: No phones/tablets/laptops/internet after 6 p.m.

Rule 10: No watching the news. No social media. No loud music.

Rule 11: Bedtime strictly 8 p.m.

Rule 12: No flaunting or flirting with the opposite sex.

Rule 13: No breaking of the marriage rules. Punishment severe.

Heaven help me if I don't obey his rules.

PART 1

'*It is not death that a man should fear, but he should fear never beginning to live.*'

MARCUS AURELIUS

ONE
FIONA

For the first time in a long while, Fiona feels a sense of excitement. A sense that no one else is going to die. For now, anyway.

It's going to be a good day, and she's sure there'll be plenty to tell Jason about in their bedtime confessional later – Rule Number 5 – when they share their deepest secrets before sleep. It brings a special intimacy to their relationship, she sees that now.

'Make Ivy's cereal, would you, Tilly?' Fiona asks her fifteen-year-old stepdaughter when she hears the doorbell.

She's surprised the teen is up and dressed, given it's the first day of the school summer holidays. But Tilly – Mathilda – is a good girl. And she's amazing with her eight-year-old little sister. They've been through a lot, those two, losing their mother only eight weeks ago. And in such a terrible way. Then the upheaval of coming to live with Fiona and their dad. While the timing made things stressful, given that she and Jason had only just moved in together themselves, the couple rallied for Jason's daughters, and Fiona has taken on the girls as if they were her own.

'Sure,' Tilly says, buttering some toast. '*Mum*,' she adds, looking up and giving Fiona a nervous smile.

Fiona already knows it's Sascha at the door with her daughter, Cora, having seen the alert on her phone. They live next door, and from the moment Sascha's head popped up over the back garden fence the day after they moved in a couple of months ago, she knew they'd be firm friends.

And likewise, Ivy and Cora, who will be in the same class at the local primary school next term. Jason insisted on waiting a few months until September for his daughters to start their new schools, with the girls studying at home for the rest of the term. Fiona would have preferred them to enrol back in May when they moved here, catching the last few weeks of the term so they could make new friends.

As a compromise in the meantime, Jason has grudgingly allowed Ivy to play with Cora – as long as Cora comes round to their house. And Sascha introduced Tilly to Amber, her friend's teenage daughter who also lives in the village. Now, at the beginning of the long summer holidays, both girls have someone to hang out with at least – even if it is just upstairs in their bedrooms. It's a start to them finally feeling settled.

'Welcome to Fiona's childcare!' Fiona sings out, though quickly lowers her voice in case any other neighbours overhear. Hollybush Close is a quiet cul-de-sac on the edge of the village with only ten houses, and she doesn't want everyone knowing her business. Her cheeks flush at the thought.

When they first discussed the idea a couple of weeks ago, Fiona had been worried about needing to register with the council as a childminder to make it official. 'Christ, I don't care about things like that,' Sascha said, waving her worries away, 'It's *you*, Fi, for God's sake. I might have only recently met you, but I trust my instincts. You're a nurse, so more qualified than most to take care of Cora. Just whack her in front of the TV with a bag of crisps and a colouring book, and you're good to go.

Anyway, it's only two days a week in the holidays. What could possibly go wrong?'

Sascha had grinned over the rim of her wine glass. She is one of those mums Fiona longs to be – carefree, relaxed, confident and self-assured. And she doesn't give a damn what anyone thinks of her. They'd been sitting outside in Sascha's garden after Sascha had held up a bottle of Sauvignon Blanc over the fence on the dot of 7 p.m. Fiona had been pulling weeds from the cracks in the paving slabs after dinner – Jason likes everything neat and tidy – and she'd looked up and smiled, noticing the condensation dribbling tantalisingly down the bottle.

After checking it was OK with Jason, finally convincing him that getting to know their neighbour wasn't strictly breaking Rule Number 4 – no leaving the house without good reason – just this once, Fiona had popped next door. She would virtually be at home anyway given that she was only going to be a few feet away, and he'd be able to hear her voice over the fence.

'Just the one small glass then,' she'd said as Sascha poured. She hadn't mentioned to her husband that there'd be wine. That would have been an instant refusal. Guilt seared down her throat as she drank, breaking two rules in one fell swoop – no drinking in the week and no lying, ever.

It was as they were finishing the bottle a short while later, when Fiona's body had long since melted into tipsy contentedness, that Sascha put the idea to her. 'So you'd really be up for it?' she checked again. 'You'll childmind Cora in the summer holidays while I'm at work on Mondays and Tuesdays?'

Fiona nodded enthusiastically, relishing the idea of cash in her pocket. She'd just have to clear it with Jason first. She prayed he'd say yes, hoping that it wasn't breaking any of the rules.

Now, Fiona watches, smiling, as Cora kicks off her trainers. 'Come on in, you two. Got time for a coffee before work?'

Sascha glances at her phone. 'A quick one,' she says, following Fiona to the kitchen.

The patio doors are open wide to the garden, a breeze wafting in from the fields beyond. It was the view that convinced Jason to take the house when he first saw the place several months ago. Remote. Private. Not overlooked. Hollybush Close is a small development on the edge of Kingshill – a picture-perfect South Warwickshire village, complete with a duck pond, a pub and a little shop and café – and Jason instantly secured number 9 with a deposit, offering to pay the first six months' rent upfront. Later, after his viewing, he'd shown Fiona pictures. She loved how the garden flowed into the fields beyond, with only a three-foot post and rail fence separating them from farmland.

'We can be free here,' Fiona whispered to Jason, staring at the photos. He linked his fingers with hers, giving them a squeeze.

'Blimey, Fi, you're taking this childminding business seriously,' Sascha says now, staring into the garden. 'It looks like Disneyland out there.'

'Just a few toys,' Fiona laughs, pouring the coffee. 'Jase put the paddling pool up yesterday, and we spotted the water slide on offer at the supermarket. Couldn't resist. The girls will love it.'

They'd managed to bring some of Tilly's and Ivy's possessions from their old house, but only what would fit in the car. It had all been rather a rush.

'I'll make sure Cora has a hot meal before you pick her up later,' Fiona says, hesitating. 'Five thirty sharp, yeah?'

'Yeah,' Sascha replies, knocking back her coffee in a couple of glugs. 'All being well.'

All being well... Fiona swallows drily. In the end, after much persuading, Jason finally agreed to her childminding –

but only if she promised to stay at home. And he wants Cora gone by the time he gets back from work just before 6 p.m.

'I know you want the money, Fi,' he said when she put the idea to him. 'But other people's kids being here when I get home from work...?' He shook his head. 'That's our time, love. Rule number three – family confessional every evening at six. No exceptions.'

'I know, I know, and *thank* you,' Fiona said, pressing her palms together, so relieved that he'd finally agreed.

Jason's rules had seemed weird to her at first, but knowing how much he appreciated order and routine, she easily got used to them. She'd never met a man so caring, so devoted and thoughtful, and in return she wanted to make him happy. The rules made things so easy between them. There was no room for bickering or arguing about who said what when, or worrying what was fair and what wasn't. Just before they were married, she'd neatly written out the rules by hand in a beautiful leather-bound notebook that they'd bought on a romantic trip to York. It seemed like the perfect use for it – holding safe their most sacred vows to each other. The promises they would live by for the rest of their lives.

'Bye, darling!' Sascha calls out to Cora as Fiona walks her to the front door. Cora glances up, flicking a wave at her mum.

'Have a great day at the riding stables,' Fiona says, noticing the sting of envy in her chest. She'd love nothing more than to be outdoors all day – enjoying the freedom... the wind in her hair, the sun on her back.

'I was thinking – why don't you book Ivy in for some riding lessons?' Sascha asks. 'Cora goes on Saturday mornings and loves it.'

Fiona pauses. 'Jason might not approve,' she says, realising how vague that sounds. 'But maybe. I'll see.'

'If he doesn't like it, then I suggest *he* doesn't go riding then.' Sascha laughs, squeezing Fiona's hand. But there's a seriousness to her tone, too. 'Maybe you could have lessons. It's a great hobby.'

Fiona bows her head and laughs, knowing that apart from anything, they wouldn't be able to spare the money. Having paid six months' rent upfront for the house, they need to be careful with spending for a while, until Jason's pay cheques start coming through. The cash buffer won't last forever – and it's only thanks to Jason that they have it to fall back on. He hasn't told her exact figures, but she doesn't think his university salary will be comparable to that of his last position as a hospital doctor.

'See you at five thirty,' Fiona says, praying Sascha won't be late as she waves her off. Then she heads back into the kitchen, noticing the girls aren't in the living room any more.

'Where are Ivy and Cora?' she asks Tilly, who's alone in the kitchen.

She shrugs, glancing up from her book. 'Dunno. I've only just come back from the bathroom. Maybe they're outside.'

Fiona goes into the garden, not instantly able to spot them. Beyond the fence, she sees a figure in the distance tracking the perimeter of the field behind their house – someone walking along the footpath. Head down, shoulders hunched. She's warned Ivy a thousand times not to climb over into the fields. And in the couple of months they've lived here, she's always obeyed.

'Oh, *God!*' she gasps, her hand coming up to her chest. 'There you are!' She laughs as the two girls pop up from behind the high-sided pool, squealing '*boo*' as they splash her with water. 'Stay in the garden, you monkeys.' She shakes her head and goes back into the kitchen.

She leans on the kitchen counter, head down, breathing slowly – in for five, out for seven. For some reason, she feels on edge, as if something is going to go wrong – her sense of excitement from earlier long gone. Giving herself a little shake, she lifts her head and looks around. Tilly has gone upstairs, leaving all the breakfast dishes strewn about. She goes to load them into the dishwasher, but as she turns, something on the floor just inside the patio door catches her eye: a folded piece of paper with her name written on top in capital letters.

She bends down and picks it up, frowning as she opens it. There are only a few words inside, printed in plain, neat handwriting. As she reads, she gasps, her hand flying to her mouth as a wave of nausea rushes through her.

I know what you did... You broke a rule.

TWO

FIONA

Since Fiona and Jason married and moved in together two months ago, she has tried to think of Tilly and Ivy as her own daughters. Admittedly, she's been thrown in at the deep end, especially as the situation was dictated by such a tragedy, but she's proud to call herself their mum. Especially after what happened to their biological mother.

Dreadful. Unthinkable.

Those poor girls. She shudders, forcing the thought from her mind. Rule Number 6 – never talk about the past – is there for a reason.

Fiona hopes Tilly and Ivy will come to feel more settled in their new home, since it's new to all of them. Though she's concerned it might be too quiet for them in a village – they were used to living in a busy town with their mum before – but she and Jason love the peace of the countryside. Still, it won't make much difference as they'll be spending most of their time at home anyway.

Rule Number 4: No leaving the house without good reason.

Fiona learnt the full extent of the rules in Jason's life as they got to know each other more. At first, she thought them silly and restrictive, but her ribbing and making fun of his strict ways soon fell away when she came to realise that they actually made good sense. He explained how they'd given a structure to his life when things around him had fallen apart. In fact, that's what drew them together in the first place – the need for stability. Not that Fiona realised this back then. He was married at the time, but Jason had gradually opened up to her, explaining how his marriage had been in trouble for a long while before he and Fiona got together, and Fiona, two years younger than him at the age of forty-three, confided that she'd also found herself adrift after a turbulent time in her life, having lost her previous job and her home.

After a lifetime of unsuitable relationships – with the men she was dating randomly ghosting her, some ending things without reason after a just few months, one lying about wanting marriage and a family, while another had gone back to his ex – meeting Jason was the best thing that had ever happened to her. He was a breath of fresh air. For years, Fiona had watched all her friends meet 'the one' and settle down, buying their forever homes, having children. After a while, she'd stopped going to all the weddings she was invited to. It was too painful having other people's happy ever afters rubbed in her face. She and Jason became each other's life raft at just the right moment.

But now, as the morning goes on after the discovery of the note on the floor, Fiona feels increasingly rattled. Did someone come over the fence into the garden, dropping the note inside the patio doors while she was seeing Sascha off at the front? Did an intruder come right into the house? The thought makes her shudder, her being alone here with the girls. Who would have written something like that?

When she asked Tilly if she'd seen anyone around, being careful not to scare her, but also gauging her to see if perhaps *she'd* written the note, her response was, 'Sorry, I was upstairs in the bathroom,' before sloping off to her room again. She'd seemed disinterested but genuine – typical of Tilly, who just wants to lock herself away in her room and chat on the phone with Amber.

She found it hard to believe that Jason had written those words either. She'd called him at work right away, making up an excuse about the dishwasher playing up just to assess his mood. If he thought that she'd broken a rule, she's certain he'd have come straight out with it, admonishing her and telling her what her punishment would be – not mess about with a note. But he was normal-sounding and affable, explaining how to remove and clean the dishwasher filter.

The only other person to have been here today was Sascha, and she can't imagine her leaving a note like that. Besides, she doesn't even know about the rules.

Upstairs in her bedroom, Fiona skims through their leather-bound notebook to see if there's a rule that will help, but apart from being honest to Jason about the note appearing in the first place – Rule Number 1: No lying – there's nothing much to guide her.

All she knows is that someone put that note inside the kitchen door. And if it wasn't Jason or the girls, it means that someone was in the house. Someone who shouldn't have been there.

As soon as she'd found it, she ushered the girls inside, telling them to play upstairs for the morning, pretending a thunderstorm had been forecast. She didn't want to take chances if there was an intruder or prowler about. They grumbled at first, but the promise of a choc ice after lunch had them quickly running up to Ivy's bedroom.

She locked the patio doors, staring out into the fields. She'll have a word with Jason later, see what he thinks about getting a solid fence put up around the garden. They might have beautiful views, but after this, she'd rather have the security of a six-foot barrier.

After tidying up the house and putting a load of washing on, Fiona grabs the ham from the fridge, then she slices up some tomatoes to make sandwiches.

'Lunch, you lot,' she calls up the stairs. For a fleeting moment, she wonders if Ivy or Cora are responsible for the note. They already pranked her by hiding behind the pool. But the handwriting is too neat, the words too adult-like and specific for it to be them.

Ivy and Cora tumble into the kitchen, chattering excitedly about ponies, and Fiona slides two plates of sandwiches onto the table along with some orange squash. Then she sees the note lying on the side where she'd left it and quickly swipes it up, stuffing it in her back pocket. She grabs a couple of apples just as Tilly takes her plate from the side, going back upstairs to her room to eat.

'Make sure you have the fruit, too.' She ruffles Ivy's hair – long and flax blonde, and usually in two neat braids, but today it's hanging loose halfway down her back in shiny waves. The sun has brought out the freckles on her cheeks and nose.

Fiona is reminded of Ivy and Tilly's mother – tall, icy blonde, angular. The girls' fair complexions, their wiry limbs, the way their faces bloom with the same countless freckles in the summer – it's a straight thought-trajectory to the woman with whom Jason fathered his children.

Both girls have inherited their birth mother's Scandinavian looks – the opposite of Fiona's own dark hair and brown eyes, her average height, her unremarkable cheekbones. *Birth mother, birth mother, birth mother...* she repeats over and over in her mind, trying to make it sound clinical and pointless. *It's not the same as* mother *– the one who takes care of them every day*, she tells herself. *Like* I'm *doing. Like Jason wanted.*

She closes her eyes, grounding her thoughts. It's not been an easy role to step into.

After lunch, Ivy stands at the patio doors in the kitchen, her hands pressed flat against the glass, her breath making a misty circle beneath her nose. Cora copies her.

'But *why* do we have to stay in?' Ivy grizzles. 'It isn't raining. There aren't even any clouds.'

'Because I said so, OK, young lady?' Fiona feels mean not allowing the girls to play outside, but, as well as the note, the figure she spotted across the field earlier is still on her mind. She wishes she'd got a better look, but she's not even sure if they were male or female. Could they have been the one to leave the note?

'This is boring,' Cora says. 'Come on, let's watch TV.' She turns to head off to the living room, her head bowed, her shoulders slumped forward.

Fiona imagines Cora telling her mum about the terrible day she had with Ivy, how she wasn't allowed to play outside, and then Sascha texting her later, saying, *Cora will be going to a different childminder from now on.*

She's been banking on this extra money so she has more freedom to buy bits for her and the girls. She hates asking Jason for extra cash. Not that he isn't generous with his money – he does cover all their expenses. But since she's not nursing any more, an income of her own would be handy. Besides, where else is she going to find a job that pays in cash while working from home?

'Wait up, you two,' Fiona says, poking her head into the living room. 'You're right. I don't think it's going to rain. You can play outside.' She can't risk Cora grumbling to her mum.

Both girls cheer, making Fiona stifle a smile as they rush out to the sandpit. Fiona puts the kettle on, keeping a close watch on them the whole time she's making her tea. Then she goes outside to sit with them, dragging the sun lounger to where she can keep an eye on them. With people walking along the public footpath in the field, she can't be too careful.

It's twenty minutes later that the alert chimes on her phone. Someone has triggered the motion sensor. She waits a moment to see if the doorbell rings, but it doesn't, so she opens the app to check who's there. There's no one visible on the live camera view now – just the familiar street scene of their cul-de-sac through a fish-eye lens. She checks the recording to see who or what triggered the alert.

Odd, she thinks, spotting the figure at her front door. She wasn't expecting anyone, and it's impossible to tell if it's someone she knows because of the motorbike helmet they're wearing. The mirrored visor is pulled down, and their black leathers give nothing away apart from showing the person is slim, tall and moving swiftly. Due to the glare of the sun behind them, the recording isn't as clear as usual.

She watches as the person puts something through the letterbox before retreating and heading back to a motorbike parked on the street. The recording ends before the bike pulls away so there's no chance of getting a number plate.

She tells herself that it's probably just the local newsletter being delivered, or a flyer about window cleaning or gardening services, though deep down, something feels off.

Fiona glances over at the girls, who are squatting down beside the sandpit, playing happily. 'Back in a moment,' she calls out, scanning the fields behind their house, checking there's no one about. Satisfied it's clear, she dashes through the house to the front door.

A chill sweeps through her as she sees the piece of paper lying on the doormat – the same type of lined paper that the note from earlier was written on.

She picks it up, her hand shaking as she reaches out for it, sees her name written on the outside. Her heart thrums in her chest as she opens the folded paper, reading the handwritten words.

You've got it coming. Everything you deserve.

Fiona stifles a gasp that sounds more like a sob, then she shoves the note in her pocket and rushes back to the girls.

But when she gets outside again, Ivy and Cora are gone.

THREE

FIONA

'What do you mean, Ivy went missing?'

Jason has barely stepped inside the front door after work before Fiona is telling him what happened, stumbling over her words as she garbles everything out. She hopes it will make her feel less on edge, less rattled, as well as distract him from what's really on her mind. A kind of rapid-fire therapy to get it off her chest, as well as a way not to *totally* smash Rule Number 1 – no lying – to pieces.

After thinking about the notes all day, she's decided not to mention them to him. Her logic being that technically it's not lying, it's just an omission – and if Jason *was* behind sending the notes, then she doesn't want him to know that she's unnerved. She'll simply take it as a quiet warning and do better. Follow the rules to the letter from now on.

'The girls were outside playing and... and...' She points out of the kitchen window in the direction of the sandpit. 'And then they weren't.' She pushes her fingers through her hair, still feeling the remnants of panic. 'God, I wish it was Friday already. I need a stiff drink.'

Her tinkly laugh goes unreciprocated, and she senses Jason

has had a hard day. While his new position at the university isn't as stressful as dealing with the patients at Radmoor Hospital, where they met, she knows it comes with its own set of difficulties. Lecturing in psychiatry can't be an easy job either, though Jason isn't one to complain.

'Where was she then?' he asks, filling a glass from the tap. 'That's assuming she's not *still* missing.' He gives her a wry smile.

'She's fine. *They're* fine. Cora went missing as well.' Fiona feels a little irked that Jason is only referring to Ivy when he knows she's been looking after Cora all day, too. She wants him to treat her childminding like a proper job, given that she's had to quit nursing completely since they moved here.

'They'd just gone upstairs, can you believe?' she continues. 'The little buggers must have somehow slipped past me when I was...' She trails off.

In her mind's eye, Fiona sees herself stumbling back into the kitchen in a daze after picking up the second note from the doormat. She stood there for a few moments, staring at the carefully written words. Blue ballpoint pen on feint-ruled paper.

You've got it coming. Everything you deserve.

'When I went back outside,' Fiona continues now, 'the girls weren't where I'd left them playing.' She remembers scanning around the garden in disbelief. She'd only been gone a couple of minutes. Then she ran to the fence at the back of the garden, her eyes darting all over the fields behind their house. There... was that a figure in the distance, on the footpath? Were they running? She couldn't be sure.

Her heart thrashed from adrenaline. 'Ivy! Cora!' she yelled, rushing over to the raised-up pool to see if they were hiding behind it again. But no – no practical jokes this time.

'Anyway, as quickly as they'd disappeared, they reappeared again,' Fiona tells Jason, swallowing down the lump in her throat. The story sounds flat and a non-event as she recounts it, especially because he doesn't know that she was already on edge from the notes. 'Turns out they'd gone to get their swimming costumes on.'

She laughs it off now, but for those few moments she was genuinely afraid that something bad had happened to the girls – that they'd either wandered off or, worse, someone had abducted them.

'God, you two had me worried,' Fiona said in a shaky voice as Ivy and Cora took turns blowing up an inflatable crocodile. 'Don't go in the water until I come outside again, OK?'

Keeping her eyes firmly fixed on them through the window, Fiona slipped back into the kitchen. She took a bottle of vodka from the back of a cupboard, staring at it for a moment before quickly unscrewing the cap and taking a couple of long swigs. At the sink, she filled the bottle with water to replace the inch or two she'd drunk. No one ever need know.

'Would you like to go first today, Tilly?' Jason asks when they're all seated at the dinner table. Fiona smiles at her husband, feeling much better now it's family time – something for her to focus on, something familiar to keep her grounded. The safe routine of their lives where everyone gets to share something with the others. Rule Number 3 – family confessional every day at 6 p.m. 'Tell us about your day?'

Tilly cuts her chicken, staring down at it. 'Do I have to?'

Fiona's heart thumps. *Tilly, no... don't kick off. Not today...*

'You know the rules, love,' her father tells her calmly, though I can see he's in no mood either. 'Just a few words to get started.'

Tilly sighs, holding her knife in her fist like a toddler and poking her meat a couple of times. She tips her head sideways as she speaks, still staring at her plate.

'Today has been OK,' she begins. 'I'm glad it's the holidays. Cora came round, she and Ivy made a load of noise, I watched three episodes of *Love Island*, phoned Amber, watched the girls play while Fi— while *Mum* did stuff.' Tilly stumbles, correcting herself over Fiona's name. Jason has insisted on them calling her 'Mum', even though she said it's too soon. 'That's about it really.'

'That show is not appropriate,' Jason says with a sideways glance at Fiona. 'If you can't stick to daytime phone and internet use rules, then I'll be forced to revise them. What about a nature documentary?' he suggests. When she doesn't reply, he says, 'And now your blessings, Tilly?'

'Today I'm grateful for... for my family,' she finishes after a pause. 'For my father and... and for my... mother.' She gives them each a quick glance.

'Me next!' Ivy trills. 'Today was sooo fun!' she babbles excitedly. 'Cora came to play all day. Like, literally from this morning to just before you got back, Daddy. And Mummy let us go in the pool!'

Fiona smiles, feeling her heart warm as the little girl speaks. She loves that she calls her 'Mummy' so readily. She's old enough to have plenty of memories of her mother, and while Fiona knows she'll never take her place, she's working hard to be a stable mother figure. It's the only way for them to be a proper family.

'We played in the sandpit and the pool and watched telly, and then Mummy got upset because she thought we'd been stolen by the bad man.' Ivy giggles as she forks mashed potato into her mouth. 'But then Mummy was happy again because she had a wine.'

Fiona turns to stone but manages to say, '*Ivy!*' in an incredulous voice, trying to feign shock. Jason would not approve of her drinking. Rule Number 7 – no alcohol, apart from one drink at the weekend. 'That's not what happened at all, you little monkey.' She feels the creep of a blush on her cheeks, praying her husband doesn't notice. She shakes her head and mouths *kids* at him.

Jason stares at her.

'Did *so*,' Ivy grumbles, scowling. 'I smelt it on your breath. Yukky!'

'Knock it off, Ivy,' Tilly says, glancing at Fiona and giving her a tentative smile. 'You know Mum and Dad don't drink in the week. Mum had some medicine for her headache earlier, that's all. She joked that it was "better than alcohol" to me, and *you* got the wrong end of the stick.'

'Ivy,' Jason warns, 'you know lying is against the rules. Do you need to have a think about what you just said?'

Ivy hangs her head. 'Sorry, Daddy. Sorry, Mummy.' She takes a breath. 'Today I'm grateful for Cora coming round to play.'

'Good girl,' Jason replies, taking a sip of his water. 'Mummy's turn now. How was your day, Fiona?' he asks, reaching out and touching her hand.

Fiona glances at Tilly, who's still staring at her plate. She doesn't understand what just happened, why Tilly covered for her like that. In doing so, she lied and broke a rule herself.

'It was a good day,' she begins, turning to Jason and forcing a smile. 'We had such a lovely time in the garden. I'm so grateful for the sunshine and for our beautiful home.'

Later, as Fiona gets ready for bed, she takes the two notes from her pocket. While Jason is in the bathroom, she slips them under the mattress on her side. She'll decide what to do with them tomorrow.

As they lie under the duvet – his breathing gradually turning into soft snores – Fiona ransacks her mind for who could have sent the notes. And more to the point, *why*. She cannot think of a single soul who would do such a thing, let alone anyone who would know about their rules. And she's terrified of what they mean for her...

It takes her ages to fall asleep, but by the time she finally drifts off in the early hours, she knows one thing for sure. She's already proved the first note to be right by breaking not one but two rules today – drinking on a weekday and lying to her husband. The first time she's broken the rules. If Jason finds out, there will be consequences. A punishment, for sure, proving the second note right, too.

You've got it coming. Everything you deserve.

FOUR

FIONA

Jason and I both worked at the hospital, which is where we *officially* met – though our very first encounter was, by chance, off hospital grounds in the local village pub a week earlier. Then, only six months later, we'd married and moved in together.

I'll never forget when he called me to his office after we'd casually chatted in the Fox and Hounds the previous week. I'd stood in front of his desk gazing into his eyes, hoping he couldn't read my thoughts, relieved not to be tipsy this time.

During the few days since we'd met at the pub, he'd been on my mind a lot. Typical me – falling headfirst for someone, allowing my heart to rule my head. Needless to say, I'd been overjoyed when he'd dropped into conversation where he worked.

He'd billed this work meeting as a kind of 'getting to know you session', since he'd only been at Radmoor Hospital for about a month. He was making his way through all the staff in the department, letting everyone know his 'door was always open', as he put it. But that's the kind of man I soon learnt he was. Caring and diligent, and brilliant at his job. Dr Jason Hewitt, Medical Director and Consultant Psychiatrist, drenched everyone in his charm.

'But I have some rules,' he wasted no time telling me as I sat in his office – not that it looked much like an office with all the pot plants and homely prints on the wall. He seemed to have really settled in.

'Rules are fine by me,' I replied with a nervous laugh, staring down at my lap. He'd already mentioned some rules in the pub – though those weren't pertaining to work. Rather, he'd hinted about the strict way he governed his personal life.

I admit, I barely listened to the list of work rules he rattled off – just obvious stuff about airing any problems or grievances we had, looking after our own mental health, making sure we took proper lunch breaks, and some stuff about patient confidentiality. He also spoke about honesty, trust, respect and time-keeping, and he mentioned interpersonal relationships at the hospital – that one certainly made my ears prick up. Overall, there was nothing out of the ordinary or *too* strict. But he clearly ran a tight ship.

I came away from the meeting wondering if he liked me too. Though deep down, I knew a man like him wouldn't be interested in someone like me – and it would be such a cliché, a doctor–nurse affair.

The irony was I hadn't wanted to be at Radmoor in the first place, but I hadn't had much choice about taking the position, almost a year ago now – not after what had happened at the previous hospital. I'd been keeping my head down and getting on with my job here, but since meeting Jason... well, it had brightened up my days knowing I might bump into him while going about my duties.

'You've got a twinkle in your eye,' someone in the corridor said as I walked past.

'It's a twinkle-in-the-eye kind of a day!' I said to the woman, who had her back pressed to the corridor wall as I passed. I gave her a wink, clutching my clipboard as I went on my rounds.

At first, I wasn't sure if the woman was a nurse or a patient – her face wasn't familiar and not all Radmoor staff wore uniforms, depending on their role, though we all wore name badges. But that evening, I spotted her picking at her food at the dinner table, a uniformed nurse passing her a little paper cup of medication, and I realised she was a patient. The poor lamb. She looked underweight and scared. She must have been new as I hadn't encountered her on my rounds before.

I say *rounds*... nursing staff like me did our best to blend in, giving the patients a sense of being at home on their journey to wellness rather than feeling like prisoners in the stark mental institution hidden beneath the luxurious façade.

On arrival, visitors or newcomers to Radmoor Hospital saw a tree-lined driveway, a honey-coloured stone mansion with plush carpets in the foyer, vases of expensive fresh flowers on antique tables at every turn, tea and cakes served every day at 4 p.m. on the dot in the visiting room, plus compassionate nurses overseen by competent and experienced doctors to get their loved ones better.

A plaque on the wooden panelling above the reception desk, staffed by a woman with coiffured hair and peach lipstick, read: *You are worthy of happiness*. There were other nauseating and patronising quotes about mental health and positivity dotted around the main building. And that was the aim at Radmoor – to pack everyone off home with a smile on their face and joy in their heart, whether it was the product of medication, therapy or the patient faking it just so they could escape.

But the reality behind the scenes was very different. Patient accommodation wasn't located in the lavish building that visi-

tors to Radmoor encountered. Outsiders never got to see North
Wing, which was more like a prison than a hospital with its
endless Victorian tiled corridors where the ECT and isolation
rooms were located. Nor did they hear the guttural wails
emanating from Jensen Ward, the high-security section of
Radmoor Private Psychiatric Hospital and Rehabilitation
Centre – a truly chilling sound when I first heard it. Police
escorts and prison guards were a common sight there.

'Hello, Susie, how are you doing?' I called out, knocking and
poking my head into the next room on my rounds. A uniformed
nurse sat on a chair in the corner looking bored. I gave her a nod,
knowing Susie must have done something bad again to warrant
a one-on-one nurse.

She was lying on her bed picking at a bandage on her forearm, and I was about to sit down for a chat, but she suddenly
lunged at me, growling and baring her teeth.

'Fuck off, fuck off, *fuck off, you crazy bitch...*' she screamed
until, between us, the other nurse and I grabbed her by the
shoulders and managed to calm her down.

'I'll come back later,' I said, knowing she'd probably get a
shot of haloperidol when the meds trolley did the rounds. I had
to remember that I wasn't there to engage with her: my job was
to check that the patients were accounted for and present in the
building. It was one of the least favourite tasks on this ward, but
someone had to do it.

I knocked on the next door along the corridor – an endless
warren with soul-baring lighting and strategically placed panic
buttons. Though Isaac Ward was still far better than the secure
units of North Wing.

When I first started, I was told not to discuss the hospital
with outsiders. That it wasn't good for the Radmoor brand.
There were four other hospitals in the group, all with the same
ethos: *Everyone deserves a future.* 'What happens in Radmoor
stays in Radmoor,' was drummed into me on my first day.

'Hi, Kevin, all OK?' I said, popping my head around his door. As soon as he heard me come in, he leapt off his bed, wafting a towel around to disperse the haze from a recent spliff. He relaxed when he saw it was just me, knowing I'd keep quiet.

'Y'all right,' he replied, lying down on his bed again. 'S'up?'

I stood there with my clipboard, sizing him up. From what I'd heard, he'd been in and out of Radmoor most of his adult life with prolonged psychotic episodes. Apparently, his wealthy parents were footing the bill.

'Helen got discharged and went home,' I told him, checking off his name on the clipboard. 'That's about it.'

Kevin lifted his chin in a nod, probably mulling over the word *home* in his mind. For many patients, him included, home was a make-believe castle in a fairy-tale land. Far, far away.

'I heard it's Chicken *Kevs* for lunch,' I told him with a wink – what he called his favourite meal. I hoped it would give him a lift.

As I turned to leave, Kevin smiled. An unfiltered grin blooming behind his wispy stubble exposing a couple of black teeth and cracked lips. 'Gwegory likey dat,' I heard him say in a babyish voice as I closed the door behind me – his little boy persona coming out.

'Oh!' I gasped, immediately bumping into someone. 'I'm *so* sorry... Doctor.'

'It's Jason, please,' he reminded me. 'Or you can just call me Doc. No formalities needed around here.'

I bowed my head, trying to hide the blush creeping up my cheeks. While I fancied him like mad – as did all the nurses – I didn't want him to know that I was crushing hard.

'Sorry, *Jason*,' I said. 'It was good to meet you in your office earlier.'

'Likewise,' he replied, giving me a broad smile.

'Just doing the rounds,' I told him, holding up my clipboard, unsure whether I should carry on or stop for a chat. The idiocy of my thinking a consultant psychiatrist would be interested in my menial task only occurred to me later when I was banging my head against the wall in my bedroom, replaying the excruciating encounter over and over, hoping to extract some tiny detail that might make me not feel quite such a loon. I'd even shown him my clipboard. *As if he needed to see your inane jottings about the patients, Fiona. As if!*

As I went over it for the hundredth time in my mind, I really, *really* wished I'd had the confidence to ask him out for a drink, or see if he fancied grabbing some food one evening after work, or maybe a movie, or if he'd like to follow me to a darkened storeroom right there and then for passionate sex. But I didn't. I kept quiet.

I *think* I kept quiet.

Sometimes I can't be sure what comes out of my mouth.

'Well, nice to see you're keeping busy,' Jason replied, walking alongside me down the corridor. It was time for my break and, as it turned out, Jason was headed to the coffee machine too.

'Always,' I replied, wondering if I should tell him it wasn't my first time working at Radmoor – though previously it had been on a temporary contract. This time, things felt more permanent, and in that knowledge, I felt more settled. I'd had something of a career setback before coming here – I hated thinking about my prior dismissal – but there was a lot more I wanted to achieve. Thankfully, my work here seemed like a solid basis for that. A nursing qualification like mine opened doors – around the world, not just in the sleepy backwaters of the South Warwickshire countryside.

'I'm still getting to know the ropes,' Jason revealed with a smile. 'As well as trying not to get lost.'

'If I can help in any way,' I said, 'then let me know.'

He smiled, holding open the door to the common room. There was only one other person in there – a room filled with

easy chairs, magazines, a fridge for sandwiches and snacks. It
was unusual for it to be so empty at this time of day.

As we stood at the drinks machine, we both reached out for
the same cup on the stack, our fingers brushing together. I
gasped, turning to face him, wondering if he felt them too – the
tiny electric shocks jumping between our hands.

FIVE

JASON

Before they go to bed that night, Jason notices his wife lift the corner of their mattress and tuck something underneath it. He was going to fetch his pyjama bottoms to put on after his shower but hesitates after seeing Fiona acting... strangely.

He darts back into the en suite bathroom. *What is she hiding?*

The thought of her keeping a secret from him makes him simmer inside. He steps inside the shower cubicle, allowing the water to scald his skin. Afterwards, he climbs into bed beside his wife, and they begin the bedtime confessional. Rule Number 5 – husband and wife must share a nightly secret.

'Honestly...?' Fiona begins, as if there is another option. She sighs.

An early warning of what's on her mind? Jason wonders.

'I had bad thoughts today, Jase. Bad thoughts that Ivy and Tilly were...' He feels her shudder. 'That they were taken from us. It was horrid.'

'It's OK, love,' Jason says with less warmth in his tone than usual. 'They're both safe and tucked up in bed. It's just your nerves. Have you been taking your pills?'

She gives a little nod.

'As for my secret,' Jason says through a disappointed sigh, 'I admit to feeling murderous at the university earlier.' Then he gives a little laugh to show he doesn't really mean it. He can't be bothered with real truths tonight. Since Fiona hasn't confessed to hiding anything under the mattress, there's an itch inside him. It physically hurts. 'Just some problems with timetabling.'

Fiona responds with a sympathetic sound and, not long after that, she falls asleep. Jason lies awake for hours, his mind stewing and going over what he saw. The only thing he knows for sure is that his wife is lying to him about something. A gross violation of the rules.

In the morning, he dithers getting dressed, waiting for Fiona to leave the room first. When she's gone downstairs, he shoves his hand under the corner of the mattress and pulls out two folded pieces of paper with her name on them. He opens them up.

I know what you did... You broke a rule.

You've got it coming. Everything you deserve.

Jason lets out a low growl, rereading the words, studying the handwriting. Then he takes a photo of the notes on his phone and tucks the bits of paper back where he found them. He isn't sure what bothers him the most – the fact that someone has sent these sinister messages to his wife, or the fact that she hasn't told him.

Either way, rules have been broken.

Either way, there will be consequences.

. . .

Jason takes his campus pass from his pocket, touching it on the swipe pad at the entrance to his university building. He started his job here three weeks ago, a month or so after they'd settled into their new home. On his first day he'd found a welcome pack from his boss left in the staff area – making him feel a bit miffed by the lack of personal greeting, as if his taking the job was a non-event to them. To make matters worse, he had no way of even getting into the department or knowing which was his office on that first morning. He'd have appreciated someone showing up to welcome him, at least.

Embarrassingly, a colleague had let him into the building, showing him where the staff pigeonholes were, giving him a quick rundown of the best place to get coffee and lunch on campus. He was grateful for the man's kindness, though he'd had to rush off, so it took Jason another half an hour to find his office – a small, cramped space on the second floor, the door to which, thankfully, the swipe card in the welcome pack opened. Though he couldn't help thinking that it looked as though its last occupier had simply upped and left, since their office was a mess of their abandoned detritus. He wondered then if it was an omen, a warning about how the department was run.

There's no denying, though, that his position here couldn't be more dissimilar to his work at Radmoor – a part of him misses being on the front line of psychiatric care, the day-to-day challenges that brings. But, despite the different – but still heady – challenges of his new job, there's something nostalgic about being back at the institution where his own medical career began at the prestigious Canonfield University. It's where his father also once studied, going on to become a Harley Street psychiatrist.

Jason sits down at his desk, gazing around at everything – the many books, papers, files and resources inherited from his predecessor. In time, he'll make the space more his own.

Thankfully, his schedule is light today with only one PhD

student meeting at 1.30 p.m., followed by a quiet session of planning lunchtime lectures for a couple of department heads. All chilled summer holiday stuff before the real onslaught of teaching begins next term. He doesn't feel particularly prepared or cut out for the lecturing, but chooses not to think about that yet. He picks up a stack of papers on the desk.

A couple of hours later, once he's dealt with a few tasks, Jason strides down the empty corridors, his footsteps echoing. The university seems like a different place without the students. Eerie, almost, with a ghostly feel after the end-of-term exodus last week. Outside, the central plaza with the student union building and campus café are all but deserted as he goes to buy his late-morning coffee and bagel. No queueing with rambunctious or hungover students as in term time.

He smiles to himself as he heads back to his office to prepare for his meeting with Rosanne, the PhD student, reminded of his own university days here – though he shudders as he recalls his second year at the medical school. Things didn't quite go to plan. But now, back working here, he's aware that in a couple of months he'll bear witness to the students' rites of passage from the other side of the fence, a different angle, almost as if he'll be reliving his training. A second chance.

Back at his desk, Jason carefully unwraps and bites into his ham, lettuce and tomato bagel, paid for in cash. There's something old-fashioned about the feel of coins and notes in his wallet. He's traditional like that. He places his bagel down and removes the plastic lid from his coffee cup. The bread seems drier today. And the coffee tastes... bitter or burnt. The coffee shop isn't on top form, he thinks, scrolling through emails on his phone as he eats.

Or maybe it's *him* who isn't on top form today. Rattled by those damn notes under the mattress.

Jason flicks to his photos app, looking at the two pictures he took earlier. Nothing about the notes makes any sense. Why did

Fiona hide them from him? Why did she tuck them under the mattress? And more to the point, who sent them? If they're important enough to keep, to *conceal*, then they're important enough to tell him about. Otherwise, she'd have simply ripped them up and binned them, giving them a quick mention in their nightly confessional.

For a second, he wonders if she's written them herself, perhaps to use as some kind of practical joke. But that's so un-Fiona-like. She might once have been a bit of a prankster, loving nothing more than a laugh, but not these days. She's grown serious, cautious, anxious – and, to be honest, he can't help thinking, she's becoming a bit of a bore.

His lunch eaten and the paperwork on his desk shuffled through several times, Jason stares at the clock on the wall. It's nearly 2.45 p.m. and there hasn't been so much as a flicker of Rosanne passing this way. He'd randomly bumped into her outside the medical building last week and they'd got chatting, her enthusiastically telling him about her research. Being the generous person he is, Jason offered a one-off tutoring session, given her field aligns with his work, and she jumped at the chance. Though in hindsight, he can't help wondering if she was... well, a bit flirtatious with him as they chatted, and hopes she didn't get the wrong impression about this meeting. He glances at his watch again. She was due at 1.30 p.m. Stupid, *stupid* girl.

He sighs, sitting with his arms folded, his legs crossed and one foot jiggling impatiently. Someone passes by in the corridor outside his office, but the footsteps come and go. Probably a janitor or security.

The longer he stares at the clock, the slower it seems to go until he's convinced the hands are turning backwards.

'Fuck it...' he whispers, feeling his body judder. Sometimes he thinks he might be better off working back at Radmoor, doing some actual good in the world. Did he do the right thing by leaving? Another shudder twists through him, knotting his insides.

There's no doubt he felt secure there, as though he had a real purpose in life. And in the short time he was at the hospital, he certainly made a positive impact on staff and patients alike. But then things... well, everything changed, and he was left with no option but to depart. And, of course, Fiona came with him. Under the circumstances, it felt like the only way out – though they knew people would still gossip, still speculate about their affair, about his wife's untimely death. Their relationship had caused ripples. A tsunami, if he's honest.

Coming back to Canonfield University had seemed like a good idea a few weeks ago when he'd accepted the post, especially as it's not far from where they live. Though he's now wondering if he's going to be satisfied working here after all. It's a far cry from what he's used to.

It's as he's packing up to leave for the day, having given up waiting for Rosanne, deciding to go home instead, that there's a sharp knock at his door. He startles, his mouth curling into a lopsided smile.

Finally, he thinks, going to let her in.

SIX
JASON

The notes are still on his mind when Jason arrives home later. As soon as he walks through the front door, he's hit by the screeching sound of young children, their shrill squeals battering his senses before he's even had time to slip off his shoes. He's not sure he's ever been cut out for family life, really, having mostly left the care of their daughters to Erika in the past. How she juggled her demanding career with raising the girls, he's not sure, but somehow she did. He's hoping that, with the rules in place, Fiona will step up to fill her shoes.

'I'm back!' he calls out from the hall, wincing as another shriek emanates from upstairs. At least the kid from next door won't be here tomorrow. *Or ever again if I get my way.*

Fiona doesn't reply – just more whooping, laughing and giggling coming from upstairs. He heads into the kitchen. His mind is still thrumming from his earlier encounter with Rosanne – he still can't believe what she said to him, or rather what she *implied*. A frown creeps across his face. That kind of talk at work, it won't do.

In the kitchen, Jason sees two plates on the table littered with the remains of what looks like pizza and chips, cutlery haphazardly strewn about, and a couple of cans of fizzy pop. There's washing up piled beside the sink, and the floor is littered with crumbs and wet, muddy footprints leading in from the back door.

'What a mess,' he says, picking up a wet towel from the floor.

He drapes it over the back of a chair, catching sight of Fiona in the garden, sitting at the patio table with a bloody glass of wine in her hand. Something inside him tightens.

'Fiona!' he booms, striding outside, wondering if his tone is too harsh considering there's a visitor sitting opposite his wife – Sascha from next door. She swings round at the sound of him approaching, while Fiona's shoulders tense up around her ears.

'Howdy, Jason,' Sascha says, her eyes flicking up and down him. Jason doesn't know if it's a scathing look or if she's mentally undressing him. 'Hard day at the office?' Then she laughs before sipping more wine, shaking her head. *The nerve of the woman.*

He approaches the table, noticing that the bottle of wine is almost empty. What the hell is Fiona playing at, boozing on a Tuesday? Rule Number 7: No alcohol, apart from one drink at the weekend.

Maybe there was substance to Ivy's accusation last night, after all. He goes up to his wife, leaning down to kiss her on the cheek. Oddly, she doesn't acknowledge him or kiss him back or even turn to look up at him. What has that bitch from next door been saying? He gives her a glare. He knows her type.

'It's not the weekend, love,' Jason says, reaching out to take the wine glass from Fiona's hand. But she holds onto it tightly. 'Darling, let me have it.'

'It's only the one drink,' she says, her voice quiet. But still, she doesn't look at him. 'Just a small glass of wine.' She stares out over the fields behind the house.

'I know, I know, but...' *It looks more like half a bottle to me... The rules, darling*, he wants to scream in her face. *Our fucking marriage rules...* Instead, he says, 'But best you don't.' Again, he attempts to take the glass from his wife's hand and, thank God, this time she relinquishes it.

'What the actual *fuck*?' Sascha leans forward across the wrought-iron table, a deep scowl etched on her face as she flashes disbelieving looks between Jason and Fiona. 'Here, have my drink, Fi,' she says, passing her glass of wine to Fiona. 'It's just wine, Jason, not bloody crack cocaine. Keep your hair on.'

Without responding, Jason reaches out and plucks the glass from Sascha's hand before Fiona has a chance to take it. Then he makes a grab for the bottle and goes to the kitchen, tipping all the wine down the sink.

'I'm sorry,' he hears his wife say quietly to Sascha out in the garden. 'It's just we have these... these sort of... Well, we don't drink in the week, that's all. Just on a bit of a health kick.' He hears her tinkly laugh. *Good girl*, he thinks.

'Riiight,' Sascha replies slowly, the word stretched out. She looks up when Jason comes back outside. 'Your idea, was it? The health kick?'

He's not sure if she's being passive-aggressive or if she's genuinely interested. 'A joint decision,' he replies, sitting down beside Fiona. 'Is dinner ready?' he directs at his wife, looping his arm around her shoulders. 'Something in the oven?'

Fiona turns to him, a vacant look in her eyes. She shakes her head – barely a movement. 'Not yet,' she admits quietly.

'Time got away,' Sascha informs him, her eyes narrowing. 'We've been chatting.'

'The thing is,' Jason tells her, 'Fiona always has dinner ready for when I'm home. I'm not sure this... *arrangement*... with your daughter is going to work out.'

'Good grief,' Sascha says, leaning back in her chair. 'Hold on... there's a message from the nineteen fifties coming in for you, Jason…' She puts a forefinger on each temple, rolling her eyes. 'They say they want you back.'

'Look, it's not like that,' he replies. 'We just have our way of doing things. That's all.' Jason stands up, tugging on his wife's sleeve. 'Come on, love, let's get on with our evening.' He stares down at her, confident she'll take the hint.

'Yes, sorry, you're right,' Fiona says after what seems like an age. She stands, thanking Sascha for bringing the wine, telling her she'll maybe see her at the weekend. That perhaps Ivy and Cora could play together at the park. They head for the hallway.

'But you're still on for childminding next Monday, right?' Jason hears Sascha asking his wife as she stands just outside the open front door, having called up to Cora that they're leaving.

Like mother, like daughter with the loud voices, Jason thinks, hovering in the kitchen doorway, not wanting to appear overbearing, but the rules are there for a reason.

'It should be OK,' he hears Fiona reply quietly. 'I'll have a word with Jase and text you.'

'What, you're seriously going to let him dictate to you like that?' comes Sascha's reply. 'Fi, it's… it's really controlling.' She lowers her voice for the last bit, but Jason still hears. He's only a few feet away.

'It's not like that,' Fiona tells her. *Good girl*, Jason thinks again. 'He's just watching out for me. Making sure I don't overdo it. And Tilly and Ivy have been through a lot lately… with… with…' She trails off. 'So routine is really important for all of us.'

'Just don't be *that* woman, Fi,' Sascha says as she's leaving. 'I know I've only known you a couple of months, but I've noticed a few things he's said that are a bit… well, *off* if I'm honest. You're smart. You're intelligent. You're a qualified nurse, for God's sake. Don't cover for an arsehole,' she adds in a loud whisper.

Drunk, Jason thinks, shaking his head.

'I won't!' Fiona sings brightly. 'See you soon. Bye, Cora!' she adds chirpily. Jason quickly darts to the sink, grabbing the dish-cloth and turning on the tap as he makes it look as though he's been washing the glasses.

'So,' he says without looking up, 'what time do you call this? When are we going to eat?'

Fiona hangs her head.

'Go on, what time is it?'

Fiona glances at her wrist, shrugging.

'Where's the watch I bought you?' Jason snaps.

Another shrug. 'It's in there where you told me to put it for safekeeping.' She points to a kitchen drawer. 'The catch still needs fixing, and I didn't want to risk losing—'

'For God's sake, Fiona! You've been drinking all evening. You don't know what time it is. And now we're going to starve. Is this in the rules?' His chest tightens as though there's a strap around his body.

'I can whip up some pasta,' Fiona says. 'The girls have already eaten.'

'So I see,' Jason replies, casting a glance over the messy kitchen table. 'Did you not consider rule number three either, our family confessional? Do you not think your time would have been better spent clearing up in here and preparing a meal for us?' He puts the dirty glasses in the sink, then dries his hands, taking hold of Fiona's arms. 'Getting pissed in the garden with that... *woman* is not my idea of a productive evening, Fiona.' He can't help the stern tone.

'I'm sorry, but—'

'No room for sorry,' he says, giving her arms a squeeze, wondering if she's put on a bit of weight. He steps back, folding his arms. 'You know what happens now,' he says, staring her in the eye. But at the edge of his field of vision, over by the door, he sees a figure lurking.

'Oh *no*... Do I have to?' Fiona says quietly, tears collecting in her eyes. '*Please*... I can whip something up for us in no time. Pasta and salad? We agreed that I could do this job, looking after Cora. It's cash in hand, Jase. It's what we need.'

'What *you* need, you mean. I don't like it. If you want more money, you only have to ask me. Is ten pounds OK?' He removes his wallet from his back pocket. Another glance at the door tells him the lurker is still watching them. 'Tilly, come out, for God's sake. I know you're there.'

'Sorry, Dad,' his eldest daughter says, slinking into the kitchen. 'I just came to get some water.'

Jason notices the way she looks at Fiona, unsure if it's disgust or pity, or some kind of silent female communication. Either way, he doesn't like it. He feels sidelined, ganged up on. All these women in the house going against him. Only Ivy seems to follow the rules and do as she's told, but now he's concerned about her being corrupted by the child from next door. He waits until Tilly has filled her glass and retreated, leaving with a backwards glance at Fiona.

'I'll tell you what's going to happen now, Fiona.' Jason takes her hands, giving them a gentle tug until she looks up at him, her eyes heavy. 'You're going to make my dinner – just mine, not yours – and then you're going to go upstairs to the spare room. You're going to take off all your clothes, keep the light on and stand up all night so that you can think about everything you've done. We'll discuss ending the arrangement with Sascha in the morning. And, more to the point, we'll discuss the notes that you hid from me under the mattress, too.'

SEVEN
JASON

Jason slept well, giving him a sense of calm once again. And after a night standing up – he made a couple of random checks on her when he needed the bathroom – Fiona seems more her usual self, too: reasonable and content, understanding and attentive as she quietly makes breakfast.

It's almost impossible for him to explain to anyone what he puts up with, how tolerant he is of her behaviour, but behind closed doors Fiona is not easy to live with. He doesn't want to come across as controlling – far from it – but experience has shown him that a firm hand is best. Which is why their marriage rules work so well, especially when he's not around. But more than anything, he just wants her to be happy.

'Do you think I could take the girls for a walk today?' Fiona asks, passing him a plate of scrambled eggs on toast.

He grabs her hand, squeezing it tightly, crushing her fingers together. She freezes before pulling away. 'A walk is not a good idea, Fiona. Rule number four – no leaving the house without good reason, remember?'

'Ooh, I want to go on a walk! Where to?' Ivy skids into the kitchen in her socks. 'Is Cora coming again today?' She puts her palms together in a praying action, batting her eyelashes up at Fiona and pouting her lips. 'Can she come on the walk too?'

'Not today,' Fiona replies. Jason notices the nervous glance she gives Ivy. Gives her *daughter*, he corrects in his mind. He must get used to that – Fiona being his girls' mother now. *Fake it until we make it*, he once told her.

His first wife's death knocked them all for six. Telling his daughters that their mother had been killed in a terrible accident, her car crushed by a lorry, the driver drunk at the wheel, was the hardest thing he'd ever had to do – made even worse by it happening the day before he and Fiona got married and moved in here.

Thing is, he can hardly tell his daughters the truth about their mother. All they really need to know is that she isn't coming back, and that they might as well get used to having Fiona as their new mum.

It's the way things are now, and Rule Number 6 – never talk about the past – is there for a reason.

To help them get over the loss of their birth mother, Jason did much research into grief, discovering a fascinating medical report specifically about children losing a parent. Admittedly, it hadn't been peer-reviewed and nor was it part of mainstream research through a university, but the blogger's principle had chimed with him. Made him think it could be a useful technique to try on his daughters. The psychiatrist in him coming out.

It was where Rule Number 8 – grieving hour every Sunday at 5 p.m. – came from. The crux of the theory is to ring-fence their sorrow into bite-size chunks and allow time-limited sessions in which to show their emotions. His daughters are not allowed to feel sadness at any other time.

'I just thought we could wander down to the stables to see the horses,' Fiona presses on, stifling a yawn as she hands Ivy her breakfast. 'Would that be OK?' Tilly saunters into the room, going up to the cooker to help her mother. 'I could even check out how much riding lessons are for the girls.'

'Wicked!' Ivy sings. 'Will Cora be at the stables?'

'Wait,' Jason says, laying down his knife and fork. 'What you really mean is that you're going to the riding school to see that woman from next door, right?' He sighs heavily. 'I can't make it any clearer that she and her wayward daughter are bad influences, Fiona.' Jason cuts his toast in half. 'The answer is no.'

'Cora is with her grandma today,' Fiona says quietly to Ivy. 'So she won't be at the stables. And I'm not specifically going there to see Sascha,' she tells him. 'She'll be busy working anyway. I just thought the girls would like to see the horses, that's all. We can take the short cut across the fields. It's a nice day and a pleasant route. I thought we could come back via the lane and stop off at the little café in the village for—'

'And you think that's safe, do you? The three of you walking alone in the remote countryside?' Jason bangs his fist on the table.

'I hadn't really thought about—'

'*Exactly*,' he says. 'You hadn't thought. Engage the grey matter, darling,' he adds with a laugh to show her he's being kind rather than bossy.

'Well, I'd really love to go on a walk, Fi... *Mum*,' Tilly says, stumbling over her words. 'And Dad, we'll be fine. The walk is popular. There'll be other people on the footpath.' She serves a plate of eggs then hands it to Fiona. 'Here you go, Mum. You have this.'

'Can we? Can we? Pretty *please*, Daddy? I really, *really* want to see the horses. Cora said there's this bay called Sparkler who's her favourite and I really want to stroke him.' Ivy sucks in a deep breath, holding it as she waits for her father to reply. Then, when he shakes his head, reiterating his decision, she lets it go in a burst of disappointment.

. . .

Before Jason heads out for work he secretly packs his gym bag with a change of clothes – dark combats, a brown sweatshirt, a beanie hat, boots – and kisses his family goodbye. Instead of driving the eleven miles to the university, he travels about a mile down the road, taking a different country lane leading from the village – the one that veers round the fields behind their house, tracking the canal before the bridge. He stops in a lay-by beside some woodland, struggling into the change of clothes while still sitting in the driver's seat. He doesn't want to be spotted.

Then he puts on his sunglasses and beanie, gets out, locks the car, climbs over the five-bar gate and strides to the side of the wooded area into a field of ripe wheat. He skirts around the edge, keeping close to the perimeter hedge as he heads back towards the village with the canal towpath a field over to his right. The route takes him close to the back of their house in the cul-de-sac. He positions himself behind the old oak tree that he often admires from their upstairs landing as he stares out across the view. It's a solid, ancient tree that gives him cover – far enough away not to be spotted, but close enough for him to watch his wife. As he squats at the base of the tree's broad trunk, he has a moment of guilt, remorse, *shame* even.

If Fiona knew what he was up to, she'd be mad as hell, accusing him of spying on her, of controlling her. But he knows it's not like that – knows that he's doing this for her safety as well as the safety of his daughters. God, if anything happened to them, he'd never forgive himself.

Jason freezes. *There, look... in the distance. That's them!* Despite him telling her several times that the walk is off limits, that she and the girls must stay at home, that it's too soon for her to be undertaking such trips out, here she is helping his two daughters climb over the fence at the back of their house before leading them across the fields.

Little specks in the distance – that's all they are – but he can quite clearly see it's Fiona, Tilly and Ivy. His daughters' flaxen hair is the same colour as the wheat in the nearby fields, while Fiona's long, almost black hair falls in a straggly ponytail down her back. But it's her bright blue T-shirt that gives her away, the one she had on in the kitchen this morning.

A shrill laugh carries up the incline on the breeze. Fiona. His wife is bloody laughing.

Jason waits, watches, bides his time until they've crossed the field and reached the stile and the public footpath sign to the east of where he's positioned – the path that leads towards the canal and the derelict old barn in the field beyond. Once they've climbed over, he leaves the cover of the tree and follows on behind them, panting as he runs across the open field to the nearest hedge, then tracking along it down to the stile. When he reaches the fence, he scans around the next field, looking for them.

There... there they are – his daughters taking big, silly strides, holding hands, their arms swinging, the breeze in their hair. And Fiona is leading the way like Dora the fucking Explorer, her phone in her hand, a black sweatshirt tied around her waist.

Something inside Jason's chest begins to burn. Like a pan boiling dry. His top lip twitches and there's a ringing in his ears.

Stupid, stupid woman, he thinks, putting one foot up on the stile, a hand on the wooden post. As he climbs over, he doesn't take his eyes off his wife as he heads towards the cover of the old brick barn – his next hiding spot – counting up all the rules she's broken today, working out what her punishment will be.

EIGHT

FIONA

Before

Later that same day – the day I had my first official meeting with Dr Hewitt in his office – I reflected on my two encounters with him while curled up in my bed, the TV on in the background.

'Doctor, Doctor, Doc-*tor*...' I mumbled as a handsome actor in a white coat strode onscreen. Medical dramas were my favourite. I chuckled at the thought of a real-life hospital romance playing out at Radmoor – though I could do without the drama part. I'd had enough of that in my life so far. Take what had happened at my previous job, for instance. My barrister told me I'd got off lightly.

Thankfully no one was around to hear my musings as I lay in bed that evening. I had a room to myself, but I shared a bathroom with a couple of others – as well as a tiny kitchen that was only really fit for microwaving meals or making a cup of tea. I was the first to admit that my living arrangements weren't ideal for a woman of my age – more suited to a student, to be honest – but for now, it would have to do. I was getting back on my feet after my last job and, while I was ambitious, I refused to be too hard on myself.

Besides, if I played my cards right, perhaps things would develop between me and Jason, and we'd fall in love and get a place of our own. I envisaged a house in a quiet area with pleasant views, nice neighbours and a friendly local pub. Maybe we'd even get a dog. But that was just me fantasising, of course...

'Two point four children and an SUV on the drive,' I said, laughing to myself as the reminder alert sounded on my phone. I hauled myself off the bed and went to the shared kitchen.

'Hey, Tanya,' I said. I reckoned she was in her early thirties. 'I didn't realise you were on duty tonight.' I eyed her pale blue nursing uniform. She also worked at Radmoor but had been there a lot longer than me.

''Fraid so,' she grumbled, glancing at her watch, seeming in a hurry. She reached round behind her and handed me what I'd come in for – my packet of pills. It saved me squeezing past her in the tiny space, and while we didn't know each other intimately, we were on trusting enough terms for me to be open about my medication.

In fact, it was quite common among medical staff. We'd had a few late-night chats about it after our work shifts ended, confiding in each other about the stresses of our profession.

I ran a glass of water, popping the pill in my mouth while Tanya busied about.

'That cough's no better, is it?' she commented, sounding concerned.

I raised a hand, trying not to spray water everywhere. 'I'm fine,' I said. 'Just went down the wrong way.' I covered my mouth and coughed again.

'I was about to order you on strict bed rest,' Tanya said in a silly yet genuinely caring voice. 'Doctor's orders.'

'I'd take orders from that Dr Hewitt,' I joked.

'Wouldn't we all,' Tanya replied, giving me a nudge.

Back in my room, earphones in and relaxing music playing, I wrote in my journal, a grin sliding across my face. When I'd started it, it had been meant to be for gratitude, but it soon turned into a stream of consciousness and ramblings that helped me decompress after a day on the wards.

I met the new psychiatrist today, Dr Jason Hewitt. Doc, he calls himself. There's something about him that intrigues me... excites me... makes me giddy... If only he felt the same. I wish I had the guts to ask him out.

Over the next couple of weeks, I tried to make it so I bumped into Dr Hewitt whenever I could. I took note of when he had a coffee break or went outside to stretch his legs and get some fresh air, making sure that I happened to be in the same place at the same time, too. Once or twice, I plucked up the courage to chat to him, and he seemed happy to engage, laughing and chatting back. I learnt that he enjoyed playing golf, preferred hiking holidays to lying on the beach, was a total horror movie geek, and that he had a vast collection of vinyl records.

I wrote furiously in my journal, detailing every word I could remember about our meetings, and every feeling I'd had during our encounters, each one seeming more special than the last. I prayed that before long I'd find the courage to see if he'd like to meet up outside the hospital.

One morning, my mind was made up. *Fortune favours the brave*, I remember my mother once telling me – though at the time she'd had two black eyes from my father's fists, so it had been hard to take her seriously given that she'd stuck with him for twenty years.

But I decided that today *was* the day to be brave – a chilly, early December day with overcast skies and a whisper of

Christmas in the air – so I engineered a reason to go to Dr Hewitt's office. Some vague excuse about the possibility of new sign-off sheets for the observations rounds. As soon as I knocked on his door, it was yanked open and, instead of Jason standing there, I found myself face to face with a woman.

A woman I'd seen around the hospital several times but had never met before. I knew she was high up, and her reputation sent shivers down my spine.

Dr Erika Norstrom – the Chief Medical Director of Radmoor Hospital.

'Yes?' she snapped. Her Swedish accent was audible even in the single syllable.

'Oh... I, sorry. I...' I tucked my hair behind my ear from where it had fallen out of my clip. I shifted from one foot to the other, smoothing down my cotton shirt. 'Is Jason... Dr Hewitt in his office?'

'No,' the woman said. She glared at me from beneath her sharply cut, ice-blonde fringe that settled halfway down her high forehead. The rest of her pale, angular face was framed by a straight bob cut, skimming the tops of her broad shoulders, which sat coat hanger-like beneath her cream silk blouse. She must have been almost six feet tall, though I spotted she was wearing heels.

'Oh, OK... I...' I stuttered and stammered through a few syllables of nonsense, my eyes darting behind her to Jason's desk.

'Do you not believe me?' she said in a bitingly cold tone. Then she stepped aside and flung the door open wide. 'See? No Dr Hewitt. Or should I say *Jason*?'

My mouth was so dry, it felt as though my lips needed peeling apart to speak. 'Sorry, I believe you. I just... I'll come back later.' I bowed my head and turned to go.

'Perhaps it's something I can help you with... Fiona, isn't it?' Her voice softened a little.

I stopped in my tracks. *She knows my name.* The eminent Dr Erika Norstrom – world-renowned researcher and leader in her field – knew my fucking name.

Something fizzed inside me. Maybe she'd read through my file, seen my CV and gone through my history. Perhaps she'd spotted something in my medical background that warranted her attention. Or, I stupidly thought, maybe I was up for a promotion. That would mean more money, maybe allowing me to get a place of my own.

All this was spinning around my mind as Dr Norstrom stood there, sizing me up, making me believe I was special. That she – one of the *powers that be* around here – had singled me out.

'No... no, I don't think so,' I said, knowing I couldn't possibly reveal the real reason I'd knocked on Jason's door – to ask him out for a drink. I squirmed inside. 'I was just following up on something we were discussing yesterday,' I lied, praising myself for quick thinking.

'Such as?' Dr Norstrom pressed on.

'It was... it was just about a patient, that's all.'

'That's *all*?' she scoffed, opening the door wider and beckoning me inside. Then she pointed to a chair by Dr Hewitt's desk. 'Sit,' she instructed, shutting the door behind me.

My heart decided it was a good time to deliver a run of anxiety-induced palpitations, but I was determined not to let my discomfort show on my face as I sat down. Dr Norstrom took a few long-legged strides and lowered herself into the chair opposite me.

Word was that she conducted ground-breaking work in the scientific research facility located on-site – and there were rumours that she used actual patients as experimental test subjects in unauthorised trials. I shuddered at the thought.

'Now,' Dr Norstrom said, leaning forward. 'Which patient did you wish to discuss?'

My mind went blank. Of course, there was no patient. I'd simply wanted to see Jason before my shift started and test the waters about asking him out. I was thinking the Three Horseshoes in town for a couple of drinks, perhaps some food, too.

'Kevin,' I said eventually.

'What about him?' she asked. The forefinger of her right hand tapped impatiently on the desk, its shiny, blood-red tip mesmerising.

'I'm not sure he's... making as much progress as he should be,' I blurted out.

'What makes you say that?'

I wanted to tell her that he'd been drinking and smoking weed again but held back. There's a strict no alcohol and drugs policy at Radmoor, though it was widely known that some inpatients who had privileges and were allowed into the nearby town would sneak alcohol into the hospital, either for themselves or for others. Booze was currency around here. But I didn't want to snitch.

I was about to make something up when Dr Erika Norstrom whipped her head towards the door, her ear cocked. 'Who's there?' she called out. 'Whoever you are, just come in.'

Slowly, hesitantly, the door opened. Dr Hewitt stood there, appearing furtive and hunched at first, but then unfurling and standing to attention at the sound of Dr Norstrom's voice.

'Come in, come in,' she said. I wasn't sure if her tone was brusque and commanding, scathing or overly familiar... or *warm*, even. It could have been any of these things. But I was more intent on reading Jason's reaction to his boss's orders as he entered, his eyes scanning around the apparent takeover of his office as he sized up what was going on.

'Erika,' he said with a nod. Then he glanced across at me, almost looking horrified to see me there. 'Nurse Fiona,' he said in my direction, barely looking at me.

'We were just discussing Kevin for some reason,' Erika said, a tinge of amusement in her voice now.

Immediately, Dr Hewitt took charge. 'Erika, I need to speak with Fiona, if I may?' He stood firm, arms folded. 'Do you want to grab a coffee with me in the common room, Fiona?' he directed at me, eyebrows raised.

I flashed a look at Dr Norstrom, then stood up and nodded when she paid me no attention. Her eyes were fixed on Dr Hewitt, making me wonder if there was a subtext I didn't understand passing between them. Either way, it gave me the chance I needed to get out of this excruciating situation.

'Well played,' I joked when we were out of earshot of Jason's office. We even shared a laugh as we headed to the common room. There were a couple of others chatting on the sofas, but they paid no mind to us.

'I came to see you, actually,' I told Jason, feeling even more nervous about the reason now. 'But Dr Norstrom opened the door instead. She certainly lives up to her reputation,' I said, laughing as I made us a couple of coffees, remembering how Jason liked his.

'You came to see *me*?' We headed out through the open French doors and onto the terrace. The views were breathtaking – one of the perks of being here each day. 'What about?'

My mouth went dry, and my heart raced. *Do it, do it, do it!* a voice in my head urged. The same voice, I should add, that has got me into plenty of trouble in the past. Impulse control has never been my forte. 'Oh, it was nothing. I was... I was just passing your office and... and I just wanted to say... good morning.'

Jason stared across at me, a friendly yet disbelieving and unnerving look in his eye, as though his pupils had grown blacker. 'Well... good morning to you, too,' he replied with a grin.

'Actually, I wanted to see if you'd like to go out for a drink with me,' I suddenly blurted out. 'You know, to the pub. Like, on a date.'

Instant death to my insides as they shrivelled and squirmed and my mind shut down, dissociating as I braced myself for rejection. A cool breeze suddenly swept up from the valley below Radmoor, flapping my hair in front of my face. For this, I was grateful. He couldn't see my anguish.

'A *date*,' Jason repeated curiously. 'Fiona, I'm very flattered...'

'It's fine, it's fine,' I said, wafting a hand at him. 'I'm sure you're far too busy, an important doctor like you—'

'No, no, it's not that. I'd love to go for a drink with you, actually...' he replied, though there was something about his expression that concerned me.

'I sense there's a but...'

He nodded. 'Thing is, I don't think my wife would approve.'

Shit, shit, shit... he has a wife! Why in the name of dating protocol did I not think of this? Of *course* a man like him would be taken – an attractive doctor with a plum job. He'd be the one with the beautiful woman on his arm, the house in the country and the two point four children at private school. A date with him would only ever exist in my head, the stuff of dreams. He was never going to be mine.

'Oh, gosh, I'm so sorry, please forgive me. I didn't realise you were married.'

Jason smiled the smile that had drawn me to him in the first place – humble and endearing, while still lighting up his face. But then he had to go and spoil it even more by saying, 'You've just met her, actually – my wife is Erika.'

NINE

FIONA

Fiona knows she shouldn't be doing this, knows that Jason would be livid if he found out. But she really, *really* needed to get out, to clear her head, and Ivy was desperate to see the horses. As they left the house, having climbed over their rear garden fence – partly to avoid the doorbell camera and partly because it's the quickest route to the footpath – she quickly glanced over into Sascha's garden next door, but she knew she'd already be up at the stables for work and that Cora was spending the day with her grandma in Little Campden, the next village.

'How far is it now?' Ivy says, sucking on her water bottle as they trudge across the fields twenty minutes into their walk. While it's not sunny today, the air is warm and humid, ripe with midges.

'Not too far.' Fiona's vagueness triggers a cascade of grumbles from Ivy, which, in turn, prompts Tilly to grab her sister's hand and begin singing. It's a song they seem to both know – one Fiona has never heard before – and, fleetingly, she wonders if it's something Erika used to sing with them. But she finds it hard to imagine their birth mother having a sing-along – in fact, from what Fiona knows about her, she finds it hard to imagine the woman even giving birth, not to mention conceiving in the first place. *Ice queen* is how Jason once described her.

'Just think of the gorgeous ponies you'll see when we get there. And if Sascha isn't too busy, maybe she'll give you a quick ride on one.'

Fiona glances across to the next field – she could swear she just saw a figure darting from behind a tree and running towards the old derelict barn. She puts her hand up to her brow, watching, waiting, but there's no one there now.

'Do you think I'll be allowed riding lessons, Fi— *Mummy*?' Ivy replies, swiftly correcting herself.

'Maybe,' Fiona says, looking back at the girls. She'll have to clear it with Jason first, though she doubts he'll agree. And he mustn't know that they went to the stables today, either. While Fiona understands why he doesn't want them to go out, that they have to be cautious, she'd have gone stir-crazy staying indoors all day again. Apart from anything, the notes she received are still on her mind, worrying her, making her anxious and look over her shoulder several times as they walk through the fields. Though at least there haven't been any more. She hates that the only explanation she can think of is that Jason must be sending them after all. Some kind of twisted warning meant to scare her into staying home, she supposes.

As they approach the entrance to Long Norton Riding Stables, there's a faint tang of horse manure in the air. The stable yard has loose boxes on three sides with a freshly swept concrete area in the middle and a yard office over in the opposite corner.

A bay horse with a white blaze on its nose pokes its head over one of the stable doors, letting out a little whinny as they approach. Ivy gambols over to stroke it, while Tilly follows on behind, and Fiona heads to the yard office to see if Sascha is around.

'Hel*lo*,' Fiona calls out, knocking on the open door and going in.

It's a rough and ready office – just a plain desk and a chair, an old PC and several planners with horses' names and lesson bookings on the wall. A few riding hats hang on the hooks behind the door, along with a couple of hacking jackets and waterproofs.

'I don't suppose Sascha is around, is she?' she says to the woman sitting at the desk. She's older than Fiona by a good ten or fifteen years and is chewing on a pencil, a deep scowl set on her make-up-free face.

'No, but I bloody well wish she was!' she snaps, as if whatever is stressing her out is somehow Fiona's fault.

'Oh, OK. Sorry, no problem,' she replies, backing out of the office. She'll just take the girls to the paddock to see the ponies, and then they'll amble to the village café for a milkshake.

'That's the thing, though. It *is* a bloody problem,' the woman says, scraping back her chair and following Fiona into the stable yard. 'Sascha didn't show up for work this morning. I've been rescheduling lessons all over the place while trying to reach her. She's got a group lesson this afternoon and—'

'She didn't come to work?' Fiona says, stopping.

The woman turns, hands on hips. Her cheeks are inflamed the same colour as the burgundy polo shirt she has on over cream jodhpurs, and Fiona notices she has some hay in her pulled-back grey hair. 'No. Most annoying. Can't get hold of her, either.' She studies Fiona. 'Are you a friend? Do you know where she is?' The woman, whose name badge reads Marjorie, seems quite flustered.

'Sorry, no,' Fiona says. 'I mean... I am a friend, yes. Her neighbour, actually. But I don't know where she is. I saw her last night – we had a drink together and—'

'Hungover, I expect then.' She tuts and shakes her head.

'No, no, far from it,' Fiona says, knowing that Sascha's

couple of glasses of mid-week Sauvignon are nothing compared to the alcoholics she's seen over the years – both in her A&E job as well as at Radmoor on the rehab unit. 'I know she intended on coming to work today. Her mum is looking after Cora.' A pang of anxiety stabs at Fiona.

While Marjorie turns and has words with one of the stable hands, Fiona pulls her phone from her jeans pocket and calls Sascha. It rings a few times then goes to voicemail, so she leaves a quick message. 'Sash, I popped into the stables with the girls to see you, but you're not here. Are you OK? Let me know. Your boss is losing her shit.' She whispers the last bit before hanging up.

After Ivy has maxed out on horse petting, Fiona calls time on hanging about at the riding stables. It doesn't seem as if Sascha is going to turn up. She looks around, wondering where Tilly has gone – but then she spots her coming over from a paddock next to the car park, a concerned look on her face. The teen glances back over her shoulder at a dark four-wheel drive vehicle as it bumps off down the lane away from the stables.

'OK, love?' Fiona asks as they head off, Ivy running on ahead.

Tilly is quiet for a moment then says, 'Something really weird just happened.' Her voice shakes and she's gone really pale. She fishes in her pocket and pulls out a piece of paper. 'A man in a car just gave me this. He wound down his window and called me over. He told me to give it to you.'

Fiona stares at it, her eyes stretched wide. It's the same type of paper that the two other notes were written on – lined paper taken from a notepad. She stops walking, snatching it from Tilly. A rush of adrenaline surges through her as she opens the note, her heart racing as she reads the two words, printed in large capitals.

RIP FIONA

For a moment, she's frozen, not knowing what to do as the sound of blood whooshes through her ears, making her panic. She quickly stuffs the paper in her pocket.

'Did you read it?' she asks Tilly, shielding her brow as she stares down the long driveway, her eyes tracking the car as it leaves the riding stables. But a second later and it's gone from sight. 'The note?'

Tilly shakes her head. 'No. No, I promise. He told me not to. Said he'd be watching me.'

'Did you see what he looked like?'

Tilly pauses, thinking. 'Not really. Just kind of normal. Like, sort of black-grey hair. He had sunglasses on, but I could tell he was middle-aged.'

'Oh my God,' Fiona whispers under her breath, not having a clue who it could be. 'It's OK, love. Don't worry. You did the right thing. Whoever he was, he... he must be muddling me up with someone else.' She attempts a laugh. 'But let's keep this between us, yeah? Your dad will only worry.'

'Yeah, cool,' Tilly says, giving a few firm nods. 'I won't say a word.'

As they trudge back along the lane to Dotty's – the little café-cum-post-office-cum-village-store in the centre of Kingshill where Fiona promised the girls milkshakes and brownies, Fiona sends a WhatsApp message to Sascha, glancing up every few seconds as she walks, her eyes scanning around in case they're being followed. It delivers with two grey ticks appearing, but they stay that way for as long as Fiona keeps her eyes on their message thread.

'It's weird. She's always on WhatsApp,' Fiona mumbles, checking her friend's 'last seen' status yet again – still showing as 5.53 p.m. yesterday evening. 'She usually replies right away.'

It's as they're almost back at the village that Fiona suddenly stops in her tracks – at exactly the same moment Tilly points to something.

'That's Dad's car, isn't it?' she says as they draw up to a lay-by. 'Why isn't he at work?'

'Good question,' Fiona says, glancing around. It's pretty much fields as far as the eye can see, apart from the village up ahead, the church spire reaching over the trees. A few sheep punctuate the field to their left, while there's a patch of dark, uninviting woodland behind the lay-by.

'Do you think Dad's come out looking for us?' Tilly suggests, her eyes flicking around. Fiona goes up to the car and cups her hand around the passenger window so she can see in.

'Maybe,' she replies, leaving a foggy patch on the glass, knowing tracking them is something he might do. Another bolt of anxiety makes her heart skitter. Inside the car, she sees a heap of clothes – the work clothes that Jason left the house in this morning. Did he take something else to change into? Did he pre-plan this – whatever *this* is?

She straightens up, peering over the roof of the car into the woods beyond. Listening. Wondering if she heard the crack of a twig underfoot. The screech of an animal. The glint of a pair of eyes. A shiver spirals down her spine.

'Come on, girls, let's go and get those milkshakes. Your dad's probably gone on one of his cross-country runs,' she says, deciding that's the best explanation, even though he should be at work, and she knows he hates running. She takes each of her daughter's hands – God, she's not got used to calling them that yet – and leads them down the road to the village in a hurry. But all she can think about is note number three burning a hole in her pocket.

TEN

FIONA

'Why do you let him do it?' Tilly asks when they're seated at a tiny table outside the front of Dotty's. Her tone is unusually direct, a scowl etched on her face, but she also sounds cautious as if she knows she's overstepping the mark. Ivy has gone inside to the toilet. 'Dad... He treats you like shit.'

'Tilly! Mind your language,' Fiona says, pretending to admire the view. To her right is a row of thatched cottages, the church, the Dog and Duck pub and the small village green, complete with a pond and set of medieval wooden stocks. To her left, the way they've just walked, is open countryside. Their street, Hollybush Close, is just a short walk beyond the church.

'Seriously, though, Fiona, why?' Tilly glances at the café door to see if her sister is coming back from the toilets yet. 'Is Dad behind that weird note or whatever it was? It seems to have upset you.'

'Firstly, it's *Mum*,' Fiona corrects. 'Your dad wouldn't like you calling me by my name.'

'But that's exactly what I mean,' Tilly says, her face colouring up into a fierce blush. 'All his stupid rules. There's one for everything. Mum's only been dead a couple of months and he expects us to pretend you're our new mother. I mean... I like you, Fiona, and you've helped Dad through a bad time, but it's all been such a rush. Such a huge change for us right after losing Mum. And it's fucking unreasonable that we're only allowed to grieve for her on Sunday afternoons.' Tilly flings an arm in the air, making Fiona jump.

'Tilly, I'm warning you, mind your language, please.'

There are tears in Tilly's eyes. 'I'm bursting with all these... *feelings*, and I don't know what to do with them. It's way too soon to think of you as our mother, however much it makes Dad feel better. It's not fair on Ivy, either.'

Tilly takes a small sip of her milkshake. Her lips quiver as she draws a breath, ready to continue with her grievances.

'We can't watch whatever we want on the TV, and Dad confiscates my phone after six every evening. We're not allowed social media, or any news or current affairs, or any shows that normal teenagers are into. He won't let you have a glass of wine if you want,' she continues, sucking in an exasperated breath as she counts the rules on her fingers. 'He tells you how to dress, he doesn't want you having a job, he barely gives you any money and expects his dinner on the table when he gets home, and don't even get me started on the fucking "family confessionals".' She air-quotes the last two words, and her mouth quivers and twists as she tries to contain her anger. 'His rules drive me *crazy*. He's not the dad I once knew. In fact, I feel like I barely know him any more.' Tilly hangs her head, suppressing a sob. 'These past few years, they've been so tough. Mum and Dad... they were apart a lot, and we've barely seen Dad. Mum tried to make things better, but...' Another sigh. 'It feels as though he doesn't even *like* us any more.'

Fiona sits staring at Tilly, her coffee cup halfway to her mouth. Is it wrong that all she can think about at that moment is how beautiful the teenager's long hair looks with the sunlight shining from behind her, kissing the crown of her head, picking out a few strands of strawberry blonde, the rest glinting gold?

She envies her beauty, her youthful and enquiring mind still fresh with the naivety of childhood, not yet tainted by adult concerns. Fiona covets her bravery in the face of the biggest loss a child can suffer – the death of a parent. And yet here she is, not only questioning her father's actions, but also sticking up for *her*... for Fiona... conceivably a candidate for a sworn enemy: the woman who took her mother's place. The evil stepmother.

You remind me so much of Erika... Fiona thinks, wishing the voice in her head wasn't so real. But then she's thinking about the way Erika treated Jason... the control she had over him, her demeaning comments, the way she kept constant tabs on him, demanding to know where he was at all times. She shakes her head, knowing this *can't* be the same. Can it...?

'The rules...' Fiona begins, wondering how to put this mess right. 'Your dad and I agreed them together, love. They...' How best to explain their marriage rules?

She knows they originated with Jason's father, Dr Frederick Hewitt – the man Jason looked up to, revered almost, from what he's told her. By all accounts, the original rules were put in place to help his mother's nerves. That's what he implied – that she suffered badly from anxiety and other ailments, though he didn't say what exactly.

'They're the foundations of our relationship. The bedrock of all we believe—'

'But you both keep breaking them!' Tilly retorts, shaking her head. 'What's the point of having them? I know you sometimes sneak a drink, and you're not going to tell Dad that we've come out on this walk. Do you each get some sick kick out of lying to each other, is that it?'

'No, Tills, it's not like—'

'Then what, Fiona? *What* is it like?' She half stands, hands resting on the edge of the table. 'I love my father, I really do, but

from where I'm looking it feels a lot like you're being abused.'
She holds her breath, waiting for her stepmother's reaction, but
there isn't one. There's an older couple at the next table, who
glance over when they hear Tilly's outburst. 'We *all* are, and it's
not right,' Tilly whispers, sitting down again.

Before Fiona can begin to process this, Ivy reappears
through the café door. 'Did you wash your hands?' Fiona asks
her, grateful for the distraction.

'Yes, Mummy,' the little girl says.

'She's not your mummy,' Tilly says sullenly, pulling her
sister close. 'You don't have to call her that.'

Ivy looks from Tilly to Fiona then back to Tilly again. 'Do
so,' she says. 'Daddy said. He told me he will be sad and die if
we don't do as he tells us.'

Tilly closes her eyes and shakes her head, muttering something under her breath.

'That's not true,' Fiona says to Ivy. 'Daddy isn't going to die,
so don't worry about that. But we do have to follow the rules,
which means, Tilly, I don't want you filling Ivy's head with all
sorts of rubbish, OK?'

Tilly stares across the fields, sucking on the straw in her
milkshake, slowly shaking her head.

'*OK*, Tilly?'

Tilly shrugs and slurps the remains of her drink. Then she
stands up, bumping the table and sloshing Fiona's coffee into
the saucer. 'I'll be home later,' she says, grabbing her phone.

'Wait... where are you going?' Fiona's body tenses. This was
not the nice morning she had planned.

'For a walk.' Tilly starts to leave, but Fiona grabs her by the
wrist. 'Get off me!' Tilly squeals, making the older couple at the
next table look round again. 'I'm going to see Amber, all right?
Or am I a prisoner now?'

Fiona freezes for a moment, then lets go of her wrist,
knowing Amber lives close by, that it should be safe. 'OK,' she

concedes. 'But I want you home by one o'clock for lunch. And... and we'll keep quiet about it, OK?'

Tilly glances at her phone screen and rolls her eyes. 'Whatever,' she says and strides off down the lane, looking back over her shoulder before turning the corner and disappearing out of sight.

Once Fiona is back home and Ivy is occupied with some colouring books in front of the TV, she calls Sascha's number again. It goes to voicemail, but she doesn't bother leaving a message. Her previous text still only has two grey ticks. Delivered, but not read. There's a gnawing feeling inside her – she's trying not to worry, but Sascha always replies quickly and it's not like her to skip work. Something inside her shifts momentarily – like a mini earth tremor. A warning. Making her want to grab onto something. She steadies herself on the wall until it passes.

'I'm just popping next door,' Fiona tells Ivy, who barely looks up from the TV. 'Don't move a muscle.' She's sure she'll be fine – she's only going to quickly check on Sascha, to see if she's home – but leaves her own front door wide open as a precaution so she can hear if Ivy needs her.

Fiona rings the bell beside Sascha's royal-blue front door, noticing her car isn't parked out the front. But she supposes it could be in the garage – Sascha sometimes puts it away. She glances at the upstairs windows, wondering if she saw one of the bedroom curtains twitch a little. It's weird for them to be closed at this time of day.

She rings the bell a second time, knocking on the frosted glass for good measure. When there's still no reply, she pushes the letterbox open and calls through. 'Sash, it's me, Fiona. Are you in there?' She can't see much through the gap, but spots some shoes strewn about in the hall, plus there are a couple of coats lying on the floor. *Odd*, she thinks. She dials Sascha's number and almost immediately hears something inside the house through the open letterbox. A buzzing sound, like a phone vibrating.

She hangs up and the noise stops. She dials again, and she hears it again.

'She's left her phone behind,' Fiona whispers, wondering if that means she went out in a hurry. She looks around the cul-de-sac to see if anyone is watching. Then, just in case, she tries the front door handle, and, to her surprise, she finds it's unlocked.

Another furtive look behind her and Fiona pushes the door open and goes inside.

'Sash, it's me, Fiona,' she calls out. 'Anyone home?'

When there's no reply, she heads through to the kitchen at the back of the house. A quick glance tells her that Sascha is not in there – but... it looks as though she's been cooking. There are some dry-looking carrots on the chopping board, as well as some potatoes that have turned a browny-grey, the colour of bruises, as if they were peeled a while ago. There's also an oven tray with two breasts of chicken laid out – each one wrapped in bacon and seasoned. Again, dry-looking.

'Weird,' she says, frowning as she scans around. 'Sascha?' she calls out, trying the back door to the garden, but it's locked. She cups her hands to the glass, seeing there's no one out there. Fiona decides to check upstairs next – but when she goes up and pokes her head around Sascha's bedroom door, she's not in there either. The bed is neatly made, though, and for some reason the curtains are closed.

Maybe she's taking a bath and got distracted or fell asleep, Fiona wonders, hoping that's why her calls and message went unanswered. As she draws up to the closed door, she hears a trickle of water – the gentle *drip... drip... drip...* of a tap. For a second, she's frozen, can't move as another mini tremor shudders through her, but it passes quickly. Just a waft of something across her soul.

'Thank God,' she whispers, relieved her theory is right, that Sascha must be home after all. Perhaps taking the day off work for some reason. She hopes she's not feeling poorly. 'Sash, it's me – you in there?' She knocks a couple of times on the closed bathroom door, but there's no reply. 'Sascha, are you OK?'

Nothing – just the sound of the dripping tap.

Slowly, Fiona lifts her hand, knowing she must go inside. She rests it on the handle for a moment, gathering herself, fighting back the rocking motion inside her body as her vision blurs a fraction. Then she levers the handle down and opens the bathroom door. When her eyes finally focus on the scene inside, her mouth falls open.

She was not expecting to see *that* – not expecting to see blood.

But, even more worryingly, there's no sign of Sascha...

ELEVEN

FIONA

That evening, Jason sits at the dinner table blank-faced. Ivy shows him her colouring book, but not even that brings a smile to his face. Fiona's heart skitters in her chest as she serves dinner onto the four plates set out on the kitchen counter. A blob of bolognese sauce drops onto the floor, landing at her feet. She can't help thinking it looks a lot like blood – the blood that was smeared all over the basin in Sascha's bathroom next door. But she doesn't want to think about that, about how or why it got there... or whose blood it is. When she'd stood there staring at it earlier, her heart rate quickening as she took in the mess, she knew that the dried, browny-red smudges weren't simply from a small cut.

Fiona screws up her eyes, blocking out the images in her mind.

'This one's yours, Ivy, and this is for you, Tilly.'

'Thanks, Mum,' the girls chime in unison, though Tilly gives her a sour look. At least she came back from Amber's house on time earlier. Fiona couldn't have coped with any more emergencies today. She just prays that they don't mention their walk, and that Tilly doesn't say anything about the note, or that she was allowed to go off to Amber's house in the first place. She feels wrung out and emotionally spent after what she found earlier. After what she *did* earlier.

'Jason, here's your dinner,' Fiona says, putting a plate in front of her husband. He gives her a brief nod.

'I will go first tonight,' Jason says, picking up his fork. 'Today has not turned out as I had hoped.' He sighs heavily. 'I have been betrayed.'

Ivy gasps, a string of spaghetti hanging out of her mouth. Tilly doesn't look up, while Fiona's shoulders tense.

'Betrayed by my own family.' He glances at the three of them in turn.

'Jase...' Fiona reaches out, puts her hand on his, but he shies away. 'Please... It's not like that, and you know it. It was just a walk to the stables, that's all.' She remembers his car parked in the lay-by, suspecting he was checking up on them. 'Let's talk about something else, and we'll discuss this later when—'

'So, you're not denying that you broke the rules, Fiona? What kind of example are you to our daughters?'

Fiona's mouth falls open, but nothing comes out. Then Tilly's words ring in her ears: *It feels a lot like you're being abused...*

Surely that's not the case? Jason wouldn't do that to her, wouldn't treat her that way, knowing everything she's been through. He's never hit her or shoved her or done anything on purpose to hurt her. He adores her, cherishes her – Christ, he was even going to leave his wife for her. Fiona feels confused, unsure of what's right or wrong, how to behave or make her husband happy any more. She's losing sight of herself, of who she really is.

'I didn't mean to break the rules, Jase. It's just that Ivy wanted to see the ponies, and I thought I could find out about riding lessons and—'

'And I told you it's too soon for all of that!' Jason's jaw tenses, his top lip curling as he tries to eat his spaghetti. But Fiona sees he's too wound up to even swallow properly. Veins stand out on his temple and his knuckles are white around the fork handle. 'You can't just go gallivanting all over the place... It's not...'

He trails off, but Fiona knows he was going to say 'safe'. She's grateful he stopped short – she doesn't want to worry the girls.

'Sorry you had a bad day, Daddy,' Ivy says. 'Can I go next?' When Jason nods, which causes a wave of relief inside Fiona, Ivy gives a blow-by-blow account of each pony she met at the riding stables. For her day's blessings, she says, 'Milkshakes.'

'Thank you, Ivy,' Jason says, withholding any further comments about their trip out. Fiona knows she's the one who'll get punished later, not the girls. 'Mathilda, it's your turn.' Jason puts down his fork and folds his arms, using her full name as if he already senses there's going to be a battle.

'I'm not doing it,' Tilly says, her cheeks flushing. 'No one gives a shit about me or how I feel, anyway.' Tilly shovels spaghetti into her mouth. 'I'm not playing your stupid games any more, Dad.'

Jason remains calm, for which Fiona is grateful, but what he says next still chills her, making her wonder if there's any truth in what Tilly said – that her father is a bully.

'Leave,' Jason says, fixing her with an icy stare. 'Get out of my sight. Give me your phone. Go to your room. Do not come out until I tell you.'

Jason holds out his hand as Tilly stands up. She plucks her phone from her back pocket and drops it on the floor, kicking it under the table. Then she goes out of the room, closing the door quietly behind her.

'Am I in trouble too?' Ivy asks, a wobble in her voice.

'No, darling,' Fiona tells her, but she doesn't take her eyes off Jason. 'Just eat up. Everything's going to be OK.'

There's a few moments' silence, followed by a couple of sniffs from Ivy, but then she says, 'Tilly says that Cora's mummy has run away,' through a couple of sobs. 'Amber told her so. Is that true, Daddy? Will Cora have to come and live with us now?' Fiona sees the concern on her face, her little nose puckered from worry.

Jason's head whips up and he glares at Fiona. 'See what you've done?' he hisses. 'Disobeying the rules leads to bad behaviour from the girls. Tilly stomping off, and now Ivy making up stories. If only you'd stayed home like I told you, if only you'd not gone to the stables, if only you'd not made friends with that woman next door or offered to childmind her stupid daughter, then none of this would have happened. It's why we have the rules, Fiona. To prevent situations like this. Do you not remember all our conversations?'

Fiona wills Ivy to keep quiet, to not say anything else that will push Jason over the edge. She knows it's best just to nod, to play along with him when he's like this – she doesn't want him to lose his temper. Besides, he's right, they *did* have many chats when they worked at the hospital – the pair of them on their secret lunchtime walks that made her heart sing as they ambled hand in hand, or huddled together in the common room with milky coffees when they had a snatched moment in their busy schedules. Sometimes they'd hunt for an empty patient bedroom, where they'd have intimate conversations before making passionate love, each of them leaving separately, their skin tingling, their cheeks flushed.

'Things won't have to be a secret forever,' Jason had reassured her at the time. 'Just until the dust has settled.'

As it was, Erika had already grown suspicious about them, and Jason had already warned Fiona about her incendiary

temper if she ever caught them together. 'Nuclear' was the word
he'd used.

At the dining table, Fiona shakes her head, shivering a little.
Surely, *surely* this isn't abuse?

'You're right, Jase. God, you're so right. And I'm so sorry.
I've been a fool. I promise we'll just stay home now. It's the
summer holidays – we can amuse ourselves here, can't we, Ivy?
And no more tall stories about Cora and her mummy, OK?'

Ivy nods, though there's still a little frown on her face. 'But
Tilly said that Amber told her—'

'Ivy, I'm warning you,' Fiona snaps.

Ivy pouts, folding her arms and bowing her head.

'Whatever you've heard, it's nothing more than village
gossip,' Jason says. 'You listen to Daddy, sweetheart. There's
nothing to worry about. Maybe Cora and her mummy just went
away this morning for a few days' break.' He gives her a reas-
suring smile, patting her shoulder, before turning to Fiona. 'As
for you,' he says in a low voice, 'there will be consequences.'

Ivy looks thoughtful again, scooping up more of her
spaghetti. Fiona can't face eating, not after what she saw earlier
next door. And she certainly can't let Jason know that she phoned
the police – not after what happened to his wife before they
moved here, him insisting they keep a low profile for a while. So
instead of using her mobile to make the call, she'd run down to
the phone box on the corner, anonymously tipping off the emergency services that something wasn't right at 7 Hollybush Close.

No, however many rules she's breaking, she won't tell Jason
that two officers came out this afternoon, checking out Sascha's
house, talking to several of the neighbours in the street, though
she didn't answer the door when they rang their bell, quickly
deleting the doorbell footage from their shared app when they'd
gone.

Something bad happened in that bathroom next door, and

with Sascha not turning up for work, it has given her an uneasy feeling. She doesn't have Sascha's mother's phone number, so can't check if she knows where Sascha is or if she and Cora are even safe. No, under the circumstances, she has done the right thing. Let the police handle it now. And say nothing about it to Jason.

TWELVE
FIONA

Before

Knowing that Dr Hewitt was married somehow made him more appealing. Wait... let me rephrase that. Knowing that he was *unhappily* married made him more appealing. As if he needed saving. To be clear, had he been loved-up and anticipating a blissful future with his wife, then I'd never have pursued things in the first place. I'm not a marriage-wrecker. Besides, knowing Dr Erika Norstrom as I did, I wasn't bloody crazy.

At first, I tried to hide my feelings – avoiding Jason when I could, changing my route as I walked around the hospital so as not to pass his office. But I still encountered him almost daily, and it wasn't long before I properly fell for him.

We seemed to go from coy looks across the common room to confessing our feelings for each other in the medical supplies storeroom in less than a month. If our passionate trysts, clandestine walks, deep chats and sneaky candlelit dinners were anything to go by, then I was *certain* that Jason was falling for me too. As far as I could see, there was only one problem standing between us.

Erika.

Even his two daughters, Mathilda and Ivy, didn't pose too many problems for a future that we now regularly talked about. Inadvertently, I'd met the girls once or twice when their mother had had no option but to bring them to the hospital and our paths had crossed in the corridor.

It was only during my most recent encounter with Erika at a supposed performance review that I became more paranoid, wondering if she'd engineered the meet because she suspected something was going on between me and her husband. Jason had warned me what she was like – domineering and ruthless, cold and calculating. He'd also told me that their relationship was dead, that they were partners on paper only. He assured me that they'd not slept together in months.

'If she wasn't nagging me, I'd worry that she'd died,' he told me once, half joking but describing how she regularly convinced him he was forgetful or stupid or a bad father. 'It's why I'm here, at this hospital,' Jason confided one lunchtime when we'd managed to escape the confines of the busy ward for a quiet walk.

'She pulled strings to get you a job here?' I said, thinking how awful it would be to have your spouse as your boss. My heart bled for him, seeing such a strong, intelligent man belittled and controlled by his wife. No one would ever have suspected what was going on behind closed doors.

Jason nodded. 'I swear it's so she can keep tabs on me,' he said. 'I only stay with her for the girls' sake.'

One day, we walked hand in hand towards the nearby market town. Radmoor Hospital was set in the countryside, but only a twenty-minute stroll to the shops. We'd taken the back route through the twisty lanes, cutting through the woods, knowing that no one would spot us. It was where we'd had our first proper kiss a few weeks ago.

High on the oxygen-rich air, Jason had taken a chance and

pressed his mouth onto mine. I hadn't been expecting it, but I didn't push him away either. Neither of us had set out to have an affair.

His hands had rested on my hips, our bodies pressed together. 'Nothing will ever be the same again now, you realise that, don't you?'

'I know.' Our foreheads touched.

'It won't be easy, you know. Forging any kind of future together.'

I'm not the one who's married, I'd been about to say, but silenced myself. Supporting Jason as he divorced Erika was a task I would take seriously. A positive change was long overdue in my life and, having finally been given a chance at happiness, I wasn't about to blow it.

'You do realise that Erika won't let me go without a fight, don't you?' he then told me, dampening my spirits.

'What do you mean?' We'd started walking again and had been chatting about what a future together might look like, where we'd live, how we'd get the girls, what we'd do for work – knowing we'd both have to leave the hospital once word got out about our affair. But then he had to go and spoil my excitement by revealing this.

After we emerged from the woods and walked further along the lane, we headed for the little sandwich shop in the centre of the market town. I asked him, 'How will we ever be together then?'

Jason looked across at me, holding my stare in a way that made me wonder if it was loving or... strangely *sinister*.

'She'd rather kill me before she let me go. But don't worry, I have an idea.'

'An idea?'

We'd gone up to the counter and ordered our sandwiches, as well as a couple of coffees. But Jason shook his head in reply, his gaze flicking about as if to say, *Not here... Let's wait until we're somewhere private...* which left me wondering what, exactly, it was that he had in mind.

When we got back to the hospital, we went inside separately so as not to raise suspicion.

'There you are, Fiona,' Liz, one of the nurses, said to me, a tinge of impatience in her voice. 'I've been looking for you everywhere. I need you to do a meds review with me.'

'I was at lunch,' I said, nodding and following her to the locked room where the medication stock was kept for Isaac Ward – a low-risk, low-security unit with many of the patients here able to go out on trips, or go home for the weekend. There was a freedom and sense of independence in this part of the hospital, where staff and patients rubbed along amiably. I knew most of the patients by name and said hello to a couple as Liz and I disappeared into the small room.

I watched as she counted out various medications, checking them off on a list while I observed. There was a very strict system in place for controlling the release of drugs. It drove me mad, but I did what I had to, knowing I'd be able to leave at two thirty for my alcohol abuse group.

It had been my idea to set up the weekly informal sessions where those with an alcohol addiction could come for a chat and a cup of tea to talk about any challenges they were facing. The powers that be – which included Erika – had deemed it a worthwhile enough idea to add to the weekly programme of group therapies. The main draw was that I'd had the bright idea of inviting patients' loved ones along to the sessions – though it wasn't obligatory – so they could better understand the challenges faced by those in recovery. Given it was my brainchild, I felt the need to attend regularly and show willing, even though there were other, more senior nurses to run it.

'Thanks, Fiona,' Liz said once we were done with the

medications. I'd been about to leave, but she stood between me and the door, a serious look spreading across her face. 'Look, tell me it's none of my business, but...' She pulled a pained expression. 'You and Doc Hewitt... Is there... is there anything going on between you and Jason?' She gave an embarrassed laugh, and her familiar use of his first name made me suspect she had a thing for him too.

'What?' I snapped back. 'No... of course there's not.' My reaction was way over the top.

Liz sighed, shaking her head. 'Good, oh, that's good. Look, I'm so sorry, Fiona.' She touched my arm, making me recoil. 'It's just that...' Another sigh. 'He has a bit of a *reputation*.' She whispered the last word, even though we were alone. 'I wouldn't want him to take advantage of you.'

A sick feeling surged through me. *She's just jealous*, came the voice in my head. *She's seen how Jason is with me – how he looks at me, slides a hand onto the small of my back when no one's looking, makes me a coffee in the common room and hands it to me with a knowing smile – and she fancies him too.*

'A reputation?' It was all I could think of to say.

'Yes, I'm afraid so. There have been several complaints recently about how... how forward he is.'

'Oh my God, that's awful,' I said, because it's what she'd expect me to say.

'Right? Shocking, really, given that he's not been here very long. Staff *and* patients, can you believe?'

No, I wanted to say. *I* can't *believe*. I wanted to yell at her that she didn't understand what he'd been through – was *still* going through – how he was being abused by his wife, by his *boss*, for God's sake. How she controlled him and wouldn't allow him any of his hard-earned money or to socialise or do anything without her.

All my conversation with Liz did was to cement my resolve to stand by Jason even more. Our relationship might have been clandestine so far, and we'd not had a chance to date openly in public like we would if we were free to do so, but there was no denying our connection, something too special to ignore. And the sexual chemistry between us was off the scale.

'Well, you needn't worry about me,' I told Liz as I headed off to the recovery session. 'I'm wise to people like Dr Hewitt.' I tapped the side of my nose, which made her smile as we parted company. As I turned away from her, I screwed up my eyes.

I headed to the room where the rehab sessions were held in order to put out the chairs, make sure there was plenty of water for everyone and get the information leaflets ready. I was in a good mood, knowing that after this meeting Jason and I would have a precious half hour together. We'd arranged to meet on the terrace for a quick tea break, and I planned on discussing the next stages of our relationship with him. A part of me was excited that he'd got a plan forming to deal with his wife.

But I was not prepared for what I found when I opened the door to room 14a: the conference-style chairs already set out in a circle, refreshments on the table at the side, a few people already sitting around, chatting among themselves before the session began.

My eyes were drawn to the far side of the room where a man and a woman were positioned together, sitting in the chairs reserved for the group facilitators.

Erika and Jason.

Their shoulders were touching, they were sitting that close – Jason looking drawn and guilty, as though she'd given him a stern talking-to, while Erika sat bolt upright, notepad and pen in hand as her bright eyes surveyed the scene. Then her stare settled on me and, as she focused, her eyes seemed to turn black.

I looked across at Jason for reassurance, but his attention was elsewhere – *on his wife*. He stared at her from point-blank range, a sneer forming on his mouth. His skin appeared sallow and grey, his eyes hollow, and his fists were clenched in his lap.

In that particular moment, he did not look happy. In fact, he looked murderous and filled with hate. Was that the effect Erika had on him?

Then, out of nowhere, it became clear what Jason's plan was for his boss, his *wife* – the only way he'd ever be able to escape her and be with me.

'Hello, everyone,' I said, sitting down as we waited for the others to arrive. I was trying to stay calm as the realisation dawned on me, but my voice wavered as I flicked another glance at the pair of them – Erika looking as though she'd rather be anywhere else, and Jason giving her daggers.

'Hello, Fiona,' Erika shot across the circle at me. Her eyes narrowed to slits.

My heart was beating so fast, it felt as though it was climbing up my throat.

And as Erika held her gaze, fixing me with her stare, I knew, just *knew*, that Jason was planning her murder.

THIRTEEN

JASON

Jason freezes as the doorbell sounds, interrupting their family confessional. He locks eyes with Fiona, who makes a move to get up from the dinner table to answer it. 'No, I'll go,' he says, putting down his fork and wiping his mouth. He doesn't want any more of the spaghetti bolognese anyway. 'I hope you're not expecting anyone.' He stands up, still reeling from Fiona's disobedience earlier – her taking the girls out for a walk – and Tilly's defiant behaviour just now.

His wife shakes her head, looking guilty as hell. *If you're lying, I'll deal with you later*, he thinks, striding to the front door.

'Oh, good evening...' Jason says to the man and woman standing there, putting on his most charming smile.

The woman, who looks to be in her forties, is dressed in dark trousers and a grey shirt, her mousy hair tied back. The man, slightly younger, has on black jeans and a navy sweatshirt. Jason's mind whips through the possibilities – maybe they're from the university, though the thought of that makes his heart thump. Or perhaps they're Jehovah's Witnesses, or collecting for a local charity. Then he's wondering if they're from

Radmoor Hospital, though he doesn't recognise them as staff. Being tracked down by anyone from there would not bode well – not after they left under such a cloud.

'We're from Warwickshire Police,' the woman says. 'I'm DI Alice Winters and this is my colleague, DC Baldwin.'

'Oh... right,' Jason says, not expecting that. He scans each officer quickly – the woman has sparkling blue eyes and pale skin, while her colleague is stocky and brown-haired with a crooked nose that looks as though it once took a pummelling. 'How can I help you?' Jason just manages to get the words out before a large, involuntary swallow closes his throat. 'Would you like to come in?' As soon as he asks the question, he's kicking himself, hoping that Fiona won't freak out when she sees them.

'Thank you,' DI Winters says, stepping over the threshold and wiping her feet. DC Baldwin does the same.

As soon as they're seated in the living room, Fiona pokes her head around the door from the kitchen where they were eating. 'Oh...' she says, glancing at each of them. 'Hello.'

'Sorry to intrude on your evening,' DI Winters says, half rising. 'We're making a few house-to-house enquiries regarding the property next door.'

'Number seven,' DC Baldwin adds.

Jason sees Fiona visibly stiffen as she grips the door frame.

'Happy to help any way we can,' Jason says. 'Darling, why don't you make the officers a cup of tea?'

Fiona nods and turns towards the kitchen again, but both detectives chime a 'no thanks' at the same time. So instead, she comes over to Jason and slides an arm around his waist. The pair sit down as one on the edge of the sofa facing the detectives. Jason feels a tremor in Fiona's leg, so he moves away a few inches, only for her to shuffle closer.

'Someone reported concerns about the family at number seven,' DC Baldwin says. 'A mother and daughter. Are you familiar with them? We know the daughter is safe with her grandmother, but we're trying to establish the mother's where-abouts and movements. Would you happen to have seen her recently?'

'Yes, we know them – Sascha and Cora,' Jason says, rubbing his chin. 'We saw them last night when Sascha came here to pick her daughter up.'

'I'd been childmi—'

'Cora had been round here to play with Ivy, our youngest,' Jason says, talking over his wife. Apart from anything, he doesn't want Fiona to get into trouble for working cash-in-hand and not declaring it. 'They both left around half past six.'

Jason remembers the wine, the stink of it on Fiona's breath, the rage brewing inside him as Sascha tried to overrule him by passing Fiona her drink, how he'd imagined beating Sascha's face to a pulp as he tipped the wine down the sink. How he sent Fiona to the spare room, making her take her clothes off and stand up all night to think about what she'd done. How, when he'd seen her and the girls trek off across the fields this morning, the anger inside him had virtually sent him insane. What was she doing, putting them in danger like that?

Punishment is imminent.

He wishes he could say all this to the police, have his wife arrested and thrown in a cell for disobeying him. That would teach her a lesson. Hell, he could even provide the detectives with photographic evidence of her dragging his daughters across the fields earlier, exposing them to danger. He'd been hiding in the barn, watching them, boiling with anger at what he'd seen while he was in there. But of course, he keeps quiet, decides the police won't see things quite the same way as him.

'And how did Ms Masters seem when she left here last night?' DI Winters asks.

'Fine,' Jason quickly replies. 'Quite cheerful, actu—'

'I was asking your wife, if that's OK.' DI Winters shoots a look at him.

Fiona turns to Jason. He nods at her, as if to indicate it's OK to speak. 'Yes, she seemed fine,' she says, while still looking at Jason. 'Sascha was fine. We'd had a nice chat and then she went home. She wanted an early night, what with work the next—'

'Don't bore the officers with silly details, Fi,' Jason says, nudging her. 'You'll be telling them what she was planning for dinner next.' He rolls his eyes and curls one side of his mouth in a conspiratorial smile with the detectives.

'Actually, we'd very much like to know if Ms Masters had discussed what she was planning to cook, or if she said anything else of interest to you, Fiona,' DI Winters says, focusing on her.

Fiona stares down at her lap, her fingers entwined as she picks at the skin on her thumb. 'Maybe... maybe soup. Or chicken and bacon. Or maybe just a microwave curry.'

'That's quite a menu,' DI Winters comments. 'Is that based on what she told you?'

Jason notices the slight blush on the crest of Fiona's cheekbones, the soft sheen of sweat on her top lip. While the officers don't know her like he does, won't be able to read the subtle signs of her anxiety, it's obvious that, for some reason, she's squirming. What the hell does she know?

'Just wild guesses, really,' Fiona says with a forced laugh. 'She was in a hurry to get Cora over to her grandma's last night – she starts work at the stables really early on a Wednesday – so I imagine she went for something super-quick like soup. Am I right?'

'It's not a guessing game,' DI Winters replies. 'We're not testing you. We simply want to build a picture of Sascha's movements over the last twenty-four hours or so.'

'Sorry,' Fiona says, offering a small smile.

'We noticed you have a doorbell camera on your front door. Would you be able to check the footage from last night?' DC Baldwin asks.

Jason arcs his head, feeling somewhat relieved. He's heard

about officers door-knocking houses with cameras fitted, gathering evidence of burglaries and car thefts and suchlike. It gives him some comfort that it's probably just a routine visit. He pulls his phone from his pocket.

'Let me take a look at the app,' he says, scrolling through the video activity of the last day or so.

Jason mainly installed the doorbell for his wife and daughters' safety for when he isn't home, so that Fiona can decide whether to answer the door or not depending on who's there. But it also tells him when she goes out. Who she has round to the house.

'It only records footage when there's movement within the detection zone that I've set at the front of our property,' he explains, though the officers already seem to know how it works. 'Other than that, I've set it to take a general snapshot of the street scene every hour. So, look, here's my wife and daughters arriving home from a walk earlier, for instance,' he says, holding out his phone while glaring at Fiona. She doesn't look up.

But wait... where's Tilly? Jason wonders when he views the clip, only seeing Fiona and Ivy returning from the walk.

'And that's me leaving for work this morning.' He shields the screen away from his wife so she doesn't notice that he's carrying a holdall, though of course she could have looked at the app on her own phone. He makes a mental note to delete that clip when the cops have gone, then if she does check, she'll be none the wiser.

Jason scrolls further back in time, not seeing anything out of the ordinary. Sascha's drive is barely in shot on the left of the footage so not of much use to them. 'Ah, here we go. Look, there's our neighbour leaving here last night with her daughter.' He hits 'play' on the clip, which also plays the audio as Sascha steps out of their front door, triggering the camera. Her voice and his wife's sound out from his phone's speaker.

'But you're still on for childminding next Monday, right?' Sacsha asks, her voice clear and loud.

'It should be OK,' Fiona replies, her voice a little quieter. 'I'll have a word with Jase and text you.'

Jason is about to hit pause, remembering what Sascha says next and not wanting the officers to hear any more of this nonsense, but DI Winters raises her hand to stop him, wanting to hear it.

'What, you're seriously going to let him dictate to you like that?' Sascha's words ring out. 'Fi, it's... it's really controlling.'

'It's not like that,' they hear Fiona reply. 'He's just watching out for me. Making sure I don't overdo it. And Tilly and Ivy have been through a lot lately... with... with...' There's a pause. 'So routine is really important for all of us.'

More silence followed by the sound of scuffling as Cora jumps down the step.

'Just don't be *that* woman, Fi,' Sascha replies. 'I know I've only known you a couple of months, but I've noticed a few things he's said that are a bit... well, *off* if I'm honest. You're smart. You're intelligent. You're a qualified nurse, for God's sake. Don't cover for an arsehole.'

FOURTEEN

JASON

Jason clears his throat, shaking his head. Then he forces a laugh. Inwardly, he curses himself for not deleting the video. But how was he to know cops were going to come sniffing about?

'That's pretty much the end of the clip,' Jason says, pausing the remainder of last night's footage. 'And there was no movement on what we can see of next door's driveway,' he adds, shoving his phone back in his pocket. 'I'm sorry, but what concerns were reported about Sascha exactly?' He squares his shoulders and sits forward. 'And what does any of this have to do with us?' He reaches out and takes Fiona's hand, giving it a squeeze. He sees DI Winters flash a look down, pleased she's noticed the gesture.

'It's an ongoing investigation,' DC Baldwin explains while the other detective writes something on her pad. 'A neighbour – well, we presume it was a neighbour, though the call was anonymous – raised concerns about Sascha's welfare. And unfortunately, it does appear that Ms Masters left her house in... a hurry or in an unplanned way. Her dinner was half prepared, and her front door was left unlocked.'

'That's a worry,' Jason says, pulling a puzzled face. 'Are you saying that she's missing? Or been taken against her will?'

Fiona covers her mouth, makes a whimpering sound.

'We can't conclude anything at this point,' DI Winters replies. 'But because we haven't been able to contact her and no one knows where she is, we're making enquiries to ascertain her well-being. Her car isn't in the garage so it's important we locate that, though ANPR cameras are scarce around here, being so rural. We also found her phone left on the hall table. Other than that, we don't know much.' She makes a note then tears the sheet from her pad, handing it to Jason. 'This is my email address. If you could send me that doorbell camera clip, I'd appreciate it. In fact, while you're at it, send me all the footage you have from the last forty-eight hours. You never know, something might show up.'

'Forty-eight hours?' Jason retorts. 'Isn't that an invasion of our privacy?'

'Well, it's up to you. I can get a judge to decide if they see it that way, if you prefer. Or you can just send it over without my having to get a court order. You might not want a judge to glean anything *else* from hearing what you've just played us. Would you now?'

'Fine,' Jason replies, biting the inside of his lip. If only the officer knew what his wife was like, how he had no choice but to put these rules in place even if they did seem controlling, then she'd be more sympathetic to his plight. Briefly, in his mind's eye, he sees himself standing up, upturning the coffee table, grabbing the heavy vase from the mantelpiece and smashing it over and over and over on the officer's head to get his point across. He takes a deep breath to rid himself of the thought.

'It would appear that you were the last ones to see Sascha – apart from her mother, of course, when she dropped Cora off for a sleepover just before seven o'clock last night,' DC Baldwin says.

'So, Sascha went straight to her mum's from here, then,' Fiona says in a thoughtful voice.

'It would appear so,' DI Waters says. 'Would she usually put her car in the garage overnight?'

'Not very often,' Fiona says. 'And especially not if she has an early start.'

'That's not entirely true,' Jason chips in. 'Sometimes it's put away. Especially if that bloke of hers is round. It's so he can park his motorbike on the drive. It's a big machine.'

Another whimper from Fiona.

'She has a partner?' DI Winters says. 'Do you have a name or know where he lives?'

'Sorry, no,' Jason replies, exerting maximum pressure on his wife's hand – a signal to her to hold it together a little longer. The officers have outstayed their welcome now, and he wants them gone.

'She once mentioned someone called Steve,' Fiona says. 'I don't know much about him. I've seen him around... though I didn't know he rode a motorbike...' She trails off, looking up at Jason. She's gone deathly pale.

'You OK, love?' Jason says, sliding an arm around her shoulder. Why the hell is she giving them all this information? It won't make a scrap of difference to them finding Sascha, but it might start them off on a trail of questions about things that are private to them. He doesn't want the whole world knowing their business, how they got together. They came here for a fresh start, dammit. That's what Rule Number 6 is for. Never talk about the past.

Jason touches his temple, feeling overwhelmed and upset by the police presence. Something begins to boil inside him, but he knows he must keep calm – for his family's sake at least. His two precious daughters are upstairs.

'I'm fine,' Fiona whispers to Jason. Then, turning to the

female officer, she says, 'I'm really worried about Sascha, though.'

'We're doing everything to locate her, try not to be concerned. If there's no news by morning, we'll get a specially trained officer to have a chat with Cora, see if she can reveal anything about her mother's plans. She's probably just gone to stay the night at her boyfriend's house and left in a hurry. No doubt she'll be horrified we're all searching for her.'

The officers stand up.

'Thanks for your help,' DC Baldwin says. 'We'll see ourselves out.'

Jason briefly stands, watching the pair leave. Fiona remains seated, staring at the wall. When he hears the front door close, Jason bends down and grabs his wife by the shoulders.

'What the fuck were you thinking, blabbing to them like that?'

'What? Jase... no, wait. If Sascha is in trouble, then I want to help.'

Jason stares down at her, wondering – for the first time since he lost his wife... his job... the hospital... *everything* – if he's done the right thing. He knew it would be tough, starting again, and God knows he loves Fiona. But sometimes... 'Sometimes, love... you've got to keep fucking quiet.'

He's not proud, but he finds himself with his hand clamped over her mouth and nose, the sinewy muscles of his forearm standing proud as she tries to pull his arm away. For a few seconds, he sees fear in her eyes, sees how she's gasping for breath as she tugs on his arm. He's way stronger than her. Could snuff her out in an instant.

But of course, he's not going to do that. He drops his hand from her face, releasing her. Fiona gasps for breath as he looms over her.

'Daddy?' comes a voice from the living room doorway,

making him whip around. Ivy is standing there, a worried look on her face.

'Hey, sweetie,' Jason pants, red-faced as he straightens up, brushing himself down. 'How's my little munchkin?' He holds out his arms for Ivy to run into like she usually does, but she just stands in the doorway, her eyes flicking between him and Fiona. Come to think of it, he can't remember the last time she ran into his arms. 'What's up, poppet?'

'Who were those people?' she asks, glancing at the front door.

'Oh, no one important,' Jason says, interrupting Fiona as she's about to speak. 'They were just doing a survey.'

'Were they police?' Ivy presses on. 'Tilly saw them out of the window and says they're police and that they're worried because Cora's mummy is missing.'

'Everything's fine,' Fiona says, standing. She glances at Jason, touching her lips. 'Let's go and make some hot chocolate, yeah?' She goes over and takes Ivy's hand. His daughter follows Fiona to the kitchen.

When they've gone, Jason sighs, going over to the window. He stares out at the street scene – the little cul-de-sac that they were so thrilled to be moving into only a couple of months ago. A fresh start, that's what it was meant to be. Not filled with secrecy and lies and disobeying the rules and nosy neighbours and the police. Why does everything feel like it's beginning to fall apart when he's tried – God knows he's tried – to put everything back together?

He spots a net curtain twitching in the front window of the house across the street. The detectives' car is parked at the end of the close, the pair of them striding from one property to the next.

Jason peers out at Sascha's front drive, where everything seems quiet, no one about. Then he catches sight of his own car parked on the front driveway. There's mud on the tyres and up the back panels from where he'd parked by the woods earlier – when he'd tracked Fiona and the girls across the fields on their walk.

He stares at the windscreen, remembering the note he found tucked beneath the wiper. Before coming back to the lay-by, he'd gone off for a walk himself, to clear his head and calm down after his discovery. But then *that* was waiting for him when he returned – someone had left it for him to find.

The dead don't stay silent forever. Her blood is on your hands.

He stared at the bit of paper, the menacing words burning his eyes as he read.

Someone else knows.

FIFTEEN

JASON

The next morning, Jason decides to go to the university. Even if he can't concentrate on work properly – not that there's much of that at this time of year – at least it gets him out of the house. And this time when he leaves, he securely locks the back and front doors, taking both sets of keys with him.

While Fiona had quickly resigned herself to her punishment – a day of being locked in at home, crafting and watching movies with Ivy, and of course preparing his dinner for later – Tilly was not at all happy about the arrangements. He tried to explain.

'I know it's hard, Tills,' he said as father and daughter sat at the kitchen table earlier. 'But it's not forever. Your mum and I... after everything that's happened, we feel it's best to keep our heads down for a bit. Until the dust settles, you know.'

He'll never forget the look of horror and shock on his eldest daughter's face as she listened. It was as if he didn't even know her – the way her eyes were filled with hate. Sure, they'd had some time apart over recent years what with him being away for work as well as the troubles between him and Erika. But he and Tilly were just starting to rebuild their relationship after her mum's death, and he'd hoped, deep in his heart, that she trusted him. That she had faith in him to do the right thing. Her expression told him otherwise.

'No way, Dad...' she whispered breathily, her whole body shaking in disbelief. 'No frigging *way* am I staying locked in this house all day.'

'It's the school holidays. There's no need for you to go out. We probably rushed things by even allowing you and Ivy to make new friends. That was your mum's idea.'

'Look, Fiona is *not* my mother,' Tilly replied in a slow and calculated voice. 'Mum only died two months ago, and this whole not-grieving-apart-from-on-a-Sunday thing is cruel. It's killing me.' Another pained expression designed to cut straight to Jason's core. 'And what's the point of us making new friends here if we're not allowed to go out and see them?'

She grabbed his arms then, making him flinch, but it was the tears rolling down her cheeks that truly ripped his heart to shreds. He saw the hurt and the pain within his daughter and yet there was nothing he could do to take it away.

'Tills, rules are rules. They're there for a reason. Things stay... well, they stay safe this way. In a few months, things will feel a lot different. You'll be over losing your mum and—'

Jason didn't realise what it was at first – Tilly's hand swiping across the side of his face, the wet globule of spit that landed on his neck. He recoiled, touching his smarting cheek, staring his daughter down. Her eyes were on fire as her shoulders rose and fell in time with her sobs.

'You're sick,' she hissed at him. 'A sick, cold bastard who—'

'Now stop!' Jason boomed. 'That's not true! What happened... Darling, you must understand that if I could change any of it, I would. I'd do *anything* to bring your mum back, but I can't. There's new research on grief in younger people... about losing a close relative. You're going to have to trust me on this, sweetheart. It's not long until the weekend now. Not long and we can get the photographs of her out, light a candle, share some memories. What do you say?'

Tilly turned away, stifling her sobs. She bowed her head and took a deep breath – partly involuntary and partly to halt an outburst. She gave a quick nod.

'Atta girl,' he said. 'Now, you look after your mum today for me, yeah?'

She turned to him slowly. 'OK,' she agreed, albeit rather flatly.

Jason stands at the counter of the university café in the plaza, the sun streaming in the window. He's ordered a cream cheese and smoked salmon bagel today to shake things up, boldly going for an iced latte instead of his usual Americano.

Suddenly, he's aware of someone beside him – someone wearing perfume that makes his nostrils flare. He glances sideways, realising it's Rosanne, the PhD student, the one who was late for her appointment on Tuesday. The one who'd made him feel so uncomfortable.

'Oh... hi, again, Dr Hewitt,' she says, looking over with a smile.

'Hello,' Jason says, nodding and glancing away. He shifts from one foot to the other. He wishes his order would hurry up. He hadn't felt entirely safe when he was alone with her in his office the other afternoon – all the things she was hinting at, implying, making his mind race. All the accusations she could make against him if she decided to turn nasty. He knows he'll have to put a stop to it. He knows what women like her could do to a man's career if he isn't careful.

'Thanks for the other afternoon,' Rosanne says, tucking a strand of hair behind her ear. She's pretty enough, he thinks. Nothing special, but a kind face. Good cheekbones. 'You really helped with my thesis.' She pauses, with Jason acutely aware that she's staring at him. 'You know, since we met the other day, I've been thinking about you, and...'

Here we go, thinks Jason, edging a step away from her.

'...and I swear I recognise you from somewhere.'

Jason's heart thumps. He turns to her. 'Really?' He puffs up his chest. 'Much of my research has been published. Maybe you've seen my name in the journals.' He hopes that suffices. Hopes that's all it is.

Rosanne shakes her head, still staring. 'No... it's your face. I recognise your face. Have you worked here long?' She tilts her head at him and narrows her eyes. Jason needs to shut this down. He swallows drily.

'I studied here many years ago,' he offers. 'Or maybe I have a doppelganger.'

'Order for Jason!' the woman behind the counter calls out, sliding his bagel and coffee onto the counter.

'I think that's yours,' Rosanne says when neither of them makes a move. Then she laughs, given that they are the only two people in the café. 'Jason... Jason...' she says, repeating his name and tapping a finger on her arm, frowning. She only knows him as Dr Hewitt from their meeting.

'It's *Jake*, actually,' Jason says, correcting the young woman behind the counter as he picks up his order. 'You mean order for *Jake*. You must have misheard me.' He rolls his eyes at Rosanne, inwardly praising himself for his quick thinking.

'Oh, OK then... *Jake*,' Rosanne says, not letting up. 'Dr Jake Hewitt... I've definitely seen you before. I just can't place where...' She pulls a face, indicating she's thinking hard.

Jason supposes he should have prepared a better comeback for this eventuality. He doesn't want to draw attention to himself and certainly not around the university. Things were different at the hospital, especially having Erika as his boss. Her ruthless ambition oozed from every pore, though most of all with her, it was about control.

People like him – even her own *husband* – had been nothing more than collateral.

Well, who's the one laughing now, Erika?

'Sorry?' Rosanne says, following Jason to the door after her order arrives. 'Did you just call me Erika?'

Jason freezes, hand on the door as he goes to open it, not realising he'd spoken out loud. 'You must have misheard,' he says, knowing he needs to be way more careful with his thoughts.

SIXTEEN
FIONA

Before

After the alcohol recovery group session had finished, with Erika giving me daggers every time I looked her way, I set about gathering up the chairs and stacking them over at the side of the room. It seemed no one wanted to help me, but I didn't mind clearing everything away. I was used to it. It was my job.

Besides, I wanted to be alone with my thoughts, having just spent the last hour and a half in the company of Jason and his wife, barely paying any attention to the patients' stories of relapse and recovery and how they dealt with their day-to-day struggles.

I pondered that word. *Wife*. I hated it. It rubbed Jason and Erika's union in my face. Their coupledom. Two hearts beating as one and all the nauseating connotations that went with that. Erika had a moniker that, as things stood, I did not have.

But I wanted it. By *God*, I wanted it.

Being labelled as Jason's mistress gave me a bad taste in my mouth. It was not who I was, or what I'd ever set out to be –

even though no one knew about our affair. But I couldn't help the chemistry that flared between us any more than he could – the pure combustion of feelings when we were together.

Jason deserved so much more than his wife offered him, and I intended on giving it to him. Where she was cold and indifferent to his needs, I worshipped him, made love to him as if it was our first time every time, and I listened to him in a way she never had. He adored this about me – that I heard him.

'It was a good session, don't you think?' came a voice from across the room. Most people had gone now, but a few remained, nurses and patients alike, milling about and chatting. I'd been focusing on clearing up, hoping I wouldn't have to speak to Jason or his wife, but, when I looked up, it seemed Erika had other ideas. It was her first time at the group session, so I presumed she was doing some kind of random quality check, to make sure it was being run professionally and of real benefit to the patients.

'Yes, it went well,' I replied, putting a load of mugs onto a tray that I was never going to be able to carry. Not in front of her, anyway. My hands and legs had suddenly started shaking.

'I'm very impressed,' she said. 'This group really offers them something unique. And you're a part of that, Fiona.'

I looked at her – her sharp features, her icy-blue eyes set beneath her slicked-back blonde hair. High cheekbones and precision-painted nails, a crisp white blouse over black trousers with a perfect crease ironed down the front, scarlet court shoes. She gave me the glimmer of a smile which, if on anyone else's face, I would have taken to be a nervous but pleasant one, as though they were apprehensive about approaching me. But in this case, I took it as the intended sneer it was. Erika was making her presence known to me and, by default, reinforcing her claim on her husband.

No two ways about it: Erika Norstrom terrified me.

'Thanks, yeah, it's a good group.' I picked up the tray, mugs rattling, my hands shaking. To my surprise, Erika reached out and took the tray from me, her strong, gym-honed arms holding it steady with ease.

'You get the door, Fiona,' she said. 'I'll take these to the kitchen.'

And that was how I came to be drying up a dozen mugs while Erika washed them one by one with Jason nowhere to be seen. Just me and her – mistress and wife – standing side by side at the sink in the small kitchen, chatting as if it were the aftermath of a WI meeting or a village fete.

'How long have you and Dr Hewitt been married?' I found myself asking when conversation about the group petered out. I was fishing for confirmation that things were on the rocks between her and her husband. It was a risky question but, looking back, I think it was to ease my guilt about what Jason and I were doing.

'Goodness, it seems like forever,' she said, with only the slightest hint of an accent – accompanied by a small laugh, which I wasn't expecting. Was this her softer side coming out? 'We were married in Gothenburg so many years ago.' She laughed again, tipping back her head to reveal her long, milky-white neck. Then she closed her eyes for a beat, as if replaying their entire married life in an instant. 'Going on twenty years. Yes, it'll be twenty years next April. That'll be a big celebration.' She looked across at me and grinned, and, at that moment, I wondered if she really *did* suspect anything about me and her husband, or if it was all in my head.

She seemed so genuine. So happy to reveal her story. So intent on sharing this moment – just two women washing up together, chatting away. Though, worryingly, it didn't sound as though she knew anything about the marital problems Jason had told me about.

Unless she was bluffing. In which case, one-nil to Erika.

'We met at the Karolinska Institutet as fresh-faced young-sters. We somehow made the logistics work, even though Jason was from England. It was love at first sight.' She flashed me another white-toothed smile. She might as well have had red love hearts for pupils.

'That sounds so... romantic,' I replied, taking another wet mug from her.

'Are you married, Fiona?' she asked, making me nearly drop it.

'God, no,' I replied vehemently. But followed it up with a gentler, 'No... no, I'm not.'

Yet.

'Well, I'm sure the right person will come along before too long. And I hope that you'll be as happy as Jason and me after all these years.'

That's when I did drop the mug, smashing it into a dozen pieces.

'She was playing with me, all right,' I told Jason afterwards, when we were out on the terrace. 'I saw it in her eyes – a death stare, if ever there was one. She was pretending to be super nice, like we were the oldest of friends.' My eyes flicked around, making sure none of the staff had clocked us. Jason had wrapped his fingers around mine, squeezing them tight. His touch – it did something to me.

'She doesn't know. She *can't* know,' Jason replied, throwing back his head and groaning. We'd watched Erika's car speed off down the long drive only ten minutes ago, so we knew we were safe. 'I've been so careful.'

'Not careful enough, I'd say.' I took a breath, launching into what was bothering me. 'Though... it was weird. She didn't seem at all unhappy. In fact, she seemed the opposite and was even telling me about where you two met, and getting excited about your wedding anniversary party next year.'

Jason scowled. 'She's bluffing,' he said smoothly. 'Don't believe a word that comes out of her mouth. You know what she's like. A master manipulator. Surely you see that?' He paused while I considered what he was telling me. 'Dear God, don't say she's got to you, too, Fiona?' He made a strange noise in his throat – a kind of choked sob. It had me hugging him, stroking his back.

'God no, no, of course I don't believe her,' I told him, though I wasn't being entirely honest. 'I see straight through her. I know it's all an act.'

I closed my eyes and Erika's face filled my mind, her searching blue eyes boring into mine as she talked about her husband. She could have been an ice queen or just someone's wife and mum at that moment – it was hard to tell. Even putting my professional head on, I felt confused and disorientated. I didn't know who to believe – her or Jason. The only thing I knew for sure was that I was betraying another woman in the most awful way.

'God, what are we going to do, Jase? I just want to be with you, but as soon as it becomes public knowledge, our time here is over. Us having a relationship – the doctor–nurse cliché – it's so against the rules.'

Jason held me at arm's length, looking directly at me. 'Rules, rules, rules. The bane of my life, yet without them, I would not have a code by which to live.'

I wasn't sure I understood his meaning, but I let him have his moment. It felt like he needed to get things off his chest, justifying our situation like I'd been trying to do. We stared over the beautiful grounds and rolling countryside beyond the terrace.

'Do you think *you* can live by the same rules, Fiona?' He looked at me again, taking my hands in his, and, for some reason, it felt as though he was testing me, making certain I was up to the job of taking Erika's place. 'My rules? I don't see a way forward for us otherwise.'

I paused, considering his question. There was no doubt in my mind that Jason was my person, my soulmate – and because it had taken me long enough to find him, I wasn't about to let him go over a few silly rules. While I didn't know the full extent of them, I doubted they'd affect me too much. I'd always be my own woman – strong-minded and independent – but, also, I knew that I had to be careful not to push those I loved away. I concluded that adhering to a few basic ground rules wouldn't hurt. I wanted to make Jason happy.

Yet... I swear there was something niggling away at me, my gut trying to tell me something – something I wasn't prepared to hear. Something I blocked my ears to. Was it wrong that I just wanted my happy ever after like all my friends? Staring out across the beautiful countryside with Jason beside me, it felt like I was so close to getting it. And if agreeing with him achieved that, then that's what I would do.

'Yes,' I replied, looking up at him with a smile. 'Of course I'll live by your rules, Jase.'

Though what Erika had said to me still niggled inside my mind, eating away at my conscience.

...I hope that you'll be as happy as Jason and me...

Suddenly, with a mischievous grin, Jason grabbed my hand and urged me to follow. I felt like a naughty schoolgirl as he led me around the side of the eighties-built wing at the rear of the grand main building. We slipped in through a rarely used door, emerging into a corridor.

'Quick, before anyone sees us,' he said in a low voice, opening the door to his office. Once inside, he wedged a chair against the handle and drew the curtains. As he undressed, turning his back to me for a moment, I slipped my phone from my pocket and propped it up near the edge of his desk, leaning it against a plant pot, camera lens facing out. I hated that I had to do this, but I couldn't get Erika's words out of my mind. Tears filled my eyes as I pressed record – I had to look after myself.

...as happy as Jason and me...

Then he came over and slid his hands under my top.

SEVENTEEN
FIONA

Fiona knows it's futile, but she tries the two back doors again, wiggling the handles, as well as checking the front door just in case she was mistaken the first time. But they're all still locked. It's her punishment for going out on a walk yesterday – being locked in the house with no way out. Trapped. All of them prisoners.

She drops down onto a kitchen chair, a cold cup of tea that she can't face drinking sitting on the table as she stares at the wall. How have things turned out like this?

Everything was fine until those notes turned up – *three* of them – their sinister words stuck on repeat in her head. She doesn't think it's coincidence that things feel off now, as if someone is watching her, following her, toying with her senses, knowing just how to get to her. Before the notes arrived, life had been ticking along just fine – they were adhering to their familiar routine to keep them safe. Sticking to the rules. But now, cracks are appearing, rules are being broken. And she's not sure if it's in spite of the notes or because of them.

Sascha's disappearance hasn't helped, of course – and the police presence in their cul-de-sac is making Jason extra twitchy.

She prays he never finds out it was her who phoned them. But now that she's discovered Sascha's boyfriend, Steve, rides a motorbike, she's even more concerned about her friend. Had it been him delivering the second note the other day? She recalls the man in a helmet putting the bit of paper through her letter-box, his bike parked on the street as he was caught on the door-bell camera. Maybe he's the type who enjoys frightening women. Fiona shudders as she wonders if he's done something awful to Sascha.

She grabs her phone to check the footage again, to see if there's anything noticeable about him or the motorbike so she can compare it if he comes round again. She plans on recording the screen so she has a permanent record of it in her camera roll, but when she checks back on the timeline, everything has been deleted – all footage apart from their own comings and goings over the last few days.

'Odd,' she says, putting her phone down and biting her lip. 'I'm sure I wasn't mistaken.' She drops her head down onto the table, taking a few deep breaths.

She knew it was never going to be easy, her and Jason making a life together. She was aware that there would be bumps along the way, repercussions even. She's not stupid. Picking up the girls from their respective schools that day eight weeks ago and breaking the news to them that not only had their mother died in a terrible accident, but that she and their dad were now together as a couple was one of the hardest things she'd ever had to do.

Understandably, Tilly and Ivy went into a deep shock, their worlds turned upside down forever, and it's only because of Jason's carefully considered rules that the family has since managed to hold it together. The solid framework he's scaf-folded around their lives has literally kept them going.

'You're not seriously going along with this nonsense, are you?' comes a voice now. Tilly.

Fiona looks up. 'Oh hi, Tilly.' She smiles. 'Staying home, you mean?'

'It's not staying home,' she says in a snarky voice. 'It's called being *locked in*.'

'If you want to be pedantic, then it's actually called keeping us safe. Your dad knows what's best for us.'

'Like, literally all the windows and doors are locked, and there are no keys! I've tried them all.' Tilly shakes her head, dropping down onto a chair. 'He wasn't always like this, you know. So controlling and... and obsessive. When I was little and Ivy was a baby, things were almost... fun. But then when we were older, he started going away a lot for work – that's where Mum told us he was anyway – and everything changed. Things turned bad.'

Fiona looks at her, not wanting to know about those times. Jason has taught her how to block things out of her mind – the irrational and dark thoughts, the unwanted feelings and emotions that follow. She locks them all away in a secret box at the back of her mind.

'We won't be stuck indoors forever,' Fiona says, getting up and tipping her tea into the sink. 'Your dad cares about us so much, that's all. He worries about us while he's at work.' *And since the police came round last night, he's been even more on edge*, Fiona thinks but keeps to herself.

'I miss Mum so much,' Tilly says out of the blue, her face crumpling. 'It's so cruel that I'm not allowed to cry for her or even talk about her.'

Fiona watches as Tilly drops her head down and sobs for all she's worth. Hot, messy tears fall from her face, making Fiona grab the box of tissues and put it beside her. Thank God Jason isn't here to see her meltdown.

'You are allowed to be sad, love,' Fiona says. 'Just keep it for Sunday afternoons. It's better that way, don't you see?'

Tilly blows her nose, looking up at Fiona through hollow

eyes. 'No, I *don't* see! None of this is right. Don't *you* see? He's abusing all of us.'

'Stop it,' Fiona whispers. 'Don't you dare talk like that. Be grateful for what you have. Count your blessings, Mathilda. Other people have it so much worse.'

She feels herself wobbling inside, her foundations shaking. She also doesn't like that a tiny part of her is wondering if Tilly is right, if Jason *is* too controlling. But then she only has to think back to their time together at the hospital, all the secret meetings they had in his office – their deep and meaningful late-night chats, the passionate sex, the merging of two lives that seemed so aligned – to know that being with him is right. It might have taken her a lot longer than most to find a life partner, but Jason has been worth the wait. They're perfect for each other, and she can forgive him a few foibles. God knows he overlooks enough of hers. Fiona loves him. And he loves her. There's no way they would have survived all this otherwise. Plus, Jason adores his daughters. Tilly needs to understand this.

'Look at this,' Tilly says, holding up an unfamiliar phone.

'Wait... where did you get that from?' Fiona asks, not recognising the device. 'Your dad will go absolutely mad! I thought he had your phone locked up.'

'Promise not to tell?' Tilly says, sniffing and wiping her nose on the sleeve of her sweatshirt. '*Please*?'

Fiona's heart pounds. She doesn't like this – it's too big a secret. So against the rules. She nods once.

'Amber gave it to me when I went to her house. It's her old one. You didn't let on to Dad that I went to see her after our walk, did you?'

Fiona shakes her head. 'No, no, I didn't. He'd have lost it.'

'Yeah, and this is our punishment for going on a stupid walk,' Tilly says, shaking her head. 'Being locked in the house. If could be for days, *weeks*, you realise?'

'It won't be. And it's not like that, Tilly. Please understand. Your dad just wants us to be safe.'

'Safe from what?' Tilly says, sounding frustrated but almost laughing. 'It's like he's brainwashed you.'

Fiona stares out of the window. Her thoughts are fuzzy, as though she's looking through the wrong glasses.

'Safe from everything,' she whispers, frowning slightly as she tries to remember. 'The way your dad and I got together,' she says, wringing her hands. 'People didn't like it. Your mum especially.' A stab of guilt jabs at her when she sees Tilly's anguish at the mention of her mother.

'Is that why Mum died?' she asks. 'Because you and Dad got together?'

They've already explained to the girls that Erika was involved in a horrific car accident. But now, Fiona thinks, Tilly is trying to piece together why she was in the accident in the first place. Tilly is probably wondering if her mum was running away from something – driving too fast, sobbing at the wheel, not paying attention after learning the news about Fiona and her husband.

But it was none of those things.

'No,' Fiona says softly, remembering the script. 'Your mum's accident was random. The lorry driver had been drinking. It was raining and there was so much spray on the motorway.'

While waiting in the car that awful afternoon, Fiona remembers seeing the expression on Tilly's face at the school gates as Jason spoke to her. At first, she was shocked and surprised that her father was picking her up. She hadn't seen him in a long while and wasn't expecting him. Fiona watched through the windscreen – the boot of the Ford SUV packed with their belongings. They'd already fetched Ivy from her primary school, pulling her out early during afternoon playtime to tell her the terrible news.

As Tilly walked over to the car, looking pale and in shock as her dad looped his arm around her back, supporting her as she absorbed what he'd just told her, Ivy quietly sobbed on the back seat, clutching her school folder to her chest. When her sister got in beside her, the girls hugged and cried for their dead mother.

Jason allowed them to be sad for a short while as they drove the twenty miles or so to their new home. But once they arrived, after they'd unloaded the car, he told his daughters to stop crying, explaining Rule Number 8 – grieving hour every Sunday at 5 p.m. – and how, at other times, they must contain their sadness.

Of course, Jason hadn't divulged precise details of the road accident to them, not wanting his daughters' minds to be filled with shocking images of their dead mother, making them even more upset. He wanted them to remember the good times with Erika, eventually find peace and be able to reminisce. But only ever for one hour at 5 p.m. on a Sunday.

'I downloaded Instagram,' Tilly says now, glancing at the door in case Ivy should come in.

'You did *what*?' Fiona squeaks. 'That's not allowed! You have a couple of useful apps on your own phone. Why are you doing this, Tilly?'

Tilly scoffs. 'Oh yeah, right – you mean the weather app and a study guide? Oh wait, and I've got a couple of boring kids' games that Dad allowed me to have, too. I know he keeps tabs on me, checking my app store account daily.' She rolls her eyes. 'I just wanted to look at social media without him breathing down my neck or monitoring what I'm doing. No other girls I know have such strict fathers. What's it going to be like when I start my new school? Is he going to escort me into my classroom? Eat lunch with me?'

Count yourself lucky you'll even be going to a school, Fiona thinks, knowing that was all down to her negotiating with Jason. Tilly has big exams coming up next year.

'Anyway, you don't need to worry. What I found on Insta has upset me too much. I've not looked at it since. If Dad finds out what I've done... God, I'll really be in for it. You won't tell him, will you? I'm going to delete it anyway... I'm so done with social media and—'

'Wait, what did you find?' Fiona reaches out and touches Tilly's hand, seeing how upset she is.

Tilly sighs, closing her eyes a moment before tapping on her screen. 'This,' she says, her hand shaking as she holds out the phone.

Fiona twists her head sideways. It's a picture – a group of people on what looks like a stage at a conference, something to do with education and science. A typical set-up – a podium, a microphone, the key speakers standing proudly as they have their picture taken against some kind of backdrop with logos on.

'What is this?' Fiona whispers.

'It's *Mum*,' Tilly replies, her voice breathy and shaky. 'It was only posted a few days ago.'

Fiona takes the phone from her, zooming in on the picture. Sure enough, Erika is standing between two men, her hands clasped in front of her royal-blue pencil skirt. She's wearing one of her trademark white blouses on top, and her blonde hair is pulled tightly back in a bun. Fiona shudders.

'Oh, *love*, this is an old picture,' she says, shaking her head and touching Tilly's hand gently. 'Look, read the caption. It says, "Science cons past and present... great to see these experts in their fields over the years." This photo was taken before the accident.' She looks away from the screen, not wanting to be reminded of Erika. In fact, she never wants to see her face again. 'Anyway, you shouldn't be looking her up. You're right, your dad would flip, so best you delete it all. If you want to see photos, he'll show you some during Sunday grieving.' Fiona stands up and paces about. 'In fact, give me that,' she says, grabbing the phone from Tilly.

'Get off!' Tilly cries, whipping the phone away. 'You have to trust me, I *will* delete it, but just let me keep the phone. That picture... I've never seen it before! I swear it was taken recently...' More sobs escape from her throat. 'So why is Mum in it?'

'Oh, Tilly... they've just posted a few photos from previous conferences, but I see how it would upset you. It's an old picture of her, that's all,' Fiona says, her mind tripping over itself. *Erika is dead... She was killed in a car crash... instant... tragic... torrential rain... drunk driver... blue lights... loud sirens...* The words Jason told her to stick to flash through her brain as she tries to make sense of it.

'What's that?' Tilly suddenly says, grabbing onto Fiona's arm, bringing her back to the moment. 'That noise...!'

Fiona hears it too – the siren screeching all around them. She rushes to the door leading to the hallway, flinging it wide open. It gets even louder.

'Oh my God, it's the smoke alarms!' she cries, heading to the bottom of the stairs. 'Ivy, come down! Quick, hurry! We've got to get out!'

As Ivy rushes down, the horror of their situation dawns on Fiona. The girls cling to each other with terrified expressions – the three of them huddled together in the hallway. They stand there, shaking, not knowing what to do as they wait for smoke and flames to engulf them, knowing there's no way out of the house. Knowing that they're locked in. Trapped.

EIGHTEEN
FIONA

'You did exactly the right thing,' their neighbour says twenty minutes later as he comes out of their house via the front door, the siren now silenced. 'False alarm. Probably dust or an insect in one of the sensors. They're all interlinked, so if one goes off, they all do.'

Fiona stands shaking on the front lawn, both girls beside her, staring at the smashed window. It was Ivy who saved the day, knowing exactly how to break through a double-glazed unit.

'The fire officer taught us what to do when they visited my old school,' she said after they'd escaped. Fiona had gone round every window in the house, but as Tilly had said, along with the doors, they were all locked. She had no idea where the keys were. Probably with Jason.

Terrified that they were about to burn to death, Fiona had been desperate. She'd followed Ivy's instructions and used the pointed end of the iron to smash in the bottom corner of the living room window. Her shoulder still ached from the many attempts it took to get all the glass broken and out of its frame. The alarms had been screeching around them as she'd worked, but she'd had no idea if there was an actual fire or not. Her main objective was to get the girls to safety.

Then, shaking and not knowing what else to do, she'd knocked on the neighbour's door the other side – number 11. She'd been too scared to go back inside the house.

'I feel such a fraud,' she says to the neighbour now, 'but I didn't want to bother the fire service when it was probably nothing.' *Too scared of what Jason would say if I caused a scene*, she thinks.

'No bother at all,' the man, late fifties with salt-and-pepper hair and a confident, calm manner, says. 'You did exactly the right thing. It's lucky I still had a spare key from the previous tenant. I used to pop in to feed her cat when she was away. I'm Graham, by the way. And my wife is Angela. She's at work currently, though she's often asleep during the day after a night shift.'

Fiona's head whips up, knowing that working pattern well. 'Is she a nurse?'

'At the hospital in Stratford, yes. We've been meaning to introduce ourselves since you moved in, but you know what it's like.'

'I'm sorry it took me banging on your door in a panic to say hello,' Fiona says, sounding far calmer than she feels.

'It's fine,' he says with a kind grin as if he deals with this sort of thing every day. There's a serene air about him that Fiona likes. 'By the way, this was on your doormat when I came out of your house just now.' He holds out a piece of folded-up paper, but Fiona just stands there staring at it. He waves it at her a couple of times, urging her to take it. 'It's got your name on it, look,' he adds when she doesn't say a word.

Eventually, Fiona reaches out and takes the familiar lined paper from him, stuffing it in her back pocket. 'Thank you,' she says, barely able to speak. There's no way she's reading it now. *In fact*, she tells herself to keep the tremors building inside her at bay, *you don't have to read it at all. You can just chuck it straight in the bin.*

'I can give you the name of a good glazier to repair your front window, if you like,' Graham says. 'They do emergency call-outs. At the very least, you'll need it shoring up for the night.'

'Oh, yes, thank you. That's kind. I... I still can't believe we were locked in our own house,' Fiona says, making sure she sounds a bit ditzy but also relieved. 'It was an accident, of course, but I'll be having words with that husband of mine, running off with our keys by mistake like that.' She rolls her eyes, giving Tilly a nudge in the ribs, sensing she's about to say something.

She prays the glazier will be able to fix the window before Jason returns, though unless she can find where he's hidden the cash that they're currently living off, she has no way of paying for it. She has no money of her own.

'Any word from your neighbour the other side?' Graham asks, tipping his head towards Sascha's house. 'It's not like her to go out and leave her house open. We've known Sascha for quite a while – she's a... a really lovely lass.' Graham pauses, clearing his throat and rubbing his nose as he ponders the situation. 'It's a worry that she didn't turn up at work, too. I heard her dinner was left half prepared, a bath run.'

'You know about that?' Fiona swallows.

'The detectives filled us in.' He glances at Tilly and Ivy, who are talking between themselves and not listening. 'They asked what we knew about you as a family, but I'm afraid that we weren't able to help them much, not having met you.'

For some reason, Fiona feels Graham is sizing her up, assessing her response and gauging her reaction. Almost in the same way that the detectives did the other evening. But, despite feeling shaky and on edge, she manages to reply calmly.

'Don't worry – we told them everything we know... They

asked us all kinds of stuff, too. My husband is a doctor, and I'm also a nurse,' she adds as an afterthought, hoping that will put Graham's mind at rest – that they're good neighbours, professional, respectable people.

But then Jason's words race through her mind... warning her about giving too much away, how people gossip and wouldn't approve of the way they got together.

Wait for the dust to settle... he's drummed into her many times. *Then you can have your happy ever after... I just want us all to be safe...*

Fiona trusts Jason. Believes everything he says. And she believes in their marriage rules, too. Or, at least, she *did.* Because as she goes back inside the house, Tilly and Ivy following, and as she goes into the kitchen, shuts the door and takes the note from her pocket and begins to read it, she doesn't think she feels very safe at all. The words swim in and out of focus, the paper shaking in her hand.

We both know it wasn't a car accident.

NINETEEN

FIONA

'To our new neighbours,' Angela says across the dinner table two days later on Saturday, raising her glass to Jason and Fiona.

'And to Sascha's safe return,' Graham adds, raising his glass. Angela gives him a sour look and turns away, her cheeks colouring.

'Her safe return indeed,' Jason says, clinking everyone's glasses. 'It's very good of you to have us round,' he continues in such a way that makes Fiona wonder if he really means it, or if it's all for show. One thing's for sure, she'll be keeping a close eye on Graham, their neighbour, from now on. Since he helped her with the alarm on Thursday, she can't help thinking that it was very convenient timing – a note happening to be on the doormat at exactly the same moment he was there. And she's already flagged the dark four-wheel drive parked outside his garage. She didn't get the exact model of vehicle that drove away from the riding stables, but there's no doubt in her mind that it was very similar in appearance to Graham's car.

As Fiona was getting ready to come out earlier – putting her make-up on, trying to do something with her hair that hasn't been cut in months – Tilly slipped into her bedroom and sat down on the end of the bed. Jason was downstairs. 'You realise he's only doing it for appearances,' she whispered, leaning closer to Fiona, who was sitting at the dressing table. 'Dad agreeing to go for dinner next door. He hates things like that really. It's only so he appears *normal*, like a decent guy.'

Fiona looked at her in the mirror as she applied lipstick. 'You're wrong,' she replied. 'Besides, your dad and I want to make a go of it around here. Get to know people in the village and fit in.'

'So how do you explain Dad locking us in the house for the last two days?' she said in an urgent hiss. 'He's got you right where he wants you, hasn't he?' She glanced at the door, listening out.

Fiona then noticed a rectangular shape in the front pocket of Tilly's hoodie. Ignoring her question, she whispered, 'Hide your phone,' just as Jason came into the bedroom.

'All ready to go?' he asked, coming up behind Fiona. Tilly curled her legs up on the bed, her knees concealing her pocket.

'Yes, I'm ready,' Fiona said, standing up. But Jason swung her round, studying her for a moment before grabbing her face between his palms. He wiped a thumb firmly across her lips.

'That's better,' he said. 'You know the rules, love. Number twelve – no flaunting or flirting with the opposite sex. I don't want that man next door getting the wrong idea.'

'Have there been any updates about Sascha?' Graham asks now across the dinner table, his eyes flicking between Jason and Fiona. Angela puts another serving dish of food on a mat, slamming it down rather too heavily, making the glasses and cutlery rattle. *Just a simple supper*, she'd said when she'd invited them over earlier that morning.

Fiona and Jason had been in the garden doing a bit of weeding, enjoying the routine Saturday task together, when Angela had popped up over the fence to invite them round that evening. Initially, Jason had gladly accepted, but then once he and Fiona were back inside the house, he laid down a few ground rules.

'You must remember rule number six tonight – no talking about the past,' he said. 'How we got together is no one's business.'

Fiona agreed.

'On that basis, we will allow our neighbours to believe that Tilly and Ivy are your biological daughters. To save questions.'

Again, Fiona agreed.

'And we will not discuss our work. With Angela being a nurse, I don't want her gossiping about us. She might know some of the same people.'

Another nod from Fiona, though she thought that one might be tricky. Work was bound to come up.

After Jason had returned home on Thursday evening, the day the smoke alarms had gone off, Fiona had done her best to hide what had happened – how she'd had to smash her way out of the house trying to save herself and the girls from... well, from *nothing* as it turned out.

But Jason knew her too well, read her like a book, sussed out that something was up within ten minutes of being home. Plus, he'd found a couple of bits of shattered glass on the living room carpet.

'You were trying to escape, weren't you?' His face stern and unmoving. 'You were trying to leave me, disobeying the rules.'

Fiona had fallen to her knees in front of him, begging for forgiveness, swearing on her life that she wasn't trying to run away. 'Ask Graham, if you like. He'll tell you what happened.' She decided not to mention the note – the *fourth* note now – having hidden it at the back of her underwear drawer.

'Who the fuck is Graham?' Jason snapped, pacing about. 'We're late for our family confessional because of you. And dinner isn't ready... *again.*'

Fiona explained how, after climbing out of the window,

she'd run next door for help. Then she told him about the glazier coming out, how he'd had a standard-sized unit in stock to repair the window, how Graham had kindly paid the bill for now.

Jason tried to keep his anger contained, but Fiona saw it, noticed the way his neck turned red and the vein on his temple pulsed as if he was about to boil over.

'Remind me to give you the cash for the window repair before we leave,' Jason says to Graham now, serving some of Angela's dauphinoise potatoes onto Fiona's plate. 'I really appreciate you covering the bill. Fiona left her purse in my car, can you believe. What a pair we are – me running off with her keys and money by mistake.' He grins that devilish grin of his – the one that makes his eyes crinkle into boyish slits, the one Fiona knows everyone loves. He has a certain way of charming people.

'Happy to help,' Graham acknowledges.

'Oh, please, take more than that,' Angela pipes up when she sees the small amount of food Jason has served Fiona.

Instinctively, Fiona puts up her hand. 'It's plenty, thank you,' she says, looking across at Jason. 'He knows my appetite.'

For a while, the two couples laugh and share stories about being absent-minded, becoming forgetful the older you get, how their respective children are more switched on than them.

'Tilly, our eldest, is babysitting Ivy tonight,' Jason says, glancing proudly at Fiona. 'She's fifteen going on thirty. Hopefully nothing will go wrong, given they're only next door.'

'They grow up so fast. Our son works and lives in Manchester now, and our daughter is in her third year at university. We get a phone call every couple of weeks, if we're lucky,' Angela says with a laugh. 'A proper empty nest,' she adds wistfully. 'But I love my work, at least,' she adds. 'Unlike some of us who've had the luxury of retiring, filling their lives with mid-life crises like sailing dinghies and motorbikes.' She half turns to her husband, giving him a brief but contemptuous stare.

Fiona goes cold, her skin breaking out in goosebumps. *Mid-life crises... dinghies... motorbikes...*

'Not forgetting all that socialising,' Angela adds sourly. 'Getting all friendly with a certain female neighbour.' She coughs, briefly covering her mouth, but it comes out sounding a lot like *Sascha* behind her hand.

'Ange, don't. Not now,' Graham shoots back in a terse whisper.

'What did you do before retiring, Graham?' Jason asks, trying to defuse the obvious tension between them as he tucks into his food. His forehead crinkles as he glances up.

Fiona is grateful to Jason for keeping the conversation going – she's not feeling very sociable tonight. Not with everything swilling around her mind. And she can't get that picture of Erika out of her mind, either – the one that Tilly showed her on Instagram. The image of her standing on that stage with a proud smile on her face keeps morphing into a smashed-up and bloody mess.

Fiona shudders, taking a sip of wine. Being the weekend, she's grateful that Jason said one glass was allowed as per the rules. She's making it last.

'Me?' Graham says, cutting into his sirloin steak. Fiona watches as blood oozes onto the plate. 'I'm a retired police detective, for my sins,' he says with a tinge of pride. 'It's been a few years since I left the force now,' he adds. 'The detectives who came door-knocking the other night, I know them well. They're my old colleagues.'

TWENTY

FIONA

By Monday morning, Jason seems more settled, and Fiona prays that life will get back on track. She also prays that there will be no more punishments and no more strange notes. It's driving her mad, wondering who's been sending them.

It's someone who knows where she lives, that's for certain, as well as someone who knows that she went to the riding stables last week. Someone who rides a motorcycle and someone who also drives a dark-coloured four-wheel drive.

She's been peeling back the net curtains in the living room regularly, keeping an eye on the RAV4 parked on Graham and Angela's drive, hoping to see who takes it out. Watching to see if Graham perhaps gets a motorbike out of the garage, or owns a mirrored visor helmet. She mulls over the reasons why a retired police detective would be interested in sending notes to someone like her.

Then Angela's words from Saturday night are on her mind again – *getting all friendly with a certain female neighbour* – making her wonder what had been going on between Graham and Sascha. Angela had certainly sounded bitter about it.

Whatever it meant, she feels uncomfortable knowing she and Jason are living next door to an ex-detective.

So, yes... while the new week seems bright and light and filled with fresh hope because Jason is in a good mood, Fiona is still rattled inside. Especially because Sascha's house is swarming with a police forensics team for a second time. Her friend is still missing.

Fiona peeks out of the front window, her finger hooking back the net curtain so she can see what's going on. Two official-looking white vans and a marked police car are parked on the drive next door, spilling out onto the cul-de-sac. The other side of their house, Graham's RAV4 is parked with its nose right up to their garage door. Jason left for work before the police arrived, and thank God, Fiona has her privileges back today – her purse, her house keys, her freedom. *Relative* freedom.

'If you go out, I'll see on the doorbell camera, remember,' Jason said as he was heading out earlier. 'Try to have a calm and quiet day, love,' he added. 'I've an easy day on campus so I won't be late home. After confessional later, we can watch a movie if you like.'

Fiona nodded, smiled, waved him off.

'Shit,' she mutters now, ducking back behind the curtain. A uniformed officer is walking towards their house, looking straight at the front window. A moment later, the front doorbell chimes. 'Shit, shit, *shit*...' she mumbles under her breath. She hadn't bargained on this. What the hell will Jason say?

For a moment, she considers not answering it, but this option is taken away as Tilly bounds down the stairs and pulls the door open.

'Oh...' Fiona hears her say in a disappointed voice. 'I thought you were my friend.'

A laugh, followed by a female voice asking if her mum is in.

Fiona takes a deep breath, fluffs up her hair and heads to the hallway. 'Morning, officer,' she says. 'How can I help?' She turns to Tilly and nods, at which Tilly heads back upstairs.

'Sorry to bother you. I'm PC Sally Oldham. We have a team in next door conducting some further forensic checks,' the woman explains, pointing to the police tape fluttering around the front perimeter of the house. Her radio crackles at her shoulder and her petite frame seems weighed down with equipment. 'And... well, I just got caught a bit short. I don't suppose I could use your loo, could I?' She bobs from one foot to the other with a pained expression.

Fiona's heart unclenches and the prickling on her neck subsides. She smiles as relief floods her. 'Oh, gosh yes, of course. Please, come in.'

'Time of the month, too,' the officer says in a low voice as she steps inside. 'The guys have it easy,' she adds, tipping her head as the two women share a knowing look. She takes off her hat, revealing short, dark hair.

'In that case, use the upstairs bathroom,' Fiona says. 'You'll find what you need in there. As you just saw, I have a teenage daughter, so I'm always prepared. She ushers the officer inside, closing the door behind her, relieved that she hasn't come round to question her about Sascha.

'My little girl is only three, so I'm a long way off all that,' she jokes.

'Who's that?' comes Ivy's voice from the top of the stairs. Both women look up.

'And this is my youngest daughter,' Fiona explains to the officer. 'Eight going on eighteen.'

Ivy folds her arms and scowls. 'I am *not* your daughter,' she says, stamping her foot. 'Tilly says you're a fake and she hates you.'

'Oh... Ivy!' Fiona says, shocked, and while she tries to laugh it off, it hurts. 'OK, *step*daughter, then,' she corrects, rolling her eyes at PC Oldham. 'Ivy, please show the police officer to the bathroom.'

Fiona watches as the officer goes upstairs and Ivy does as she's told. In the hope it might get her into the officer's good books, Fiona goes and puts the kettle on. She figures a mug of tea to take back to her boring sentry duty will be welcome.

'Thanks for that,' the police officer says a few minutes later, poking her head into the kitchen. 'I'll be off then. And don't worry, we won't be bothering you any more. The rest of the team are guys, so they can duck into the fields behind the house.' She laughs. 'We're not allowed to use the bathroom next door while we're working in there.'

'Of course,' Fiona says smiling. 'Oh... I thought you might want this.' She slides a travel mug of tea and a chocolate biscuit bar across the counter.

'Magic,' the officer says, coming right into the kitchen. 'Thanks. Now if only everyone had good neighbours like you...' She takes a sip, staring at Fiona over the rim of the mug. 'Your youngest lass is sparky, isn't she?' she continues.

'Ivy?' Fiona laughs. 'A live wire.'

'Bet it's hard being a stepmum.'

Fiona nods. Those prickles on her neck are back.

'Do they live with you full-time, or do you share residency with their birth mum?'

Fiona swallows. 'Oh... I'm afraid the girls' mother passed away,' she explains. 'So they're with us full-time.'

'Gosh, I'm so sorry to hear that. Sounds... unexpected?'

'It was. Out of the blue. A motorway accident. A drunk lorry driver crushed her car.' Fiona shudders. She hates recounting the story. Rules 1, 2 and 6 whip through her mind.

'Those poor girls. Their poor father. When... when did it happen?'

Fiona can barely speak now, she's so anxious. She had not been expecting a grilling this morning, let alone from a police constable. And Jason will surely be giving her another one when he gets home later – *You let a police officer into our home without me being there? Are you crazy?*

'Just a couple of months ago, actually,' she replies, praying there are no more questions.

'Were the girls' parents already divorced?' the officer asks, convincing Fiona this is way more than idle chit-chat. It's some kind of fact-finding mission. Brownie points for the constable if she unwittingly discovers a secret.

'Yes, yes, they were.' Fiona decides to leave it at that, knowing she's not a good liar.

'And how have you settled into the area?' PC Oldham presses on. 'My old colleague, Graham, lives next door the other side of you.' She grins. 'Funny, that. He said you'd only been here a short while.'

Fiona nods, grateful for the slight change of tack, though she doesn't find Graham living next door the least bit amusing. With what she's learning about him, she finds it sinister and creepy, if she's honest, and if she knew Jason wouldn't go mad, then she'd be reporting him for potentially sending the notes and therefore harassment to the... well, to the police. And if it's true that he's had an affair with Sascha, then she bets they'd be very interested in that, too. Though she's heard stories of how they close ranks, protect their own. They probably wouldn't take her seriously. 'We thought a fresh start for the girls was a good idea. New area. New schools. New friends.'

The officer seems surprised but gives a nod. Fiona wills her to leave, but she stands her ground. 'Ivy was telling me upstairs that you childmind Sascha's daughter. Cora is safe with her grandma, by the way.'

'Yes, I'd heard she was at her grandma's house,' Fiona says, gripping the worktop behind her. 'I wouldn't say I was a child-minder, exactly,' she continues, adding a laugh. 'Just helping out a friend a couple of times, really.' The blush burns her cheeks.

PC Oldham nods. 'And nothing she said last week gave you any cause for concern?'

'No, nothing.'

'And your husband? He gets on with Sascha OK?'

Fiona shrugs. 'He didn't really know her, to be honest. She was more my friend. And barely a friend, really, given that we've not been living here long.'

'*Was?*' the officer says, tipping her head sideways. 'We've not found anything to suggest that Sascha is dead,' she adds, picking up her tea and heading towards the door. She turns back, facing Fiona. 'Let's not give up hope just yet.'

Fiona can't just do nothing. She's restless and anxious. Having taken the risk and deleted the doorbell footage of the police officer coming into the house earlier, as well as Amber arriving to hang out with Tilly – Fiona agreed to her visit as long as Tilly keeps it secret from her father – she prays Jason has been too busy at work to look at his doorbell app. Thing is, she knows his phone will have received alerts.

With this in mind, she decides to take another risk by switching off the camera for a short while as she leaves the house. The two older girls promised they'd keep an eye on Ivy, who's in the living room watching a Disney film, and Fiona promises she won't be long. She spotted the old bike in the garage soon after they'd moved in and, given that Jason has taken the car to work, it's her only option if she wants to get to the next village without having to walk three miles.

Little Campden is down a steep hill – a hairy moment for Fiona as the brakes take an age to slow her down as she enters the village, the breeze blowing her hair behind her. But a tight squeeze with both hands and her trainers trailing on the tarmac, and she eventually draws to a halt at the green beside the pond.

'Excuse me,' Fiona asks a man with a terrier on a lead, 'do

you know where the village hall is, please?' He looks as though he's lived here a long while and would know.

'Down Chapel Lane to your right there, and it's just before you get to the new houses,' he says in a deep, croaky voice.

Fiona nods and pedals away, certain that she remembers Sascha saying her mum lived next door to the village hall, how handy it is for her bridge nights and the youth club that she runs. *It's got to be worth a shot*, she thinks.

Halfway down Chapel Lane, Fiona spots the sign outside the village hall. It's single-storey and built from red brick and stone, with black metal railings out the front. There's a notice-board filled with posters about various clubs and upcoming events.

She gets off her bike and wheels it along beside her, drawing up to the white cottage the other side of the hall. The front garden is small but neat, filled with red roses in full bloom and a lavender hedge leading up to the front door. She leaves the bike propped against the wall and opens the gate, going up the paved front path. It seems dark through the windows, but someone must be home because she can just make out the flickering of a TV screen. Going by the bright colours, it looks like a kids' show.

She knocks a couple of times with the brass knocker and waits. And then the door opens.

'Yes?' a woman says.

Fiona instantly knows she's got the right house – the likeness between mother and daughter is obvious, though Sascha's mother appears younger than Fiona had imagined. Admittedly, she's not an expert on maternal looks, given she hasn't seen her own mother in well over a decade, and her father since... since he died when she was a teenager. She shudders, not wanting to think about that.

Fiona supposes the fine lines around the woman's eyes put her in her early sixties, and her clothes – skinny jeans and a faded grey T-shirt, along with bright pink clogs – give her a youthful appearance. Her hair, dyed almost black with a few strands of grey at the roots, is pinned into a messy updo.

'What do you want?'

'I'm Sascha's neighbour,' Fiona says, thinking she doesn't sound like herself at that moment. What the hell is she doing? Why didn't she take Jason's advice and just stay home? No good will come of this. But then if Sascha is in danger, how can she just do nothing?

'Sascha's neighbour?' the woman repeats, looking her up and down. Fiona hears Cora in the background, then the little girl appears at the door, sidling up beside her grandmother. 'You're that new family?' she asks, making it obvious that Sascha has discussed them.

'Yes.' Fiona nods, smiling down at the little girl she looked after last week. But she doesn't reciprocate. Rather, her eyes look red and swollen as if she's been crying.

'I see,' the woman says, turning to Cora. 'Go and play upstairs, darling, there's a love.' When Cora does as she's told, giving Fiona a lingering look as she goes, the woman adds, 'Well, then. You'd better come in.'

TWENTY-ONE
FIONA

Before

It was official. Jason and I were as good as a couple – and we had been for an entire week. I was so excited and in love, I could hardly contain myself. If we passed each other in the hospital corridors, the knowing looks he gave me virtually set me alight.

Of course, we couldn't tell anyone else about *us* yet – as Jason regularly reminded me, that would only scupper things in the long run. But as far as things were concerned between the pair of us, our relationship was official. We'd finally admitted our love for each other – almost six months after we'd first met in the pub at the start of November last year. For the last seven days, I'd been walking around with an inner glow that only two people in the world knew about.

We were in love. Jason was going to leave his wife. I'd never been so happy.

However, neither of us was stupid enough to believe we'd be able to stay at Radmoor after our secret came out – that would have been insane. For a start, Erika would have made our lives a misery, and the senior staff would frown upon our relationship.

Besides, we were ready for a fresh start and both confident that
we'd be able to get jobs elsewhere.

Apart from anything, I was relieved to know I'd finally be
leaving shared accommodation. I hated it – living like a student,
cooped up with the others – but now I could spend time
browsing property websites because with Jason's financial
resources, we'd be able to afford somewhere decent.

We'd decided we'd rent first, just for six months to give us a
feel for an area and decide if we wanted to buy. We figured
staying within the county would suit us – but still feel like a
new start. And we both loved the countryside around here. We
planned on getting a dog and going on long hikes.

I was so happy.

But then everything went bad. *Worse* than bad.

One afternoon in late April, Jason told me that he'd got cold
feet. That he couldn't leave Erika and the girls. That he'd be
destroying their lives if he abandoned them.

He didn't seem to care that he was destroying mine in the
process.

My life was upended in an instant.

It was as though I was reliving everything bad that had ever
happened to me. I was drowning in a whirlpool of emotions,
swept along by a downward-spiralling current, and there was
not a damn thing I could do about it.

My response? Easy. I went drinking alone in a pub. By this
point, I was numb inside but wanted to feel even *more* numb.
Obliterate every last drop of feeling I had left. To those who
didn't know me, I must have looked like a hopeless down-and-
out propping up the bar of a village pub a couple of miles from
the hospital while drowning my sorrows, praying that no one
who knew me from the hospital would come in.

Usually after work I kept myself to myself and, after a shift,
I'd be relaxing or watching TV or sleeping. But meeting Jason
had changed everything. He'd given me hope. A reason to live.

A reason to plan. It made me realise that a life without him by my side wouldn't be worth living.

And now that had been taken away from me. I felt empty, bereft, as though someone had died. I didn't know what to do with the feelings bubbling inside me and could barely concentrate on work. Jason had broken the news to me so casually, so cruelly, when I'd gone into his office earlier that day.

'I can't give you what you need, Fiona. I'm ending things between us. Our relationship is over.' He was sitting at his desk, staring up at me, fingers steepled under his chin.

I was blindsided. Kicked in the face. Didn't feel real.

I stood there for a moment. Mouth open. I shook my head, slowly at first, my frown deepening and my eyes widening. Then I turned on my heels and ran – I had no idea where I was going, but the corridors in the hospital always seemed endless, so I just kept running and running, tears streaming down my face.

I bumped headlong into Liz, a fellow nurse, and she held me and cradled me and allowed me to cry on her. I didn't let on what had happened, but she told me to forget about work for the rest of the day, that someone else would do the observation rounds and the couple of group sessions I had later on. She insisted I take time out. To go to bed and sleep.

Instead, I walked the couple of miles to the village pub and strode up to the bar, proceeding to knock back three or four or five large wines in the space of a pissed-off hour while aimlessly scrolling Instagram and Facebook in the hope of distracting myself and making my sitting at the bar alone appear not quite so pathetic.

But all those happy lives and loved-up couples on social media only served to make me feel even more wretched. Why wasn't *I* allowed my happy ever after?

I'd been at the bar almost two hours when I became aware of someone standing nearby – a man just a couple of feet away from me. I hadn't noticed him come in, but now the heat radiating from his body seemed to caress my cheek.

I turned sideways, checking him out, wishing in my heart of hearts that it was Jason standing there... We'd met in this very pub six months ago. This exact same spot. This exact same way – me at the bar, pissed. Him coming in for a quiet drink.

I don't know if it was the alcohol doing something to me – admittedly, I'd had far too much already and was finding it hard to focus – but something strange happened, and I felt myself transported back in time to that night last November. The night that had changed both our lives. I'd been equally drunk back then, too.

'Coke Zero, please,' I'd heard the voice say to the bartender all those months ago. From the corner of my eye, I'd seen a man with his wallet in his hand as he leant forward on the counter. He was tall and had an exaggerated profile, prominent yet straight nose, a strong jaw dashed with stubble, and a mop of black curls that appeared unruly yet perfectly styled at the same time.

I kept glancing at him. Sideways snapshots emblazoned on my mind. When I think back to that moment, I fell in love with him after about ten seconds.

'Bag of cheese and onion too, mate,' he'd added in a deep voice that seemed to echo around him. Then he'd paid and sipped his drink, the ice cubes clinking as he made no move to find a table. I'd slid my empty wine glass forward to Gary, the lad who'd already served me a few drinks. I couldn't really remember how many at that point. I'd planned on quitting in the new year. Dry January and all that. It would be easy enough.

'On the hard stuff, eh?' I'd said, glancing across at the man. I didn't care if he thought I was chatting him up. I *was*. Not something I'd have ever done without the wine swilling around inside me. I was drunk enough not to give a shit what anyone thought, yet not too far gone not to make sense.

The man had laughed. 'Not on a school night,' he'd joked, raising his glass at me. I did the same with my replenished drink. 'It's the rules,' he'd added.

'The rules?' For a moment, I considered that he was a teacher. Probably a head teacher, I reckoned, as my eyes brazenly swept up and down him. Judging him. Appraising him. 'A disciplinarian, eh?'

Jesus fucking Christ, Fiona...

He'd had the good nature to smile then, rather than give me the incredulous eyebrow-raise and wide berth that I deserved. He stood his ground at the bar.

'A doctor, actually,' he'd replied after some thought. 'I'm Jason, by the way.' He'd turned to face me properly then held out his hand.

I'd stared at it, analysing its anatomy as though I was treating him in an A&E cubicle like I'd done more times than I could remember in my last job when people came in with broken fingers or sprained wrists.

I'd had an insane desire to kiss it. Lift it up and bring his fingers to my mouth, leaving the faintest trail of saliva on his skin. Marking my territory.

These thoughts made me cringe now. My low mood, the alcohol, plus my first few heady gulps of the man I would marry were an intoxicating mix.

'Fiona,' I'd replied, praising myself for not saying anything else that would have me marked as unhinged. Something inside me fluttered. No, *flapped*. Like a bird trapped inside a cage. 'As you can see, I don't care that it's a school night,' I'd added, raising my glass to him. 'Nor do I have any rules.' I seem to remember hiccupping then.

'Fair enough,' Jason had replied, offering me his crisp packet. 'Rules aren't for everyone. But it's how I live.'

I'd thought about this, staring at the opened packet he was holding out to me. It seemed an oddly intimate gesture, sharing his crisps with a stranger. There we were, in the beamy pub, a log fire blazing, only half a dozen customers in that night, with him already offering me something. Giving me something. His attention *and* his crisps. It had felt like the kindest thing anyone had ever done for me.

'So you're a doctor, eh?' I'd said, taking a crisp and munching it.

Jason had smiled. 'Indeed. A psychiatrist at Radmoor Hospital, if you know it. It's only a couple of miles away, but to be honest, it feels like it's in the back of beyond.'

I'd stared at him, my heart skittering. *To be honest...* I'd swilled that around my mind, as though I was tasting wine. 'Are you always so honest with strangers?' I'd asked, cringing inside again, despite my outward grin.

'Only the pretty ones,' he'd replied, almost making it sound like a confession.

I'd taken another crisp from the bag lying on the bar.

'And yeah, I know Radmoor,' I'd laughed. 'I'm a nurse there.' I'd smiled, waiting for his reaction, to see if he recognised me, but he didn't seem to. Radmoor was huge and had many different wings and departments, and hundreds of employees. I'd have certainly remembered his distinctive looks if I'd seen him around. 'I've been there over a year now, though it feels like my entire life. Before that, I was a trauma nurse at the General.' I'd gulped another large mouthful of wine. Drowning it all out. 'How long have you been at Radmoor?'

'Not very long,' he'd replied. 'A matter of weeks.'

Vague, I'd thought. *Deliberately so, or is he teasing me, making me work for it?*

'Is it a temporary position, or are you there long term?'

Give it up, Fiona. Let the poor man enjoy his Coke and crisps in peace.

'I'm not sure yet. To be honest.' He'd added the last bit with a wink. 'I'm going to see how it goes.'

I'd laughed. No, it was more of a snort. 'Well, I for one like that you're so honest with me,' I'd said, which despite continuing on my cringe trajectory seemed to tickle him.

'The rules, innit,' he'd said in a put-on accent. A far cry from his upper-class inflection.

'So, what's with all these rules then?' I'd found myself asking. Truth was, if I didn't keep the conversation going, I was concerned he might get bored and go and find himself a table. I could hardly sidle up and join him.

'It's a more mindful way of living, I suppose,' Jason had admitted. 'Second nature now, but I have a list of guidelines for my life. I stick to them. Like a set of morals to live by.'

'Right,' I'd said, feeling a little taken aback even in my tipsy state. I wasn't sure I liked the sound of all that. It sounded a bit... cult-like. 'You mean like a religion?' I tested.

'No... no, far from it,' he'd replied with a laugh. 'It's nothing sinister. Just my own boundaried way of living. It's how it's always been. It suits me.'

'Go on then,' I'd said, feeling brazen. 'Tell me one of your rules.'

Jason had paused to think, a smile set firm on his face. 'OK. Since you asked...' He had taken another slug of Coke, enjoying keeping me in suspense. 'Rule number twelve – no flaunting or flirting with the opposite sex.'

I'd rolled my eyes, laughing. 'Very funny. Wait, don't tell me – especially extremely tipsy women in pubs, right?'

'*Especially* those.' His eyes had crinkled as he smiled, then he'd beckoned Gary over and pointed to my almost empty glass. 'Another one for the lady, please. And a whisky on the rocks for me.'

I'd watched as he paid, thanking him for my drink when he

slid the glass of wine that was surely going to end in my down-fall across the bar.

'Cheers,' I'd said, glancing at his whisky. 'You're a rule-breaker, then, too.'

He'd raised his glass back at me. 'Only for very special people,' he'd replied, sipping his drink while not taking his eyes off me.

'I like your style. Though I thought your rules were going to be more Ten Commandments-like, if I'm honest.'

'What, you mean like *thou shalt not kill?*'

The way he'd said it – no, the way he'd *looked* at me as he'd said it – gave me the chills. His stare had almost physically hurt as I held it for as long as I could, but it was no good. I blinked. I lost. I turned back to my drink, lifting the glass to my lips with a shaking hand.

But it wasn't Jason. The man leaning against the bar to my left now *was... not... Jason.* Of course it wasn't Jason. That night last November was long gone. A figment of the past that I'd never get back. The random man standing next to me took his pint and went to join some friends across the other side of the pub. I was on my own again with my overwhelming thoughts.

Jason did not want me. He'd dumped me. He wanted to stay with his wife. He would never kiss me again... never make love to me again... He'd never laugh with me or stroke my cheek or make me a coffee again. We'd never browse houses online together again, imagining ourselves curled up together beside the fire, everything in our lives perfect and happy. We'd never go on weekend breaks or summer holidays or decorate a Christmas tree or go to the cinema. And we'd never cook a meal together or make silly home movies or take photographs or...

I couldn't stand it. That he didn't want me. That he'd

ditched his plan to leave her. To deal with her. To get rid of her. I thought I was going to die.

I hated that he wanted Erika instead.

It made me want to kill her.

Then it came to me.

'Oh my God, I know what to do...' I whispered, staring straight ahead at the bottles racked up behind the bar. My heart was pounding. '*I know what to do...*' my lips mouthed. 'I know how to make this right...' The lad behind the bar raised his eyebrows at me talking to myself.

My vision blurred and swam as I opened my phone and pulled up the most recent video of Jason and me together. I had loads of them. Photos as well. I often looked at them when I was alone at night or when Jason was with his wife. This was the video I'd secretly filmed two weeks ago when we'd had sex in his office, though I never once thought that I'd have to use it.

I tapped out a text message to him, my fingers shaking as I kept mistyping the words, my eyes blurry from the alcohol, none of them coming out as I intended.

> *Jason... can't live without you. I need you in mine life. I want to be with you be liked we planned I'll die without you. Don't break up with me. begging u. I'll sent sex video to your wife then you;ll be sorry. Shit will hit fan and youll loose ewvery-thing. Job and her and your kids and money. Try me, not jokinh xxxxxxxx U play by my rules now*

And then I hit send.

It was another forty-five minutes until he arrived – after a bit of back-and-forth texting, me stupidly telling him that I was drunk in the village pub, and him panicking, trying to talk me round, begging me not to tell his wife, saying that he'd love me forever, that he had been wrong to break up with me, that we could still have our happy ever after.

Even though I wanted to believe him – *God, I wanted nothing more* – it was impossible now. I was fuelled by rage.

And I'd not followed his rules. I'd pretty much broken every single one by blackmailing him like that. It would take a lot of work on my part to come back from this betrayal. But even more on his part.

I'll never forget the look on Jason's face when he entered the pub, his long dark overcoat trailing behind him, his shoulders glistening from the rain. He was upset, of course – I'd done a terrible thing – but behind the fear, anger and disappointment in his eyes, I still saw deep compassion inside him. It was how he did his job, after all.

'There she is,' he said, his voice weary and resigned. He pointed at me from the doorway, directing three male nurses my way, their uniforms crisp and white. One of them was unwrapping a syringe as he approached.

I struggled – of course I did – and I put up a good fight. But I wasn't able to overpower them – it's what they were trained to do, after all. And once the haloperidol was coursing through my veins and my muscles became relaxed, my mind fuzzy, especially after all the alcohol I'd had, the world around me faded fast.

But I do remember my handsome doctor's face as they manhandled me past him, all the pub customers staring as they bundled me into the waiting ambulance to take me back to the hospital. Back to my ward, to my treatment, to my medication. Back on full-time patient observations with a nurse by my side. Back to a life in hospital that I didn't want to live.

PART 2

'Freedom is obedience to self-formulated rules.'

ARISTOTLE

TWENTY-TWO

JASON

Jason has never once doubted his love for Fiona. Not even after she sent him the blackmail text threatening to tell his wife about their affair.

His decision to break up with her back in April hadn't been an easy one, especially since his relationship with his wife had deteriorated over recent years. It had started with the usual stuff between married couples – sex had gradually dwindled to nothing, she was more interested in her career and their daughters than giving him attention, and Erika barely seemed to notice if he was at home or not. But once the rot set in, so did his wife's controlling ways.

Fiona, on the other hand, was the opposite: attentive, a good listener, always there for him if he needed to vent about work... or vent about anything, really. Her sense of humour aligned with his, and they were effortlessly comfortable in each other's company, simply being able to *be* without expectation. And of course, the physical connection between them was insane.

So understandably, Jason had felt like the worst person in the world when he'd told Fiona that he would not be leaving his wife after all. There was no easy way to break the news to her and, as he'd half expected, it had tipped her over the edge. While Erika was familiar territory for him – a safe place in a tough world, and they'd been through a lot together – the main reason was their daughters. He'd had to think of them. Divorce would be gruelling for all concerned, but especially so for Tilly and Ivy. Though if he'd known about the compromising sex videos in Fiona's possession, then he'd have thought twice about the way he'd handled his decision to end it with her. A spanner in the fucking works.

Ultimately, and after much thought, it was the existence of the videos – and his inability to get rid of them – that had made Jason go back on his decision and choose Fiona over his wife. He felt certain that blowing up his daughters' lives and having all his dirty laundry aired – Erika would make sure they'd know what he'd done – would be way worse for them than having divorced parents. Though of course, either of those options would be preferable to a *dead* parent as far as his girls were concerned. It wasn't an easy decision, but staying with Fiona seemed like the right thing to do. And he *was* in love with her, after all. It wouldn't be for nothing.

He must admit, though, she hasn't always been easy to live with. And he's aware that sometimes he comes across as controlling or bossy when all he wants is for his new wife to be happy and safe, considering the places her mind could take her to. If he hadn't implemented the rules, heaven only knows where they'd be now.

It's hard to believe all that was three months ago now – a drunken Fiona being unceremoniously brought back to hospital from the pub. It wasn't the first time it had happened on her long road to recovery.

Jason admits that she has been one of his more challenging cases.

Not a day goes by that he doesn't feel wretched for

reporting her that night, for having her dragged back to Radmoor Hospital like a wildcat. He'd led the three male nurses to where she was – drunk and vulnerable in the Fox and Hounds, which she'd walked almost two miles along country lanes wearing high heels and no coat to reach.

She was a liability to herself, and it was Jason's job to protect her.

But there was no denying he loved her – that he *still* loves her – even though he knew it was wrong. So very, very wrong.

A doctor–patient affair.

Of course, he'd had to consider himself, too. Intimate relations such as this were a big no-no in his profession. Her vulnerability was at the forefront of his mind during every single moment of their relationship. Throw an expensive private hospital with a crack legal team into the mix, plus a huge dose of crazy from Fiona, and it did not bode well. He needed to handle things very carefully. He'd already made enough mistakes, and his whole life could come crashing down around him if he didn't think things through.

The night the three male nurses manhandled her back from the pub, Jason had gone with her in the private ambulance. After they arrived at Radmoor, where she'd been an inpatient for almost twelve months this particular time – though he'd only been her doctor for less than half that – he sat with her in her bedroom, watching over her and making sure she didn't throw up and choke, or hurt herself some other way. There was a full-time observations nurse there too, of course, which he was relieved about, and her room was checked for sharp objects, blades, cords, laces, belts, pens, plastic cups, crockery... anything she could harm herself with.

He considered that she might be moved to a more secure ward in the morning, but the poor woman was too out of it to make a fuss that night – the sedative had put her into an almost catatonic state.

Because of her other mental health issues – psychoses, PTSD, depression to name a few – Fiona had a tumultuous relationship with alcohol, though this was her first relapse in a while. As a long-term inpatient at Radmoor, she'd tried all the tricks in the book, from self-harm to running away to hunger strikes to promiscuous behaviour with other patients. She'd once gone through a phase of concealing her medication and saving it up for 'a rainy day', she'd confessed to the medics who'd resuscitated her after she'd swallowed the lot and been found passed out in the hospital grounds.

Now, as Jason sits alone in his car, not wanting to go to work at the university today, his mind elsewhere, he wonders how he can keep his wife – his *new* wife – and daughters safe. It seems Fiona is still in self-destruct mode, even though she got what she wanted – him and her together, finally away from the hospital, his first wife dead and the pair of them living the perfect life that she'd always dreamt of. A ready-made family, a beautiful home, a loving husband.

The strange thing is, he wasn't even angry with her for what she did. He'd never truly wanted to end his affair with her in the first place – but Erika had grown suspicious. She had a sixth sense, sniffing out the pheromones that he and Fiona left behind like a vapour trail around the hospital.

But with all the evidence Fiona had against him – intimate videos and photos of them together, him in compromising situations with a patient – she could have whatever she wanted. The proof against him was damning. If it got out, it would ruin his life. He just hated the way she'd gone about it.

I do love her... he kept reminding himself when things felt tougher than usual. *I really, really do...*

Of course, as Jason expected, Erika threatened to have him transferred to a different hospital as her suspicions grew – being his boss, she had the power to do that – but when Jason swore on his life that there *was* no affair, that Fiona meant nothing to him, that she was a psychiatric patient, for God's sake, she eventually backed off, preferring him to stay at Radmoor where she could keep regular tabs on him.

This gave Jason time to reassess, to rethink his life's plan. And, given how busy Erika was with other work outside of the hospital, it meant he could still see Fiona daily, even if it was only in a professional sense.

He was being pulled in two directions.

'What a bloody mess,' Jason says now, starting the car and continuing his journey to his new office at the university.

He grips the steering wheel tightly, wondering how his life got to this point. Not only is he eaten up by guilt every single day for plotting to leave Erika, for what happened to her, for what his daughters have gone through, now he's also received a strange note that, if he's honest, has got right beneath his skin. Appearing under his car windscreen wiper and similar to the two notes Fiona received, it's making him feel sick from the inside out.

The dead don't stay silent forever. Her blood is on your hands.

He can't stop thinking about those words. Hand-printed in plain capitals. It *has* to be the same person sending them. Was this note perhaps also intended for Fiona? Did the sender believe it was his *wife* who had parked the car in the lay-by that morning? Perhaps they assumed she'd be the one to find it on her return. He hasn't told Fiona about it, not wanting to worry her.

He wished he could believe that whoever sent it probably wasn't thinking in that much detail... That it was just some random kids, a prankster, someone with a vindictive streak who despises newcomers to the area. Villages can be funny, closed-off places, and they are still outsiders as far as the locals are concerned. Though he senses, from the wording, that it's way more targeted than that.

But what Jason *does* know for certain – and he can't tell a soul about – is that he was the last person to see Sascha the morning after she disappeared. But that is a secret he'll be taking to the grave. He did it to protect his wife.

As he walks to his office in the medical school building, Jason smiles, saying hello to a few people. He barely knows anyone here yet, but he hopes that will change at the start of the academic year. He's keen to become a part of the place that was the beginning of his career as a doctor, the institution where he began his training.

Aged eighteen, fresh-faced and eager, he'd come from one high-pressure environment – Melton College, one of the UK's top public schools – and tumbled right into another – Canonfield University. It had never been in question that he'd follow in his father's footsteps, and his grandfather's before that. In fact, the men in his family were all medics or lawyers or dead. There was no other way.

His mother had died when he was eight, and as an only child, Jason struggled growing up under his father's huge, dark shadow. It was in his blood, programmed into his DNA that he'd go into psychiatry, private practice, continue the family tradition on Harley Street.

Two months after his mother's death, Jason was sent off to preparatory boarding school, and subsequently on to Melton College, where his father and his father's father had all been pupils. The gold-embossed boards of fame lining the walls in the grand dining hall bore the name Hewitt as far back as the school's long history went. With his forebears all being head boys, prefects, sports captains and scholars, Jason had a lot to live up to.

Now, as he strides along the university corridors, he shakes his head, rids himself of the old memories. Things are different now, no need to dwell on the past. His father, who passed away three years ago, has no power over him any more – aside from the legacy and trust he left, setting out the mean and controlling way in which he is allowed to use the family money. There *is* that.

At exactly the moment Jason turns the handle on his office door – and just as he realises it's locked – he hears a voice a few feet away. A *woman's* voice. It makes him startle.

'Hi, again...' she says, coming up to him.

Jason turns, seeing Rosanne standing there. She's grinning, has her head tilted to the side, and there's a definite twinkle in her eye. Is it just coincidence that they keep bumping into each other, or is she engineering it?

'Hi there,' he replies, feeling in his pockets for his swipe card. He'd come into the building on the back of someone else holding the door open for him, so he hasn't had to use it yet today.

'We must stop meeting like this,' she says with a laugh, as if she's read his mind.

A quick nod from Jason as he checks the pocket inside his jacket. No card there either. *Damn...* he thinks, figuring he's either left it in the car or at home. He delivers a quick smile, hoping she'll go away.

'It came to me last night where I recognised you from,' Rosanne presses on.

Jason freezes as he searches in his briefcase. He doesn't want to have to call security to let him in. He looks up.

'It did?'

His heart thumps.

'Uh-huh, it sure did,' she says in a provocative way that makes Jason wonder how far she's going to take this – pretending that she recognises him as a sly way of seducing him.

He's seen it before – students and patients alike, though Fiona was always different. Being a psychiatrist gives him a certain power, he's learnt during his career, and especially over women.

'Here,' Rosanne says, taking something from her bag. 'Use my swipe card. It works for the whole department.'

Jason stares down at it. 'Thanks,' he says, taking it and opening his office door. 'Would you like to come in?' he asks.

This, he thinks as he flicks on the lights, *needs nipping in the bud.*

TWENTY-THREE

JASON

Jason knows that if people discovered the extent of their marriage rules, the strict guidelines that frame and contain their lives, they would never understand.

But these are the lengths he has to go to in order to protect Fiona, to keep her safe – from herself as much as other people. He doesn't want her relapsing, with alcohol as well as taking a dip with her treatment plan for her psychoses, which is why he has put the rules in place. And besides, they both willingly agreed to the rules.

When Jason was a child, his father had employed a similar set of rules in their household. His father was a man to be feared in many ways, with those around him knowing their place, not daring to break the rules or push back against him. Because of this, he'd commanded respect, and the rules system had worked well. Until Jason's mother went and killed herself.

While Jason has no intention of pushing Fiona to her limits as his father did to his mother, the rules that he was forced to live by growing up have certainly taught him that strong boundaries are useful for those who need a little extra help – and indeed he's continued to live by them himself for much of his adult life. No harm in a bit of a helping hand when life gets tough.

'Mummy's turn,' Jason says later that evening when they're all sitting round the dinner table. Rosanne coming to his office earlier is still playing on his mind – her saying those things to him. It's not right. He looks at his beautiful new wife, knowing she'd be horrified if she knew. 'You've outdone yourself, by the way, darling,' he says, taking a bite of the home-made quiche. 'Delicious.'

Fiona smiles, but for some reason he senses Tilly bristling the other side of him. She's not getting used to calling Fiona 'Mummy' as he'd hoped, and her unease has now spread to Ivy.

'What does Mummy have to tell us about her day?' Jason looks at Fiona, taking another mouthful of food, trying to gauge her mood. 'Best potato salad I've ever tasted, too.'

He strokes her leg under the table, and she gives him a nervous smile. A smile that puts him on red alert. He's never quite sure what she'll get up to when he's out, if she'll try to run away or leave him or do something equally reckless. He trusts her... he *thinks*... not to get drunk. She mostly seems to be in a good place as far as alcohol is concerned these days, especially given the medication she's on – just one or two slips lately.

But now that she's not going to group therapy – she so enjoyed helping the nurses organise the sessions at Radmoor, even suggesting the idea of an alcohol group for patients and partners – he's having to keep a closer eye on her progress. Psychosis is only ever just around the corner for Fiona, often with unknown triggers. The only reason he feels comfortable leaving his daughters at home with her is because Tilly is old enough to look after Ivy should Fiona become unwell. It's why he allows his eldest daughter a phone in the day in case she needs to call him. When they moved here, he took her old phone and bought her a new one with a different number, putting only his and Fiona's details into the contacts. The past is best left in the past, he explained to her.

'Nothing much, really,' Fiona tells everyone. 'It was just a normal day.'

'Did you go out?' he asks. 'Any sign of him next door?' He tips his head in the direction of Graham's house. Since they went round for dinner on Saturday night, it's been playing on his mind that their neighbour is an ex-cop. He'd have rented another house if he'd known, figuring he's likely the nosy type, never minding his own business. There'd been a couple of motion sensor alerts on his phone earlier, but by the time he got round to checking them – after he'd dealt with Rosanne in his office – there was nothing to see on the app. A false alarm, he supposed, which sometimes happens if the sun is at the wrong angle, triggering the sensor.

'I haven't seen Graham,' Fiona says, silencing a cough with some water. 'And I didn't go anywhere today. I'm sure I didn't.'

Tilly flashes Fiona a look, then glares at Jason.

Something's up, he thinks.

'Did Tilly have a friend round today, by any chance?' Jason asks Fiona as she stands at the bathroom basin. They're getting ready for bed. 'I'm not cross, by the way. I understand she needs social contact.' Jason bites back his real thoughts about that.

'No,' she mumbles without looking up at him, toothbrush in hand.

'Any idea where this came from then?' He holds up the scarlet hoodie – a garment he's never seen before.

Fiona turns from the basin, toothpaste all around her mouth. She freezes for a moment, studying the sweatshirt. It's subtle but Jason sees the flare of her pupils, the tension in her jaw a split second before she stifles a sob, dropping her tooth-brush onto the floor.

'Oh...' she whimpers. 'Oh no... oh *no!*' She begins to shake.

'Hey, hey... it's OK, love. Stay calm, you're safe...' Quickly, Jason throws the sweatshirt down the other side of the bed so it's out of sight, wondering what it is about it that has upset her. He's learnt some of her triggers, but not all.

Fiona drops down on the bed, her mouth still foamy from toothpaste and her eyes wide and fearful as she curls up. Jason grabs his work bag and fumbles with the combination lock, rummaging through various bottles and packets of pills. He has a decent supply.

'Here, take these, love,' he says, handing her a couple of diazepam tablets. He gives her a glass of water, then fetches a warm flannel to wipe her face. She's shaking, sitting in her underwear on the bed.

'That... that sweatshirt,' she says, clutching her arms around her body. 'It's... it's...'

Jason kneels down in front of her, peeling her arms free and holding her hands. Beneath the minty toothpaste smell, her breath is stale, and she has mushroom-coloured rings around her eyes.

'What is it, love?' he asks again, wondering if the bright red colour was the trigger. She's mentioned that in the past before – something about her father's red bow tie.

'It's... it's *Sascha's* sweatshirt. She left it here before... be-fore...' Fiona whispers breathily, her voice petering out as she draws her knees up on the bed, hiding her face behind a curtain of hair.

TWENTY-FOUR

JASON

Jason is exhausted. Bone-deep tired – from holding down his new job at the university, dealing with Fiona's changeable moods, and shouldering his daughters' grief.

And what makes matters even worse is that Fiona is starting to doubt that she killed Erika...

'Out of the darkness comes light,' were her words to him the night before they left Radmoor as he tried to make her comprehend what she'd done. He'd wanted to shake her, drumming it into her, but he'd held back. He explained the seriousness of her crime, and, eventually, she seemed to understand what he was saying.

Her first reaction was to stare at a blank wall, in some kind of altered state as she swayed from side to side, grasping the horror of her actions. But then, almost gleefully, she reminded him that Erika's death now allowed *them* to freely marry. She almost seemed *pleased* by what she'd done. Fiona might as well have had blood on her hands as she'd stood there, talking about it in such a matter-of-fact way.

Of course, given everything she had on him, all the photographic evidence of their doctor–patient affair, there was no question that he would have to cover for her, concealing her crime. She wasn't in charge of her own faculties. Fiona had little idea of the gravity of the situation or the consequences. And worse, Jason knew it was all his fault. He should never have allowed it to happen.

He also knew that he had to feed a more palatable story to his daughters about their mother's death – there was no way they'd want to be anywhere near Fiona if they thought she'd murdered their mother. Tilly would be reporting her to the police in a flash.

His body shakes from the mess of it all.

Jason parks his car at the university, wiping his hands down his face. Then he gets out and opens the tailgate to retrieve his briefcase. On seeing the bright red fabric of the sweatshirt poking out from the side, he twiddles the combination lock, opens the case and shoves Sascha's sweatshirt back inside. He didn't want to leave it lying around at home, upsetting Fiona again.

As he heads through the campus, he's not sure how much work he'll get done today – he has so much on his mind that continuing with his own research seems about as likely as a trip to the moon right now. He stops in at the plaza café to grab a coffee before heading towards the medical faculty.

It's as he's walking towards the building, about to cross the virtually deserted campus road, that he sees three marked police cars parked outside the entrance on double yellow lines. There's one uniformed officer standing beside a vehicle, the officer leaning on its open door as he talks into his radio. His eyes flick about, hovering on Jason briefly, before glancing further down the road. Then he looks back at Jason again.

For a moment, Jason freezes, his heart thundering in his chest. A whooshing sound fills his ears, and his mind is suddenly flooded with images of Erika, how he's been expecting the police to arrive at their house, arrest Fiona, cart her off to a custody cell, charge her with murder.

He can't let that happen. He's been so strict about them staying indoors. Staying safe, staying hidden. *I love her... I love her... I love her...*

He's snapped back to the moment by the sudden approach of a vehicle to his right – an ambulance. He sees the officer beckoning it to the front entrance of the medical building, indicating it should park by the main door. When the green-uniformed paramedics get out, it seems there is no urgency to their arrival. They stop and chat with the officer for a few moments before removing a gurney from the back of the ambulance, plus several medical bags. Then the officer directs them into the building, pointing to an upstairs floor.

Jason is about to turn and leave, unable to deal with the intense feelings this scene is stirring inside him. His boss will understand if he takes the day off, he thinks, but then he halts, touching his head as his vision turns blurry.

It's just stress, he thinks, forcing himself to remain calm. *You've been under an enormous amount of pressure... Breathe, man, breathe...*

As he regains his balance, he decides that he's going to go home and take a sick day, that he'll reschedule his only meeting for another time.

He's about to return to the car but suddenly he's back there – feeling as though he's twenty years old again as he struggles and sinks in the mire of his medical studies right here at this very university. Everything became too much for him. He was drowning under the pressure of his studies, not being the strong, go-getting man everyone expected him to be. Nothing like his father.

Instead, he was a let-down. A stupid, hopeless loser.

Then his father's red and angry face is leering down upon him, his fists pummelling the air around him.

Even now, he sometimes still hears his father's voice – admonishing him, mocking him, belittling him. *You're a Hewitt, goddammit! Hewitts never give up!*

Then he feels the hand, vice-like, as his father grabs him by the throat...

'You all right, sir?' comes a voice.

At first, Jason isn't sure where it's coming from.

It's not his father's angry tones any more... No, this voice is showing *real* concern.

'Sir, can you hear me? You were swaying a bit there. I thought you were going to pass out.'

When he focuses properly, Jason sees the uniformed officer from across the road is now standing beside him, holding onto his arm in a vain attempt to support him.

'Sorry,' Jason says, squinting at him. He's not very old, though older than he was when he was struggling at med school. 'I'm OK, thanks,' Jason admits. 'Reckon I'm going down with something. I'm going to head back home. Work can wait for another day.'

'Where is work, sir?' the officer enquires, silencing the radio attached to his shoulder. 'Is it in the medical building?'

Jason stares up at the 1970s-built structure – nothing much to look at, but a hothouse for some of the most pioneering medical minds today.

He nods. 'Yes, it is. Is there a problem in there?' he asks, flicking a nod towards the parked police cars, the ambulance.

'It's going to be sealed off for the foreseeable,' the officer explains. 'There's been an incident.'

'How awful,' he says. 'What kind of incident? Is everyone OK?'

'I can't say at this stage, sir, but I'm sure a statement will be released in due course – by the police and the university.'

'I hope my colleagues are all OK,' he says, even though he hasn't really got any of those yet.

'Put it this way,' the officer says, turning to head back to his car, 'whatever they've found in that office, it'll be coming out in a body bag.'

TWENTY-FIVE
JASON

Before

The relationship between a psychiatrist and their patient is a complex one and is, in many ways, not dissimilar to that of a marriage, with trust and respect at the core. And not forgetting the secrets to be kept.

I first consulted with Fiona a few weeks after I took up my position at Radmoor – and about a week after our chance meeting in the pub that night. While it was frowned upon for some patients to leave hospital premises while undergoing treatment, especially to go to the pub of all places, it was certainly unwise for Fiona to consume large amounts of alcohol given her medication and psychiatric history. But legally, she wasn't sectioned or doing anything wrong by going to the Fox and Hounds. And of course, when I met her at the bar, I had no idea she was a patient.

I remember our first official session in my office well. From the outset, it was clear that the poor woman was living in some kind of altered reality or fantasy world as though she was stuck in the past – a past that had not treated her kindly. And it was also clear that she soon formed a strong attachment to me.

It wasn't the first time a patient had developed feelings for me. For any mental health professional, there's a danger of transference – where a patient overlays the feelings and emotions for someone else in their lives onto the medical professional – which can easily turn into obsession. I've never found it helpful to explain the nature of transference to a patient who is experiencing it because it's a most intriguing way of getting to the root of the matter. I like to experience it. Observe it. Work with it.

Except I did not believe Fiona was experiencing transference at all. I knew she was genuinely falling in love with me.

And the problem here wasn't how I should handle the strong emotions she was experiencing – rather the problem was that I was falling in love with her, too.

None of this was covered by my rules or in the grand plan I had for my life when I started working at Radmoor.

'Take some slow, deep breaths,' I told Fiona as she lay on her bed in hospital that terrible night, after I'd watched three male nurses bring her back to the ward. She was barely able to focus, and I'm not even sure she recognised me.

In Fiona's small, soulless hospital bedroom, I glanced over at the nurse assigned to twenty-four-hour observations. The irony didn't pass me by – how Fiona, who was convinced that *she* was a nurse at Radmoor, had taken it upon herself to do the observation rounds, checking up on the patients each day. The real nurses working at the hospital had indulged her fantasy behaviour, humouring her, and I'd condoned it, too. It kept her occupied and gave her a purpose.

While Fiona was indeed a qualified nurse, she was no longer registered to practise, and it was important she worked through her traumas in her own way. After all, she was doing no harm.

But as I stroked her head that evening, watching her brain take her on a perilous journey as she sweated the alcohol and antipsychotic drugs out of her system, I knew I had a problem.

In her text, Fiona had told me she had a secretly recorded video of us having sex at the hospital. And, in a drunken fit just a couple of hours ago, she had threatened to send it to my wife. Whatever else happened, I needed to erase it from her phone.

'If you fancy a break,' I said to the nurse, 'I'm happy to watch over her.'

Initially, she shook her head. It would be more than her job was worth to abandon her watch – even to a doctor such as me. If anything happened to Fiona during her absence, then she'd be culpable. But I saw the flicker of temptation on her face and ran with it.

'There's chocolate cake in the staff room,' I told her. I'd seen her stuffing her face several times when she thought no one was looking. 'Must be someone's birthday.'

The nurse licked her lips. Ran her hands down the folds of her uniform. Stretched. Then she gave a quick glance at the door, flicked her eyes to Fiona, who was sleeping now, and stood up.

'Thank you, Doc,' she said, clearing her throat. 'I appreciate it.'

'No problem.' I nodded at her, adding a confident smile. The second she was gone, I grabbed Fiona's handbag from beside the bed, rummaged through it, found her phone and unlocked it by waking her up just enough for the face recognition to work. Then I scoured through the videos in her photo albums.

What I discovered shocked me. There were hundreds of pictures and videos of me going about my duties at the hospital – walking in the grounds, sitting in the common room, talking to staff members in the corridors – pictures taken covertly during our consultations, and more videos of us kissing as well as our other sexual encounters. It seemed her obsession with me knew no bounds.

I sat there for a moment, staring down at Fiona, stroking her sweaty hair as she lay on the bed.

The problem was I *liked* that she was so into me – seeing all this evidence of our affair gave me a warm feeling inside – the exact opposite of how my wife made me feel. I was especially touched when I saw that Fiona had made a special folder in which to put all the images. It stirred something within me, latent feelings that I'd long since forgotten.

But the pictures and videos had to go. I couldn't risk them being sent to Erika. While my marriage was not perfect, while we were often at loggerheads – our strong personalities often clashing – the fact was that we had two amazing children who I refused to hurt. And not only that, but Erika had moved mountains to get me this position at Radmoor, one of the most prestigious psychiatric hospitals in the country.

I felt torn in two. How could I throw all that away for what others would see as a brief fling? No one would understand the deep bond between me and Fiona, how it had caught us both by surprise. And people especially wouldn't understand that I was involved with my patient – albeit one with whom I had a special understanding. It hadn't been out of choice, us meeting and falling in love. Fate had intervened while simultaneously throwing a huge spanner in the works.

I was doing my best at damage limitation, but I also knew where my heart lay – right beside the woman on that hospital bed.

After I'd deleted all the images on Fiona's phone and then cleared the deleted folder, a thought struck me. What if Fiona had them stored elsewhere – perhaps emailing them somewhere for safekeeping? She wasn't stupid.

It was easy to get into her email account – the app on her phone was already logged in – but it was just as I heard the nurse chatting to someone outside the door in the corridor that my worst suspicions were confirmed. In her sent folder, I saw that Fiona had recently emailed all the images to another account in her name that a quick attempt showed me I did not have access to.

I tossed Fiona's phone back into her handbag just as the nurse came back into the room.

'All fine here,' I said. But inside, I felt sick, wondering where else Fiona had sent the pictures – or worse, *who* else she'd sent them to. Erika was at home with the girls, and while it was not unusual for me to spend the night here at work, I knew my wife would be coming to the hospital tomorrow. Did she already know?

I looked at the nurse as she settled back into her chair, feeling pathetic as, for a moment, I wished that she would engulf me in her motherly arms, tell me that everything would be OK, that nothing bad was going to happen.

'You've got a little bit of...' I touched my lip, indicating to the nurse that she had chocolate around her mouth. And then with a final glance at Fiona, I headed back to my office. It was time to make a plan.

TWENTY-SIX
FIONA

Fiona sits on the edge of the sofa not knowing what to do with herself. Jason has not long gone to work. Being Tuesday, she should be looking after Cora again today, but Sascha is still missing. It's been almost a week now, with no further news. As far as she knows, Cora is still with her grandmother.

She doesn't understand how, in the space of a few days, things have gone so wrong – her life seeming to have veered so far outside of Jason's rules that it doesn't seem possible that she was ever following them in the first place.

But she was. She knows it. To the letter… That is until the little cracks started showing. Making friends with the woman next door because she was lonely – though perhaps Jason was right about Sascha when he said he wished they'd never met her, that she was a bad influence, tempting Fiona to break the rules. And taking on a job she wasn't mentally equipped to deal with – looking after someone else's *child*, for heaven's sake. Not to mention the occasional swig of vodka to help her get through the day. Lying to Jason about the notes. Exposing her and the girls to danger by going on a walk, knocking on the other neighbour's door, allowing Tilly to have a friend over

– knowing she has a secret *phone*, of all things. The list goes on.

All the risky behaviours that Jason has warned her about. She's been doing them.

He's been so good to her, so understanding and tolerant, especially given how confused she's been in recent months. And while she desperately wants to believe it's because he loves her as fiercely as she loves him, she can't help worrying that he's only with her because she still has all those compromising photos and videos of them together – him a doctor, her a psychiatric patient.

Even though Erika is dead and there's nothing to be gained by sending the pictures to her any more, Fiona knows she can still do a lot of damage to Jason professionally. A man like him having an affair with a vulnerable person like her – a bomb would go off in his life if she reported him to the powers that be at Radmoor, or the General Medical Council. But then she's not exactly squeaky clean either – what she's done is *way* worse. More than anything, she wishes Jason had kept what she'd done to Erika to himself. Ever since she found out, her mind has been haunted with images that are far too heavy for her to carry around. She's rotten inside, contaminated, and she knows she's a criminal. Nothing but lowlife scum who should be locked up, the key thrown away. She'll never be able to repay Jason for looking after her, for protecting her like he has.

Without thinking, she reaches out and picks up the coffee mug sitting on the side table. Then she hurls it at the television. It's only when the mug falls to the floor, its handle smashed, dregs of coffee dribbling down the TV screen, that Fiona thinks of the consequences. The house was fully furnished when they rented it. They must pay for any damage.

She stares at the broken mug, feeling nothing inside. Yes, that's all she wants. To *feel* again. Even when Jason told her that she'd killed his wife, his words didn't reach the core of her. She didn't feel anything – no remorse, fear, guilt or even satisfaction. Nothing. She was dead inside.

Now, she feels the *tic-tic* of a muscle twitching under one eye as she scans her mind, trying to recall details of what she did, the awful things Jason described to her, as well as how he helped cover for her. *That's something*, she thinks, *to prove his love for me*.

Fiona knows she causes trouble. She knows she's a lot to deal with, that sometimes she goes off the rails. She can't help it. She knows that sometimes she hurts Jason, too, which, when she's lucid again, makes her sad. The last thing she wants is to upset the man who saves her life literally every single day.

She loves Jason. He loves her. They are a team. They live by the rules.

Though most of the time, Fiona lives under a cloud of shame.

Shame for hiding away when she was a child and her father was free with his fists, her mother taking the brunt of his anger. It was Christmas Day when, aged four, she first remembers witnessing the violence. Fiona was playing with her new doll, and her mum wanted to watch the Queen's Speech, but her father hadn't long rolled in from the pub blind drunk, laying into her because his lunch had gone cold. Fiona had hidden behind the sofa with her hands over her ears, waiting for it to be over.

Then there was the shame for not telling anyone what her father did to her mother year in, year out, winter, summer, day or night and for any reason he chose – hurting the kind, sweet woman who, despite her bruises and black eyes and split lips, still managed to read her only daughter a bedtime story every night and tuck her into bed.

And the shame Fiona has carried with her ever since *that* night – the night that was special for no particular reason other than it changed the course of her life – when, aged sixteen, she turned and walked away from it all. The *drip... drip... drip* of the bathroom tap still sticks in her mind to this day. Marking the moments of her life.

Homeless yet free, it was three weeks before she made the first attempt on her own life, ending up in a psychiatric unit for seven months because she refused to eat.

And then, when she'd managed to turn her life around thanks to the foster family she was placed with, there was the shame she felt for falling behind with her studies, for not having made any friends at college when she eventually took her A levels a year late because she felt like a freak with those bandages around her arm as the other students gossiped and stared.

She was *so* ashamed that she lugged around the guilt of what she'd witnessed her father do to her mother for years and years and years, never telling a soul. Every single minute of every single day still tainted by him. When she closed her eyes at night, trying to get to sleep, all Fiona saw was his angry face – his saggy jowls, his big belly, the greasy strands of hair swept over his bald head.

But oddly, it was his bow tie that she remembered the most. A red satin one that he wore that first Christmas when he tried to strangle her mother. She'd focused on it, fixed her eyes on the shiny scarlet fabric. She'd just stared at that bow tie, waiting for it all to be over. Waiting for her mother to breathe again. Waiting until the next time.

And the shame was still there when, years after she'd qualified as a nurse, and many years since her father had died, Fiona was assigned to an urgent trauma case one shift at the general hospital. Nothing out of the ordinary in A&E on a busy Saturday night. Road traffic accident. Three dead at the scene. Two fighting for their lives. She worked with the rest of the team, cutting up the man's trouser legs as she snipped off his clothes, the ambulance crew handing over to the hospital doctor.

Then she cut off his red bow tie...

Her focus was sharp and diligent as she got the IV line into the back of his hand, listened closely to the precise orders of the lead trauma medic as she went with the patient for a CT scan, accompanying him back to A&E for further treatment and monitoring. There was already hope he would pull through.

But as Fiona went about her work, it felt as though something was lodged in her eye – a fragment of glass – and however hard she rubbed, it wouldn't come out. An interruption from the past – something bubbling up inside her that she couldn't control as she rushed about the busy emergency department.

It wasn't her father's bow tie that she'd cut from the patient's neck – he was long since dead – but to her, it had certainly felt like it. A random man who'd been wearing a similar tie at the time of the car accident had unwittingly triggered his own demise.

Knowingly injecting a fatal dose of medication into his IV line that resulted in his almost immediate death gave Fiona a temporary release from the shame that coursed through her veins, though the drug-like effect within her had a short half-life. But it had caused her to feel a little twinge of *something*... though she wasn't sure what.

Over the coming months, she narrowly escaped being charged with murder or manslaughter when her defence team found evidence that the wrong drugs dose had been signed off by the trauma doctor in the first place. But nonetheless, she was struck off from nursing ever again for not noticing the error, for administering it without double-checking with a colleague as was the practice. As a trained and experienced nurse, she should have known better. And indeed, she had. But she'd done it anyway.

. . .

Fiona suddenly stands. Sascha is still missing. She has a sinking feeling in the pit of her stomach – as though her insides have been scooped out. It's the same feeling that she had when Jason told her what she'd done to Erika. How he'd found her broken and bloody body, how he'd promised to help her by covering up what she'd done.

At first, she hadn't believed him. She remembered nothing. How could she have done such a thing – *killed a woman*?

It was the same feeling she had aged sixteen when she walked away from her father's dead body, his bulk almost entirely filling the small space of their bathroom floor.

The same feeling at the hospital, when the machine hooked up to the patient in the red bow tie flatlined, pronouncing his death.

'Oh my God,' she whispers, her trembling fingers coming up to touch her lips. 'I... I must have killed Sascha, too.' But then... she's not sure. Not certain of anything any more.

Suddenly, there's a peal of laughter from upstairs, followed by heavy footsteps as Tilly and Amber run down to the hallway. The pair of them bound into the living room, suddenly stopping when they see Fiona standing beside the TV, the broken mug at her feet. She knows she looks a sight in her grubby tracksuit bottoms and the T-shirt she slept in, her hair a mess.

'Hi, Fiona,' Amber says chirpily. There's something about the teen's voice that grounds Fiona, that brings her back to the moment with a grateful smile. She's a lovely girl.

'Hello, Amber,' she replies. 'It's good to see you. Would you two like some tea? I have cake, too.' She heads towards the kitchen and both girls follow.

'So, what did Sascha's mother say to you when you went to her house?' Amber asks, making herself right at home as she slumps down at the kitchen table. 'It's all well weird, I reckon,' she adds, pulling a face at Tilly. 'Like, Sascha just disappearing. Someone told me that her bath was full of blood. And that her dinner plate was smashed all over the floor. Maybe there's a murderer on the loose.' She pulls a concerned face.

Tilly gasps, looking horrified. Fiona hands them a slice of cake each.

'Who told you I went to see Sascha's mother?'

'News travels fast around here,' Amber says, taking a bite. 'Bill said that you asked him directions to the village hall, then he saw you coming out of Evelyn's house when he passed shortly after. He's my great-uncle – the old chap with the terrier,' she adds. 'Everyone knows everyone else's business around here,' she says, laughing, her mouth full.

Fiona nods slowly, though she can't be bothered explaining that there was no blood in Sascha's bath – rather just a few smears in the basin – and that Sascha's dinner was not on the floor. It was left half prepared on the side. But still, she feels unsteady as the memory flashes through her mind.

The blood in the bathroom... the drip, drip, drip of the tap...

Cora's grandmother – Sascha's mother – the woman who lives in the cottage next to the village hall in Little Campden, introduced herself as Evelyn when Fiona tentatively stepped inside her home yesterday. The place was small and cluttered and already filled with a feeling of loss, of sadness, of no hope whatsoever.

'Please, sit,' Evelyn said, flicking her eyes to the open-tread stairs that led up from her tiny living room. She'd sent Cora upstairs. 'Have you got news about Sascha?' She perched on the edge of her seat. 'I'm so worried. She's my only daughter.'

'I'm sorry, I don't,' Fiona told her. 'But if there's anything you need, I'm here to help. Sascha has been so kind to me since we moved in a couple of months ago.'

Fiona decided not to mention how Jason admonished her for having a new friend, how he thought Sascha was a bad influence, always popping round with wine, deliberately forcing Fiona to buck the rules. And then the childminding job... 'It's too much, Fi,' he'd said, shaking his head and sighing. She knew his concerns were for her own good, but she'd wanted to feel normal and fit in so badly. Thinking back, she *had* started to feel a bit affronted when Sascha kept picking holes in their marriage, implying that Jason was treating her badly when she didn't understand the first thing about their rules. Sascha wasn't one for holding back, and, once or twice, Fiona had actually found her quite overbearing. If she was honest, she resented it when she poked her nose in.

But still, she desperately wanted to know what had happened to her, find out that she was alive and well. Because the alternative was too unbearable to consider.

'Do you know anything about Steve?' Fiona then asked, making Evelyn's head whip up. 'Sascha's boyfriend.' She remembered what Jason had said – that he rode a motorbike. Then she recalled the doorbell footage of a biker delivering the second note. The same footage that had since been deleted from the doorbell app. She has no idea if the motorbike is relevant or just coincidence.

'That piece of shit is *not* my daughter's boyfriend,' Evelyn shot back quickly. 'He might be Cora's father, but I've warned him to stay away. That if he ever goes near Sascha or my grand-daughter again, then I'll fucking kill him.'

TWENTY-SEVEN

FIONA

'Steve is Cora's *father?*' Fiona asked, shocked, watching the anger rise within Evelyn. But it was soon diluted by tears, her shoulders dropping down again, and her sinewy fists unclenching as she let out a few stifled sobs. A mother and grandmother... desperate.

'Unfortunately, yes,' Evelyn said through stringy lips. 'I warned her. I warned her years ago not to get involved with him. His family have disowned him. Or should I say, Steve won't have anything to do with *them*. The Maddocks family are well known around here. Six brothers and three sisters – Steve being the second-eldest brother. People steer clear of their street cos all those lads have been in and out the nick since they were teens.' She sucked in a breath and continued. 'But they ain't all bad, that's the thing. They've tried to turn their lives around. Tried to do right.' Evelyn looked away, muttering something under her breath.

'That sounds tough,' Fiona said, seeing how distressed the poor woman was. 'I knew Sascha had started seeing someone, but I didn't realise they had history.'

'They go way back. They were at school together, and

they've been on-off ever since,' Evelyn told Fiona. Then she got up and went to a small sideboard where there were several bottles of spirits. 'To calm my nerves,' she added. 'Want one?'

Fiona stared at the bottle of supermarket-brand whisky that Evelyn was holding up. She swallowed, seeing there was over half a bottle of the stuff remaining. She imagined herself alone with it, caressing its shape, bringing it to her lips, closing her eyes, taking the first glorious sips. The feel of it burning a spicy hot line down her throat.

'Bit early for me,' Fiona said, holding up her hand and looking away.

Evelyn sat down again with half an inch of whisky in a tumbler, her hands shaking.

'Do you know where Steve lives? Might Sascha be with him?'

Fiona was beginning to realise that she and Sascha can't have been as good friends as she'd imagined, because she hadn't mentioned any of this during their chats over wine or coffee. Perhaps she'd only been interested in befriending her for cheap and easy childcare, which seemed to all start when Fiona had revealed that she was a nurse. Though she hadn't mentioned that she'd been struck off for negligence – no, she'd kept that detail to herself.

Evelyn immediately shook her head. 'She's not with him.' Her face was stony as she stared at the fireplace.

'You've checked?'

'Look, you'd do best not to ask any more questions,' she said, stiffening again. 'If you know what's good for you. You've asked too much already, and I've *said* too much. I'm warning you, keep out of business that's not yours. Especially Maddocks business.'

Fiona was shocked. 'But maybe Sascha went there to—'

'She's not with him, OK?' Evelyn yelled. 'Sascha wouldn't just leave Cora like that. If she'd gone to be with him, then she'd have taken her girl with her. I just don't get it. She's got a nice house, a good job, was finally getting her life on track.'

Was? Fiona thought, remembering PC Oldham's words when she'd needed to use the toilet earlier that day – *We've not found anything to suggest that Sascha is dead*, she'd said when Fiona had accidentally used the past tense. She shuddered at the thought of Evelyn knowing something.

'Can you just tell me where Steve lives?' Fiona asked again, knowing it would probably be easy enough to find out if Evelyn wasn't forthcoming. 'Or his family. You mentioned "their street"?'

'I've warned you, keep your nose out,' Evelyn growled, her eyes narrowing to suspicious slits.

Fiona shrugged. 'I... I thought I could ask if they know anything – as Sascha's concerned friend. You never know, they might open up to me.'

Evelyn scoffed. 'Yeah, if you give 'em a kilo of cocaine, maybe.' She drained her glass. 'Their place isn't for the likes of you,' she continued. 'It might be cute cottages and church fetes here in Little Campden, but two miles down the road in Long-bourne it's a different story. Show your face on that council estate, and you likely won't leave with it,' she added, standing up to indicate it was time for Fiona to leave. 'Final warning – stay out of it.'

Fiona followed her to the door, wanting to go anyway. With her mind in overdrive about what could have happened to Sascha, she felt uncomfortable – the first flickers of dissociation kicking in. Like she was seeing something out of the corner of her eye – though when she turned and looked, it was gone.

'If I can do anything,' Fiona said, standing on the doorstep, 'please let me know.'

Evelyn gave a terse nod. It was just before she closed the door that Fiona spotted Cora crouching on the open-tread stairs behind her, her hands gripping the banisters, the little girl darting back up when she caught Fiona's eye.

'Fiona... Fiona... Mum...? *Mum?*'

Fiona jolts at the sound of Tilly's voice. 'Gosh, sorry... I was miles away.' She sees Tilly's and Amber's eyes flicking down her front, a worried look on their faces.

When Fiona looks down, she sees she's covered in carrot cake and frosting – all over her T-shirt and tracksuit bottoms, plus her hands are smeared with it too. Not only that, but she has a sharp knife brandished in her right hand and there's something soft and sticky under her right foot. More cake.

'What... what are you doing?' Tilly sounds nervous.

'You OK, Mrs H?' Amber chimes in, dropping to a squat with a roll of kitchen towels. 'You've gone right pale.'

'Come and sit down, Fio— *Mum*,' Tilly says, taking the knife from her and leading her to a chair at the kitchen table. 'You started slicing up all the cake, dropping it on the floor like a machine that wouldn't stop. You sure you feel OK?'

A familiar line of pain cuts across Fiona's forehead, joining up the bolts of electricity she feels at her temples.

'I... I'm fine,' she says, though her vision doesn't feel right. Everything looks a little darker, a little blurry.

She has a sudden desire to fall into Jason's arms, to be wrapped up and engulfed by him, have him tell her everything is going to be OK before he gives her some pills to calm her racing mind.

Yes, pills. That's what she needs. Jason and his pills.

The kitchen door suddenly opens, making Fiona whimper. She feels so on edge.

'Dad?' Tilly says, twisting round from cleaning up Fiona's hands with a wet cloth. 'What are you doing home so early?'

TWENTY-EIGHT

FIONA

'It's OK, girls, I'll take over from here,' Fiona hears Jason say. He puts down his briefcase and takes off his jacket.

Why is he home before lunch? she wonders, though she's so relieved that he's back. Maybe it's the evening already and she's been slicing cake for much longer than she thought. Things aren't clear in her mind.

'What's up, love?' Jason asks as he sits down, looking at her intently. He takes her hands in his. 'You don't look well.'

Fiona shrugs, not knowing what to say. Her life doesn't feel like her own any more.

'Why is that bloody girl here *again*?' Jason asks when the two teens are out of the room.

Fiona just stares at him.

'Never mind, we'll sort that out later.' He lets out a sigh. 'Have you taken any pills other than your usual meds?'

Fiona shakes her head. 'No.'

'For God's sake, how much did you drink?' He sniffs around her mouth.

'Nothing. I haven't had anything. Just cake and some whisky.'

Fiona sees Jason close his eyes for a beat. Truth is, she's not sure if she's had anything to drink or not. It feels as though she might have done – her mind is woozy and giddy, and her thoughts are sluggish – but she doesn't remember opening a bottle or drinking anything apart from tea. Then she remembers throwing a mug at the television.

'Evelyn had whisky yesterday,' she tells Jason, wondering if that's what he means. 'But I swear I didn't have any.' She realises her mistake straight away.

'Who the *hell* is Evelyn?' he booms.

'Cora's grandma,' she replies, hanging her head. 'Please, don't punish me... I went to her house in Little Campden yesterday. I was only trying to help. She's worried about Sascha, too. Do you think Steve has done something bad to her? He's got a motorbike and... and I saw him at the door... and there's all the horrid notes I've been getting and...'

Fiona touches the side of her head, squinting.

'No... no, that's not right. That's not what I mean.' She shakes her head in frustration. She knows what she wants to say, but it won't come out. 'Do you think what happened to Erika...' She swallows, terrified to let the memories out. 'Do you think the same thing has happened to Sascha?' Her heart pounds from the frightening images flashing before her eyes. She's not sure if they're memories or her mind playing tricks.

Oh God, what have I done?

Jason gets up and goes to check outside the kitchen door to make sure the girls aren't eavesdropping.

'Are you intent on breaking *all* our marriage rules?' he growls, looming over her and grabbing her arm. 'Fiona, you have got to listen to me, OK?'

She stares into his eyes – dreamy and smoky grey with those long lashes that she fell for within minutes of meeting him in the pub that night. Chatting him up. Eating his crisps. *Good times*, she thinks with a smile. *Long gone.*

'I do not want you leaving the house. I do not want you speaking to Cora's grandmother any more. Whatever has happened to Sascha, we need to keep out of it. That woman has caused us nothing but grief.' He takes a deep breath, holding back the full force of his anger. 'Where is your phone?'

Fiona rises slightly and pulls it from her tracksuit pocket. 'Here.' She's used to handing it over. Then she remembers that she forgot to switch the doorbell alerts back on. She watches as Jason flicks through her apps.

'Google Maps has logged you going to Longbourne yesterday as well. What were you doing there?'

He's speaking to her like she's a child.

'I... I... After I was at Evelyn's house, I thought I'd see if I could find Steve,' she tells him. 'I know the police will have spoken to him, but I wanted to find out if he knew anything about Sascha, hear it for myself. Evelyn told me that he lives in Longbourne, so I went looking for him. But also...' Fiona trails off, wondering if it's wise to tell Jason about her suspicions. 'Look, I'm petrified that I did something bad to Sascha. I'm so worried that I hurt her – or *worse* – during one of my episodes... like I did to Erika. I just wanted a tiny clue that she's OK, that she's still alive.' She shields her mouth with her hand as she speaks, keeping her voice low. 'And not only that, but someone's still sending me threatening notes. I've had four now. I shouldn't have kept it from you, but I didn't want to worry you. I... I'm really scared, Jase. I saw someone on a motorbike put one of them through the letterbox last week.'

She has no idea how the first note ended up on the kitchen floor and hates the thought of someone leaving it there for her to find. A stranger creeping into the house from the fields while she and the girls were at home is too horrid to contemplate.

'What if it was Steve that I saw delivering the second note on the doorbell camera?' she whispers, deciding that it's best not to even mention her concerns about Graham next door, that she's got suspicions about him too. It's all too much. But mainly, she's concerned about what she might have done to Sascha... that she's had another dissociative episode and struck again.

On hearing all this, Jason covers his face, wipes his hands down his cheeks, dragging down the skin.

'And you didn't think to tell me any of this? Rule number one, Fiona. No lying. Which part of that do you not understand?' He grabs her again, giving her a shake.

'But I didn't—'

'Stop – just stop! I don't want to hear any more of your lies. You need to stay out of things that don't concern you.'

You look tired, my love, Fiona thinks, barely hearing his words or accepting the gravity of what she's done. She wishes more than anything she wasn't such a burden on him. Wishes she had control over her thoughts, over her actions.

'Is it work?' she asks. 'Making you so exhausted?' She knows it's not. She knows it's *her*. She'd do anything to make things right between them again.

'God, don't talk to me about work.' Jason goes to the fridge and takes out a bottle of Peroni, knocking the top off with the opener from the drawer. Fiona watches as he takes the first few swigs, cold and refreshing as she imagines the liquid slipping down her throat. She doesn't think it's a good time to mention Rule Number 7 – no alcohol, apart from one drink at the weekend. Is everything falling apart in their lives – is that what's happening – the rules no longer keeping them safe?

'What upset you at work?' Fiona goes to the sink, turning on the tap with her elbow to wash the rest of the cake off her hands. She's reminded of scrubbing up at the hospital... and her mind begins to veer back to that night, that busy Saturday in A&E almost two years ago when everything went bad. When she lost control of herself and obeyed the voices in her head, costing her career. She can't predict when they'll come, the voices – or what they'll make her do – but they're always there, lurking, waiting.

'The police were at the university. Swarming all over the medical school,' Jason tells her. 'And an ambulance.'

'That's a worry.' Fiona suddenly feels light-headed, as if she's in the scene he's describing – as if she's really there. But then she's not sure if it's the university or the accident and emergency department... or at Radmoor or at Sascha's house. Everything is so muddled in her mind.

She plunges her hands under the tap.

Stay real, stay in control, stay in the moment, she tells herself, focusing on the hot water as it splashes over her skin.

'Did you find out what was going on?' she asks, trying so hard to sound normal and in control. *I can do this,* she thinks, drying her hands. 'I hope no one was hurt.'

'No idea,' Jason replies. 'But they wouldn't let me in. It looked serious.' He stares at Fiona. 'But more importantly, I need to know if you've been anywhere else – yesterday or today. I don't like punishing you all the time, but you keep breaking rule number four and leaving the house without good reason. Good reason means a medical emergency or if I need you to pick me up in the car. Is that so hard to understand?'

'I've not been anywhere else,' she replies. 'Cross my heart and hope to die,' she adds in a silly voice, a smile creeping across her face.

'With a cherry on top?' Jason grins, coming up to her and grabbing her wrists, clamping them together at his chest as he pulls her close.

'Cherries on top are for promises,' she tells him, liking that he hasn't stayed angry with her for long this time. 'But I *promise* I haven't been anywhere this morning. I've just been at home.'

A couple of jagged memories flash in front of her mind – bolts of lightning illuminating the room... *Sascha in her house that night... Erika walking to her car in the dark... Both times it was raining. So much rain... So much blood... Drip... drip... drip...*

Then there's something warm on her mouth – Jason's lips as he kisses her. She closes her eyes and falls into his embrace, grateful that he came home early from work. Almost as if he knew she needed him to take care of her.

'I love you,' he tells her, his hands running up her spine. Tingles flood her, as though she's drowning in him.

'Love you too,' she whispers back.

He tilts up her chin with one finger. 'But please, don't go out again, OK?' He shakes his head, sighing, and Fiona rests her head on his shoulder, her arms wrapping around his back.

'OK, I'm sorry,' she whispers, sliding her hands down into his back pockets – somewhere to rest them – but in one side, she feels something. She pulls out a folded piece of paper – a *lined* piece of paper that makes her blood run cold.

'What's this?' She opens it up, staring down at the words.

The dead don't stay silent forever. Her blood is on your hands.

She looks up at Jason – wide-eyed and terrified as she wonders who the note is referring to. Then she stares down at it again, half expecting it to catch fire.

It's the handwriting that she can't take her eyes off – the neatly printed letters going in and out of focus the more she stares at them... the more she *recognises* them. Her heart beats faster as her suspicions grow. Suspicions about herself. About what she might have *done* – what she might have blocked out or imagined, her mind concocting stories about where the notes came from to protect herself. She knows she's capable.

She looks up at Jason, her hands clasped under her chin. 'I'm so scared I killed Sascha, and... and now this... It's *me*, isn't it? This handwriting, it looks like mine. It's almost like I'm trying to confess – my unconscious mind speaking out. Oh God, Jase... *I* wrote these notes, didn't I?'

TWENTY-NINE
JASON

Before

The master plan that I formulated that night – the same night Fiona was hauled back in a drunken state from the pub – with my fingers steepled underneath my chin as I sat in my office at Radmoor, rocking back and forth in my desk chair, went something like this:

Run away.

That was it. The sum of three hours' contemplation by a highly qualified medical professional with a gun pointing at his head.

Run for it. As if I could outrun a bullet.

There was a knock at my door. I quickly shoved the half-bottle of whisky back inside my drawer. It wouldn't look good – a doctor drowning his sorrows. While I wasn't officially on duty, I was aware of the consequences of drinking while on hospital premises.

'Sorry to bother you, Doc, but Fiona Fisher is asking for you,' the nurse said. 'Would you have a moment?'

I looked at my watch – shocked. It was almost 7 a.m. I'd

been awake all night, drinking whisky and pondering my predicament. Erika had messaged me from home around 9 p.m., checking on me, and I'd replied, letting her know that I was fine, that I was bedding in for the night here. There were no further messages from her, so I assumed she'd accepted what I'd said. And surely if she'd received any incriminating videos from Fiona, all hell would have broken loose by now.

Though I had to admit, that wouldn't be Erika's style. No, knowing her, she'd continue as normal, keeping her powder dry, then strike when I was least expecting it. Lashing out with a career-crushing, soul-destroying retaliation in one fell swoop. And, of course, she'd take Fiona down with me – though as things stood, there wasn't much further for that poor woman to fall.

'Of course I have a moment,' I told the nurse, glad to be of some use. Thankfully, it was set to be a quiet workday, so still wearing the same clothes from yesterday, I strode down the network of corridors in Isaac Ward to Fiona's hospital room.

To my surprise, when I knocked and went inside, she was sitting on her bed, looking as though she'd already showered, styled her hair, dressed in clean clothes and even applied a touch of make-up. I can't deny, she looked fresh-faced and... well, she looked *well*. She certainly put me to shame in my crumpled shirt and trousers that smelt faintly of body odour, and certainly of stress. I'd even managed to get some mayonnaise from yesterday's lunch down my shirt, resulting in a greasy stain on my chest. My stubble and unkempt hair completed my stressed and anxious no-sleep look.

'Fiona,' I said, pleased to see her looking so well. Though I was surprised, given she should have been, at the very least, suffering from the clutches of a wretched hangover. 'How are you feeling this morning?'

She looked up at me, her dark eyes seeming full of remorse.

That's what it looked like to me, anyway. Perhaps things weren't as dire as I'd imagined.

'Fine,' she said in a neutral tone. Then she looked at the nurse hovering in the doorway, giving her a nod. The nurse turned and left, shutting the door behind her.

I frowned, sitting down on the bed, taking Fiona's hands in mine once we were alone.

'I was so worried about you, darling,' I said, wanting her to know that I was having second thoughts about ending our affair, that we could still, in time, carry on seeing each other.

I also needed to work out how best to handle Erika first – as well as mitigating the risk of Fiona sending her the videos that she'd got secreted away. Erika's email address was easy to find online, but Fiona would also see her around the hospital before too long and could simply show her. I needed a contingency plan. Something to cover my own back, should the need arise.

'Look, I just wanted to say that I'm sorry for causing trouble in the pub last night,' Fiona began. 'I didn't mean to get so drunk. It's just when you told me that we were over, that you didn't want to be with me any more... I... well, my world fell apart.'

'It's OK, I understand,' I told her, hardly able to believe that she was being so reasonable. 'It was a big shock for you. My head was all over the place and I feel so torn in two. But I shouldn't have told you like that, it wasn't fair.'

She thought for a moment, nodding. 'And don't be fooled by all this, either,' she added, sweeping a hand down herself. 'My head hurts like it's being crushed in a vice, and I feel as though I could throw up at any moment. Serves me right for drinking so much, eh?'

'My poor baby,' I said, pulling her close and cradling her in my arms. I needed her to feel as though I cared, as if there was still hope for us. And it was true – I *did* care for her. But I was still having trouble reconciling my love for Fiona with my marriage to Erika and, more importantly, the pain I would cause our daughters. It was a matter of weighing up who I feared the most.

My body stirred as she ran her hands down onto my thighs, making me twist away slightly. 'Not now, darling,' I said. 'The nurse could come back at any moment.'

'Then *when?*' There was a disappointed look on her face. 'Tonight?'

I shook my head, frowning. 'Not tonight. Erika will be at the hospital from this afternoon and will be here until late. She'll expect to see me.'

It was the look on Fiona's face then that reminded me she was still very unwell, unstable and teetering on the edge of an emotional precipice. However much I wanted to be taken in by her put-together appearance, the effort she'd made to look nice and behave reasonably, beneath all of that she was still fragile and vulnerable. She did not want to accept that she had to wait, bide her time – and I admit that, deep down, neither did I.

'That *bitch*,' she whispered, leaning forward to kiss me. 'She's ruining *us*, do you not see that? She's stealing our happiness.' Her tongue traced around my lips, making it hard for me not to respond. 'I could *kill* her.'

'I know, I know, it's so unfair, darling. Just be patient a little longer. It's my daughters... a divorce won't be good for them. Tilly has exams soon and—'

'But what about *us?*' Fiona said, tugging on the fabric of my shirt. And my heart. I gave a quick glance towards the door. 'We had so many plans. Our new life together – including your girls. We had it all worked out.'

She did have a point. What had happened to our dreams – the life we'd spent so many illicit encounters discussing – our excitement growing as we plotted the rest of our lives together? Had I been kidding myself all along that it was even possible – leaving everything here at the hospital without repercussions or backlash? Leaving Erika without her and the board of directors kicking up an almighty stink because I'd run off with a patient?

'Perhaps it was all just a crazy fantasy,' I suggested, knowing almost immediately that was the wrong thing to say.

The slap was short, sharp and stung like hell. But I probably deserved it.

'No,' Fiona whispered. 'You're lying to *yourself*, Jason. You want me, I *know* you do, you're just too cowardly to face the consequences.'

She snarled at me. Her anger building. I knew she was right.

'You think you're this high-and-mighty doctor, going on and on about your father being an eminent psychiatrist on Harley Street, with your flash house and important wife and two beautiful daughters.' She laughed, scoffed at me. 'Well, let me tell you something, Jason Hewitt. Sorry, *Dr* Jason Hewitt... you're none of those things. You have nothing. You're empty – dead inside. When it comes down to it, you're no better than me. Making all those plans, making me think you'd actually go through with them, that we had a future... nah, you're as fucking crazy as I am.' She laughed and spat at me then, a foamy globule landing in my crotch just as the bedroom door opened and the nurse returned, a cup of tea in her hand.

Again, I deserved her vitriol. I quickly stood up before the nurse saw how close we were sitting, and then I headed towards the door.

'Nearly froze myself to death outside,' the nurse said, chuckling as she sat down again, settling herself in for another long, boring stint of making sure Fiona didn't hurt herself. 'Serves me right for having a fag,' she chuckled at no one in particular, her cough turning into a chesty hack. 'I should pack it in, or it'll be the death of me one day. And I'll have no one to blame except myself.'

She continued chattering as she picked up her magazine,

but I was already leaving Fiona's bedroom with her words ringing in my ears.

It'll be the death of me... No one to blame...

But what if there was *someone to blame?* I thought, heading back to my office to freshen up before Erika arrived. Someone to blame who had a big grudge against my wife?

I went into my office and sat down, thinking, thinking, thinking. My hare-brained idea to 'run away' had just evolved into a new plan that might actually allow me and Fiona to finally be together.

THIRTY

JASON

Ever since he left the university two hours ago, Jason has felt the pressure inside his head building. The sight of the police cars, the ambulance arriving, then the officer asking if he was OK...

No, I'm not fucking OK... was what he'd wanted to say.

But of course, he hadn't.

The officer had told him that whatever it was inside the medical building wouldn't be coming out alive.

His mind darts back to what possessions might be in his office on the second floor, what traces of himself he left behind. An image of Rosanne flashes before his eyes – her offering him her swipe card when they met in the corridor, the hopeful look she gave him as he invited her into his office.

You were on my mind last night...

Jason really, *really* wishes she hadn't said that. It wasn't right, had made him feel uncomfortable.

His head has been swimming with thoughts of what the police will have found as he drove home, speeding away from the campus as he headed back to his family – not certain home was where he wanted to be, either.

If he is honest with himself, he has felt displaced and out of sorts since he left his position at Radmoor. He has to stop blaming Fiona for it.

She is ill. She is not herself. She needs protecting.

Now, he grips the wheel tightly, driving *away* from home again after having only been back briefly, when he found Fiona covered in cake, on the edge of one of her strange turns. Goddamn he loves her fiercely, but she pushes him to his limits.

Suddenly, a horn blares, making him jam on the brakes. He almost ran a red light. Then there's a screech as the car behind him comes to an abrupt stop. He loosens his tie, wiping the sweat from his top lip with the back of his hand.

'It's OK, it's OK, everything is OK,' he mutters to himself, shoving the car into gear again with a graunching sound and driving on when the lights change.

After he'd arrived home earlier, finding Fiona upset, he'd leapt straight into action, taking care of his wife. Then Fiona found the note that had been left on his windscreen tucked inside his pocket. He cursed himself for not disposing of it. She looked up at him with her big doe eyes, watched as he ripped up the bit of paper, tossing it in the bin. Getting rid of the evidence.

He knows full well that she didn't write *any* of the notes they've received.

But it suits him that she believes she did.

Longbourne is only five miles away according to the map on Jason's phone, and while he doesn't have an actual address for Steve, he remembers the approximate location of the street Fiona visited from the log on her phone.

He slows down as he enters the village – not as attractive as Kingshill or Little Campden, especially as it has a main road cutting through its centre. But it's pleasant enough and has a petrol station at least, which he pulls in at to get fuel.

'I'm looking for Drakes Avenue,' Jason says when he goes

inside the small shop to pay. A young lad is serving and barely gives him eye contact. Jason hands over twenty pounds then fishes in his pocket for some loose change. He hands over another twelve pence, having overshot at the pump. 'Any idea?'

'Drakes Avenue?' the boy says, almost sounding surprised. 'Good luck with that,' he adds.

'Good luck?' Jason says. 'Why would I need good luck?'

But the boy just laughs and looks away before serving the next customer.

When he's back in the car, Jason consults the map on his phone, trying to convince himself that he's doing this recce for Fiona. That it will ease her worry if he can just have a quick chat with Steve, see if he knows what might have happened to Sascha – and maybe even probe to see if it was him who sent the notes. But more than anything, he needs to get a sense of what the people involved in Sascha's life know, where their suspicions lie.

The houses down Drakes Avenue seem pleasant enough at first glance – pairs of local authority semi-detached houses built in the 1950s, Jason guesses by the look of them. With typical long front gardens and views over the fields on the edge of the village, there are about ten houses in total.

Each property has some kind of vehicle parked on the front drive – though none of them appear particularly road-worthy, judging by the state of them. A couple are virtually rusted away, while others are missing tyres and haphazardly propped up on jacks, and one or two have no glass in the wind-screens.

But the preferred method of transport around here seems overwhelmingly to be motorbikes. There are at least twelve or fifteen of them parked on the driveways – all gleaming and cared for.

Jason cruises down the street, not sure what or who he's looking for. He doesn't like the thought of Fiona coming here –

arriving on her push bike, of all things. And there's not a soul about, which gives the street an eerie feel.

A shudder runs through him, so he decides to leave, not liking the vibe of this place one bit. He's not surprised that Fiona left as soon as she got here. He pulls the car to a stop, puts it into reverse and backs up into one of the driveways to turn round, deciding to head home.

But when he glances in his rear-view mirror to finish the turn, he's surprised to see... to see several pairs of hands pressed against his back window. He swings around in the seat.

What the fuck?

Three or four men are standing right behind the tailgate of his Ford, their palms pressed against the glass. He can't see their faces, but their arms are covered in greeny-black tattoos. Jason snorts. What are they expecting to do, stop a car from moving?

He shakes his head, not needing to reverse any further anyway. He puts the car into first gear and is about to drive forward when he sees another four men standing right in front of his bonnet, also with their hands on the car. They've seemingly come from nowhere, too. He presses his foot on the brake.

'Fuck's sake,' Jason mutters, his heart rate ramping up a notch. He gives a couple of polite toots on the horn, grinning widely through the windscreen and waving his hand in a sort of salute. But the men just stand there, each of them with unruly beards and wild hair, large beer guts, wearing oily jeans and an assortment of leather jackets, cut-off denim waistcoats and heavy chains around their thick necks.

He presses the button to put the window down an inch. 'Sorry, didn't mean to come onto your property,' he calls out of the narrow gap. 'Just got a bit lost. I'm heading off now, if you could just step aside. Sorry again,' he says, adding another grin.

One of the men lurches forward over his bonnet, pressing down hard with his palms, denting the metal. The car rocks. Then another man joins in... and another and another. Soon, there are about nine men surrounding his car at the front end, rocking and shoving it until he begins to feel quite nauseous.

He puts the window down a bit further, not knowing what to say to them. If he puts his foot down and drives off, one of them is bound to get hurt. Then they'll take down his registration number and report him to the police – and he can't have them doing that. Obtaining fake number plates was hard enough – copies from another Ford SUV, the same model and colour from a guy down at the pub near Radmoor who knew someone who knew someone else. It's just until things settle down, until it's safe to update his car documents to the new address. But meantime, he can't risk being flagged up on the police system.

Jason is about to ask one more time if the men wouldn't mind moving, but he suddenly finds himself choking, gasping for breath, as a beefy arm comes in through the window and grabs him by the shirt collar, pulling it tight around his neck before smashing his face against the steering wheel.

THIRTY-ONE

JASON

After being hauled out of the car, Jason finds himself splayed across the bonnet, his right cheek pressed against the metal, still warm from the engine. There's a knee in his thigh as one of the men pins him against the radiator grille, and several hands weigh down on his back and head.

'Let me up! Let me *go*...!' Jason's voice is muffled and distorted given his mouth is clamped against his car. He tries to wriggle free, but he can't fight against their collective strength.

'What you after, dickhead?' one of the men growls.

'We see you prowling about,' comes another gruff voice.

'Nothing, that's the thing. I'm after nothing.' Jason cringes at the sound of his public-school accent compared to the men's voices – reason enough for a beating alone.

'Don't believe ya,' comes another voice, which is quickly followed by the shrill tones of a woman further away.

'Jesus Christ, let him be!' she shrieks.

Thank God, Jason thinks, his limbs shaking and trembling as he feels himself released with a shove. He half slides down the front of the bonnet but manages to save himself. He stands up to find he's surrounded by nine or ten burly men, most dressed in biker leathers and denim. He feels as though he might piss himself at any moment.

A couple of the men are suddenly shouldered apart as someone weaves between them. A woman steps through – much shorter and skinnier than the men, and older, too, going by the strands of grey in her black hair.

'Who the fuck are you?' she says, standing with her hands pressed on her hips, elbows wide. She's wearing jeans, black leather knee-high boots and some kind of rock band T-shirt. At first glance, Jason reckons she could be in her late fifties, maybe her sixties. Her make-up-free face is hard to age.

'I... I'm Jake,' he says, thankfully having the name in reserve after the café incident with Rosanne the other day. The fewer people who know that he's called Jason, the better.

'Righto, Jake the Peg, what the fuck you want, coming down here? This is Maddocks territory. You stupid or something?'

'I had no idea it was... some kind of territory,' Jason says, trying not to shake. He doesn't want to show his fear. 'Apologies for the intrusion. I'll be going now.'

'No one comes down here for nothing,' the woman presses on. 'It's a dead end. You a cop, or what?'

Jason laughs, almost relieved she thinks that. Still, the irony doesn't pass him by. 'No, God, no,' he says. 'Bloody cops. Pigs, the lot of them.' Somehow, in his accent, it doesn't sound the way he intended.

'Depends on what you done wrong, eh?' the woman says, laughing. 'They're not pigs if you're squeaky clean, are they now?' She walks around him, sizing him up. 'You come for... you know, some food?' She folds her arms across her front.

'What?' Jason edges towards the open door of his car. His heart is thumping, and his hands are sweating. He just wants to leave. 'Thanks, but I'm not hungry.'

'Jesus wept. You looking for Mary Jane?' the woman says, seeming to lose her patience.

Jason stares at her, wondering who Mary Jane is – and also wondering if it's worth mentioning that he's really looking for Sascha. Maybe this Mary person knows her. He shakes his head quickly, unsure how to reply.

'Ganja, mate,' the woman goes on. 'Skunk, weed, grass. Hash, pot, fucking marijuana,' she says, baring her yellowing teeth.

'Oh. I see,' Jason says, wondering what the hell kind of street he's stumbled upon. 'No, I don't want drugs. Sorry for the misunderstanding.'

'Check out his boot,' the woman says to the men, ignoring Jason's reply. One of the men tramps round the back of Jason's SUV and opens the tailgate, pulling something out. Jason's heart sinks when he realises that he's left his work bag in there.

'It's locked,' the man says, holding it up.

'Then I'm sure our new friend here will unlock it,' she says. 'Won't you?'

'Under normal circumstances, I would, yes, but I'm a doctor, you see, and in a bit of a hurry... to, um, to get to the hospital.' He prays she'll buy his excuse.

'We'll try not to keep you then,' the woman says as the man dumps the bag on the car bonnet. '*Doctor.*' She gives him a sharp shove.

Jason stumbles, steadying himself on the bonnet before twiddling the combination locks randomly, pretending he's trying to open it. It's stuffed full of all the medication and drugs that he took from Radmoor when he left – drugs that he's not entirely authorised to have in his possession. Well, they're drugs that he shouldn't have at all, but he knew he'd need them for Fiona.

Shit, he thinks, the urge to piss himself growing stronger. Though he's wondering if there's a deal to be done here.

'Get on with it then, Doc,' the woman says. 'I ain't got all day.'

'Sorry, sorry,' Jason says, touching his head and sounding flustered. 'My memory isn't the best under pressure.'

'Does this help jog it along?' the woman says, giving the burly man beside her a nod. He whips out a flick knife, the blade shooting into action and pointing right at Jason.

'Yes, yes, it does indeed,' Jason says with a dry mouth and a nervous smile. 'The code has literally just come to me.' He fingers the lock barrels and opens the leather bag with shaking hands, realising that the red sweatshirt is still stuffed in there, concealing the boxes and packets of pills beneath.

'What's that?' the woman says, pointing at it. 'Take it out and hold it up,' she orders. After staring at it for a moment, she reaches out for the crumpled garment – the red sweatshirt with *Good Times* printed across the back in a stylised font. Jason hadn't noticed the words before – he'd been more focused on dealing with Fiona and getting it out of her sight after she'd had such a strong reaction to seeing it.

The woman draws closer to Jason – she's a foot or so shorter than him – but nonetheless, she squares up to him, her clenched fist grabbing hold of his shirt and pulling him down towards her with surprising strength.

'Where the fuck did you get this?' she hisses, holding up the sweatshirt with her other hand.

Jason wants to recoil, but he's surrounded by the men as they close in.

'Owww!' he yelps, feeling a sharp pain in his shin bone as the woman kicks him.

'I said *where did you get this*?' Jason swears there are tears in her eyes.

'I... I'm not sure exactly. It was just lying about at home, so I picked it up.' Frantically, he tries to think of a good reason why he might have a missing woman's sweatshirt in his possession, without landing his daughters or Fiona in trouble too.

'Lying about?' the woman scoffs, kicking him again. Jason

flinches. 'I believe the lying bit, at least.' She walks away a few paces, shaking her head.

Jason is frozen, not daring to move a muscle. From the corner of his eye, he reckons the car door is about six, maybe eight feet away. He could make a dash for it but doesn't fancy his chances, surrounded like he is. Even if he got in the car, these men would soon have him out again.

Slowly, the woman turns round, her hands gripping the red sweatshirt, her knuckles white as she clutches the fabric.

'Get him inside Andy's house, boys,' she says in a monotone voice. 'And bring his doctor's bag, too.'

THIRTY-TWO

JASON

There was a time in Jason's life when he'd have done anything to please his father. Anything at all. But the more he went out of his way to make his father like him, the more the man seemed to despise his only son.

Dr Frederick Hewitt, FRCPsych, top Harley Street psychiatrist to the rich, the famous and anyone prepared to pay his extortionate fees, did everything in his power to avoid having to deal with Jason once his wife Nancy had passed away. Jason always believed, as he'd been told, that it was cancer that got her – *riddled with it*, his father had once said. Though when he was thirteen, having not long started at Melton College, some of the other boys – whose own parents socialised with Jason's parents – told him that his mother had taken off one day with a bottle of pills and a rope. She'd been discovered a week later by the groundsman in the woodland at the edge of the family home.

Jason refused to speak for an entire term after he'd heard this – until the headmaster stepped in and punished the boys responsible for spreading the rumours, even expelling one of them. His father was telephoned but refused to come to the school to comfort his distraught son, saying he was too busy and that it was character-building for Jason to deal with the bullies and gossipmongers himself.

So, that's what Jason did. By the time he was fifteen, having stewed on his father's wisdom for years, he'd finally had enough and stabbed someone in the thigh with a splintered plastic Biro casing, narrowly missing an artery, and was nearly expelled. His father's donation towards the new Astroturf hockey pitch sorted out that little problem.

Why all this is flashing through his mind now – as he's staring at a nicotine-stained ceiling, lying supine on the kitchen table in a house in Longbourne while surrounded by a group of angry men and a violent woman – is beyond Jason, but it is. Clear as day. He supposes it's not dissimilar to being strapped to the wall bars in the gymnasium at Melton College and urinated upon by a gang of older boys. He'd just had to grin and bear that, too, getting through using pure grit rather than physical strength.

'I said where did you get this from?' the woman yells, waving the red sweatshirt over his face.

Jason jerks as he's shoved to the side, feeling a hand slide inside his back pockets as he's frisked. His wallet is pulled from his trousers, and he hears it being riffled through, the sound of cash being taken out. There's only about a hundred quid in there – the bulk of his stash being safely hidden at home. It's what they live on day to day, and even Fiona doesn't know where it is.

'Take my money,' he says weakly, trying to avoid the question. 'You can have my bag, too. It's good-quality leather. But please, leave me with the tablets. My... my patients need them.'

Jason suddenly recoils, his head snapping to one side as something solid connects with his jaw. The woman's fist, he realises, when his vision returns to normal. He tries to sit up, but one of the men shoves him back down.

'Where did you get it?' she repeats, shoving the sweatshirt

in his face, smothering his mouth and nose so hard that he can't breathe.

He tries to fight back, but his arms are pinned down. He coughs and splutters into the fabric, his mouth opening as he gasps for air. There's a ringing sound in his ears, and it feels like he hasn't taken a breath for ages, even though it's probably only a minute or so.

Then, suddenly, he can breathe again. Jason sucks in hard, screwing up his eyes as he draws in air. The woman has removed the sweatshirt from his face.

'I... I found it at home,' he gasps, bluffing again. 'I think it belongs to one of our daughters.'

'You have daughters?' the woman says, leering down over him. 'How old?'

Jason shakes his head, wishing he'd not mentioned them. The woman prods her knuckle between two of his ribs, making him yelp. 'Fifteen and eight,' he says.

'Names?'

'They're called... they're called Rose and... and Anne,' he says, blurting out the first names that come into his head. He doesn't want these wretched people to know anything about him or his family. But then he remembers Rosanne at the university – her coming into his office yesterday, what happened between them, the lies he's going to have to tell... and he's wondering if the choice of random girls' names wasn't quite so random after all. Another bloody mess he doesn't want to think about.

'Well, Dr *Jason* Hewitt,' the woman says, waving his driving licence about over his face, 'I'm gonna ask you one last time what you're doing down Drakes Avenue. And if I don't believe what you tell me, I'm gonna get Andy here to break both your fucking legs. OK?' The woman glares down at him.

Jason is terrified, feeling about nine years old – like the helpless little boy his father abandoned when he forgot to pick him up from boarding school one Christmas.

'I... I was just hoping to... well, to see if I could find a guy called Steve. I heard he lived around here. I wanted to see if he'd heard from Sascha. That's all. But it really doesn't matter. I was getting petrol anyway and—'

'So you know them – Sascha and Steve?'

The woman's face hardens, the lines around her eyes seeming to grow deeper, more concerned, and there's... yes, there's fear in her eyes now, Jason thinks. Him mentioning their names has done this to her. What does she know?

In fact, he thinks, what do they *all* know? The men are muttering among themselves, grumbling and shifting about, clenching their fists.

'Look, I don't really *know* know them, if you see what I mean,' Jason continues. 'But I know *of* Sascha... a bit.' He feels his cheeks and neck burn crimson.

Another punch to his jaw, but this time it's delivered by one of the men and he hears a cracking sound – fist on bone.

'Where do you know Sascha from?' Her voice is urgent now. 'When did you last see her?'

He has no idea who this woman is or why she's so keen to get the information, but Jason senses there might be a bargain to be had. Although he's not sure people like them uphold their promises.

'If I tell you, will you let me—'

Jason's head spins sideways, his neck cracking from the force of the blow delivered to his nose this time. A second later, he tastes blood as it trickles down the back of his throat. He spits and coughs, but it's dribbling from his nose now too, running down his cheek as he turns his head.

The woman shoves the sweatshirt in his face again, but it's not to suffocate him this time. She's wiping up the blood with it.

'Get him up,' she says to the two men pinning him down.

His back is stiff and sore as they haul him up. He didn't have a chance to see much when they manhandled him in here, but the small kitchen is grimy and littered with dirty dishes, stained mugs, ashtrays and drugs paraphernalia from what he can make out. Oddly, there's a vase of fresh flowers on the windowsill. The burly men seem to fill the entire space with their bulk, though it's the woman who commands the greatest presence.

'You've got one more chance to tell me how you know Sascha and Steve. After that, I can't be held responsible for what the boys will do to you. Fair?'

'Fair, definitely very, very fair,' Jason says. 'Sorry, I should have just told you that we live next door to Sascha. She's our neighbour. Lovely lady, and Cora is a very sweet girl. Everyone in our street is very concerned about her. We hope she's found safe soon. That's why I came, to find Steve, to see if he knows anything. So I could let my wife know, really. She's very worried about Sascha, you see. They're good friends. I... I just want to put her mind at rest. I mean, I don't even know Steve really. Apart from that he rides a motorbike and—'

'Shut up!' the woman barks. 'Get him out of this kitchen,' she then says, stepping away from the table, still clutching the now bloody sweatshirt.

Jason stiffens as the two men lift him under the shoulders and drag him out of the back door, past a couple of chained-up dogs – some kind of banned breed, he thinks, as he glimpses them snarling. They shove him and his bag in through the driver's door of his car, then laugh loudly, giving the roof a thump as, with shaking hands, Jason starts the car and drives off as fast as he can.

As he speeds away, glancing back in the rear-view mirror, he swears he sees a little girl's face in an upstairs window of the house, her palms pressed up to the glass. When he twists round to look again, she's gone. But he'd swear... he'd swear on his goddamn *life* that it was Cora looking out at him.

THIRTY-THREE

JASON

Before

Over the next couple of weeks, things slid into more of a routine at the hospital – with me making sure that my consultations with Fiona were limited to predictable and safe matters only. With her medication tweaked, the moods and angry outbursts seemed to settle somewhat, and she became more engaged in hospital life again. She finally understood that if we were to be together properly, we would have to bide our time.

Soon after her drunken episode at the pub, I'd laid down some strict ground rules with her – no walks together on hospital premises – or anywhere, for that matter – or meeting in empty bedrooms, or her outstaying her allotted session time in my office. During our regular consultations, I stuck to talk of how she was progressing and her medication rather than our usual excited chats about a future together.

'Darling, please understand – it's just until... until we're able to leave here,' I'd told her by way of appeasement – but it was also true. I loved her still. I wanted to be with her, but I also knew how unstable she was. As long as she had those compromising videos of us, the power was tipped in her favour.

It was not a healthy way to start a relationship, I realised, but for the future protection of my career at the very least, I needed a way to strike back at her should the need arise. I had to take some of the power back.

'Trust me, making Erika suspicious about us will only hinder us being together.'

The look on her face told me she grudgingly agreed with my reasoning, though her simmering resentment against my wife was growing – which was, as it happened, exactly what I wanted.

There had been several team meetings recently about Fiona's potential discharge in the next couple of months, which had also made her feel unsettled. She was an NHS patient in a private institution and that came with certain budget restrictions and a time limit. The powers that be wanted accountability reports, positive results, a detailed treatment plan and, before long, that her care be relinquished to a community mental health team. But I promised her that we'd be long gone by the time any of that happened.

Anyway, Fiona did not have a home or a community to return to, having lost her nursing job under such unfortunate circumstances. With no money coming in, she'd been forced to give up her flat and had no idea where all her possessions had gone. When she had been sectioned under the Mental Health Act the first time, she'd assumed that her landlord had got rid of her stuff. With no living relatives, she'd had no one to turn to for help. She'd been swallowed up by the system.

During some of our first sessions together, I'd noticed that Fiona was often confused about where she was living and, despite being told countless times that Radmoor was her home for now, she often believed she was back living in her old house share, that other patients in the hospital and even some of the nurses were her roommates.

On paper, Fiona's life was a sorry situation. It was clear how she'd come to rely so deeply on our doctor–patient relationship. I was all she had.

'I saw her earlier, your wife. She was giving me death stares,' Fiona hissed through pursed lips about two weeks after her drunken incident when we crossed paths at the coffee machine. It was in the patients' common room, but staff often grabbed a coffee from there as it was closer than the actual staff room for this wing of the hospital.

'Try to keep out of her way,' I advised Fiona, heading back to my office, not wanting to engage with her in case we were spotted. But Fiona followed me, grabbing my arm when we were alone in the corridor. Of course, I could have called for help, alerted staff members that a patient was harassing me, but where would that have got me?

'Erika said she's going to *kill* me, Jason,' Fiona told me with terror in her eyes, her body shaking. 'Don't you get it? She's plotting things. Plotting my murder.'

Her voice was crazed, and her pupils had grown huge and black. It wasn't the first time she'd suffered with paranoia. At that moment, I thought she looked beautiful.

'And you're next, Jason!' she continued. 'I know she's out to get us, you've got to believe me... She's jealous of me, jealous of *us*... We need to get away from here...' Her breathing was fast and panicked.

When I reached my office, I allowed her in, shutting the door quickly behind me. I was about to explain that while Erika was indeed suspicious of interactions between us, I had no reason to believe that she was going to harm either of us, that she should calm down, but Fiona grabbed me and kissed me.

And I'm afraid I succumbed. I admit, my behaviour was no better than hers – that of a mental patient in crisis.

All the bad somehow melted away when we were together – our bodies blending in a way that seemed to strengthen me. She made me feel like a man again – something I'd not experienced from Erika in a long while. My wife's cold, indifferent ways had left me with an ache inside, and Fiona seemed very adept at soothing it.

She was dangerous, exciting, devilish, and her being a patient made it all the more exciting. If our relationship had any chance of moving forward, I knew the path would be fraught with problems.

Or more to the point, I knew the path first had to be cleared.

'There's Tilly and Ivy to think about,' I told Fiona after the kiss had turned into more. 'I won't allow them to get hurt.' I held her as we sat on the window seat, staring out across the grounds of Radmoor. This place was a sanctuary for both of us – me from my marriage, and for Fiona, it was a respite from a world that she didn't fit into.

'They'll live with us, of course,' she said matter-of-factly, not even needing to be asked if she'd be their stepmother.

'I don't think Erika would allow that,' I said with a brief laugh. 'But I love your optimism.'

Almost immediately, I realised I shouldn't have laughed. I'd seen that look in her eyes before – a milky glaze coating her irises. The colour drained from Fiona's face, making her seem even more ghoulish. She thought I was mocking her.

I desperately wanted to avoid an episode. It would spoil everything – so I decided on a diversion. Erika was away for a few days, so I threw caution to the wind.

'Let's have a romantic weekend away,' I said, feeling spontaneous. 'We could go to York.' I tried to think of somewhere she'd like. 'I know this little guest house. The beds are feather-soft, there are beams and open fires, the floors are wonky and the linens are luxurious... We could go on walks and eat nice food and browse the bookshops and—'

'Sold!' Fiona said, the shroud of whatever demon had been threatening to engulf her suddenly lifted. Was that all it had taken – the promise of a weekend away? 'I'll go and pack. Will you drive or will we take the train?'

'Oh, the train, don't you think?' I said, and she immediately agreed. 'I'll pack a picnic and champagne, and I'll read poems to you on the way.'

'And when we get there, we'll find a cosy pub and hold hands across the table.'

So that's what we did. Within the hour, Fiona and I had gathered our stuff together – she wasn't on hospital observations any more and was not currently under any mental health sectioning either, so a weekend away was not out of the question. She was allowed to leave for a day or two and signed out under the guise of visiting a friend. In fact, for many patients, it was encouraged to help with reintegration into society and family life. And with my wife away, no one ever needed to know that Fiona and I had gone together.

We were so excited. The spark reignited. The journey up north went smoothly, the pair of us sitting side by side on the train, holding hands and not caring who saw our shared kisses. It was such a special time. We checked in at the Abbeydale Guest House, making love on the plump bed before we went out exploring. We wandered the cobbled streets hand in hand, checking out York Minster, peering in all the shop windows – Fiona bought a scented candle and a dream catcher, while I bought a second-hand copy of *Great Expectations* from a quirky bookshop that seemed to have endless floors. In a quaint gift-shop, we chose a leather-bound notebook – the type with rough, handmade paper and a lace to tie it up – buying it together.

'Perfect for writing the rules in,' Fiona said with a sparkle in her eye – something I'd not seen in a long while, showing me she was willing to go along with the system, that she was still invested in us. This time away together was just what she'd needed. Just what *we'd* needed.

'Here, have some more wine,' I said later as we sat in the beamy restaurant beside the roaring log fire. Fiona held out her glass, stopping me when it was half full, I was pleased to note.

'How's the steak?' she asked.

'Melt in the mouth,' I replied. 'And your rabbit stew?'

'Best ever.' She licked her lips.

Back at the guest house, I drank fine whisky in the bar while Fiona had a cup of tea, chatting with other guests – a couple over from the States celebrating their thirtieth wedding anniversary, and another young couple on their honeymoon – they'd got married the day before.

'So romantic,' Fiona whispered at me, the firelight twinkling in her eyes. 'We're surrounded by love.'

'We shouldn't be the odd ones out,' I said to her, gazing into her eyes. If I didn't want to lose her, I knew I had to take our relationship to the next level soon. She was only going to wait so long for me to sort things out with Erika.

'How so?' she replied.

'Marry me, darling,' I said, slipping from the leather chair and getting down on one knee. I took her hand in mine, bringing it to my lips as she stared down at me. 'I want you to be my wife.'

'Oh my God,' she whispered back, her face lighting up. 'You really mean it this time? You want to be with me?'

'Yes, of *course* I do. I'm so sorry for everything I've put you through, but the time has come to show you how much you mean to me. I am one hundred per cent committed to you, and I want to be with you forever,' I replied, still clutching her hand. 'I know things have been difficult lately, but I honestly can't live without you, Fiona. I don't *want* to live without you. I need you. I want you in my life. We'll make it work somehow.'

I slipped an imaginary ring on her finger, trying not to think how wrong it all was. All the hurdles I still had to overcome.

'Then you shall have me,' she replied, the grin blooming on her face as she admired the non-existent diamond solitaire. 'But what about...' She flashed a look at the other couples beside us, not wanting to be overheard. 'What do we do about your wife?'

THIRTY-FOUR
FIONA

Fiona is relieved Jason isn't going into the university today. He doesn't look very well and needs time to rest. 'Here, drink this,' she says, handing him a cup of tea. He sits up in bed, bleary-eyed after a fitful night of tossing and turning, despite going to bed early. She's already asked him several times what's wrong, but he's avoided answering.

'Thanks, love,' he says, taking the tea. 'Sorry I've been so out of sorts.'

'You poor thing,' Fiona replies, sitting down on the edge of the bed. She was worried about him when he went off in the car yesterday, returning later in the afternoon with a bloody nose. He was acting strangely, too, though swore there was nothing wrong, that it was just a careless accident.

'My face connected with the corner of the car door,' he'd told her yesterday, rolling his eyes. She sensed he was lying, blatantly breaking Rule Number 1 into a thousand pieces.

'After you went to bed, the girls and I watched a movie. Nothing inappropriate, so don't worry. They're both still asleep now,' she says, smiling. 'I thought I'd let them have a lie-in,' she tells him, praying he won't be angry that because of this, they missed their bedtime confessional. He was asleep when she finally came up.

'Thank you,' Jason replies.

Weird, Fiona thinks. He's not usually so amenable if she breaks a rule.

'Is your nose still sore?' She doesn't believe his story. She knows a punched face when she sees one. She shudders, recalling the times her father let rip on her mother.

'I'll live,' he replies.

'Jase... tell me what really happened,' Fiona says. 'Who did this to you?' Something inside her shifts as memories shuffle for space in her head – *split lips, black eyes, bruised cheeks*. She forces them back down.

Jason sighs. 'OK, OK. I went to Longbourne yesterday. I know the police are doing all they can, but I wanted to see what I could find out about Sascha, maybe find Steve and have a chat with him. I hate seeing you so worried about her, and I didn't want you sneaking back there again.'

'Oh God, Jase, it really wasn't a nice place. That's why I left in a hurry.'

After she'd visited Evelyn's cottage, something hadn't sat right with her. Something wasn't adding up. The woman had been on edge, nervous, as though she was speaking under pressure or even covering something up. Fiona had a sixth sense for that kind of thing. And Evelyn had become quite angry when it came to discussing Steve, her daughter's supposed boyfriend, her granddaughter's father.

It was what had made her cycle the couple of extra miles to Longbourne where the Maddocks family live, hoping to find out more. She hadn't minded the bike ride – exercise always helps her mood – but as soon as she'd cycled down Drakes Avenue, she was pedalling out of there again as fast as she could. Seeing what the street was like – a group of shady-looking lads hanging out, leering at her as she passed, a couple of the residents yelling at each other, throwing punches – it was enough to put her off. She was still worried about Sascha, of course, but more worried for her own safety.

'Did someone in Longbourne do this to you?' she asks Jason, gently touching his bruised nose. She shudders as, in her mind's eye, Erika's face overlays his – blood oozing from *her* nostrils, a vacant death stare. Then the image morphs into Sascha...

She stifles a gasp with her hand, not wanting these thoughts, but sometimes she can't help them, doesn't have control over what she lets in. And she can't help the voices, either, telling her what to do – they're embedded within her, part of her DNA. Her brain nurtures them, fosters them, breeds them and twists them into unmanageable monsters populating her head. Then the monsters take over, making her do terrible things... But the consequences of *not* doing them are more awful.

Her heart races and her palms sweat, every cell of her body vibrating to a different frequency. A feeling she knows only too well – the vibration of madness. The toxic switch of her brain chemistry as she loses control.

Please no...

'I... I didn't mean to kill her, Jason... I really didn't, you have to believe me...' Fiona clutches her head, shaking it from side to side to rid herself of the feelings. But she's consumed, her brain on fire with the memories – memories of what she did just before they left the hospital. 'I can't stand it... dear God, I can't trust myself...'

Jason is suddenly on his feet, rummaging through his doctor's bag. Just the sight of him doing this has a calming effect on her. He hands her a couple of pills, which she washes down with a glug of his tea, and this kind act – of being cared for, of being medicated, of being stroked and held – is enough to avert a full-blown episode.

His strong arms make her feel safe as he cradles her, rocking her back and forth as they sit on the bed together until Fiona's eyes droop shut.

When she was thirteen, Fiona ran away from home. It wasn't planned or premeditated, rather it was a visceral reaction to the situation she found herself in – the only way out of a life that consisted of watching her father beat up her mother regularly, followed by both her parents pretending that everything was absolutely normal. It had been this way for as long as she could remember.

The funny thing was, as she sat on a bench outside the train station, thinking about the violence she'd left behind, she already missed her dad. She'd learnt how to deal with his rages, his outbursts, his temper, and how to dodge his fists from a young age. It was simple really – all she had to do was be nice to him or avoid being around him. Appease and placate. Or run and hide.

As she sat alone on the railway platform bench, she didn't know what to do with the feelings left inside her – the baggage that she'd unwittingly brought with her. The unspent fear that had protected her for so long still raged in her mind, except now it had nowhere to go.

Fiona ran to a nearby wastebin and puked.

Back on the hard bench, freezing cold and without money or possessions, she wondered if this was what happiness felt like.

Her time alone was short-lived, and the next morning, while walking up and down the high street as she waited for the shops to open, plucking up the courage to nick a sandwich because she hadn't eaten in nearly twenty-four hours, her time was up. Marlbury was a small town and people talked. Gossip spread fast, especially when the police alert went out and everyone was looking for her.

A hand came down on her shoulder as she waited outside a grocery shop, and she didn't even flinch or try to run away. Instead, resignation flooded her, and she almost felt relieved that she'd been caught.

'Miss?' a woman's voice said – middle-aged and pleasant. There wasn't a single bruise on her face. 'Are you OK?'

Fiona nodded, looking at her, marvelling at how... how *normal* she seemed.

'Where's your mum, love?' she said, her eyes flicking around. 'Why are you out with no coat in this weather?'

Fiona shrugged, wondering if this nice lady would take her in, become her new mum – because as things stood, she was mightily angry with her own. Angry for allowing herself to be treated that way by her father. Angry for allowing her own daughter to witness it. And angry as hell that she hadn't taken Fiona away from the violence and got them both to safety. She knew her rage was misdirected, that it should have been aimed at her father, but if it hadn't gone somewhere, the only other place to aim it would have been at herself. Which, over the years, was exactly what happened anyway.

Fiona stood there, staring up at the woman. It wasn't that there weren't words to come out, a story to tell – there were plenty of those. Rather, they wouldn't come out in the right order, in a way that would make sense. In a way that didn't make her sound crazy, because that's what her father had called her once when she'd begged him to stop, her mother unconscious on the floor.

As things turned out, when Fiona didn't say a word to the nice lady, she took her by the hand and led her to the police station. Within an hour, she was back home, hiding in her bedroom and wedging the back of a chair under the door handle.

From that moment on, she decided that whenever she felt afraid, she'd become someone else entirely, become that nice lady's daughter in order to protect the *real* Fiona from everything bad in her life. She talked to Nice Lady often in her head, and soon she began to reply – her new mother's soft, kind voice comforting her, telling her what to do. Gradually taking over. Gradually getting revenge.

When she wakes, Fiona is alone. She's not sure how much time has passed as she splays her arms out either side of her, feeling around the bed for Jason. But he's not there. Whatever he gave her wiped her out.

She sits up, trying to get her bearings, her mind fuzzy and heavy, but it's also warm and relaxed. It's the best feeling in the world.

But the feeling is short-lived as suddenly the door bursts open and Jason strides in.

'Where are Tilly and Ivy?' he says, a concerned look on his face.

'What do you mean?' Fiona asks, feeling light-headed as she sits up.

'The *girls*,' he says, rushing up to the bed. 'They're not in their rooms. They're not anywhere in this house. My daughters... they're gone.'

PART 3

'We suffer more in imagination than in reality.'

SENECA

THIRTY-FIVE

FIONA

Fiona can't believe this is happening. Can't believe that Tilly and Ivy have run away. After everything she's done for them, all the sacrifices she's made, this is how they repay her.

That's what one part of her believes, anyway – the part that listens to Jason, always doing as he says, following the rules – no phones after 6 p.m., no social media, no watching the news, and everyone in bed by eight o'clock sharp. It's the part of her that won't put a foot out of line.

But as she sits in the passenger seat of Jason's car, a pain forming between her temples, the buzzing in her ears getting louder, she can't help wondering if there's another part of her trying to speak up – a part that she's not heard from in a very long time. The part that's stayed silent since she was a little girl.

She wishes it would go away. Leave her alone.

She thinks this part is the *real* her, and it's scaring her.

'Slow down, I feel sick,' she says, grabbing the dashboard as Jason takes a corner too fast. 'You need to drive carefully on these narrow lanes,' she adds. 'What if the girls are walking along the road?'

At this, Jason brakes. 'And they said nothing to you about this? Nothing to hint they were unhappy or going to run away?'

Fiona remembers Tilly grieving for her mother, missing her terribly and feeling bereft that she wasn't allowed to attend her mother's funeral. How she'd gone against the rules and down-loaded Instagram, showing her a photograph of Erika that she'd found online, convinced it meant she was still alive, not wanting to believe that whoever had posted it had, as they'd stated in the caption, used an old picture. Fiona could hardly reveal the truth in order to prove she was wrong – that her father had hidden her mother's dead body, that he'd disposed of her.

You killed her... evil bitch... it's you *who deserves to die!*

Fiona covers her ears and screws up her eyes as the voice fills her head. She remembers the empty horror of Jason telling her what she'd done, how she had no recollections of her terrible crime. She'd seen his lips moving clearly enough, explaining her dreadful actions, but nothing, just *nothing*, would seal the link between what he was saying and her reality.

Suddenly, there's a sharp prod in her side.

'Get a grip, Fiona! Keep your eyes open for the girls.'

'We should call the police,' she says, wiping her nose on her sleeve. This is not how she expected today to have gone. Not how she expected the last two *weeks* to have gone if she's honest.

She'd been so excited about the childminding job, earning a bit of money and making a new friend. Since leaving the hospital, the life Jason promised her hasn't yet materialised, what with him insisting they lie low for so long, not being able to leave the house, live out their dreams, the happy times they'd long fantasised about. Abiding by the rules for fear of what might go wrong if they *don't* stick to them doesn't seem such a good idea any more. She feels as though she's in a prison. Being perfectly honest, she feels as though she's still at Radmoor.

None of this is what she signed up for when she and Jason

got married. She thinks back to his proposal in York on their romantic weekend away. It had all been so perfect.

And now look at them – her new friend has been missing for over a week, and their daughters have run away.

'Tilly hasn't even got her phone with her,' Jason says, his knuckles white as he grips the wheel. 'And how the hell did they get out of the house? I swear I locked the doors!'

Fiona daren't mention that it's because of *his* stupid rules that Tilly doesn't have her phone. 'After the smoke alarm went off the other day, I made sure the keys were by the door in case—'

'So it's *your* fault they've run away...' He shakes his head, thumping the steering wheel. A strange growling sound rumbles in his chest.

Fiona feels even more sick now, and there's a ringing in her ears. A hissing getting louder and louder, making her want to stick something inside her head because she knows it means the voices are coming.

'Go and ask inside the shop,' Jason commands Fiona as he parks outside the small village store in Longbourne, about four miles from their village.

She gets out of the car and rushes inside, standing in line at the checkout before asking the cashier if she's seen two girls.

The woman shakes her head, disinterested, glancing at the next customer.

'Here, this is them,' Fiona says, showing her a picture on her phone.

'Sorry,' she says, barely glancing at it. 'Not seen them.'

Despondent, Fiona is about to go back to the car, but the customer behind her taps her on the shoulder. An older lady with a yellow headscarf and a brown coat.

'Wait, I saw two girls getting off the bus,' she says. 'They were in Stow earlier. I was about to get on the same bus to come back to Longbourne. I'd stopped the night at my daughter's house, you see. I go there once a month. It keeps me busy and—'

'Was this them?' Fiona thrusts her phone at the woman. She has no interest in hearing about her overnight jaunts with her daughter.

The woman studies the picture that Fiona took of the girls at the riding stables just a week ago. *How can so much have happened since then?* In the photo, both girls look happy as they pose, Ivy reaching up to attempt rabbit ears with her fingers behind Tilly's head, though she isn't quite tall enough. Tilly giving her little sister a prod in the ribs, making her giggle just as the photo was taken.

'Yes, dear, that's them. Pretty young things. I mainly noticed them because of that woman they were with. She seemed like a nasty piece of work, snapping at them. I felt sorry for them but didn't want to interfere. I mind my own business, I do. The older girl had her arm around the younger one and looked responsible enough, though she was clearly upset. She was asking other passengers if they'd seen her phone, seeming very distraught about it. She tried to get back on the bus to find it, but that woman wouldn't let her. She was panicking that she'd lost it.'

'Oh my God, her *phone...*' Fiona says, suddenly remembering.

The secret phone that Amber gave her.

She has no idea who this nasty woman might be, but this news gives her a shred of hope – she needs to get the phone number from Amber, preferably without alerting Jason. God knows what he'll do if he finds out Tilly has a second phone – and worse, that she *knew* about it. She just prays that Tilly managed to find it so that she'll be able to contact her.

'Where did the bus originate, do you know?' Fiona asks.

'Here, of course,' the woman says, looking at Fiona as if she's

SAMANTHA HAYES

unhinged. 'It's the shuttle bus between Longbourne and town. It stops in all the villages around here. Us pensioners wouldn't survive without it, living out in the sticks like—'

'OK, thank you,' Fiona says, rushing back to the car.

'Well?' Jason says, revving the engine as she gets in.

'Tilly and Ivy were spotted getting off the bus in Stow earlier,' she tells him breathlessly. 'Someone in the shop saw them,' she continues. 'Apparently, the girls were... they were with a woman,' she adds, not liking the sound of that.

'What woman?'

'I... I don't know,' Fiona replies, which is the truth at least. She balls up her hands and closes her eyes. 'Look, I think I know how to get in contact with them, but we need to go to Amber's house first,' Fiona blurts out, hating how forgotten and unloved Tilly and Ivy would feel if she didn't do everything in her power to get them back. 'And for God's sake, hurry,' she snaps, surprising herself with her authority.

Jason sighs and puts the car into gear, making a U-turn and following the signs back to Kingshill. Then Fiona directs him to Amber's house, remembering the directions Tilly once gave her. It's when they're at the top of the street that Jason slows down, scanning the house numbers as they draw close.

'It's that one,' Fiona says, pointing at a neat modern house up ahead. Jason comes to a stop on the opposite side of the road, and then they both fall silent, the engine purring as they stare out of the windscreen.

There's a police car on the drive, and a pair of uniformed officers standing at the door.

THIRTY-SIX
FIONA

'We can't just sit here and do nothing,' Jason says, flicking the sun visor down even though there's no sun. He hasn't taken his eyes off the police officers across the street. 'What are we doing here, anyway? Do you think Amber's mother is the woman Tilly and Ivy were seen with? Unless my daughters are inside that house, then we're wasting precious time.' He slides further down in his seat, turning sideways.

'I don't know,' Fiona says, shaking her head and taking a deep breath. 'Look, don't be cross, Jase, but... but Tilly has a second phone. Amber gave her old one to her. *Please* don't be mad... She just wants to be like the other girls and...' She trails off, finding it hard to get the words out. 'They've both been through so much.'

Her thoughts are suddenly filled with that terrible day – the day they picked Tilly and Ivy up from their schools. The rain was sheeting down, wetting the girls' faces along with their tears, soaking their hair and clothes as they were told the terrible news. The image of their mother's dead body was already emblazoned on Fiona's mind.

Along with the lies she's told. The secrets she's kept.

'It's time, Jase... I need to confess,' she whispers, unclipping her seatbelt. 'I'll go over and tell the police everything. What happened... What I *did*...' She stares across the road, where the officers are still standing on the doorstep. This is her opportunity to put everything right. Her hand goes to the door handle, but Jason leans over and bats it away.

'What the hell are you talking about?' he snaps at her, spit flying from his mouth. 'Have you gone *completely* mad?'

Fiona isn't sure if Jason is angry about Tilly having a spare phone or because she wants to turn herself in. Probably both. He's been protecting her all this time, putting himself at risk for her, and she's about to blow all that. Whatever happens, she'll always love him for having her back.

'Jason, I murdered your *wife*,' she whispers, barely believing her own words. They fall from her lips so calmly. So matter-of-factly. 'I'm so sorry that you were the one who had to break it to me, the one who had to deal with the fallout and... and get *rid* of her.' Fiona can't imagine how Jason must have felt – hiding his wife's body, orchestrating them both leaving their jobs, their lives together the very next day – yet still he stuck by her. 'And as if all that wasn't enough, I'm desperately worried about what I did to Sascha. Everything that's happened... it's all my fault, I *know* it. If I confess, then you won't have to run and hide any more. You and the girls will be free to rebuild your lives.'

Tears roll down Fiona's cheeks and she screws up her eyes. But all she sees is Sascha's happy face when they were drinking wine in the garden... followed by an image of her lying on the bathroom floor, covered in blood. The *drip... drip... drip...* of the tap.

Jason stares at her for what seems like forever, his shoulders rising and falling in time with his angry breaths. Then he glances out of the windscreen, across to Amber's house.

'Get down,' he hisses, leaning sideways over the gear stick. He pulls Fiona down too. 'The cops... they're leaving.'

'Jase... it's my chance to make things right,' Fiona pleads in a whisper, pulling away. 'Let me go...'

'You think leaving me is the way to make everything better? I gave up *everything* for you, Fiona. I love you. We have the girls to care for... when we find them.' Jason sounds so sincere, confusing Fiona. She doesn't know what to do. 'Don't give up on us,' he begs, gripping her hand. '*Please.*'

Their faces are close, their frightened breaths warm on each other's cheeks as they huddle over the handbrake together.

Fiona gives him a quick nod. Tears stinging her eyes. 'OK,' she says, sniffing. 'OK. I'll try to stay strong.' She grips his hand in hers and, soon enough, they hear two car doors slamming shut, an engine starting and a car driving away.

They both sigh out as they sit up, relieved the police have gone.

'Oh God,' Jason says. 'That girl's coming over, look...' His hand automatically goes to the ignition key.

'Wait, it's fine,' Fiona says. 'I want to speak to her. She knows the number of Tilly's phone.'

Jason makes an angry sound in his throat, but she ignores it, winding down her window as Amber approaches. The girl pads across the tarmac wearing sheepskin slippers, comfy fleece shorts and a baggy sweatshirt on top. Her long brown hair is wild and unbrushed, and her arms are folded across her chest.

'I thought it was you,' is the first thing Amber says as she bends down to peer in through the window. 'I saw you from the doorway. The cops were here a moment ago.'

'What did they want?' Jason snaps from the driver's side. Fiona gives him a prod and a sideways scowl.

Amber glances back over to her house. The front door is still wide open. 'They were asking Mum and me about Sascha,' she says, her eyes flicking around the interior of the car. 'They've been doing the rounds again.' Though Fiona can't help wondering if she's lying, especially as they didn't seem to go to any other houses. Plus, Amber seems a bit jumpy, not like the confident, cheery teen who's been hanging out with Tilly the last few weeks.

'We came to see *you*, actually, Amber,' Fiona says. 'I need the number of the phone you gave Tilly.'

Amber immediately backs away.

'Wait, it's OK,' Fiona says, holding up a hand and getting out of the car. 'You're not in trouble, and neither is Tilly.'

Jason gets out of the car too, coming round to her side.

'You weren't supposed to know about that phone.' Amber glances at Jason, clearly more fearful of him. 'Tilly said that you confiscated hers, that you're so strict and—'

'Don't worry, Amber, it's fine,' Jason says in a voice that Fiona rarely hears these days. Calm, soothing, comforting and kind. The Jason she fell in love with. 'We're not cross with you. If anything, I'm cross with myself for being too firm with her. Too many rules,' he adds with an embarrassed laugh. 'I thought I was helping them after their mum died,' he explains sheepishly. 'But I know they just want to fit in, be like their friends. I'm going to treat them to a new iPad soon. Make it up to them.'

Fiona's head whips round. This is all news to her. Still, if it gets Amber onside then she doesn't care.

'The phone number?' Fiona says, stepping closer. She holds out her phone for her to put it in. 'It's just that Tilly and Ivy took off somewhere earlier without telling us where they were going, and—'

'Like, you mean, they've run *away*?' Amber sounds shocked.

'Kind of,' Fiona admits, though the truth hurts. This is all her fault. 'I mean... I'm sure they're fine, but we're just a bit concerned.'

Amber nods slowly, her eyes flicking between Fiona and Jason.

'Did they mention anything to you about where they might

have gone?' Jason says, stepping closer. Fiona sticks out her hand to stop him. He'll spook her if he's not careful.

'No,' Amber replies quickly. She pauses for a moment, biting her lip, before beckoning Fiona to pass over her phone. 'I'll put the number in your contacts,' she says, sounding torn.

'Thank you,' Fiona says after she's done it, tucking her phone in her pocket again. She doesn't want to make a show of calling Tilly straight away, demanding they come home immediately. She senses she needs to keep Amber's trust. 'I appreciate that,' she adds, patting the girl's shoulder.

Suddenly, a woman's voice calls out from the doorway across the street – Amber's mother wanting her back inside.

'Just a moment, Mum,' she yells back, raising a hand at her. 'Look,' Amber says, turning back to Fiona, 'if it helps to keep them safe, the phone I gave Tilly is still logged into my iCloud account. I could try to locate it in Find My, if you want.'

'Yes, please!' Fiona says, shooting a wide-eyed look at Jason. 'We're so worried about them. We just want them back.'

'No problem,' Amber says, taking her own phone from her pocket and tapping on the screen. 'It's just loading,' she says. 'Signal's not the greatest around here.'

'Is that it?' Fiona says, pointing at a dot on the screen as she peers over Amber's shoulder. Jason stands the other side of her. 'Is that where Tilly's phone is?'

Amber shakes her head. 'No, that's my new phone – this one.' She taps her iPhone then zooms right in on the map that's appeared. 'See? It's showing us here just outside my house. And look, that's my MacBook and my AirPods located inside my house.' She points across the road.

'So where is the old phone that you gave Tilly?' Fiona asks, watching as Amber zooms out on the map. A moment later, another blue dot appears on the screen, a few miles east of where they are now.

'It's right there,' Amber whispers, zooming in again. It takes a few seconds for the map to appear in detail, but when it does, Amber is able to locate the street. 'Looks as though they're in Little Campden,' she says, pointing at the screen. 'Which is weird as I was expecting it to show them at...' Amber trails off.

'Expecting to show them where?' Fiona asks, but Amber shakes her head, reluctant to continue. 'Amber, *tell* me! It's important,' she shouts, knowing that her pupils have flared, making her eyes seem dark and dangerous, that her cheeks have flushed, that she's scared the teenager by getting right up in her face. 'God, Amber, I'm so sorry. It's just that with Sascha still missing, I'm... I'm worried. We both are.' She looks to Jason. 'Please, tell us where you thought they'd be.'

Amber frowns, looking uncertain. 'I... I thought they'd have gone to the old field barn, yeah? You know, the one between your house and the riding stables. I probably shouldn't let on, but sometimes we hang out there. It's just like this secret place, y'know?' Amber clears her throat. 'We'd have a smoke, maybe a drink, too, but never in front of Ivy so don't freak out.' She stares at the ground.

'Jesus Christ,' Jason says angrily, pacing about.

They went there to get away from us... Fiona thinks, hating that she hasn't made them happy. She's tried, God knows she's tried, but she's not been well. Leaving hospital so suddenly... it's taken its toll on her mental health. She's not sure she's cut out to be a mother. Not sure she'll ever replace Erika.

'Thank you for locating them,' Fiona says with relief, handing back Amber's phone. 'It looks as though they're close. We'll go and get them.'

'I know which house they're in if it helps,' Amber chimes, looking up. 'It's showing them at Evelyn's place next to the village hall. They're with Sascha's mother.'

THIRTY-SEVEN

JASON

Before

After we returned from our weekend away in York, there was a lot to arrange before our wedding – not to mention the effort of containing our excitement. We didn't want anyone finding out about our plans, preferring to keep things quiet under the circumstances. Besides, neither Fiona nor I cared for a big fancy wedding – just a small, meaningful ceremony was perfect for us.

But there was still one problem – my wife. I could hardly marry Fiona while still legally wed to Erika, so it would be far easier for all concerned if she was dead.

Conveniently, Fiona had already expressed a desire to kill her, so, while unconventional and extremely risky – and leaving me feeling like something of a psychopath – this did seem the most logical solution. Plus, any threat of Fiona sending compromising videos to Erika was instantly eradicated. If in the future she should threaten to blackmail me professionally with the copies she'd got stored elsewhere, then all it would take would be a gentle reminder from me of what she'd done to my wife. Problem solved.

We were sitting together in my office late one evening, the leather notebook set out between us as we fine-tuned the rules of our marriage. Fiona had the neatest handwriting, so she was listing them out.

She didn't realise it, but the rules were only there to keep her safe, to prevent her from doing anything impulsive or acting out what the voices in her head often told her to do. I was already familiar with the system, convinced that it was a solid framework for her to live by; strict boundaries for when there were no hospital walls to contain her madness, no group therapy sessions in which to expunge her demons. No nurses to watch over her full-time. At some point, I would have to get a new job so wouldn't always be there to take care of her. While Tilly was responsible and competent, I still needed Fiona stable and functioning and well enough to care for my daughters. She would become their mother in all senses of the word.

Money was going to be a worry long term unless I secured employment, but for the first few months, I'd made provisions – as long as we lived within our means. Having known my marriage to Erika was on the rocks a long while before meeting Fiona, I'd been withdrawing small amounts of cash from our joint account wherever possible, secreting it away in a briefcase hidden in the boot of my car. Plus, there was the drip-feed of the family trust, set up by my father purely to prove his ongoing hatred for me long after his death. Erika had no access to that, and I'd already made sure to withdraw the funds, also holding them in cash.

I doubted Fiona would ever be well enough to work again, and certainly not as a nurse. Her suspension from the General Hospital, the ensuing enquiry, the negligence case and her dismissal had made certain that her nursing days were in her past. Though the fact that she already had form for being capable of murder suited my plan.

Despite her medication, Fiona's psychotic episodes were

still hard to predict. For now though, it also suited me not to
shatter her fantasy world when the episodes happened – for
example, her belief that she worked at Radmoor rather than
being a patient in it.

The truth was, her own reality was too painful to bear, and
my longer-term plan involved stretching Fiona's imaginary
world just a little further, rather than destroying it. So strong
were her fantastical beliefs, it wasn't difficult to plant seeds in
her mind. Seeds that would soon grow to bear fruit for our
future.

All things considered, it was going to be rather easy to get
Fiona to murder my wife.

In the week preceding our wedding, I'd managed to secure a
rental property in a village about twenty miles from Radmoor. It
hadn't been easy, finding a private landlord that wouldn't ask
questions. But as luck would have it, I'd chanced upon a sign up
in a local shop: *House to rent, fully furnished. Call Barbara and
Dave on...*

When I'd phoned the UK mobile number, it had rung with
an overseas ringtone. One pleasant conversation later, and I'd
discovered Barbara and Dave had moved to Spain a few years
ago and preferred to rent their home the 'old-fashioned way'.
Too tight to pay agent's fees, I suspected, or let their mortgage
company know what they were up to, but it worked in my
favour. Barbara entrusted Margaret from Kingshill's post office
to collect the first six months' rent in cash and pay it into their
account, with just one simple tenancy agreement to sign for our
lease.

'That's all *ours*?' Fiona had said when I showed her the
photos I'd taken on my house tour. She'd grabbed my phone and
scrolled through. Her mouth hung open, her eyes wide.

'Every single wall of it,' I told her as she examined number 9
Hollybush Close.

'But... what... when...?' She had so many questions and her

face reflected the delight of a child. 'It's perfect! I love it! The girls can have a bedroom each!'

'It's ours for six months to start with,' I explained when she'd calmed down. After that... well, I didn't want to think about what came after that. I was banking on finding a job before too long.

On the day of our wedding, everything was set in place. We planned on leaving Radmoor right after the ceremony. I'd already checked that the car was full of petrol; Erika had happened to drive my Ford to the hospital yesterday shortly before her demise – we sometimes swapped cars – though it didn't really matter which vehicle she'd arrived in because she wouldn't be leaving in it again... though I was yet to explain all this to Fiona for fear of overloading her. I instructed Fiona to pack essential items only as space was limited in the car. And besides, we could rebuy anything that we needed in time.

There was no doubt that feathers would be ruffled once we got married, so a swift exit and lying low for a few months was in our best interests.

We felt like Bonnie and Clyde.

'You look radiant,' I told Fiona, who was admiring her reflection, smoothing down her blue, lacy dress in the mirror. It was clear from the look in her eyes as she turned around to face me that she was as much in love with me as I was with her.

While the legal side of our marriage would have to take place at a registry office another day – we'd simply grab a couple of witnesses off the street for that – this was the part that was most important to us both. The exchanging of rings and vows – or should I say *the rules* – in front of our loved ones.

Except there were no loved ones.

How could I invite my daughters when they knew nothing

of their mother's death yet? She'd barely been gone a day. And Fiona hadn't had contact with her family in years.

We were to be married in the patch of woodland at the edge of Radmoor's grounds – which might seem like a risky choice of venue, being at the hospital, but we picked it because of how meaningful the spot had become to us. We'd spent many hours wandering through those trees, sitting on stumps, leaning on the fence overlooking the countryside, talking, chatting, planning and dreaming. And, of course, lovemaking when the weather allowed.

The little glade at the southern edge of the woods where the bluebells grew in spring was where the ceremony was to take place – just us, the celebrant and the wildlife. And it wouldn't take long – a matter of a few minutes, really.

'Would you do me the pleasure of marrying me, Fiona Fisher?' I asked, holding out my arm to her as she smoothed down her hair and adjusted the hat and veil she wore.

'Why, of course, Dr Hewitt,' she giggled, taking my arm. What a pair we made as we sneaked out of the hospital towards our wedding spot.

I kept an eye open for anyone watching us – a doctor accompanying his patient would not normally raise eyebrows, but given we were both dressed rather smartly, Fiona in her lacy dress and me in a grey morning suit, we were likely to draw attention. Though as luck would have it, we made our way out of the building without a problem. Along the way, I picked a small bouquet of wildflowers for my bride.

'No hitches getting hitched,' I joked as our walk broke into a run, the pair of us careening through the woodland.

We laughed all the way, our arms windmilling, finally coming to a stop by the waiting celebrant, who was holding our leather-bound notebook and wearing a smart velvet robe.

There we stood, just the celebrant to witness our special union as we took it in turns reciting our vows, followed by a solemn recital of the rules – again, taking it in turns to read them out. After we were finished, we kissed, but then Fiona became twitchy and nervous, whispering in my ear as her eyes flicked about.

'Isn't... isn't this where you said you buried Erika?' she asked – my fault for divulging that I'd dragged her body down here under the cover of darkness last night, describing how I'd concealed her in a shallow grave. I don't think it had fully sunk in yet, what I'd told her she'd done.

'Rule number two,' I whispered back, tapping the leather-bound notebook. 'We never talk about *You Know Who*.'

Then I took Fiona's hands in mine, whispering to her how much I loved her as I put Erika from my mind, allowing the rest of our lives to begin.

THIRTY-EIGHT

JASON

'You fucking *idiot*,' Jason spits at Fiona as he drives off. God, he wants to thump her.

'What? Jase... no, *don't*—'

'Now that Amber knows the girls have run away, she'll phone Tilly and warn her that we're searching for them, you realise?'

Fiona shakes her head. 'I'm sorry, Jase, I just want to find them. I didn't think—'

'There we go,' Jason snaps, ramming the car into third gear as he takes a bend too fast. 'Not thinking. Do you *ever* actually think, Fiona?' he growls, flashing her an angry look. 'Do you ever engage your brain to work things out?'

'Stop it,' Fiona whispers, her head tucked down as she grips the seatbelt strapped across her. 'Stop being so hateful. I'm doing my best.'

Jason grips the wheel as he takes the country lanes at speed. Several times he jams on the brakes to avoid hitting oncoming traffic, and several times he bumps the left wheels up on the grassy verge to avoid a collision. He's seething. Everything is slipping through his fingers – all his carefully thought-out plans and contingencies and rules... all of it has turned to mush. All because Fiona can't follow a few simple orders.

'Idiot!' he yells out of the window at the delivery van making its way past them. The driver recoils at Jason's angry gesture. 'Which way?' Jason snaps when they reach a crossroads. He's boiling over with rage.

'Left,' Fiona says quietly, looking at her phone to check. 'It's not far. Sascha's mother lives in the next village. I went there—'

'Yes, yes, I know you did!' comes Jason's angry retort. 'Yet another example of your disobedience. Rule number four, Fiona. No leaving the house without good reason!'

Fiona sighs beside him, and, from the corner of his eye, he catches her hanging her head. Has he pushed her too far? Snapped at her one too many times? He doesn't mean to be... well, *mean*. He just wants to keep her safe. To keep them *all* safe. And right now, with his daughters missing, he feels he's done anything but that. He's failed his family, and it feels as if everything is falling apart.

'Turn down that street and look for the village hall,' Fiona says quietly once they've entered Little Campden. 'Evelyn's cottage is next door to it.'

A moment later and Jason parks the Ford outside the house. Fiona unclips her seatbelt and they get out.

'After you,' Jason says, holding open the garden gate. She goes up the path and knocks several times on the old front door of the red-brick cottage, the pair of them staring around as they wait, but there's no reply.

'Great,' Jason says, hands on hips. They knock again, but still no one answers. 'See? Just as I predicted. Amber must have warned them we were coming.'

'But why would they even want to run away?' Fiona says, shaking her head. She steps over to the front window with its wonky glass panes, cupping her hands around her eyes as she peers in. 'It's quite dark in there. I can't see much. Oh, wait...'

Fiona angles herself to get a better look. 'I think I just saw someone on the stairs, but they darted back up.'

'Try calling the phone number Amber gave you,' Jason instructs, shaking his head in despair. He should be at work, earning a living to support his family, not dealing with this hysterical nonsense in some woman's front garden.

Fiona pulls her phone from her pocket and does as she's told. Then, from behind the thin glass, they both suddenly hear a phone ringing.

'Hang up and dial it again,' he demands, also peering through the window. Sure enough, a phone on the coffee table lights up as it rings. 'Oh, that's just great. Tilly's phone is in there,' he says, standing back from the window and shaking his head. 'But where the hell is Tilly?' Jason lifts a couple of plant pots, looking underneath in case there's a door key – but he finds nothing.

'Perhaps we should go round the back,' Fiona suggests. 'They might be out in the garden.'

'You see, now you're thinking, Fiona,' he says, taking her by the hand and leading her down a side path to the back of the cottage, but there's no one in the garden. 'Check under the mat,' he instructs when they reach the back door.

'No key,' Fiona says.

'And no one in the kitchen, either,' Jason adds, looking in through the window. He curses under his breath.

'Jase, look...' Fiona calls out, pulling a hopeful face as she stands with her hand on the back door handle. 'It's open.' She pushes the door inward. 'Should we go in?'

'Of *course* we go in,' he says, striding past her. 'Hello?' Jason calls out boldly, heading into the kitchen. 'Anyone home?'

Fiona follows him and, when no one replies, they go through to the living room at the front. The cottage is a two-up, two-down with little space for anyone to hide.

'Did you see that?' Jason whispers to Fiona, pointing up the stairs. 'I swear there was someone on the landing.'

Fiona's eyes are wide as Jason goes to the foot of the stairs to check.

'Hello, anyone up there?' he yells. 'Come down! Tilly, Ivy, is that you?' He peers up, but it's too dark to see. Fiona taps him on the arm.

'Look, this is the phone that Amber lent Tilly,' she says, picking it up from the coffee table. 'I recognise the yellow smiley face sticker.' Fiona tucks it in her pocket. 'I don't understand why it's here, but not the girls. Tilly would never want to be without a phone, Jase. It's a worry—'

'I know it's a worry!' he snaps, feeling agitated. 'And if you'd stuck to the rules, she wouldn't have even had it in the first place. You *lied* to me, Fiona. And this is the price we're now paying for that. Go upstairs and see who's there,' he says. 'I'll see what I can find down here.'

'You want *me* to go up? Alone?'

'Shout if you need help,' he says, turning her towards the stairs.

While she's gone, Jason goes into the kitchen and roots through some drawers and cupboards. But there's nothing of interest. Just as he's about to give up and call Fiona down, suggesting they leave, he finds a bathroom tucked away off the back hall beyond the kitchen. He needs to use the toilet so takes the opportunity, wrinkling his nose at the smell when he goes in.

'Holy Christ,' he says, lifting the lid of the toilet. 'Disgusting.'

There's no water in the pan, which fills the room with a sewage smell, but he's desperate so he relieves himself anyway, hoping for Evelyn's sake that she has another bathroom upstairs to use. This one needs ripping out.

He shuts the lid and flushes, but nothing happens. The

handle is loose, and no water comes from the cistern. Sighing, Jason lifts the porcelain lid of the tank just at the same time he hears a voice chiming out from the living room.

'Cora, Nanny's home... Are you OK, sweets?'

The hairs on the back of Jason's neck bristle – and not only because Evelyn has come back. Crammed inside the toilet cistern are dozens of clear plastic packets of white powder.

'What the *hell*...' He daren't move now that Cora's grand-mother is back home. She'll have a heart attack if she finds a strange man in her bathroom. Carefully, barely breathing as the woman's footsteps get closer, Jason replaces the cistern lid. But one side of it slips from his hand, making a loud clanking sound as it lands back on the tank.

Frozen from fear, he can only assume that he's just stumbled on a massive drugs haul. Does she even know she has this in her house? Wondering if the day could get any worse, Jason decides he'll wait until things go quiet again – perhaps Evelyn will go upstairs to find Cora, getting distracted by Fiona – then he'll creep out of the back door. But suddenly there's a noise right behind him.

The sound of the bathroom door opening just a few feet away.

Slowly, Jason turns round, his eyes focusing on the woman standing there. She's dressed in black leather trousers and a heavy metal band T-shirt, and her dark hair is pulled back. She has a grim, determined look on her face. Her sinewy arms are outstretched and rock-steady as she aims the shotgun barrel right at him.

'What the *fuck* are you doing in my house?' she growls, coming even closer before pressing the gun up against his throat.

THIRTY-NINE
JASON

'*You?*' Jason croaks, trying to back away from the cold metal pressing against his neck. His heart pounds as he recognises the woman from Longbourne – the same woman who had him pinned down on the kitchen table. '*You're* Sascha's mother?'

'Fucking shut up!' she barks, shoving the shotgun barrel harder against him. Jason dares to lower his eyes, seeing her right forefinger wrapped around the trigger, her knuckle white. 'Answer me, you piece of shit scum! What are you doing in my house?'

Jason swallows – feeling the cold metal of the barrel dig into his Adam's apple. 'I... I... we were just looking for my daughter, Tilly, and her sister Ivy...'

'*We?*' the woman snaps. 'And that's not what you said your kids were called.'

Shit, Jason thinks in a panic, realising his mistake too late. There's a chance – just a *slim* chance – that if Fiona hears a commotion, realises Evelyn has come back, she'll have the sense to slip out of the house unnoticed and raise the alarm. *Dear God, let her do that...*

'I mean *I*,' he corrects. '*I* was looking for my daughters. I was told they were here. I knocked on your door – I swear I did – but no one answered. Then I saw Tilly's phone on your table and when I tried the back door, it was open. I'm so sorry to intrude.' He ignores her remark about names.

'Looks like you made yourself right at fucking home.' Evelyn eyes the toilet, jabbing the gun in his throat again.

'Yes, sorry. I got caught short. Your toilet doesn't seem to be working, though. I can pour a bucket of water down it to flush, if you—'

'Shut your fucking mouth and tell me what you're *really* doing in my house.'

'Looking for my daughters, I swear! And I should be asking you why Tilly's phone is in *your* house. My girls are missing! The police are all over it, so if you don't want to be arrested, then—'

'You called the police?' Suddenly Evelyn doesn't sound quite so cocksure.

'Yes,' Jason lies, daring to lift his chin to make himself appear confident. 'Of course I did. What would you expect me to do?'

'Who told you your kids were here?'

To Jason's relief, the woman backs off a step or two, releasing the pressure on his throat. But the gun's barrel is still pointing directly at his head.

'Amber, Tilly's friend from Kingshill. Long story, but she was able to track Tilly's phone to your house.'

'I see,' Evelyn says. Jason sees the cogs of her brain whirring. He has no idea why this unsavoury woman has popped up in his life again, but he doesn't like it. He likes it even less that she appears to be about to shoot him.

'Have you seen them? One a teenager, one aged eight.'

'I have, as it happens,' she says matter-of-factly, despite the gun she's wielding. 'I was on the bus to Stow with them earlier. They seemed lost so I helped them out, that's all. Decent lasses.'

Jason is confused – but also distracted as he thinks he hears a noise somewhere in the house.

'You went to Stow with them, Evelyn?' he says loudly, almost shouting her name, praying that Fiona will hear, realise what's happening and then go for help. 'Why don't you put the gun down? No one need get hurt,' he says, again loudly.

Evelyn makes a noise in the back of her throat, scowling at him.

'Anyway, being on the same bus as them doesn't explain why you have Tilly's phone in your house,' Jason says, braving it despite being terrified.

'That's because... it dropped from the girl's pocket when she got off the bus,' she tells him quickly. 'Then they rushed off before I could give it back, so I brought it back home with me to keep safe before handing it in. I've been out ever since, walking the dog.'

Right on cue, an old-looking white and tan Jack Russell terrier clacks into the downstairs bathroom, looking up at Jason before letting out a couple of snarly yaps.

'Cut it out, Charlie,' Evelyn snaps back, and the dog skulks out again.

Jason doubts she had any intention of giving the phone back, probably going to nick it instead – and it's a strange coincidence that Evelyn just happened to encounter his daughters on the bus earlier. He can't help thinking it was pre-planned – or, at the very least, that she'd seen them as easy targets to prey on.

'Look, why don't you just put the gun down?' Jason suggests, trying not to react when he hears a little girl's voice coming from the kitchen.

'Nanny will be there in a moment, poppet!' Evelyn calls out, twisting her head sideways while keeping the gun pointed at Jason. 'Stay out there like a good girl.'

'Your granddaughter?' Jason asks, wanting to keep her engaged for a bit. It must have been Cora he spotted in the upstairs window of that wretched house in Longbourne. He has no idea why or how he and Fiona have been dragged into Evelyn's dirty world, but he knows he's got to get them out of it.

Evelyn nods, the scowl on her face getting deeper. She doesn't seem to know what to do, the pair of them stuck in a stalemate – though she seems to be edging towards the bathroom door, as though she's the one being held hostage.

'Yeah, and she misses her mum,' the older woman says with a quiver in her voice. 'And I miss my daughter,' she adds with a sniff as tears pool in her eyes.

'Look, we have something in common right now,' Jason says, hoping to play on her emotions. She's blocking the doorway, and even if she wasn't pointing a shotgun at him, he'd still have to shove her out of the way to escape. 'My daughters are missing too. I know how awful it feels.'

He waits for it to sink in.

'If you just put that gun down, then maybe we can help each other. You know, compare notes. Sascha was at our house the night before she disappeared, and you saw my daughters just before they vanished, too.'

Something inside Jason unravels as, slowly, he witnesses Evelyn lowering the gun. A moment later, and it's hanging down by her side, looking as though she's about to drop it. If it falls to the floor, it could go off accidentally.

'Look, why don't we go and put the kettle on and see if we can figure out what might have happened to them, eh?' Jason continues. He dares to reach out towards the gun. 'Shall I put this somewhere safe? Do you have a gun cabinet?' He doubts that very much, nor a licence, but he just wants to get the damn thing off her then get the hell out of this house. He prays Fiona has already made it out of the cottage safely.

'I dunno...' Evelyn says, her voice weak, yet she seems resigned to handing over the weapon. Jason senses that she doesn't want this standoff any more than he does. 'My girl... my

Sascha... I can't stand her not being here. Seeing Cora so upset about her mummy, it's killing me...' A tear rolls from one eye, and Jason dares to take a step towards her, his hand outstretched as if he's taming a wild animal.

'That's it,' he says, his hand almost on the gun. 'We'll make everything OK. We'll find Sascha, and we'll find my daughters too. Everything's going to be fine...' He uses his most caring doctor voice to win Evelyn's trust, and he swears he just about has it when there's another noise – this time from the front of the house.

Evelyn stiffens, gripping the gun again and brandishing it at her waist.

'What the fuck was that?'

'Nothing, nothing,' Jason says. 'Just the wind, I think. A door banging.'

'You're a cop, ain't you?' Evelyn says, her eyes flashing wide. 'Did they send you? Is that why you're sniffing around my toilet cistern, eh? Think you're so fucking smart. Or maybe you're one of Steve's lot and he's—'

'You *have* to believe me, Evelyn. I'm here to find my daughters. I'm not a cop and I have nothing to do with Steve. Look, put the gun down and—'

Suddenly, there's another sound, much louder this time – a sharp bang, unmistakably coming from the living room, as if someone is smashing through the front door.

Evelyn tenses, aiming the shotgun directly at Jason's heart. Her arms are rigid and her pupils huge as she reanimates into full red alert.

'Police! Police!' resounds from the other room – a chorus of loud voices as they rampage through the downstairs.

Evelyn swings round at the sound of them, and Jason takes his chance. He lunges at Evelyn, shoving her by the shoulders so the gun is pointing at the ceiling, before wrenching it from her with both his hands gripping the barrel.

Three strong yanks later and Jason has control of it. He braces the butt against his shoulder as he aims it at Evelyn, giving her a couple of hard kicks with his right foot to get her away from him. Being older, weaker and shorter, she stumbles backwards, crashing into the bathroom wall, banging her head and sliding down to the floor as she cries out in pain.

Jason aims the gun down, pointing it right at her head, his finger on the trigger just as the bathroom door is kicked in by the boot of a police officer. Seeing what's happening, the officer yells out to his colleagues for back-up.

'Suspect has a gun! Suspect armed!' He reaches for his taser, pulling it from its holster and pointing it directly at Jason. 'Put the gun down now!' the officer yells at Jason, who swings round to face him, the gun's barrel now aiming at the officer's face.

The officer brandishes the taser. 'Last chance! Put the gun on the floor!' he yells again, his voice loud and commanding. Another officer appears behind the first, also with a bright yellow taser in his hands.

Jason draws breath. 'But I wasn't going to—'

'*Now!* Drop your weapon!' the other officer yells.

As Jason changes position, trying to explain what has happened, the barrel of the shotgun lifts higher towards the officers.

'*Taser, taser, taser!*' shouts the first one, preparing to discharge the stun gun.

FORTY

JASON

'Stop! Don't shoot!'

Jason freezes, his eyes wide as he realises what's about to happen. Slowly, he places the shotgun on the ground, not taking his eyes off the police as he raises his empty hands above his head.

It barely takes the officers a second to put their weapons back in their holsters and lunge at him, removing the shotgun to a safe place before manhandling him to the ground. Jason's arms are forced behind his back, and he feels one of the officer's boots in the lower part of his spine, pinning him down. His face is pressed sideways on the cold, filthy floor, the stink of piss even worse down here.

He hears a woman's whimpering – Evelyn sobbing to the police about her ordeal.

'Oh my God, I was so scared,' she wails. 'He was going to shoot me. Thank God you came.'

'Jesus Christ!' Jason screams as best he can, given his mouth is flattened on the tiles. 'I was *not* going to shoot her! She was about to—'

Then he hears the words he never wanted to hear.

'I am arresting you on suspicion of possessing a firearm with the intent to injure...' As the officer cites several other wrongdoings, he hears them, but he also doesn't hear them. He can't believe this is happening.

'I was not going to injure *anyone*,' he shrieks as the two officers haul him upright. There's another officer present now, assisting Evelyn, escorting her from the bathroom. 'It's not even my shotgun! If you'd arrived a few minutes earlier, you'd have seen *her* aiming it at *me*, for God's sake!'

'But we didn't see that, did we now?' one officer replies in a patronising tone. 'Come on, co-operate so we can get you cuffed. If you struggle, we'll nick you for resisting arrest as well.'

A moment later, Jason's hands, which are still pinned behind his back, are secured together with cold metal handcuffs.

'You're making a terrible mistake,' he says, twisting his shoulders round in protest. 'I was about to call *you*, for heaven's sake,' Jason rants as he's led out of the bathroom. 'That woman is crazy! She was about to...' He trails off as, to his horror, he sees Evelyn in the kitchen pointing to a sweatshirt on her kitchen table, showing a female officer.

'The fabric is red, but you can clearly see the bloodstains,' she says, lifting it up. 'The dark crusty bits there, look. There's no doubt this top belongs to my missing daughter. And I swear *he's* got something to do with Sascha's disappearance,' she says, giving Jason a sly look, adding a sob for the officer's sake. 'He had it with him when he broke into my house, see, like it was some kind of trophy or something. Oh, dear Lord...' Evelyn wobbles and touches her temple. 'If you do your testing stuff on it, you'll find Sascha's DNA or some of her hairs proving it's hers, and the blood... it could be hers *or* his.' She jabs a finger at Jason as he's led through. 'My Sash wouldn't go down without a fight.'

'You lying old bitch!' Jason snarls. '*You* did that when you punched me in the—'

'Enough already!' the officer booms in his ear. 'Get that sealed up in an evidence bag, would you, Leanne?' he says to the constable. She nods in return.

As Jason is taken through the living room, he glances up the stairs to see if there's any sign of Fiona, but it seems quiet. *Dear God, let her have got away*, he thinks as they go outside through the smashed-in front door. A red battering ram lies on the carpet beside splinters of wood.

There are two marked police cars stationed outside the house, and a few neighbours have gathered on the street to see what's going on. Someone is filming the scene on their phone as Jason is led out of the cottage. He has no idea who called the police – or, indeed, why. He feels a hand press down on the top of his head as he's ushered into the back of the car, an officer getting in beside him.

'Where are you taking me?' he asks, about to say so that he can let his wife know. But he decides against that. The less they know about Fiona's involvement, the better. *The less they know about* anything *the better*, he thinks, as his mind frantically tries to work out how he's going to get out of this mess. All he wanted was to find his missing daughters, to take them and Fiona back home, keep them safe, follow the rules, have a happy life together. But now this...

He can't help the couple of choked sobs that work their way up his throat.

Get a grip, you big baby! a voice booms in his head. *Grow up, you useless snivelling little prick! You don't deserve to call yourself a Hewitt.*

As the car starts and the driver pulls away, Jason stares out of the window at the street outside Evelyn's house. And that's when he realises his Ford is not there.

Thank God. Fiona has got away.

·   ·   ·

The cell is stark and grey and cold, but not quite as grim as he'd imagined. He's often wondered what it would feel like to be locked up – like the patients in the high-security wing at Radmoor – and now here he is, experiencing similar himself. It's noisy in the police station – constant shouting and swearing and protests as other prisoners are locked up or escorted out. Also similar to Radmoor, he thinks, having visited the secure wing many times in the past.

When they brought him in, Jason remained calm and dignified at the custody desk as he was being checked in, causing no problems for either of the arresting officers, or the custody sergeant booking him. They took his possessions, including his phone, the laces from his trainers and his belt, making a list of everything. Not that he had much on him anyway.

Now he sits on the single bunk, knees drawn up to his chin, a rough grey blanket slung around his shoulders as he takes shallow gulps, trying to stifle the sobs. His father's voice is still there, deep inside his head, telling him what a pathetic failure he is. It's as though he never died at all.

An hour later – or maybe it's five, ten, twenty hours, he's not sure – a detective and a uniformed officer arrive at his door, the clanking waking him from a fitful, uncomfortable doze.

'You're on, Mr Hewitt,' the female detective says, hands on hips in the doorway. She beckons him over with her head.

Jason recognises her to be the officer who came to their house last week enquiring about Sascha's disappearance – DI Alice Winters. Her piercing blue eyes flick all over him, making him feel uncomfortable.

'This way,' the male officer says, leading Jason out of the cell. He's already been asked if he wants a duty solicitor with him for his interview, but he declined. Though having spent time stewing in the cell, he's beginning to think it might have been a good idea after all, even if just for advice about a 'no comment' interview. But then surely that's almost as good as an admission of guilt – accepting representation – isn't it? An innocent man does not need a lawyer. His whole body shivers. He doesn't know what's best any more.

Once seated in the interview room, he looks around. There's only one window, up high with wired glass and bars on the outside, but it's not open. It's not even cold outside, but the involuntary shudders run through his body every few seconds, as though he's got a fever.

Another plainclothes officer joins DI Winters – DI Rachel something or other, almost a carbon copy of her colleague – and the pair chat in low voices. Jason can't be bothered listening or trying to work out what they know or what evidence they have against him. If he's honest, he can't believe this is even happening, him sitting here in a police interview room after being arrested for brandishing a gun he doesn't even own. A gun he was trying to prevent going off in his face. He lets out a weary sigh as the officer explains they'll be recording the interview.

'Can I just say,' Jason begins, 'as a medical doctor and upstanding citizen who has never been in trouble with the law or even had so much as a parking fine, I am utterly innocent and was *not*, contrary to your beliefs and what it may have seemed like at the time, about to shoot the woman whose house I was in.'

'OK, we'll get to that in a moment, Dr Hewitt,' DI Winters says, reciting their names for the recording, as well as stating where they are and the date and time. 'Right, so firstly, do you admit that you were in Evelyn Masters' house without her permission, having broken into the property while she was not at home?'

'Well, yes, but... but it wasn't like that,' he says. 'You have to believe me. I was looking for my daughters. They'd left our house, you see. I didn't know where they were. I'd tracked

Tilly's phone to Evelyn's property. The back door was open and—'

'How old are your daughters, Dr Hewitt?' DI Rachel Whatever asks.

Jason swallows. 'Fifteen and eight.'

'And you didn't – or *don't* – know their whereabouts?' She sounds incredulous.

Jason shakes his head, staring down at the table. 'No.'

'So they're missing?'

'I... I don't know. I think so, yes.' Jason stares down at his lap.

'Missing since when? Have you reported it? Is there an incident number?'

'No,' Jason replies in a voice that doesn't sound like his. He feels empty and desolate inside. 'I haven't. Not yet.'

FORTY-ONE

JASON

Before

I can't deny, there were many times over the years that I wanted to murder Erika – and I'm sure she felt the same about me. To stop myself from going through with it, I would play out the scene in my head, imagining what it would be like to watch her take her last breath, snuffing her out. Each occasion, it was a different scenario – sometimes I strangled her, sometimes I shot her, sometimes I stabbed her, and sometimes I pushed her off a cliff. It would all play out in slow motion while I watched on, scrutinising every moment of her death.

But in her make-believe demise, the worrying thing was that I never felt a damn thing, not a shred of emotion as she reached the end of her life. Which told me everything I needed to know – there would be no love lost between us when it happened for real.

I should say that this wasn't always the case – I'm not hard-hearted or some kind of sociopath. Far from it. But we both admitted that we'd grown apart these last few years, as often happens to couples after decades of marriage and the stresses of children, when careers and modern life get a stranglehold over the early flushes of new love.

We'd met at Karolinska Institutet in Sweden when, aged twenty, I took a year overseas partway through my medical studies. Erika was a medical student there herself, and we first encountered each other in the most mundane of places – the canteen queue at lunchtime. If I hadn't heard my name called out from somewhere across the hall, if I hadn't swung around abruptly, I'd never have accidentally swiped the tray of hot food from Erika's hands as she stood close behind me. And I'd never have been on my hands and knees at her feet, apologising frantically and immediately cleaning up the mess, offering to buy her another lunch as she towered over me with an amused smile on her face.

It happened to be my lunch break too, so we sat together – yes, she forgave me for my clumsiness – her eating a mushroom stroganoff and me a smoked salmon salad. Even after we'd finished, we sipped tea and chatted as if we'd known each other all our lives. For the next few weeks, we continued to meet up for lunch when our schedules allowed, sharing a table and each of us looking annoyed if anyone else should join us, interrupting our increasingly intimate chats. Not intimate in a sexual sense – rather, intimate in a vulnerable, personal way. Nothing was off topic.

'So you never really knew your mother?' Erika reflected back at me as I explained how she'd died under tragic circumstances when I was eight, that I'd never got over it. But I didn't mention that I'd never forgiven my father. 'It must have been so hard, being sent away to boarding school at such a young age.'

Her gentle yet clipped accent did something to me, I admit, and my interest in the Oedipus complex had not been in vain. It gave her emotional authority over me, her kind words caressing me in a way that was foreign both in sound *and* because I'd never experienced such a feeling before. Her constant kindness often made me want to cry, and it was only my father's stern voice ringing around my head that prevented me breaking down at our lunches.

Then one day, I plucked up the courage to ask her out on a date.

'You took your time,' she said slyly, glancing sideways at me with a wink as we walked arm in arm. Erika was about two inches taller than me, more so in her wedge-heeled boots. And I liked that about her – enjoyed looking up to her in so many ways. She was brilliant in mind, body and soul.

'I wasn't sure you'd say yes,' I admitted. 'To a clumsy Englishman who knocked your food from your hands.'

'I always say yes to clumsy Englishmen,' she replied as we headed to the cinema. Of course, I didn't understand a word of the film, and Erika had to keep whispering the plot in my ear, with people sitting around us getting increasingly annoyed by the interruptions. Then one time when Erika was about to explain something, I turned my head towards her and stole our first kiss.

The softness of her lips became just a hazy memory as, decades later, I imagined poisoning her or hiring a hit man to take her out. I didn't know what had happened to our deep chats, the laughter we'd shared, the long walks we'd taken in the rain; the cooking together, the reading together – she loved it when I recited poetry – and the just being together doing absolutely nothing. All of it had since hardened into an uncomfortable shell that didn't fit my soul any more.

I didn't mean to fall out of love with her.

I didn't mean to fall in love with Fiona.

I'll never forget those few minutes it took me to change the course of Fiona's life – the point at which there became a *before* and an *after*.

'Fiona,' I said an hour before we were to be married. We were in her hospital room – nothing unusual there as I often had reason to be in and out – and my hands were set squarely on her shoulders while our faces were close. She was wearing her pale blue lacy dress, looking angelic with her light make-up and freshly washed hair, ready for our wedding. But I wanted to make sure she understood, completely grasped the seriousness of what I was about to tell her. 'Listen to me. Erika is dead. Do you understand?'

There. It was out. The gravity of it hanging in the air between us like a smog. Though she had no idea what she'd done.

'Oh my *God*,' she whispered. 'I... I don't believe it. That's terrible. I'm so sorry.'

She stared vacantly over my shoulder for a while, then her eyes latched back onto mine. A muscle on her cheek danced. 'But... but, dear God forgive me, but it's *not* terrible, is it? For us, I mean.'

I sighed, wondering if the news was sinking in. She seemed completely unperturbed, but I needed her to understand what she'd done, accept the seriousness of her crime.

'The answer to that is yes *and* no,' I admitted, feeling wretched for my girls, who, at that point, knew nothing about their mother's very recent death.

'But surely it means we can be together now,' Fiona stated, her hands clasped under her chin. 'Without Erika getting in the way.' She looked so naive, so innocent, and I was about to blow her world apart. 'Doesn't it?'

'Fiona, what you don't understand is...' I hesitated. This would be the hardest sentence I'd ever have to say in my life. Well, apart from breaking the news the next day to my daughters. 'Fiona, listen – *you* killed her. Do you hear me? You murdered Erika.'

For a while, there was nothing. Just silence and staring as

Fiona took in what I'd told her. Behind her vacant eyes, I imagined her brain scanning through recent memories, even rummaging through older ones, in the hope of digging up a clue that would trigger the terrible realisation that yes, she had indeed killed Erika Norstrom during one of her severely psychotic episodes.

'But...' she uttered quietly. 'But... no, no I did not.' She emitted a nervous laugh.

I gripped her hands, bringing them up to my chest. 'Yes, my darling, I'm so sorry, but you did. Do you remember in our sessions how we talked about your mind blocking out traumatic events? It's a protection mechanism, because of the terrible abuse you witnessed as a child.'

She gave a little nod. A frown.

'It's happened again,' I told her. 'Forcing memories won't bring them back.'

She shook her head, a frown sitting at the top of her nose.

'But... how did it happen? Where? When?' she asked quietly, as if she was asking a friend to remind her about a shopping trip they'd been on. 'Am I in trouble with the police? I really don't recall—'

'Details don't matter,' I told her. 'Knowing the minutiae of what happened is simply going to traumatise you more. Your brain needs space to process what you've done and—'

'If it's true, then... then I need to turn myself in,' she said, quite calmly, pulling away from me. The expression on her face told me that she was finally accepting of her crime – she had no reason to disbelieve me, her doctor and her fiancé – but it also told me that she was intent on doing the right thing and give herself up. But I didn't let go of her. There was no way I would allow her to tell a single soul what she'd done. No one had witnessed Erika's demise, and I wanted to keep it that way.

'No, Fiona, you must not do that. What about *us*? What about our future and everything we've got planned? You were right when you said that it's all possible for us now that Erika is gone.'

She bit her lip, torn, frowning, a soft sheen of perspiration forming on her face.

'I think you're right. I *did* do something terrible, didn't I?' She sat down on the edge of her bed, the horror of what had happened dawning on her. 'It's gradually coming back. I sense it. I *feel* it. There's something in there...' She touched her forehead, and I lowered myself down beside her, giving her time to absorb the news. I wanted it to sink in. For her to know, to fully understand, that in no uncertain terms she'd killed my wife. That she needed protecting from herself.

'Fiona, listen to me,' I said. 'I will take care of you. I will help you. Do you trust me?' I lifted her chin with my finger. She had tears in her eyes.

'Oh my God, what have I done? I don't believe it... not again... I'm *evil*... It's all so terrible... What did I do? I mean, *how* did I...?' It was clear she wasn't going to let up until I gave her something to process.

'It was thankfully quick. You strangled Erika with a laptop cable,' I informed her, keeping facts to a minimum. 'Listen, Fiona, you are a patient here at Radmoor. Do you understand that? If you turn yourself in, you're never coming out of here. *Ever.* You'll be incarcerated in North Wing for the rest of your life.'

'Can I see her?'

I shook my head. 'No... Fiona, no. That would not be helpful for you. I've already dealt with her body. She's at peace now, buried in the woods. No one saw me. No one knows, but I had to protect you. I couldn't let you go down for this – not since you've been making such good progress. Do you hear me?'

Fiona frowned. 'I... I don't know. My memory is so patchy. I hate it that my brain lies to me... covers things up.' She let out a whimper.

'Look, it's not the first time you've killed someone, is it, Fiona?' I gently reminded her. 'And you didn't recall that immediately either, did you? It's why the judge was more lenient. Because of your mental health. But there might not be a second chance this time.'

She nodded, finally accepting what had happened – that somehow, a psychotic episode had been triggered and she'd behaved in a similar way. And after a little more coaxing, she also believed that I'd taken care of everything.

'All we need to do is lie low for a while,' I told her. 'Keep ourselves to ourselves, with you and the girls staying home as much as possible. We'll stick to the rules, and we absolutely must *not* attract any kind of attention from the police. Do you understand? Do you think you can do all that, Fiona?'

In reply, she simply gave me a vague nod.

FORTY-TWO
FIONA

Fiona sat in the car outside Evelyn's cottage for as long as she dared, her knuckles white as she gripped the steering wheel. She felt terrible for leaving Jason inside, but she knew he'd want her to get out. She stared straight ahead through the windscreen, her body motionless. Should she drive off, abandoning Jason to his fate if Evelyn called the police, or go back inside to help him, risking getting caught herself? For a while, the indecision made her do nothing, Cora's whining from the back seat irritating her, making her nerves jangle.

Shortly before, when she'd gone upstairs in the cottage, she'd found the main bedroom empty. She'd then checked the second bedroom, just wanting to get back downstairs to Jason so they could leave before Evelyn came back.

She'd been hit by a musty, stale smell, and a pair of grimy lilac curtains were drawn across the small window. Boxes and piles of old magazines were strewn everywhere, plus heaps of old clothes and bedding shoved on the floor to one side.

'Hello?' Fiona had whispered from the doorway, convinced she'd just heard something – a snuffling sound coming from behind some boxes. 'Who's there?' Then she'd caught sight of a pair of eyes in the corner, looking up at her, blinking. 'Cora? Is that you?'

Silence for a moment and then a small figure had emerged. The little girl had stared up at Fiona with tears in her eyes.

'Oh, sweetheart,' she'd whispered, holding out her hand. 'Come here, I won't hurt you.'

Those last few words had echoed through Fiona's head... *I won't hurt you...* and she'd wondered just how true they were – how much control she really had over her actions.

Cora had hesitated but then clambered over the boxes to Fiona.

'Did your grandma leave you all alone?'

Cora had nodded.

'You must feel scared. Do you know when she's coming back?'

Cora had shaken her head. 'Is Ivy here?' she'd then asked, her face suddenly brightening.

Fiona had swallowed. 'No, I'm afraid not,' she'd said in a shaky voice. 'Not today.'

'Where is she?' Cora had folded her arms in front of her, scowling. 'Did she go off to find her *real* mummy?'

'Cora!' Fiona had gasped, wishing she'd kept her voice down. 'You know I'm Ivy's real mummy. Don't say things like that.'

'You're not! Tilly told me. And Ivy hates you. I bet they've gone to find their proper mummy so they can have her and not you.'

A shudder had run down Fiona's spine then, every nerve in her body suddenly on red alert. What was the child talking about? Had she even heard her correctly? The girls had gone to find their *mother*?

Then, as if it had been someone else witnessing it, she'd

seen a hand reach out and roughly grab Cora's upper arm. Her head had whipped back.

'What do you mean, they've gone to find their mother?' Fiona had snapped, regretting it instantly when Cora's cheeks turned bright red, her bottom lip quivering. Maybe the girls were heading to the crematorium where Jason had told them Erika's ashes were interred – a lie, of course, but they couldn't tell them the truth.

Cora had begun to cry.

'Oh my God, I'm *so* sorry, Cora. I didn't mean to hurt you. Look, how about we go and find Ivy so you two can play together? I'll make you some brownies and you can play in the pool again. Does that sound nice?'

Cora had sniffed, staring up at Fiona. 'You *promise* we can go in the pool and not just watch TV?'

'Cross my heart and hope to die,' Fiona had replied, at exactly the same moment they'd suddenly heard a woman's voice yelling out downstairs.

How Fiona got the child out of the house without them being discovered, or without the child calling out to her grandmother, she had no idea. But she did. Sitting in the car as she gripped the steering wheel, she swallowed, glancing out of the side window at Evelyn's cottage. There was no sign of anyone – though she'd heard a terrible commotion as they'd left. It sounded as if a fight was about to break out.

Evelyn had sounded angry as hell, yelling at Jason as they'd crept downstairs. Fiona had held her breath as she'd opened the back door, praying it wouldn't creak. Once they'd got outside, Fiona had dragged Cora by the hand, dashing round the side of the house and onto the street where the Ford was parked. Thankfully, she had the keys in her shoulder bag, after Jason had given them to her when they'd arrived.

'Quick, get in the back. Put your seatbelt on,' Fiona had instructed, opening the door for Cora. Getting in the car herself, she fumbled with the keys and started the engine, glancing back at the cottage in case Jason should come running out.

But he didn't – and he still hadn't. Fiona wasn't sure how long she should wait.

'Is Grandma cross with Ivy's daddy?' Cora whined from the back.

'I don't know,' Fiona said vaguely, trying to ignore the child's questions, indecision gnawing at her conscience. Her foot hovered over the accelerator, one hand on the gear stick, ready to go. 'Come on... come *on*,' she muttered as the ringing in her ears started up – a sign she was getting stressed and anxious, that her brain was overloading.

'Where's Mummy?' Cora chimed again from the back. '*I want my mummy... Where's Ivy...? Where's Tilly...? Where are we going...? What's Grandma doing...? I want Mummy...*'

Cora's incessant questions cut through Fiona's head, making her cover her ears and screw up her eyes. But then she was flooded with images of Erika – her eyes bulging as she imagined herself tightening an electrical cable around her neck... Then she saw Sascha in her mind, her body bloodied and beaten on the bathroom floor when all she wanted to do was cook dinner, take a bath... Ivy and Tilly still missing... their fate unknown.

Then it was Amber's voice she heard, her words cutting through her jumbled thoughts... *I thought they'd have gone to the old field barn...*

It was the piercing sound of sirens that snapped Fiona back to the moment – sirens that were getting closer. Up ahead, she saw two police cars speeding round the corner towards Evelyn's house. Without needing to think about it any longer, Fiona shoved the car into gear, took the handbrake off and pressed down on the accelerator, driving away from the cottage and using all her self-control not to speed away. Drawing attention to herself was the last thing she wanted to do.

'Where are we going?' Cora asked from the back.

'We're going to find Ivy and Tilly,' Fiona said, glancing in the mirror, giving the little girl a smile to reassure her. Her arms were shaking as she gripped the wheel. 'Because I think I know where they are.'

FORTY-THREE

FIONA

Now, Fiona drives fast, bumping over potholes, skidding around corners on the country lanes. A couple of times, she jams on the brakes to avoid cars coming the other way, one hooting as they narrowly miss each other.

'Where is it, where *is* it...?' she mumbles, leaning closer to the steering wheel. She squints as she rounds another bend, the sun suddenly dazzling her. She flips down the visor just as she spots the lay-by on the left.

She pulls over and unclips her seatbelt, swinging round to look at Cora.

'Come on, get out. You'll have to come with me.'

The child will slow her down, but she can't leave her alone in the car. Perhaps her presence will convince Ivy, and therefore Tilly, to come home if she finds them hiding where she suspects they are. She'll bribe them with chocolate brownies and fun in the paddling pool. Then Jason will come home, and they will all laugh with relief, and she will cook a nice dinner and they will have plenty to talk about at the family confessional tonight, and then Jason will collect up all their phones and they can watch a Disney movie, then it will be bedtime and he will give her some pills and—

'F*iona*!'

There's a bang on the driver's side window. Fiona whips her head round to see Cora standing on the lane, thumping the glass.

'Are you coming? I want to see Ivy!'

For a moment, Fiona remains frozen, but then she gets out of the car and helps Cora climb over the wooden post-and-rail fence leading to the field to the side of the wooded area. There's a steep hill this way, but it avoids having to push through the thicket of trees.

When they reach the top of the incline, hand in hand, Fiona has beads of sweat on her face. She takes off her sweatshirt and ties it around her waist, revealing a white T-shirt beneath. They trudge across the undulating field until, in the distance, Fiona spots the back of their house in the cul-de-sac.

'Not far now,' she tells Cora, veering east in the direction of the old oak tree and the riding stables. But it's not the stables they're heading to. No, it's the red-brick field barn that has just come into view beyond the next hedge. The barn where Amber told her Tilly and Ivy sometimes hang out.

Fiona and Cora climb over the final stile, heading towards the barn nestled in a cluster of trees.

'Are we going to the hideout?' Cora asks. 'Ivy told me about it. She said it was creepy.'

Fiona gives her hand a squeeze. 'Don't worry, it won't be creepy. And anyway, I'm here,' she says, feeling apprehensive when she spots the smashed-in windows as they approach the barn. 'We might even spot a pony nearby.'

'Will there be ponies inside the barn too?'

'Maybe,' Fiona says as they draw up to the building. As they skirt around the outside of it, she wonders if it's even safe to go in. Part of the roof and one gable end wall have caved in, with many of the slates missing, and there's broken glass and crumbling bricks everywhere.

When they reach the other side of the barn, Fiona notices that the old stable door is closed. Part of her hopes it's locked so that no one could be inside, and then she can head back to the car and go home, where she'll find Jason and the girls waiting for her, all of them happy and smiling, and things can get back to normal.

But as she puts her hand on the old metal latch, pressing down on the lever, she senses that won't be the case.

She stops.

'Cora, go and sit under that tree over there,' she instructs, pointing to a spot where the little girl can wait. She doesn't want her to get injured or scared. She pulls her phone from her pocket, unlocking it. 'Here, you can play a game.'

That seals it for Cora, and she skips off to the base of the tree.

Fiona pushes the door open and steps inside. Until her eyes grow used to it, she's met with almost total darkness, as well as a fusty, animal smell with... with something else, too. The smell of something decaying. The smell of...

Fiona retches, clapping her hand over her mouth as the stink permeates her nose, her mouth, her ears... everything.

'The smell of *death*,' she whispers, wishing she'd got her phone so she could put the torch on. She shuffles further into the barn, taking her sweatshirt from around her waist and pressing it over her mouth and nose. The smell is revolting.

On the opposite wall, there's a window with an old board propped up against it, seemingly only held in place by cobwebs. She tugs at it a few times, eventually dislodging it and sending it crashing to the barn floor. A shaft of light streams in, highlighting the cloud of dust. When it's settled, Fiona stares around the interior of the barn, which is, as she suspected, filled with rubble from the roof and part of the end wall collapsing. She hates the thought of Tilly and Ivy coming up here alone.

On the back wall is a brick-built feeding trough with metal bars, and in one corner is a large stack of chopped firewood that looks as though it's been collected over the years from fallen trees. And there are a couple of bits of farm machinery – possibly ploughing or raking attachments for a tractor, while at the other end of the barn is what was once a stack of straw bales, but it has now disintegrated and mostly fallen into a rotting heap.

And that's when Fiona sees the foot poking out from under the straw.

A female foot, judging by its size and the pink and white trainer on the end of it. It's twisted at an odd angle.

Fiona recoils, stifling a scream as she presses the sweatshirt harder against her mouth. But she can't help the muffled exclamation when a rat runs out from under the straw near the leg, scuttling across to the other end of the barn, its long tail trailing behind.

'Oh my God, oh my God, oh my *God*...' she squeals into the fabric. 'What the hell...? *Who* the hell...?'

She takes a couple of steps closer to the foot in case there's something about the trainer or lower part of the leg that will identify the poor person buried under the straw. They're wearing blue denim jeans, a pale grey sock and the trainer. She gasps as she spots the blood spattered around the bottom of the jeans – dark, crusty and long since congealed. Another retch forces up Fiona's throat.

This is not good. This is not good at all, she thinks, frantically trying to remember the colour of the girls' trainers. The foot looks too big to be Ivy's, but it's about the right size for Tilly. Though she doesn't think she has pink trainers.

Deciding she must be brave, Fiona kicks some straw out of the way, revealing another leg, although this one is bent back in an unnatural position as though several bones are broken. And on this leg, there's an even larger patch of dried blood halfway up the jeans.

Fiona searches around for something to move the straw with so she doesn't have to touch it. She spots a few gardening implements propped up against a wall – including a long-handled fork. She shovels the straw out of the way, careful not to hurt whoever is under there – though she suspects they're long past feeling pain.

'Oh, dear *God*,' she says as a hand and arm are revealed. As she clears away more of the straw, it's obvious that it's a woman – especially when she uncovers the torso. She feels sick and light-headed, and her vision swims in and out of focus as she sees the blood-soaked clothing the woman is wearing – a once grey and green cotton top, now cracked and crusty with dark brown congealed blood. A mass of flies suddenly swarms out from under the straw, buzzing past Fiona's head.

She yelps, recoiling and batting them away, screwing up her eyes as their droning gets inside her head. When she opens her eyes again, there are no flies any more, but she still hears them... a *buzz, buzz, buzz* inside her brain, driving her mad as she frantically starts swiping away the straw over the body's head.

'Please don't be Tilly,' she wails, chucking the fork aside and dropping to her knees to finish uncovering the body by hand. She grabs masses of the loose straw, swiping and brushing it aside, finally revealing the blue-purple-almost-black face of the decomposing body beneath.

'Oh, dear *God*,' she says, feeling a rush of relief when it's not Tilly. But she immediately realises who it is, the buzzing inside her head growing even louder. 'Sascha... no, oh Christ no... *Sascha...*' she sobs as she sees her friend lying dead and bloody and decomposed in front of her. She knows for sure it's her because of the small butterfly tattoo just visible on the side of her neck.

Just as she's about to get up, her hand presses down on something hard and metallic beside the body's arm. When she looks down, the buzzing in her head stops – everything falling silent as she sees the item lying there, trying to work out what it means. Trying to work out how it got there.

It's Fiona's wristwatch – the silver one that Jason gave her as a gift not long after they got married.

She picks it up to check, but there's no doubt it's hers. Engraved with her name and a loving message from Jason on the back. The faulty catch is undone, and the glass face is cracked. The buzzing in her head starts up again just as another fly escapes from the body.

Fiona leaps back, screaming as she covers her ears, screws up her eyes, but there's no escaping the voice in her head: *You did this. You killed Sascha!*

FORTY-FOUR

FIONA

She feels contaminated and dirty, as if her body is crawling with insects. Flies laying eggs under her skin, worms squirming inside her mouth and ears. Bugs in her hair, beneath her clothes, her skin erupting with blisters.

Fiona drops the watch down again and rushes for the barn door, squinting as she charges outside into the sunlight, stumbling on a pile of bricks. She needs to get away – from her dead friend, from the dirt, the infections, the bugs. From what she did.

She gasps for fresh air.

The memories are like a broken mirror in her mind – each piece containing a small part of what she did.

'Cora! Cora, come now!' she yells, seeing her still sitting at the base of the tree.

Cora looks up slowly. 'Hang on, I just need to finish this—'

'Now!'

She can't let the child witness the horror inside the barn. If she sees her mother in that state, the trauma will never leave her. It will eat her up from the inside out, shaping her into a person like... like... *Like me*, Fiona thinks, holding out her hand to the little girl. 'Come on!'

Cora quickly gets up and trots along beside her as they head briskly back through the fields towards the car.

'Where are we going? Where's Ivy? Wasn't she in the barn?'

'Stop asking questions,' Fiona snaps, breathless. She just needs to hold it together until she can get help – and before she hurts anyone else. Just needs to stay focused on reality, grounding herself and keeping the anxiety and dissociation at bay. *Not long now*, she tells herself as they approach the lay-by. She fixes her eyes on the trees ahead, the car just coming into view beyond.

'But you said I could play with Ivy,' Cora whines as they climb over the final stile. Fiona holds Cora's hand as she swings one leg over the wooden rail, then the other, before jumping down into the lay-by the other side.

It would be so easy to shut her up, the voice says. *To snuff out her little life, drag her body back up to the barn. Bury her beneath the straw with her mother for the flies and the rats to feast on. Will you do it? Go on... Do it... do it... do it...!*

'No, no... stop it!' she cries, covering her face. 'Go away! Get out of my head!'

'What's wrong, Fiona?' Cora asks, looking back over the fence at her.

At the sound of her young voice, Fiona feels a moment of clarity. She stares down at the child, knowing she doesn't want to harm a hair on her head. But then she didn't want to harm Erika, either.

Yet she *did*. She knows she did.

Similarly, she has no recollection of injecting the medication into the IV of the patient brought into A&E that night. Just the awful aftermath of the investigation, enquiry, court cases, dismissal and the end of her career.

Yet she did that too.

And now Sascha – her new friend. The friend that was nothing but kind to her. The friend who worked hard and was a good mother. The friend who was trying to make a go of it with Steve, Cora's father. The friend lying dead and rotting, looking as if she was beaten to death on a barn floor.

Yet she did that too. How else did her watch end up at the scene?

'Nothing's wrong, sweetheart,' Fiona says, trying to sound normal. 'Ivy and Tilly weren't in their hideout.' *Thank God*, she thinks. 'But I think I know where they might be. Shall we go and see them?'

The truth is, Fiona has no idea where they are. But she's certain what she must do now to save this little girl's life. To protect her from an unknown fate that she wouldn't be able to stop if her mind sank her into that dark place again.

Fiona has become too good at switching. Too good at protecting herself from her father's anger. Too adept at becoming someone else entirely to hide from the trauma of what she did. Too skilled at forgetting all the bad things she's done.

'Buckle up, sweetheart,' Fiona says shakily once they're in the car. She puts her destination into Google Maps. 'Twenty-five minutes,' she whispers. The time it will take to get back to Radmoor Hospital. Less than half an hour until she can turn herself in, protecting Cora... Tilly, Ivy, Jason and anyone else who might cross her path in the future and happen, by coincidence and bad timing, to trigger something so evil lurking inside Fiona that she kills them too.

As she nears her destination, she grows more and more anxious. Nothing about the scenery looks familiar as she drives first along A roads and then country lanes. And nothing in her life feels familiar any more, either. She has no idea when she last took her tablets, or if they were even the correct dose. At Radmoor, she would get regular blood tests to monitor her medications, but since they left, Jason hasn't had access to labs. He's been so stoic, hardly complaining at all about having to take the job at the university when she knows how much he misses his work at the hospital. He did it all for her – to protect her, to save her, to be with her.

I love you, Jason, says the voice in her head.

'Are we nearly there yet?' another voice says – high-pitched and young.

Fiona glances in the rear-view mirror and smiles. 'Not long now.'

A few minutes later and she drives past the pub where she and Jason first met. But the memory barely touches her, as if it belongs to someone else. The relationship that followed – their clandestine meets, their walks around the hospital grounds, their lovemaking, their late-night chats, their exciting plans, their romantic trip to York, their marriage ceremony in the woods – all so perfect. Yet all so wrong.

Fiona grips the wheel, grateful that her emotions are stone-cold right now. She's happy to feel numb with nothing to trigger her. Content to be driving along with nothing but empty space in her mind. Fleetingly, she wonders what Jason is doing right now. If he's OK. If he escaped Evelyn's cottage unscathed. She knows the police were heading there – she watched them pull up outside in her mirror as she drove away.

The sun flickers through the trees – almost blinding her with its staccato flashes as she drives. 'Oh my God!' she cries, jamming on the brakes.

Her foot slips off the clutch, making the car lurch and stall. Tilly and Ivy are standing in front of the car, their hands spread out on the bonnet, the pair of them inches away from being run over. They're staring at her through the windscreen, their faces pale and shocked.

'It's Ivy!' Cora squeals from the back seat, unclipping her seatbelt and opening the door.

'No, stay there, Cora, it's dangerous on the road,' Fiona says in a voice that doesn't sound like her own – robotic and flat. She gets out of the car and stands beside it, staring at the two girls. 'There you are,' she says, meaning it to come out in a friendly, relieved way. But instead, her words sound cold and serious, making them step back a couple of paces.

'Come on, Ivy,' Tilly says to her sister, taking her by the hand. 'Just keep walking.' They turn to go.

'No, wait!' Fiona calls out – this time, sounding a little more like herself. Her vision swims and swirls, the sunlight in her eyes. She sees a flash of red on Ivy's T-shirt. Spots the red ruck-sack slung over Tilly's shoulder. More dizziness. More voices crying out through the years – a little girl lost. *Her.*

'We're not coming back with you,' Tilly says over her shoulder, holding Ivy's hand as they walk off. 'You and Dad...' she says scornfully, stopping briefly. 'It's all so wrong.'

'I know, I *know*... and it's fine... I understand you don't want to come back home,' Fiona says, surprising herself. *Do it, do it, do it...* the voice in her head growls. *Get them in the car...* 'But I'm happy to give you a lift wherever you like. It's dangerous walking out here on the lanes by yourselves. I nearly ran you over! You were lucky it was just me.'

'Come with us, Ivy!' Cora bleats through the open window. 'Please! Get in!' She beckons frantically with her hand to her little friend, giving her an enticing grin.

Tilly stops. Her shoulders hunched around her ears. She turns round. 'It's definitely just a lift?' she says, sounding wary. Fiona has no idea how far they've walked, but she can't imagine Ivy managing much further if they've come from Stow. 'You're not going to take us back to Kingshill?'

'I *promise* it's just a lift,' Fiona says reassuringly, smiling as she opens the passenger doors, her fingers crossed tightly behind her back. 'Just a lift to wherever you want.'

FORTY-FIVE
JASON

Before

A wedding *and* a house move – two big life events on the same day. It had been a lot to organise in a short space of time. I was concerned that Fiona would become overwhelmed, triggering some kind of unstable episode for her, but even after I'd told her about Erika's death, her mood had remained remarkably even.

I was proud of the way she handled everything – trusting me, relying on me. Deep down, I had a sense things were going to be OK, and besides, I'd got a briefcase full of medication, allowing me to continue with her treatment plan for many months yet. Not entirely legitimately obtained, but I was operating under emergency conditions, knowing we'd need to lie low for a good few months. Everyone would be out looking for us, what with leaving work without giving notice, and I knew the police would want to talk to me about Erika. It's always the husband – or in this case the *estranged*-husband – that they look to first.

'When we're settled in our new home, I'm going to take you shopping and buy you a wedding gift,' I promised her, already knowing I was going to get her a watch. Every time she looked at it, she'd be reminded of me. Of *us*. Of the time passing. Of the rest of our lives together.

Fiona looked across from the passenger seat of my car, smiling at me as we drove away from Radmoor as newlyweds. No backwards glances from either of us. Still wearing her pale blue lacy dress, the damage inside her was invisible to the naked eye. What other people would see when they met her was a happy, content, carefree woman with her future ahead of her. What *I* saw was all of that, but my trained eye had a secret spyhole into her interior world – a world filled with trauma and mistrust. A world in which she had no allies. A world from which there was no escape from the voices in her head. The only exit route for her was to become someone else entirely. To switch personalities for as long as it took to gain respite.

It was textbook psychiatry. And an easy diagnosis for a doctor such as me. I was also acutely aware how much our respective pasts overlapped on the trauma stakes, so from the moment I'd first learnt her patient history at Radmoor, I'd taken extra care not to project or transfer my own past sufferings onto her.

'Oh, it's *perfect*,' were Fiona's words when we first pulled up outside number 9 Hollybush Close on move-in day. Our wedding day. 'I still can't believe it's ours.' She got out of the car, not taking her eyes off the house, a grin plastered on her face.

Tilly and Ivy were quietly sobbing in the back of the car, and I virtually had to prise them out when we arrived, though I did understand their reluctance. They'd been taken out of school unexpectedly by a father who… well, I'd admit that I hadn't been around much for them lately – and then they'd been informed that their mother was dead. Oh, and I'd also had to tell them that I'd left my work at the hospital – promising them that I wouldn't be going back, that I'd take a job without such gruelling hours – and that they were moving in with me

and my new wife with barely any of their possessions. My heart
bled for my girls.

Earlier, though, I *had* made a quick dash home for a few of
their things – grabbing a soft toy for each of them, a few clothes,
some books and a couple of board games. I thought having some
familiar items might help them settle in more. Before leaving my
old home, I'd opened the garage door to see what else we might
need, and Fiona had taken a shine to a picnic basket set among
the camping stuff that Erika and I had only used a couple of
times, so I threw that in the boot too, promising her we'd go on a
family day out soon. But under the circumstances, I'd not
wanted to hang about long, so I locked up the entire house
securely, knowing that before too long it would have to be
packed up and sold. Though that was a problem for another
day.

As we unpacked the car at Hollybush Close, I caught sight
of several of our new neighbours' curtains twitching upon our
arrival. I smiled to myself. Give it a few months for the dust to
settle – perhaps a year to be on the safe side if I was able to
renew the lease – and I knew we'd fit in around here, making
friends while out on walks, chatting to people in the local pub,
inviting people round for dinner. In the autumn, Fiona was
keen for the girls to start at the nearby schools and make new
friends, though I still thought home-schooling was best. I knew
Fiona would soon make this house a home, and I was certain I
would find work before too long – in fact, I already had my eye
on a position at the university only ten miles away. It was where
I'd trained as a doctor – another reason why I was drawn to this
location.

But still, I felt it necessary to impress upon my family that,
for now at least, we must keep ourselves to ourselves. Let things
settle. A fresh start such as ours needed careful planning.

'There are a few house rules,' I announced to my daughters
when I brought our luggage inside, locking the front door. I

instructed Fiona to close all the curtains even though it wasn't dark yet. Tilly and Ivy stood in the living room, looking around at the unfamiliar furniture that came with the rental, their eyes red and sore, their fingers interlinked. They were still snivelling even though I'd already explained how the contained grieving time on Sundays would work: Rule Number 8.

'We don't want your stupid rules any more,' Tilly shot back. 'Mum hated them, and so do we.' I'd never seen her sneer like that before. At one point, I thought she was going to spit at me. 'We just want to go home. We want Mum back.'

'Oh, *Tills*,' I said, reaching out to touch her arm, perhaps give her a hug.

'Get off me!'

Ivy started crying then, hurling herself on the sofa and sobbing into the cushions. Fiona tried to comfort her while I tried to talk sense into Mathilda.

'Darling, look. None of this is ideal or what any of us expected, I know that. Please believe me when I say that I love you and Ivy more than life itself, but Mummy isn't here any more, and we must make the best of things. It's the three of us and Fiona now, OK?'

'No, it's not fucking OK, Dad! Not fucking OK in the least!' She flung her hands in the air, paced about, rattled and tugged at the locked front door and whipped back the living room curtains to bang on the glass. I yanked her back when she did that, closing them again. She was snivelling and panting and had the demeanour of a wild animal.

'It will take time, my darling, but I promise you, we will get there. We all will. Your mum wouldn't want you to be like this, would she? All upset and hysterical? She'd want you to be happy and settled.'

Tilly scoffed, sneering at me as she stood there, arms folded, her breaths shallow gulps. 'You have no idea what Mum would want. You two were barely speaking in the end! And she bitterly regretted you being at Radmoor. She hated having to see you there every day.'

Fiona was comforting Ivy, but I knew she was listening, tuning in. And I hoped she realised that not everything Tilly said was true. But this was a child's view of a complicated marriage. I couldn't expect Tilly to understand our nuanced relationship.

I'd already warned Fiona to keep her mouth shut about what had really happened to Erika last night. My daughters might one day come to terms with their mother dying in a car accident, but they would not accept murder. And especially not murder committed by their new stepmother. Tilly would go straight to the police if she knew the truth.

'Your mum was a beautiful person inside and out, Tilly,' I reassured her. There was a lump in my throat as I said the words, confusing me greatly. 'And no one can predict when accidents are going to happen. It's why we must strive to appreciate every moment with our loved ones. Trust me, darling, there will be a full investigation into the motorway pile-up, and an enquiry into why that lorry driver was over the drink-driving limit. I won't rest until we get justice for your mum, OK?'

Tilly dropped down onto the sofa then, seeming exhausted. There was so much grief inside her, it was blocking up all the exit routes, which was why I'd proposed the Sunday grieving time, along with some other rules for my daughters to abide by.

'You'll find that our daily family confessionals will bring a sense of peace and well-being to all of us,' I tried to convince Tilly. Ivy didn't seem to be listening and kept dozing off in a fitful sleep. 'And the time you'll have without the internet and your mobile devices is time to be cherished, not a punishment. You'll see.'

I also explained that, under the circumstances, I felt it best that the girls didn't attend their mother's funeral. At first, Tilly protested, demanding she be allowed to come, but when I explained that a crematorium was no place for an eight-year-old and that Ivy would benefit more from having her big sister at home to comfort her, she reluctantly agreed. By this point, Tilly was too broken to fight back. I knew she just needed time.

We spent the rest of that first day unpacking the few clothes and belongings we'd brought with us, trying to make the place seem homely. Then I made a quick trip to the local supermarket, stocking up on enough food to last a couple of weeks. I paid in cash, thanking my past self for the funds I'd squirrelled away.

When I returned home, still sitting in my car on the driveway, I saw our next-door neighbour, a woman from number 7, standing on the drive in front of her house. She was talking to a man sitting astride a motorbike, the engine rumbling, his helmet on. The woman, around the same age as Fiona, seemed to be having words with the man, looking exasperated and throwing her hands in the air. Then she shook her head and walked back towards the house, ushering a little girl on the doorstep inside.

I saw the child waving as the man rode away on his motorbike, though he didn't see her. Before the woman shut the door, she happened to glance my way as I was getting out of the car with the groceries.

We locked eyes for a moment, her face breaking into a smile as she raised her hand. 'Welcome to the village,' she called out, making her way over. 'I'm Sascha.'

But instead of replying, I hurried inside and shut the front door, locking it behind me.

FORTY-SIX

FIONA

'Look, just tell me where we're going,' Tilly demands from the passenger seat.

'I told you, just a quick stop-off first, then I'll take you wherever you want,' Fiona replies, sensing Tilly's nervousness. She's already asked three times, checking they're not heading back to Kingshill.

Inside Fiona's mind, there's a battle kicking off. She's trying hard – so, *so* hard – to keep the voices at bay. To keep the other part of her from taking over. She doesn't want to be *that* Fiona today. Doesn't want to sleepwalk through events over which she has no control. For once, she needs to do the right thing and turn herself in. She knows she is unwell. She knows she needs help. She knows she has done bad things. It's all over now.

'Keep going, keep going,' she mumbles under her breath. 'You're nearly there... nearly there. Then everyone will be safe...'

She recognises this stretch of road from her many illicit walks to the pub in search of alcohol – an easy way to obliterate the pain inside her. Getting blind drunk provided a respite when trauma prised open the cracks in her life.

But she can't do this alone any more. Knows that she's a danger to others – as well as to herself. She glances in the mirror, seeing Ivy and Cora chattering away.

They deserve a future, Fiona hears a voice say, gripping the wheel as she approaches the entrance to Radmoor's long driveway. *A future that I had stolen from me...*

She nods vehemently, agreeing with the voice in her head. But then another, louder one takes over, almost deafening her.

You're a murderer! Sick and twisted! Those three girls are sitting in a car with the woman who killed their mothers... Are you going to tell them what you did? Blood everywhere... drip... drip... drip...

As she stares through the windscreen, Fiona is suddenly back there, aged sixteen as she gazed down at her father on the bathroom floor. She'd lived her life trying not to be noticed by him. Leaving for school several hours too early. Hiding in her room when he got home from work.

It was the noise, his chest-bursting cries, that had caused her to stop outside the bathroom door as she'd crept past on the way to her bedroom. She held her breath as she listened, finally daring to go in when his grunts subsided.

She sensed something was wrong.

She pushed the door open and stood there just watching him, fascinated, wondering why he was lying on the floor twitching and wheezing sporadically. She almost admired his bulk as it filled the floor space next to the bath. A giant felled.

A grimy vest sodden from sweat clung to his fat, hairy torso. Baggy, white-grey underpants contoured the shape of him beneath. Blood from a gash on his head – from where he'd hit himself on the basin – spilt onto the tiles, a large puddle forming. She turned her head sideways, bewitched by the way it became thick and mahogany so fast. *Like paint*, she thought, bending down and dipping in her finger. She sniffed it, unflinching at the metallic tang, knowing that the same stuff was flowing through her veins, too. The same toxic, good-for-nothing DNA that had driven him to torment her mother every day of her life. Fiona was made from the same matter. No better than the useless lump of flesh lying on the floor at her feet.

She kicked him in the back. His fat rippled.

Her mother was out cold on the bed next door – not from a beating this time, rather from the bottle of vodka that she consumed every day to help her forget. To cleanse her palate for the next round. Except now, there wouldn't be another round.

Fiona turned and walked away from her father's semi-dressed body. She didn't know what had happened to him, but she left without a backwards glance.

A heart attack, Fiona overheard much later after her mother's screams had led to an ambulance arriving. So much panic in the house. *If only someone had been there to call for help... Got to him sooner... Chance of survival.*

Fiona stayed in her room, a small smile curling up her lips as she heard those words. The *drip... drip... drip* of that bathroom tap marking the seconds of her life.

'No, stop!' Fiona cries now, her face crumpling from the horror movie inside her brain.

Do it... Don't do it... Get rid of those brats... Save them... No good will come of this...

Don't give up! Run away while you still can... Turn yourself in...

Fiona gasps, braking hard as she leans forward over the wheel, staring out of the windscreen, sweating, shaking, barely able to function. Her thoughts are all over the place, tumbling through her mind, contradicting one another. Making her feel as though she's going mad. *More* mad.

She blocks her ears, screwing up her eyes and shaking her head as she waits for it to pass.

Drive on... a gentle voice tells her. *You OK, Fiona?*

It doesn't sound like one of her voices. There's a hand on her arm.

'Fiona?' Tilly asks, facing her. 'Are you OK?'

Fiona shudders – a gentle tremor at first, building up to her entire body juddering and rocking. Vaguely, she's aware of Ivy grizzling from the back seat, of Tilly stroking her shoulder, whispering kind things to her.

'Hey, hey... it's OK, Fiona. It's going to be OK...'

When she turns, she sees the honest eyes of the teenager – her pupils wide, her head nodding in reassurance. A little smile on her face. Her hand feels warm and kind – something Fiona has not felt in a long while.

'Is it?' she asks. 'It's going to be OK?'

'Yes, of course it is. Everything is going to be fine. All you need to do is drive into the hospital and then everything will be OK.'

She's lying! She's a traitor! Get rid of her – get rid of them all!

Fiona's vision clears just enough for her to see that Tilly has taken hold of the steering wheel and is turning it to the right, pointing it towards the iron gates of the hospital.

'That's it,' she says kindly. 'Just press the accelerator. We're nearly home...'

Home... Fiona thinks, uncertain if the word makes her feel safe or terrified.

Don't be stupid! Ditch the girls... drive off!

'OK, OK, OK...' Fiona mumbles, blocking out the voices as she leans forward, focusing on the driveway ahead. 'I can do this... I've got this...'

'You *have*. You so have!' Tilly tells her, keeping a gentle hold of the wheel as they cruise down the tree-lined drive towards the main building of Radmoor Hospital. 'You're doing great, Fiona,' she says.

'Home,' Fiona whispers as they pull up outside the stone portico. 'Yes, I think I'm finally home.'

. . .

No one notices the Ford parked in front of the hospital with three frightened girls inside. No one knows that Fiona tells them to stay put or sees her get out and go round to the tailgate, feeling like a robot following orders. She knows she's being driven by something – something familiar, yet also something diseased and broken living inside her. Something bad lurking within that makes her hurl things out of the boot – shopping bags, a tool kit, a coat, a pair of wellington boots. She doesn't know exactly what it is she's looking for, but she knows it's in here somewhere. Then she spots the picnic basket, and the voice tells her to unfasten the wicker lid.

She does as she's told. It's the picnic set they brought from Jason's old home, deciding to keep it in the back of the car ready for the family day out they've not yet had. As she rummages among the plastic plates, the cutlery, the salt and pepper shaker, chucking it all out, she imagines them all sitting on a tartan rug, nibbling on sandwiches and strawberries, the sun shining, a glass of prosecco, ball games and ice cream. It was all a lie.

Then Fiona finds what she's after – a sharp chopping knife.

She turns it over and over in her hands, the five-inch blade glinting in the sunlight, listening intently as the voice tells her what she must do.

'Get out,' she says to the two younger girls in the back. Not harshly, but not kindly either. After a moment's hesitation, they do as they're told. They've both spotted the knife. 'Hold hands,' Fiona instructs before taking hold of Cora's wrist and leading the pair of them round to Tilly's side of the car. 'You get out now, too,' she says, and, slowly, Tilly does as she's told, not taking her eyes off the knife pointing at the side of Cora's neck.

'Wait, what are you *doing*?' Her eyes flash up to Fiona's face, then back to the knife. 'Put that thing down, for Christ's sake. Someone will get hurt!'

Fiona ignores her. 'Hold your sister's hand. Follow me. One wrong move from any of you and the child gets it,' she says, not even recognising her own voice. She leads them across the gravelled parking area reserved for doctors' cars and up to the hospital entrance – a stone portico in the grand main building.

The four of them walk up the steps in a line, towards the warm, welcoming lights of reception. It's been a long while since Fiona has set foot in this part of the building, with her ward being in another section of the hospital. They go through the old double doors with polished brass handles and walk across the plush, burgundy carpet. She hears Ivy sobbing beside her, while Cora says nothing. Tilly hasn't taken her eyes off her since they left the car, flashing glances at the knife pointing at the girl's neck.

The receptionist looks up.

'Oh!' she exclaims, half standing up, but freezing when she realises what's happening.

'It's OK,' Tilly blurts out, keeping her gaze fixed on Fiona. 'Please don't be alarmed. Stay calm if you can. No sudden moves.'

'What on *earth*...' The receptionist, wearing a cream blouse and a navy skirt, comes out from behind her desk, approaching Fiona cautiously. 'How... how may I help you?' Her eyes flick to the knife.

'I... I want to see a doctor,' Fiona says calmly, making it clear that she has a weapon, brandishing it at Cora. 'And I'll only see Dr Hewitt.'

FORTY-SEVEN

JASON

'You're being released under investigation,' DI Winters tells Jason after the two officers have questioned him for several hours, including a reprimand for not sending them the doorbell camera footage they'd requested. Informing them that it had mysteriously deleted itself hadn't gone down well – they said they'd now have to apply to the court for a warrant to retrieve the missing files.

'For God's sake, you've got to believe me. I'm a doctor. I was not trying to kill Evelyn!' he protested earlier in the interview, having repeated several times that the uniformed officers had walked in on the situation at the cottage just as he'd finally managed to defuse it by getting the shotgun off her. He'd also told them about the stash of drugs in Evelyn's toilet cistern. 'Look,' he eventually capitulated, knowing this admission was a last resort. 'Phone Radmoor Hospital. Give them my full name – Dr Jason Henry Hewitt FRCPsych. I used to work there.' He sighed, realising that as his departure had been rather sudden and without notice, they might not hold him in the best light, but still, they couldn't deny his credentials. He prayed it would go some way to upholding his character.

'And where is it you work now, Dr Hewitt?' DI Winters asked.

Jason paused. He hadn't wanted to mention the university at all, given that he was so new there, and especially as he wasn't certain how much longer he'd stay in the post anyway. He'd got a bad taste in his mouth about the place now.

'Canonfield University.' An image of his office swept into his mind – all the books and stacks of papers and student files and course materials... and Rosanne as she'd sat on the corner of his desk looking at him in that certain way – the certain way that some women have that says one thing yet, when put to the test, means quite another.

DI Winters made a quick note in her file. 'How long have you been working there?' She glanced up.

Jason wrinkled his chin. 'Not long. A few weeks. Preparing for the new academic year.' He wasn't feeling in the mood for chit-chat. 'Look, my father was an eminent Harley Street psychiatrist, Dr Frederick Hewitt,' he sputtered out in a final attempt to show good character. 'You've got this all wrong. I shouldn't be sitting here. It's a waste of police resources.'

'Do you know a woman called Rosanne Clarke, a PhD student at Canonfield, by any chance?' DI Rachel Whatever asked, raising her eyebrows hopefully.

Jason's stomach spasmed, delivering a pain right under his heart. For a second, he wasn't sure whether to be more concerned that he was having a heart attack or about what the detective had just asked him. 'I don't think I do, no,' he forged on, a weight seeming to press down on him.

Her sitting on the corner of my desk like that... legs splayed out, all those questions... going on and on and on... She should have kept quiet. Not probed and dug and grilled me about where she goddamn recognised me from...

He ran his finger around the collar of his shirt, feeling his underarms prickling from sweat.

On and on and on...

'Canonfield has come up in another ongoing investigation,' she told him.

'Is that the assault case?' DI Winters asked, turning directly to her colleague. Jason was all ears.

DI Rachel Whatever nodded, holding her eyes closed for an extra beat. '*Murder* case, actually,' she corrected. And when her lids opened, her focus was directly on Jason. Unblinking.

'Right,' DI Winters said, snapping her file closed. 'We have a couple of calls to make, some things to check out, so don't run away.' She grinned as both detectives exited the room together, gone for nearly twenty minutes. A uniformed officer sat with him.

As he waited, he presumed they were about to charge him with all sorts – possession of a firearm, intent to kill or injure Evelyn, breaking and entering. His mind flicked back to the university. To Rosanne. *Aren't you that woman's husband... Erika Something... Erika... Erika Norstrom...?* she'd asked over and over and over. Her hair had got everywhere, her limbs thrashing. He'd had to put his fist in her mouth to keep her quiet, the other hand crushing her neck. But she'd stay silent now. The next day, he'd watched from his car as the body bag had come out of the building on a gurney an hour after the paramedics had first gone inside.

Jason is collecting his belongings from the custody desk – with DI Rachel Whatever stuck to his side since they left the interview room – when DI Winters approaches him. 'There's been a development,' she tells him. 'It's about your daughters... We believe we've found them.'

Jason heaves out a sigh of relief. 'Oh, thank God. Where are they? Are they OK? When can I see them?' He feels tears welling up but does not want to show weakness in front of the detectives.

'We'd like to take you to them,' DI Winters suggests, 'if that's OK with you?'

At first, Jason is reluctant, wondering if it's some kind of trick, but he quickly realises he has very little choice in the matter. His car wasn't outside Evelyn's cottage when they arrested him earlier. He prayed that Fiona was back home safe with the girls, that they would take him home, too, and they could put this unfortunate incident behind them. One thing he knows for sure though is that there will be a strict tightening up of their marriage rules. He won't allow this to happen again.

'OK, so I don't want to distress you, Dr Hewitt, but you should be aware that there's a bit of a situation going on at present,' DI Winters says twenty minutes later as they're driving along a country lane. He's sitting in the back of an unmarked police car with a male uniformed officer either side of him. She glances at him in the mirror. 'It's to do with a woman called Fiona Fisher... She's currently at Radmoor Hospital. And she's with your daughters.'

Christ, how much worse can this get? Jason thinks, wondering how he'll be able to talk his way out of whatever trouble she's got them into now.

'What kind of situation?' he asks, trying to remain calm. With a bit of quick thinking, he's certain he'll be able to handle it.

'We don't want to alarm you but, she's... well, Fiona has another child with her, too. A girl named Cora. I'm afraid she has a weapon and is threatening to hurt her if we don't comply with her wishes. The other girl's father has also been called and is on his way. Fiona has been asking for you, saying you're the only doctor she is willing to see. We're hoping you can help defuse things.'

'You mean... she's taken the children *hostage*? Oh my God, that's dreadful,' he says as DI Winters gives him a solemn nod in the rear-view mirror.

Frantically, he tries to think of a plan as they speed to the hospital, how he can get through to Fiona, coax her to release the girls. He needs to get his daughters, and Cora, out of harm's way.

'I'll help any way I can. But you need to understand that Fiona has been under a huge amount of stress lately. She's not been herself at all. But with the right medication, I believe she'll make good progress again. One thing I can assure you of is that she is not...' He was going to say violent but suddenly changes his mind. In order to protect himself, it's very likely that he'll need to prove that she is *exactly* that. 'She's very unlikely to harm a child. But still, we need to play this very carefully.'

Ten minutes later and the unmarked police car parks outside the main hospital building. Over to one side, he sees his Ford stopped haphazardly on the gravel, three of the doors left wide open and a uniformed police officer standing sentry nearby. Across the other side of the expanse of gravel are about six or eight police vehicles, some marked with neon yellow and blue, some not. Outside the main entrance, there are two ambulances waiting, their rear doors wide open.

The police escort Jason inside, the two uniformed officers flanking him. He swallows drily as he goes up the steps and crosses the threshold – he'd never expected to be back here again.

'Dr Hewitt,' the receptionist says. 'I'm so glad you're here.' She stands up when he comes in and is about to go up to him, but DI Winters puts up a hand to halt her.

Jason gets his bearings, looking around the reception area. It's like nothing he's ever seen before, the entire place swarming with police – officers in protective clothing, plainclothes officers huddled together discussing the situation, paramedics on standby. But suddenly all eyes are on him.

'The doctor is here,' an officer says, and DI Winters leads him up to another plainclothes officer – a man in his mid-forties.

'Dr Hewitt, thank you for being so obliging,' he says. 'We have a delicate ongoing situation that with your help, I believe we can prevent from escalating. At present, the hostage-taker has requested to be placed in the conference room down the corridor, insisting that no one else apart from one police officer be present, positioned at the opposite end of the room to Fiona and the children. That's the best we could negotiate for now. At this point, we're working on the assumption that she's dangerous and will harm one or more of the girls if we don't comply.'

Jason wipes his hands down his face, closing his eyes briefly. 'Good God,' he says. 'She's not a well woman.' He tries to collect his thoughts. 'As her former psychiatrist, I will try to help however I can.'

The detective nods. 'Phase one is to get all three girls released unharmed. We have a trained negotiator on hand and a taser unit present, and an armed response team is on the way. After that, her arrest and ongoing treatment will be dealt with by the courts and the hospital jointly. But look, one thing at a time.'

'Agreed,' Jason says. 'What do I need to do?'

'Right. Fiona insisted that you were brought to her. She refused to talk to anyone unless you were present. She said something about it being in the rules. We have no idea what rules she's referring to, but at that point she was very on edge and, we believe, close to harming the child. We had no choice but to comply.'

Jason nods, his expression serious as he thinks. 'OK, I understand. Do you want to take me to her?'

'Shortly, yes. First though, it seems as though you're the person who knows her best of all. Would you say that's fair?'

'Very fair,' Jason agrees.

'She's made a claim that she killed...' The officer appears uncomfortable, seeming uncertain in his approach.

DI Winters interjects. 'Fiona is claiming that she murdered Sascha Masters – the subject of an ongoing missing persons enquiry. She told us where the body is supposedly located. We've got a team en route now to confirm facts. But having said that, Fiona also claimed...' Winters tucks a strand of hair behind her ear, shifting from one foot to the other. 'Look, there's no easy way to say this, Dr Hewitt, but she's also insisting that she killed your wife, Erika Norstrom. She's been saying it on repeat for the last hour.'

Jason sighs, shaking his head. 'She's worse than I thought,' he says, trying to sound concerned, but also vague. *This could all still work in my favour if I'm careful*, he thinks, following on as he's led down the corridor.

At the entrance to the conference room, they're met by a police negotiator waiting outside a set of double doors, along with several other officials. The negotiator – a woman in her fifties – looks a whole lot calmer than Jason feels right now. She gives DI Winters a nod and then has a brief chat with Jason before knocking on one of the conference room doors, opening it slightly.

'Fiona, Dr Hewitt is here, as you requested. Is it OK for him to come in?' The negotiator has the door open a crack and, across the other side of the large room, Jason sees four figures bunched together in the corner. Fiona is standing up, a knife gripped in her right hand, the blade pressed underneath Cora's chin. Under the circumstances, Jason thinks the child looks calm. Not so his own daughters, though, both of whom are sobbing silently as they crouch down on the floor behind Fiona, Tilly hugging Ivy close.

'Yes,' Fiona says, her voice sounding weary and defensive at the same time. 'No one else though, just him.'

The negotiator turns to Jason. 'In you go. Stay just inside the door. Keep your talk light and friendly and non-threatening. Our aim is for her to send the children to us while she remains at the other end of the room. Do not approach her, whatever she says.'

Jason nods solemnly, taking a breath as he steps inside. Behind the door, he catches sight of a young, uniformed officer standing in the corner.

'Hello, Fiona,' Jason says, turning to face her. 'It's good... it's good to see you,' he adds, not knowing what else to say. 'Hello, girls. Everything's going to be OK.' He raises his hand briefly, but then he sees Fiona's forearm stiffen, the blade pressing up under the child's throat. Tilly and Ivy let out a couple of sobs.

'You came,' Fiona says weakly, the slightest glimmer of a smile forming on her face. Behind the semi-open door, Jason hears the officers discussing something, a flurry of activity from the corridor.

'Of *course* I came,' he says. 'I wanted to see you, Fiona. And the girls, too. You must be really hungry and tired. What would you say to a nice drink and a meal?' It's the only thing he can think of, but he sees Ivy nodding hopefully in the corner. Fiona remains frozen, her eyes flicking between him and the door. 'Does that sound nice?'

Nothing, just Fiona staring at the door located to his right.

'If you send all three girls up here to me, I can get them ready to go out. Then you can freshen up, too. We could go to the pub nearby, the Fox and Hounds. You like it in there. A bottle of wine by the log fire, some good food. How about it?' He's hoping to prey on her weakness, tempt her with her life-long nemesis – alcohol.

'Just step to your left a bit,' Jason suddenly hears the negotiator say in a low voice from the corridor. 'Someone else is
coming in.'

Jason does as he's told without taking his eyes off Fiona in
case she does something stupid. Behind him, he hears the door
creaking, then spots Fiona's eyes growing wide, her mouth
falling open.

'No!' she shouts, raising her arm and yanking back Cora's
head to expose her neck. 'No, no, *no!*' Her cheeks colour up and
she begins to sway, not taking her eyes off the person who has
just entered the room.

'Hello, Fiona,' a voice behind Jason says.

He swings round to see who it is, his mouth also dropping
open when he sees her.

'Oh my God,' he says, recoiling. '*Erika?* What the hell are
you doing here?'

FORTY-EIGHT

FIONA

'*Mum!*' Tilly cries out from where she's crouching behind Fiona. 'You're alive!'

Ivy bursts into tears when she sees her mother. 'Mummy, oh Mummy, I want you...' she wails, holding out her arms, followed by more cries from both girls.

'It's OK, darlings,' Erika calls back. 'I'm here... Just stay where you are and do what Fiona says. Everything will be OK, I promise!'

Fiona stares down the conference room, unable to believe her eyes as she sees Erika standing there. She watches as the woman she killed turns to Jason, gives him a brief nod and says hello. She can't work out if it's a friendly, pleased-to-see-you type of greeting, or if they're angry with each other. But more than anything, she can't work out why the woman Jason told her *she'd* murdered is standing right there at the other end of the room, alive as anything.

Stay real, stay grounded, she tells herself, but already the floor is starting to rock beneath her.

'Hello, Fiona,' Erika calls out, lifting her hand and giving a small wave.

Fiona lets out a whimper, her hand shaking as it grips the knife at Cora's throat. The ringing in her ears is getting louder.

'I... I don't understand,' she finally says, wanting to sit down, though she can't relinquish her hold on the child. She's her only security to negotiate the terms of her return to hospital, given what she's done. If she can't strike a bargain, she knows she'll be going straight to prison.

But everything has changed now with Erika standing forty feet away. The woman she was meant to have strangled.

'You're... you're supposed to be dead,' Fiona says. Her voice is croaky and clogged with confusion.

'No, Fiona, I'm not dead. The police knew you were upset about that, so thought it would be a good idea if I came to see you. So you can see I'm alive and well, OK?' Erika's voice is kind and soothing. 'And... and they told me you had Tilly and Ivy with you, too.' She takes the smallest step forward. 'I've really missed them, so thank you for looking after them.'

Fiona feels her head starting to shake – left to right – then her shoulders begin to shudder. Her legs feel like jelly, and she doesn't think they'll hold her up much longer.

She looks at Jason. 'But... but you told me she was dead. You told me that I *killed* Erika.' Her voice is barely a whisper.

Cora lets out a whimpering sound and, behind her, Fiona hears Tilly telling her to be brave, to keep still and everything will be OK.

'Fiona,' Jason says. 'Listen to me, you're mistaken. I understand you get confused, but there's no need to worry. Erika is right here, look. She's not dead at all. You did not kill her.'

'Why... why are you doing this?' she replies, feeling tears welling in her eyes. 'You told me I murdered your wife. You told me you buried her body, that you'd protect me and keep my secret. That we'd have a nice life together. That you'd make me better.'

She can't take her eyes off Erika Norstrom – the woman

who caused her so much torment when she was here at Radmoor. But the strange thing is, she looks so different to the woman she remembers – Jason's high-powered and glamorous wife in her pencil skirt and stilettos who virtually ran this hospital single-handedly. She looks nothing like that now.

The woman standing at the other end of the room has mousy, slightly greasy and dishevelled hair and is wearing a baggy T-shirt with jeans and scuffed trainers. There's not a scrap of make-up on her, and nothing about her is vaguely like the sophisticated international research doctor that she remembers from before.

It's Erika – she can see that clearly from her face – but it's also *not* her. This version of her looks mumsy and... and *normal*. The type of woman you wouldn't look at twice in the supermarket, or if you saw her fetching her kids from the school playground.

'*Why*, Jason?' Fiona feels the hot sting of tears in her eyes.

'We all just want the girls to be safe, Fiona,' he replies, avoiding her question. 'And Cora too,' he adds. 'Cora's father is on his way.'

Cora lets out another sob and Fiona feels the child trembling against her legs.

'Fiona, I understand you're upset,' Erika says, the Swedish accent that Fiona remembers still there but less harsh, less clipped and commanding. 'But I have not come here to make you feel bad. The police rang me and told me that my daughters had been found so I came here straight away. We've been looking for them for two months now. I'm so grateful to you for taking care of them.' She smiles nervously.

'What are you talking about?' Fiona says, feeling more confused than ever. She twitches a couple of times, trying to silence the voice in her head, but it's not shutting up. It's telling her to do things – to hurt the child, and then hurt herself. *Take back control...* it tells her. *It's the only way to end this.* 'You're wrong! They're *my* daughters. Tilly and Ivy belong to me and Jason. He's *my* husband now. We're married! You're still trying to ruin everything. You think you're the boss of this place, all high and mighty, but look at you now. You're nothing. I doubt you could run a jumble sale, let alone a hospital like this.' Fiona scoffs, feeling strangely confident again. 'You're a charlatan, Erika Norstrom, that's what you are!'

'No... no, look, I don't work here, Fiona,' Erika replies calmly, glancing at Jason. 'I've never worked here. You're mistaken. But I understand things can get muddled. I promise, everything will be fine, but I need you to put the knife down and allow the girls to come to me.'

Fiona laughs, tipping back her head. 'No way,' she spits. 'You're lying! I know you work here. I saw you every day! Are you saying I'm mad, is that it?' Another laugh.

Erika turns to Jason and whispers something in his ear, making him nod. But then one of the double doors opens and the police negotiator calls out in a crisp, clear voice, 'Fiona, we have Cora's dad with us out here.'

Fiona's eyes flick to the door.

'Would it be OK if he came in, too? He'll remain at this end of the room beside Dr Hewitt. Like us, he's on your side, Fiona, but he'd really like to see his daughter.'

Another pause, which Fiona fills with a whimpering sound, not knowing what to do. Then she sees the negotiator, who she'd told to stay out of the room, step just inside the door.

'Can you confirm if it's OK for Steve to come in?' she says, her hands clasped in front of her.

Fiona doesn't know if it's OK or not. She doesn't think she knows anything any more.

'Fiona, look, Steve isn't angry with you,' the negotiator continues. 'None of us are. We understand how you're feeling. He just wants to say hello to Cora. Will you let him?'

Before she can stop herself, Fiona nods. 'OK. But no one

else. Just him. And stay back.' Maybe if she goes along with these people, they will help her. The woman in the corridor does seem kind, she thinks, and more than anything, that's what she needs right now – kindness. She wishes there was a rule for that. Perhaps Jason could add one in.

'Daddy!' Cora squeaks when she sees her father step into the room, the blade of the knife pressing against her throat. Fiona slackens her arm just a little to allow the child to speak without getting hurt.

'Hello, sweet pea,' the man says. He's tall and dressed in jeans and a black T-shirt. He has a bushy brown beard and leather boots. *Sascha's boyfriend*, Fiona thinks. The man with the motorbike. 'Everything's gonna be OK now Daddy's here. You believe me, sweetness?' His voice is croaky and on edge, and his hands fidget by his thighs.

'Yes, Daddy,' Cora says. 'Where's Mummy?' she asks, making Fiona tense again.

Suddenly she sees flies swarming, smells the hot, sweet stench of death, sees Sascha's decaying skin – *her* wristwatch lying beside the body.

'I killed her!' Fiona blurts out. 'I killed your mummy!'

Cora immediately bursts into tears, and then Fiona hears something spattering to the floor, followed by a hot, damp feeling seeping through her trainers. The child has wet herself.

'It's true!' she spits out, almost snarling at her audience. 'Go and see for yourselves. My watch is up there with her body in the barn and—'

'*No!*' Steve yells, lunging towards her. But Jason pulls him back, grabbing his arm and swinging him round to a stop.

'Keep back!' Fiona cries, feeling a panic swell inside her. Her mind is barely hanging onto reality as it is, but then the doorbell video clip of the man in the motorbike helmet posting the note through the letterbox plays in her head. She screws up her eyes, trying to make it go away.

I know what you did... You broke a rule...

You've got it coming. Everything you deserve...

'It was *you!*' she yells out, jabbing a finger from her free hand at Steve. 'You put that note through my letterbox. I saw you on our camera. You were threatening me and my husband. Admit it! You're the one who should be in trouble, not me!'

'Wait, what are you talking about...?' Steve says, raising his hands and looking puzzled.

Fiona sees an image of a black car driving away from the riding school, the driver handing Tilly a note... then the screeching of smoke alarms, all of them in a panic as she and the girls tried to escape from the house... Graham, their neighbour, finding a note on the doormat... The note in Jason's pocket, believing the handwriting was *hers*...

She doesn't know what's real any more.

'Fiona, *please*, can't you just let Cora and Ivy go?' a voice says. At first, Fiona isn't sure where it's coming from, but then she realises it's Tilly behind her.

She turns slightly to see the teenager crouched in the corner, pressed up against the wall.

'Take me instead. You can still have the knife, but just let Ivy and Cora go. *Please...* I'm begging you, Fiona...' Tilly lets out a frustrated sob.

'Shut up!' Fiona yells. 'Stay where you are and keep quiet. You don't know what you're talking about.' She turns her attention back to Steve. 'Admit it was you who sent all those notes, so the police know what you did, that you were harassing me. Stalking me and my husband.'

'No, I really *don't* know what you're talking about...' Steve insists, shrugging and glancing through the semi-open door at the officers in the corridor, shaking his head.

'Admit it!' Fiona screams.

'Look, if you mean the letter or whatever it was that I put through your door a couple of weeks back, yeah, that was me.

But it wasn't *from* me. I found it dropped outside your house on the pavement. It had your name on it, so I thought I was doing you a favour. I remember Sascha telling me her new neighbour was called Fiona.'

'I don't fucking believe you!' Fiona shrieks, yanking back Cora's head.

'Wait, stop!' Tilly cries out, creeping out from behind her. From the corner of her eye, Fiona sees her approaching slowly. Then she feels a hand on her arm. For a moment, it feels pleasant, the touch of another human. But then she recoils. 'It was me. *I* sent the notes.'

Silence as she takes this on board. Fiona feels herself swaying again. Her vision blurring. Could it be true?

'I... I wanted to upset you, make you scared and freak you out... you *and* Dad. Just like you'd upset Ivy and me. Losing our Mum *destroyed* us, and despite us being nice to you, we hated you for it. It felt like... like you were the cause of it all – one day Mum was there and then she wasn't and you'd taken her place. I wanted to ruin your life, too. And Dad's. I... I didn't know what else to do.' Tilly bows her head and draws breath, holding back her tears as best she can.

'Look, I put the note under Dad's car wiper. When I left Dotty's café, I didn't go straight to Amber's house like you thought – I went back to the lay-by instead. And there was no man at the stables passing me a note, it was just *me*. Our neighbour, Graham, found the one I'd left for you next, when the alarms went off. I started out just writing random stuff that I thought would upset you, but when I saw that photo of Mum on Instagram... something just didn't feel right, like you were lying to us. Maybe it was something in my unconscious that made me start thinking that you or Dad had done something awful, I dunno... I just wanted the notes to upset you, not even realising that I was actually on to something.

'It's only just dawned on me now that you and Dad

kidnapped me and Ivy. I don't think it's even hit me yet. I trusted you both. I was blind to the clues, what with losing Mum and the shock of having to leave our schools, live in a different house, get used to a new stepmother right away... it was all too much. We never wanted to live with you, being kept like prisoners, following Dad's rules. But you made us believe we had no choice, that our mum was dead.' The look on Tilly's face is pure disgust.

'You were not prisoners, you stupid girl,' Fiona spits back. 'How ungrateful! You have fantastic lives with two parents who love you. Yet you threw it all back in our faces.' She turns to the others. 'That's teenagers for you.'

'You told us our mother was *dead*!' Tilly repeats, stepping in front of Fiona. 'We believed you! You're sick in the head. You're crazy!'

Fiona hears the buzzing in her ears... sees the flies in front of her face. She wants to bat them away but she can't let go of the girl... it's all over if she does that.

'Get back...' Fiona shouts at Tilly. 'Get away from me. You don't know how good you've had it—'

'That's not true,' Tilly whimpers, retreating a step. 'What about all Dad's stupid rules and lies about us having to lie low and hide away? He told us we had to leave our old lives behind, that it was time to move on. We couldn't do anything or go anywhere, and even when we did go out for that walk with you, where were we supposed to run away to? You'd told us Mum was dead, and we believed you. We had no other relatives to contact – we never got to know Mum's family in Sweden because they cut her off when she ran off to England with Dad. And Dad has no living family, either. We literally had no idea you'd...' Tilly glances over at her father, at the police officer, at her mother, at Cora's father, at the negotiator standing in the doorway. She chokes back a sob. 'We had no idea that we were *kidnapped*, that everyone was out looking for us.' Tears roll down her cheeks. 'So while we hated the situation, we literally had nowhere else to go. And there was no reason to ask for help because we didn't realise what you'd done until now. You were our only lifeline. We needed you for our safety. We *relied* on you. I suppose in the end we just got used to it, tried to make the best of it. Like, this was our life now.

'It was only when I confessed how unhappy I was to Amber late last night when she called me for a midnight chat that I knew something had to change. I've never opened up like that before, but it all came flooding out. She... she said we should run away to teach you both a lesson, so that's what Ivy and I did early this morning before you were up. I didn't even know where we were going.' Tilly draws breath, then continues. 'But... but please...' She points at Cora, shaking her head. 'For the love of God, Fiona, I'm begging you, *please* let Ivy and Cora go free.'

'What, and get arrested for murder?' Fiona scoffs, though she feels something inside her loosening, wanting nothing more than for this standoff to end. 'So... so Amber *did* call the police, then,' she mumbles as her mind whirs, slotting into place the barrage of text messages from Amber that had lit up the screen of Tilly's second phone just after she'd left Evelyn's cottage with Cora.

Worried about you Tills. Where ru?

Ur dad and F came here, they're angry, out looking for you, acting creepy af...

Tills tmb pls getting freaked out now...

Txt back or getting help...

Right, calling cops now.

Sent police to Evelyn's house... tracked ur phone...

Wot u said last nite about them, it's not OK. Stay safe...

Fiona is tired, she's scared, and she just wants the voice in her head to go away, to be able to relax her arms and put the knife down and not have to hold onto the child any longer.

'But... but I killed Sascha,' she whispers. 'I... I need assurances first. I need to know what's going to happen to me... I can't go to prison. Dear God, don't send me there...'

And I need help, she thinks, even though she can't say it. The child whimpering against her, making her feel strange inside... something unfamiliar brewing in the pit of her belly as she stares down at the girl – her little shoulders juddering in time with her pitiful sobs, the messy parting in her soft hair, the grubby cuffs of her sweatshirt.

'I've tried to get better, I really have...' Fiona fights back the tears. 'Jason, you've been a good doctor and you've done your best for me, but I'm no good for you now. I want to come back to Radmoor, but I need promises that there will be no charges for killing Sasch—'

'Wait!' Steve interrupts. 'Look, you're not going to get into trouble with the police for that, OK?' he says, dropping his head into his hands. He takes a deep breath before looking up and continuing. 'Cora, I'm so sorry, sweetie, please forgive me for having to say this, but Fiona... I know who killed Sascha. And it wasn't you.'

FORTY-NINE

JASON

The room falls silent as everyone takes in what Steve just said.

I know who killed Sascha…

'This is ridiculous,' Jason blusters, glancing at the police in the hope they will intervene. But for some reason, they seem intent on allowing this dangerous situation to unfold. 'We must stay focused on what Fiona wants, how we can help her going forward. Then I'm sure she'll release Cora unharmed. Her mental state is on a knife edge, for heaven's sake.' He hisses the last bit towards the police negotiator who's standing just inside the door, only a few feet away from him.

'Listen to my doctor,' Fiona responds, ignoring Steve. 'He knows me. He knows what I did… and none of this is his fault. He… he was trying to protect me and the girls. Jase, I know you followed us when we went on that walk to the riding stables. When the girls went on ahead…' Fiona screws up her eyes at the memory, trying to piece things together. 'Sascha must have been tending to the ponies in the field and that's when I…' She trails off as a series of sobs interrupts her. 'God, I don't know… Every-thing's such a blur. Maybe *that's* when I killed her… My watch is still at the scene, I know that much! Go and check.'

Jason's heart clenches as he sees his wife's distress and confusion – or is she even his wife now that Erika is here? He's not exactly shocked to see Erika alive and well. The thing is, he'd never wanted to lie to Fiona, but he got swept along with plans, swept along with protecting himself. If Fiona had believed his wife was still alive, she could have done all kinds of damage to him and his career with those videos. He shouldn't have messed with her mind, knowing how vulnerable she is, the way she'd dissociated before... but making her believe she'd killed Erika was insurance for him. If only she'd stuck to the goddamn rules.

She looks pitiful and he wants to help her, but he must also tread carefully. He managed to convince the police that he hadn't broken into Evelyn's house for malicious reasons, and that he wasn't about to shoot her. He doesn't want to get into more trouble with them now – not after everything. All he wants, if he's honest, is his old job back here at the hospital and for things to be as they once were. He didn't realise how good he'd had it.

'Listen to me,' Steve says, taking a step closer to Fiona. 'If you let Cora go, I can prove that you didn't harm Sascha, OK? Then you won't be in any kind of trouble, and there's no reason for you to hold onto any of the girls, OK? You're making a terrible mistake, Fiona. Let them come to safety and I will tell you what happened.'

Fiona looks confused, a little nervous tic pulsing under one eye. Jason knows all too well that her mind protects her by blocking things out, that she can't trust her own recollections.

'But I know I did it...' she whispers, sounding unsure. 'I know I killed Sascha.'

Another pitiful whimper from Cora as she's pressed against Fiona's legs.

'You mean just like you thought you'd killed my mum?' Tilly pipes up from behind, pointing towards Erika. 'I *told* you he was abusing you, that Dad was gaslighting you and treating you badly, but you wouldn't listen to me. He's been abusing us all! I even showed you that photo of Mum online, wondering what the hell was going on, convinced it was recent. But we were so brainwashed, we didn't even believe what's been going on right under our noses! For God's sake, just let the girls go. You can keep me.'

Fiona's head whips around, her arm still clenched around Cora's neck, the knife still at her throat.

'Tilly, no, that's not fair,' Jason calls out. 'I've only ever had your best interests at heart. *All* of your best interests.'

'Fiona, we fell for it as well, don't you see?' Tilly continues, imploring her. 'You could have escaped too, but like us, you didn't. We were all scared. All broken. But now's your chance to set yourself free, to get better. You don't have to believe what he says. Listen to Steve, Fiona. Listen to what he has to tell you. You have nothing to lose, right?'

Fiona gives Tilly a glance then looks down the long room at Steve. She gives a small nod.

'Send Cora to me first,' Steve says.

'Not a chance,' Fiona replies, tightening her grip on the little girl.

Steve takes a deep breath. 'Cora, sweetie, everything is going to be OK, please trust Daddy, OK?'

Cora makes a whimpering sound.

Steve takes another deep breath followed by a couple of steps towards Fiona, edging closer to his daughter as he begins.

'I don't speak to my brother often as my family are a bad lot, but it was him who saw what happened...' He glances nervously behind him, checking that the collection of police officers gathered in the corridor can hear him. 'My brother told me everything – that there'd been an argument, between Sascha and her mother, Evelyn. They've never got on properly those two, sparks always flying. Sascha had already dropped Cora off at her mother's house in Little Campden last Tuesday evening, but then an hour or so later, she found out through a text from my sister that Evelyn had taken Cora up to Andy's house in Drakes Avenue. That's the street in Longbourne where all my brothers live.'

Steve shakes his head, wipes his hands down his bearded face. Even from his three-quarter-angle view, and despite the man's large size, his manly demeanour, Jason sees the sweat seeping out of him. He's nervous as hell, and his eyes are fixed on his daughter.

'Sascha didn't want Cora mixing with any of that lot, and I agreed. As I said, I don't have much to do with them any more – they're a bad lot, always on the wrong side of the law – but years ago, Evelyn got caught up in it all. It's drugs, county lines stuff, with serious money involved.

'Initially, they were using Evelyn's house in Little Campden for all the wrong reasons – taking it over as a trap house for a while when the cops were all over Drakes Avenue. To start with, they gave her no choice, taking advantage of her living alone, of her older age. But then they realised that because she ran the local youth scheme for disadvantaged kids in the village hall right next door to her house, she had perfect access to what they needed – vulnerable teenagers in need of money and something to do. The kids trusted her, saw her as a grandmotherly figure when their lives at home were fraught and impossible. Evelyn became someone for them to turn to – for drugs and a listening ear. And the parents knew no better, believing their youngsters were getting involved with wholesome activities. Evelyn liked the money, of course, and soon she was in way too deep to get out of it.' Another look to the door from Steve, where the police are on standby.

'Anyway, Sascha was so angry with her mother for taking Cora to Drakes Avenue that night, so she just dropped everything at home and rushed off to fetch her back. Her car might still be up there somewhere, though more likely it's been broken up and sold off down the scrappy by now. She told me she was going to ask *you* to look after Cora the next day instead, Fiona. She trusted you. She thought you were her friend. She'd hate that you're doing this to her daughter.'

A clever move by Steve, Jason thinks, as he sees Fiona's grip on Cora relax a little.

'I... I liked her too,' Fiona whispers back. 'She made me feel useful, as if I had a purpose again. She made me feel... how I once *used* to feel.'

Steve continues, taking another couple of steps closer to Fiona, only about five feet away from his daughter now. 'Evelyn and Sascha got into a fight up at Drakes Avenue when Evelyn wouldn't give Cora back from inside the house. There was a blazing row between the two women. Evelyn even threw a few punches. I don't want to go into too much detail right now...' Steve looks at his little girl again, fighting back a sob. 'Not with Cora here... but... oh God, there was an accident. Sascha ran out onto the road just as one of my brothers came speeding up on his motorbike...'

Steve covers his face again, hangs his head as his shoulders judder up and down. Cora echoes her father's pain with sobs of her own, covering her ears and screwing up her eyes.

'Then... then afterwards, when there was nothing they could do, they decided to move her... There was talk of a barn up by the riding stables where Sascha worked. After they'd done it, two of my brothers went back to Sascha's house, made sure there was some of her blood in the bathroom to take the heat off them, to make it look like something had happened to her in her house.'

Steve takes a breath, calming himself down before continuing.

'Look, I've not said anything about it until now because they're a bad lot, my brothers. I know I should have told the police, but I had to believe Evelyn when she threatened that I'd never see Cora again if I grassed on them. You don't mess with that lot – they make people disappear, no problem. Then Cora wouldn't have *either* of her parents. I wasn't thinking straight. I just wanted to protect my little girl. Please let her go!'

Silence as everyone takes on board what Steve has revealed.

'You're doing really well, Fiona,' a voice says from the doorway. When Jason looks over, he sees the police negotiator has come into the room. 'Don't worry about me being in here, I'm simply here to take care of your well-being, OK? I don't want anyone to get harmed, and that includes you, Fiona. We know you've been through so much, and we want to help you.'

Surprisingly, Fiona manages a small nod, her gaze flicking across to Jason.

'It's not his fault...' she stutters. 'Jason was just trying to protect me. We fell in love. And our marriage rules kept me... they kept me safe.'

Jason hears Erika make a noise in the back of her throat, but she keeps quiet, knowing how serious the situation is.

'Fiona, we understand,' the negotiator says. 'I'd like the opportunity to talk to you about everything somewhere a bit more comfortable. It sounds like you've been through so much. You've been very brave.'

'I don't know,' Fiona replies. 'I want assurances... I can't go to prison... Inside my head, it's...' Her face crumples as the tears flow. 'Every day is so hard, as if I'm constantly fighting against the voices. But then I realise that I'm just fighting against myself. I try to be cheerful, really I do, and I tried to be the best mum for—'

Suddenly, Fiona lurches sideways, her head whiplashing from the jolt. Jason is frozen to the spot as he watches the scene unfurl in front of his eyes – a tangle of bodies and arms and yelps and cries.

Steve has lunged at Fiona, grabbing her arm that's holding

the knife, managing to wrench it away from his daughter. He's way stronger than Fiona, but she still has a tight grip on it, and her other arm is clamped around Cora's neck, refusing to let go. Steve crushes Fiona's wrist, but the knife is now just inches from his face.

'Cora!' a voice calls out. Tilly rushes forward, crouching down by the little girl, pulling at Fiona's arm to get her free.

'Tilly, no, get back!' Erika screams down the room at her daughter.

Suddenly, there's a shrill scream. 'Owww!' Fiona's face burns scarlet as she whips her arm away from Cora. 'You bit me!' she wails, staring at the red marks on her forearm.

Tilly doesn't hang about. 'Run!' she cries, shoving Cora away.

For a second, the child hesitates, looking up at Fiona and her father, who are locked in a stalemate, then she kicks Fiona hard in the shin before running off.

The moment of pain gives Steve the break he needs to force Fiona's arm away from him, twisting it up at an unnatural angle behind her back.

Instantly, she drops the knife and doubles forward, crying out in pain. It's Tilly who dives in to grab the weapon, springing to her feet again and grabbing Ivy's hand, dragging her out of the corner where she's been cowering. They dart down the length of the conference room towards the others, running into their mother's arms, allowing themselves to be engulfed by her embrace.

FIFTY

JASON

Jason stands there, feeling numb as he watches three uniformed officers swoop on Fiona, swiftly getting her lying prone on the carpet, one with a knee in her back as they cuff her and then get her upright. They're not rough with her, but firm and decisive in their actions. She doesn't put up a fight.

'Fiona Fisher, we are detaining you under Section 136 of the Mental Health Act,' the female officer says, sounding breathless. 'We believe you need urgent care and assessment because of your mental health, so we're taking steps to keep you safe. Given that you're already in a psychiatric hospital, you will be assessed by a doctor and mental health professional here as soon as possible. Do you understand me?'

Fiona doesn't reply, rather she stares down the room at Jason, her gaze connecting with his. In that moment, they could be anywhere – taking a walk in the hospital grounds, sitting in his office during one of their consultations, on the train to York for a romantic weekend, sitting round the dinner table for their family confessional. Rule Number 3 – one of his favourites. Jason smiles to himself.

'I love you, Jason,' Fiona calls out. The officers lead her

towards the door, where there are now several nurses waiting to take care of her.

'I know, Fiona, I know you do,' he says back, touching his fingers to his lips and blowing her a kiss. A quick glance around tells him nobody sees.

It's hard to absorb the scene in the hospital conference room – Erika, his wife, very much not dead, sitting at the side of the room with Tilly and Ivy huddled against her, an officer waiting with them, making sure they're OK.

Steve holding Cora tightly, the little girl balanced on his hip while he speaks to another officer in semi-coded language about the ongoing investigation into his missing, now presumed dead partner.

He watches as Fiona is escorted out into the corridor... then off to the high-security North Wing of the hospital where she will be assessed, sectioned and her treatment continued. Jason doubts very much that there will be a warrant for her arrest at present – not until her mental health has stabilised.

As for him, he feels shell-shocked and exhausted. Drained doesn't come close to describing the empty, hollow feeling he has inside. Facing his wrongdoings as a doctor is now unavoidable.

Everything is over.

'Jason,' DI Winters says as she approaches him.

'All's well that ends well, Detective,' he replies. 'Though most people around here call me Doctor or even *Doc*, if you don't mind.'

'Of course, I understand,' she says kindly. A male police officer joins her, along with another doctor he recognises vaguely – a psychiatrist, though he's from a different wing of the hospital. But Jason has seen him around.

'Hello, Doc,' the psychiatrist says to him. 'How are you feeling?'

'A bit shaken, if I'm honest.'

While it feels good to share how he's doing, Jason doesn't much care for the strange feelings brewing inside him. Feelings that unnerve him, as though there are the beginnings of an earthquake inside his belly. And especially with all these people crowding around him.

'OK, Doc,' DI Winters says gently, placing a hand on his arm. She pauses a moment, studying him, shaking her head in a pitying way, almost looking as if she's about to apologise to him. 'Like we've done for Fiona, we are also detaining you under Section 136 of the Mental Health Act. Dr Murray here and I both agree that you need urgent care and assessment. No need to feel concerned, Jason, you'll be taken good care of, and all your needs and rights will be met. You'll be kept here at the hospital in familiar surroundings, at least.'

'Wait... what are you talking about?' Jason says as the roaring sound fills his head. He clutches at his face, feeling reality slipping from his grasp as he breaks out in a sweat. He feels sick and weak, as though his legs are about to give way. 'Is this some kind of joke?'

'He was a patient on Isaac Wing before he ran off a little over two months ago,' he hears the psychiatrist telling the detective. 'But we'll be transferring him over to Jensen Ward in North Wing now. It's the high-security unit,' he adds.

DI Winters nods, exchanging a few details with the doctor, while several nurses in white uniforms encircle Jason.

'Wait... what the hell's going on?' Jason asks, his eyes shooting between them. 'At the police station you told me that I was free to go!'

'We released you from police custody, yes,' DI Winters confirms. 'But you're now a suspect in the Rosanne Clarke murder case at the university—'

'That's absolute rubbish! I barely even knew the woman.' *Though it turned out she knew quite a lot about me*, he thinks, his mind flicking back. *A shame for Rosanne that she recognised me from the newspaper reports* – Manhunt for Escaped Psych Patients Continues. *That she wouldn't let it drop.*

'Jason, when we arrested you and took you into custody at the police station earlier, we quickly found out about your situation here. During your interview, we contacted the hospital, confirming that you were previously a patient, that you had absconded with another patient and abducted your daughters. We brought you back here because of this, plus the ongoing investigation into Rosanne's murder, and because of your mental health. You need to continue with your treatment. Plus, it was our belief that your presence would help bring the situation with Fiona to a peaceful conclusion.'

'That's not true! I was a doctor here! I was *Fiona's* doctor!'

'Jason, no... you're not a doctor, or Fiona's doctor. You never qualified. I'm so sorry to—'

'What are you doing? Get off me!' He tries to shrug free from the nurses' grip. 'Where are you taking me? I want to go home with my wife!' He stares over at Erika, who's sitting with their daughters, cradling their heads against her shoulders, shielding them from what's happening. 'Look, talk to *her*! Erika is the boss of this bloody place, and she'll have your guts for dinner if you don't get your hands off me now! Erika – get over here and tell them who you are! And tell them that I'm a doctor, for Christ's sake!'

'Doc, come on now,' one of the male nurses says, keeping a firm hold on him. 'Erika isn't the boss here, and you know it. We've told you this more times than I care to count. Can you remember what it is your wife does?'

'Don't talk to me like I'm a bloody idiot,' Jason shoots back, yanking his arm free as the nurses flank him either side. 'I'm a psychiatrist, a qualified doctor who used to have a top job here, and for your information you have no right to—'

'Jason, listen to them... *please*. They're trying to help you.'

Erika is now beside him, taking his hands in hers. She has a weary look on her face.

'Order them to stop, Erika! Make everything OK like you always do.' Jason feels close to... so close to *something*, but he's not sure what. Every cell inside him vibrates and buzzes, and frankly he's a little bit frightened now. 'You're Dr Erika Norstrom, research professor and—'

'Jason, no, stop,' Erika says kindly, squeezing his hands. He must admit that, at this precise moment, she doesn't look much like a high-powered medical director – what with her grey roots showing, her eyes sunken and tired, her face lacking any make-up. But then, he supposes, she has been through a lot today, too.

'Jason, listen to me. I'm head of the science department at a high school near where we live. I'm not a doctor, my love. I never have been. I'm a teacher. Do you understand? I am Swedish and we met at Karolinska when you...'

She trails off, shaking her head, closing her eyes.

'Love, you're not at all well. You haven't been well for...' She shoots a glance at the ceiling as her eyes fill with tears. 'A long time. But you've been *really* struggling with your mental health since your father died three years ago. You'll get better, though, I know you will. You've come so far... this has just been a...' She swallows, almost choking on her words. 'It's just been a little blip.' She gives him a kind smile. 'We've all been out searching for you, you know!' She sniffs and smiles again. 'Hunting high and low. Especially because you took the girls this time. That wasn't OK, Jase. You had me worried sick. But look, I'll still come and visit you every day like I usually do. And when I'm able and you're a bit better, I'll bring Tilly and Ivy if they want to see you.'

Jason glances over to where his daughters were sitting, but notices that a female police officer is guiding them out of the room, along with Steve and Cora. Tilly gives him a glance back over her shoulder as she leaves, her face expressionless.

DI Winters steps in, taking Erika aside, but Jason hears what's being said, even though he can't process what's happening. The reality of this situation does not match up with what's inside his mind.

'Because of what he did,' Winters begins, 'abducting your daughters without parental rights, along with fellow patient Fiona Fisher, he'll likely have to go through the courts eventually. Though that will be a matter for the CPS and his mental health team to decide further down the line. For now, he'll be held in the high-security ward here, until a further sectioning can be put in place by a doctor. Unfortunately, he won't be able to leave the hospital or have any freedoms like when he was on Isaac Ward. But that may change again going forward, depending on progress.'

'I understand,' Erika says, sounding weary. 'I just want what's best for him. It was such a fight to get him a place here at this hospital.' She sighs and, in her tired eyes, Jason sees a glimpse of the woman he met at the Karolinska Institutet all those years ago, the bright young scientist from Stockholm who fell in love with a man who was already trying to run away from his past – even though he was only twenty. Already a med school drop-out, having never completed his training at Canonfield University where his father and grandfather and many other generations of his family had all become leading medics, Jason had fallen at the first hurdle of life.

In an attempt to save face, he'd taken himself off travelling for a while, scraping a living by doing dead-end jobs. It was where he'd met Erika, while he was working in the canteen at her university – a temporary position until he decided to move on. Except, for a long while, he didn't move on. He fell in love and moved into Erika's student accommodation while she worked hard for her chemistry degree.

Once Erika graduated, the pair married and moved to England, with Erika landing a decent teaching job, and Jason picturing what it would have been like to have followed in his father's footsteps.

'I was always good at imagining things,' he tells the nurses as they lead him out of the conference room and across the quad at the back of Radmoor Hospital towards North Wing.

They humour him with idle chit-chat, quite used to dealing with people like him, Jason thinks, smiling to himself as they walk down seemingly endless corridors, stopping for security clearance along the way. Then, finally, they arrive on Jensen Ward.

'I learnt to be anything I wanted from a very young age,' he tells another nurse with blonde hair and a pretty smile as the handover into the assessment ward begins. He thinks he might recognise her from somewhere, perhaps the last time he was sectioned and put in here. 'You see, in my mind there are simply no rules. No one telling me what to do. In my head, I'm free as a bird. It's helped me survive.'

FIFTY-ONE
FIONA

Three months later

'I can *smell* him, you know,' Fiona tells Louisa, the nurse. Her eyes are wide with excitement. They're playing cards, and Fiona isn't winning, but she doesn't mind. 'He's near, isn't he? He's getting closer, isn't he? Is he here, on Jensen Ward yet?' She keeps repeating this, which makes the young nurse assigned to her smile. 'Is he coming yet? I think I hear him coming.' Fiona claps her hands.

'Maybe. You'll have to wait and see. It's all been approved though.' Louisa smiles, sweeping back a strand of hair.

'You mean it's been approved by the powers that be?' Fiona isn't quite sure who they are but knows they're important. 'Do you mean I have to wait and see, like it's a surprise?' Fiona sits forward on the edge of her seat. 'I like surprises.' Then she plays a card, shaking her head. 'No, actually, I *don't* like surprises. Can I see him now?' She cranes her neck, looking around the day room. 'Is it today?'

'Yes, Fiona. Your visit is arranged for today,' the nurse says patiently, playing her card. 'But he won't be coming in here. You'll be meeting him somewhere else.'

'How long have I been here in North Wing again?' Fiona feels fiery today, her nerves playing with her body as her skin dances with excitement.

'About three months now,' the nurse tells her.

She's got her new dress on – Erika had it sent in for her. It's a sweater dress in navy blue wool. Quite itchy, but she likes it now that it's getting colder outside. Not that she goes outside or gets cold. Erika is nice, she thinks.

And Erika is not dead, she knows that now, too. It's in her brain to remember forever. Which is a good thing, and she *also* knows that Erika isn't the boss of the hospital – someone whose name she can't remember does that job. That's what they keep telling her – the powers that be. But then she gets confused because Jason said that she killed Erika, but it turns out she didn't. She thought she'd killed Sascha, too – that's Cora's mum – but she didn't kill her either. She knows she gets a bit muddled sometimes. It's probably just that. Getting muddled again. But then some days, when she's sitting beside the window with the fat globules of rain running down the toughened glass – not even a sharp object will break it; she knows because she tried – she thinks she did kill *someone* once. But she can't quite remember who. Or when. Or where. Or why. Or how. Or if it was all just made up in her head like the others.

Drip... drip... drip...

She bashes the side of her head with her hand. Maybe she killed herself. It feels like it sometimes.

'Don't do that,' Louisa says, pulling her hand away. 'You'll give yourself a headache.'

Fiona pouts then looks at her watch. 'Jason gave me a watch as a wedding present once,' she tells the nurse. 'But it's not this one. The police had to keep it, but they said I could have it back one day even though it's broken and has blood on it and we're not even married. That's what they said. Cora told them that her mum stole it from me because she needed money, and she was going to sell it, but then she didn't. The catch was broken, that's why it fell off and got smashed. Look, it's two forty-eight. Is it nearly time? I don't really want that watch back because it's dirty now. Is he coming yet?'

'Soon,' Louisa replies, her eyes crinkling as she laughs. 'You're a chatterbox today, aren't you?' She's been waiting with Fiona since the 7 a.m. handover, and will be with her until 6 p.m. tonight, when a night nurse will be by her side until morning. They've told her she is making good progress, but they said her journey is a long one. She's not sure where she's going.

At a team meeting several weeks ago, it was decided that Fiona's progress would be further benefitted by a visit with Jason Hewitt. She had been asking for him repeatedly, and Jason had been pining for her, too. Given their close bond as patients on Isaac Ward, it was deemed that he would also benefit.

It was an unusual situation and had required special clearance by several psychiatrists, as well as being put before a medical panel of experts for a final decision. Given that male and female wards were separate areas on Jensen Ward in the high-security unit, a neutral meeting place had been arranged. And if their visits had a positive effect on both patients, then it would become a regular occurrence – perhaps once a month. Erika, Jason's wife, had given her blessing.

'One step at a time though, right?' Fiona says, standing up then sitting down again. She plays a card. 'That's what they tell me. That one step is the start of a journey.'

'That's right,' Louisa says, studying her hand of cards. But then another nurse approaches and whispers something in Louisa's ear. 'Looks like it's time, Fiona. Are you ready?'

Fiona stares at Louisa. 'I'm ready,' she says, standing up and smoothing down her dress.

. . .

At first, she doesn't recognise Jason. He's lost weight and has grown a beard, which she thinks makes him look a bit funny, but she reckons she could get used to it. Somehow, he doesn't look like a doctor any more – just a man with a sad air about him; a man who wishes things had turned out differently. A man that, if she'd passed him on the street, she wouldn't have noticed and, if pushed, she'd have probably commented on his sallow skin because it looks like he's not seen the sun in ages.

She stands there looking at him, their eyes connecting, her mind flying back in time to when they met. Even though the powers that be have explained to her that Jason was never her psychiatrist on Isaac Ward, that he's not even a qualified doctor, let alone *her* doctor, he will always be Doc to her. Her Doc.

That's what he insisted everyone on the ward called him. Fiona smiles at that memory. And she enjoyed her consultations in his office, talking over her problems with him, even if it turned out that it was just his hospital bedroom a couple of corridors along from hers. He'd tried to make it into a consulting room with a notepad and pen on the table by the window, and a second chair for her to sit in. He watered his pot plants weekly. And Fiona didn't mind imagining. Because without imagination, how do you know where the real parts are? That's what Jason once said.

In the meeting room now, there is a semicircle of chairs. Jason has three people sitting to one side of him – a doctor and two male nurses – while there is another chair next to Jason for Fiona. Her nurses and another doctor will sit beside her.

'I brought you this,' Fiona says, forgetting to say hello to him. 'I made it.' She holds out the folded piece of paper to him. 'It's a card. You can open it.'

'Thank you, Fiona,' Jason replies, taking it and looking up at her. 'Sit down. How are you? It's been a while, eh?'

Fiona nods, tucking her dress beneath her as she lowers herself onto the chair.

'I like the card, thank you. Is it us?' He looks at the picture – two people sitting together. 'What's that on the table between them?'

Fiona looks embarrassed. 'It's the notebook with our rules,' she whispers.

'"To Jason, happy to see you, from Fiona,"' he reads. 'That's nice, thank you. Sorry I didn't make you one.'

Fiona shrugs. 'What have you been doing?'

'Lots of things,' Jason says. 'Painting. And some exercise. We do book club and Erika comes to see me. There's a court-yard I can go in, but I don't bother.'

'Erika came to see me, too,' Fiona tells him, remembering the one and only time she's had a visitor. 'She was nice. Not angry, but I think she was just hiding it. She said it helped her, seeing me. Helped her work things out in her mind. To get closure.' Fiona shrugs, wrinkling up her nose from embarrass-ment. She feels squirmy inside. 'She told me that one day I might be able to see the girls. She says they ask things about me. Imagine that! It would be like old times again.'

'That's nice,' Jason says. 'Erika is my wife,' he tells her, frowning.

Fiona nods. 'Yes, she is.' Then she's silent for a moment, thinking, making sure she doesn't talk about the bad things because she knows the powers that be are listening. They're sitting all around them. 'Do you want to go on a trip?' she asks. 'Like we used to? Do you remember?'

'Of *course* I remember,' Jason says, leaning forward on his chair beside her. He grins, the shine of his smile showing through his beard. Then he laughs, saliva collecting in the corner of his mouth. 'We had such a good time in York.' He wipes his lips on the back of his hand.

Fiona laughs with him. 'Oh my God, the journey up. Do

you remember when that nurse caught us on the train? She found us hiding under the duvet on your bed and asked what we were doing.'

'On our way to York!' Jason says in a silly voice, his smile widening.

'Away for the weekend!' Fiona chants back, sticking her nose in the air.

'They must have thought we were mad,' Jason says, and they both burst into fits of laughter, looking at each other, rocking back and forth in their chairs as if no one else is in the room.

Just them. Quite alone.

Just them and their pain and their wounds and their suffering and their scars and their hopes and fears and dreams and nightmares that they will carry around with them for the rest of their lives, despite all the medications, despite all the talking therapies, despite all the group sessions. It's what makes them real. What keeps their souls alive, because without the hurt inside, there is nothing left of them. It's who they are. Who they've become.

'Shall we go to York again now?' Jason asks.

Fiona nods enthusiastically. 'Oh my God, like... yes! Hundred per cent yes!'

'First class, of course,' Jason says. 'We could stay in the same guest house.'

'Where you proposed to me.'

'Where you said yes to me.'

They look at each other, lost in memory, lost in imagination, lost in each other.

'We did OK, didn't we?' Fiona asks, her voice tentative, uncertain. 'Living our lives? Having our little family? They say we got things wrong. That we shouldn't have done it. But Jase, tell me we coped, that we managed, because all my life that's what everyone's told me – that I can't do things. That I'm useless. That I'm broken.'

Jason looks into Fiona's eyes. 'We did our best,' he says, nodding. 'We lived by the rules, Fiona. You can't do more than that.'

'I'll never forget, you know. I'll never forget what we had. And our little wedding ceremony... it was perfect.' She remembers walking down to the woods in her fancy dress, each of them reciting the rules to a celebrant who had felt so real at the time. She giggles at the memory.

They're both still for a moment, letting the past percolate. Allowing their minds to sync.

'Look, hurry!' Fiona suddenly says. 'The train's about to leave! All aboard.'

They get on, settling into their first-class seats, the pair only vaguely aware of the other people sitting around them as they head north for York on their romantic weekend away.

They stare out of the window as the countryside speeds past, their minds taking them on a journey. Fiona's hand slides across her lap and onto Jason's leg. His fingers reach out and clasp hers, gripping her tightly. He pulls her closer to him, leaning forward for a hug.

Fiona does the same, nervously wrapping an arm around his back.

After a moment, with his face buried in her hair, Jason whispers, 'I found her, you know...' His mouth is pressed so close to her ear, it's as if he's inside her head. 'I found Sascha in the barn.'

Fiona freezes, letting his words settle in her mind.

'It was when I followed you on your walk to the riding stables,' he continues, his words only heard by her. 'She was lying in the dirt by the haystack, staring up at me, her face crusted with blood. She spoke to me. She was still alive.'

Fiona holds him tighter, hardly able to believe what she's

hearing. 'What did she say?' she whispers directly into his ear, the sound of the train almost drowning her out.

'She said... "Help me... please..." And then she blinked twice.'

'What did you do?' Fiona whispers back. The train rumbles on, the green of the countryside a blur as it speeds past. Like their lives – a smudge on the universe.

'I told her she broke the rules. Then I smothered her face until she went quiet. After that, I covered her up with straw,' Jason whispers. 'She looked so peaceful, so I left her. It was better that way.' He hugs Fiona harder, the pair of them turning to look out of the train window. 'We're all just passengers, you know,' he continues. 'Passengers in our own lives. We can go anywhere we want. Live wherever we choose in our imagination. No one can stop us.'

'As long as we follow the rules,' Fiona whispers back, giving Jason's hand a little squeeze.

A LETTER FROM SAMANTHA

Dear Reader,

Thank you so much for reading *The Marriage Rules* – I really hope you enjoyed it! If you want to be kept up to date about my new books, please click on the link below to sign up (you can unsubscribe at any time you want).

www.bookouture.com/samantha-hayes

This book began life when an editor and an author sat down for lunch one day and began discussing ideas… I knew I wanted to write about a married couple who seemingly had everything 'sorted' in life – but what if, unbeknown to others, they lived by a strict set of rules, their *marriage rules*, and that things weren't quite as perfect as they seemed?

Thus ensued several hours of brainstorming where my characters began to take on a life of their own… and my editor and I began asking lots of questions. What if one of them was unwell – perhaps they were a patient in a psychiatric hospital? And what if their doctor wasn't to be trusted? And, more importantly, what if nothing was as it seemed…?

I really wanted to give my readers a 'through their eyes' experience as Fiona's and Jason's stories, both past and present, unfold. Believing they've each found their soulmate and moving into their new home, on the surface, the couple seem to have it all. But things soon start to fall apart when their neighbour,

Sascha, disappears, and the cracks in their perceived realities begin to show.

At times, it was a challenging book to write given that the reader is very much seeing the characters' realities from their point of view – from inside the mind of a person who is not well, and while it's a tragic story in many respects, I hope the twists and turns along the way took you by surprise!

If you loved this book and have a couple of minutes to spare, then I'd so appreciate a quick review on Amazon to help spread the word – just a few words are fine! Thank you so much.

In the meantime, I'm rolling up my sleeves and forging ahead with my next psychological thriller – and if you haven't read all of my other books yet, there are plenty to choose from on Amazon!

With warm wishes,

Sam x

facebook.com/samanthahayesauthor

x.com/samhayes

instagram.com/samanthahayes.author

ACKNOWLEDGEMENTS

As always, I'd like to say a massive thank you to my amazing editor, Lucy Frederick, for having the patience of a saint as we whipped this book into shape! I really appreciate all your hard work. And big thanks also to my regular editor Jessie Botterill for brainstorming this book with me. That was one wild lunch!

Of course, massive thanks to Sarah Hardy and all the publicity team at Bookouture for letting the world know about this book, and to DeAndra Lupu for copyediting, Jenny Page for proofreading and Lisa Horton for superb cover design – I appreciate all you do. And, as ever, my sincere thanks to everyone at Bookouture for publishing my books.

Big thanks as ever to Oli Munson, my agent, for looking after me, and everyone at A. M. Heath.

And I truly mean this when I say HUGE thanks are due to all the amazing bloggers, reviewers and readers who shout out about my books – I truly appreciate you spreading the word, and I know my fellow authors feel the same. You guys rock!

And last but not least, much love to Ben, Polly and Lucy, as well as the rest of my family.

PUBLISHING TEAM

Turning a manuscript into a book requires the efforts of many people. The publishing team at Bookouture would like to acknowledge everyone who contributed to this publication.

Audio
Alba Proko
Sinead O'Connor
Melissa Tran

Commercial
Lauren Morrissette
Hannah Richmond
Imogen Allport

Data and analysis
Mark Alder
Mohamed Bussuri

Editorial
Lucy Frederick
Melissa Tran

Copyeditor
DeAndra Lupu

Printed in Great Britain
by Amazon